BY J. R. WARD

THE BLACK DAGGER BROTHERHOOD SERIES

Dark Lover

Lover Eternal

Lover Awakened

Lover Revealed

Lover Unbound

Lover Enshrined

The Black Dagger Brotherhood:
  An Insider's Guide

Lover Avenged

Lover Mine

Lover Unleashed

Lover Reborn

Lover at Last

The King

The Shadows

The Beast

The Chosen

The Thief

The Savior

The Sinner

THE BLACK DAGGER LEGACY SERIES

Blood Kiss

Blood Vow

Blood Fury

Blood Truth

THE BLACK DAGGER BROTHERHOOD WORLD

Dearest Ivie

Prisoner of Night

Where Winter Finds You

NOVELS OF THE FALLEN ANGELS

Covet

Crave

Envy

Rapture

Possession

Immortal

J.R. WARD

A WARM HEART IN WINTER

• A CALDWELL CHRISTMAS •

POCKET BOOKS

New York London Toronto Sydney New Delhi

Pocket Books
An Imprint of Simon & Schuster, Inc.
1230 Avenue of the Americas
New York, NY 10020

This book is a work of fiction. Any references to historical events, real
people, or real places are used fictitiously. Other names, characters,
places, and events are products of the author's imagination, and any
resemblance to actual events or places or persons, living or dead, is
entirely coincidental.

First Pocket Books paperback edition November 2020

POCKET and colophon are registered trademarks of Simon & Schuster, Inc.

For information about special discounts for bulk purchases,
please contact Simon & Schuster Special Sales at 1-866-506-1949
or business@simonandschuster.com.

The Simon & Schuster Speakers Bureau can bring authors to your
live event. For more information or to book an event, contact the
Simon & Schuster Speakers Bureau at 1-866-248-3049 or visit
our website at www.simonspeakers.com.

Interior design by Davina Mock-Maniscalco

Manufactured in the United States of America

10 9 8 7 6 5 4 3 2 1

ISBN 978-1-9821-5970-2
ISBN 978-1-9821-5971-9 (ebook)

Excerpt(s) from LOVER AT LAST: A NOVEL OF THE BLACK
DAGGER BROTHERHOOD by J. R. Ward, Copyright © 2013 by
Love Conquers All, Inc. Used by permission of New American Library,
an imprint of Penguin Publishing Group, a division of Penguin
Random House LLC. All rights reserved.

Destiny is never wrong.
And love is never wasted.
—Lassiter

GLOSSARY OF TERMS AND PROPER NOUNS

ahstrux nohtrum (n.) Private guard with license to kill who is granted his or her position by the King.

ahvenge (v.) Act of mortal retribution, carried out typically by a male loved one.

Black Dagger Brotherhood (pr. n.) Highly trained vampire warriors who protect their species against the Lessening Society. As a result of selective breeding within the race, Brothers possess immense physical and mental strength, as well as rapid healing capabilities. They are not siblings for the most part, and are inducted into the Brotherhood upon nomination by the Brothers. Aggressive, self-reliant, and secretive by nature, they are the subjects of legend and objects of reverence within the vampire world. They may be killed only by the most serious of wounds, e.g., a gunshot or stab to the heart, etc.

blood slave (n.) Male or female vampire who has been subjugated to serve the blood needs of another. The practice of keeping blood slaves has been outlawed.

the Chosen (pr. n.) Female vampires who had been bred to serve the Scribe Virgin. In the past, they were spiritually rather than temporally focused, but that changed with the ascendance of the final Primale, who freed them from the Sanctuary. With the Scribe Virgin removing herself from her role, they are completely autonomous and learning to live on earth. They do continue to meet the blood needs of unmated members of the Brotherhood, as well as Brothers who cannot feed from their *shellans* and injured fighters.

chrih (n.) Symbol of honorable death in the Old Language.

cohntehst (n.) Conflict between two males competing for the right to be a female's mate.

Dhunhd (pr. n.) Hell.

doggen (n.) Member of the servant class within the vampire world. *Doggen* have old, conservative traditions about service to their superiors, following a formal code of dress and behavior. They are able to go out during the day, but they age relatively quickly. Life expectancy is approximately five hundred years.

ehros (n.) A Chosen trained in the matter of sexual arts.

exhile dhoble (n.) The evil or cursed twin, the one born second.

the Fade (pr. n.) Non-temporal realm where the dead reunite with their loved ones and pass eternity.

First Family (pr. n.) The King and Queen of the vampires, and any children they may have.

ghardian (n.) Custodian of an individual. There are varying degrees of *ghardians*, with the most powerful being that of a *sehcluded* female.

glymera (n.) The social core of the aristocracy, roughly equivalent to Regency England's *ton*.

hellren (n.) Male vampire who has been mated to a female. Males may take more than one female as mate.

hyslop (n. or v.) Term referring to a lapse in judgment, typically resulting in the compromise of the mechanical operations of a vehicle or otherwise motorized conveyance of some kind. For example, leaving one's keys in one's car as it is parked outside the family home overnight, whereupon said vehicle is stolen.

leahdyre (n.) A person of power and influence.

leelan (adj. or n.) A term of endearment loosely translated as "dearest one."

Lessening Society (pr. n.) Order of slayers convened by the Omega for the purpose of eradicating the vampire species.

lesser (n.) De-souled human who targets vampires for extermination as a member of the Lessening Society. *Lessers* must be stabbed through the chest in order to be killed; otherwise they are ageless. They do not eat or drink and are impotent. Over time, their hair, skin, and irises lose pigmentation until they are blond, blushless, and pale-eyed. They smell like baby powder. Inducted into the society by the Omega, they retain a ceramic jar thereafter into which their heart was placed after it was removed.

lewlhen (n.) Gift.

lheage (n.) A term of respect used by a sexual submissive to refer to their dominant.

Lhenihan (pr. n.) A mythic beast renowned for its sexual prowess. In modern slang, refers to a male of preternatural size and sexual stamina.

lys (n.) Torture tool used to remove the eyes.

mahmen (n.) Mother. Used both as an identifier and a term of affection.

mhis (n.) The masking of a given physical environment; the creation of a field of illusion.

nalla (n., f.) or *nallum* (n., m.) Beloved.

needing period (n.) Female vampire's time of fertility, generally lasting for two days and accompanied by intense sexual cravings. Occurs approximately five years after a female's transition and then once a decade thereafter. All males respond to some degree if they are around a female in her need. It can be a dangerous time, with conflicts and fights breaking out between competing males, particularly if the female is not mated.

newling (n.) A virgin.

the Omega (pr. n.) Malevolent, mystical figure who once targeted the vampires for extinction out of resentment directed toward the Scribe Virgin. Existed in a non-temporal realm and had extensive powers, though not the power of creation. Eradicated.

phearsom (adj.) Term referring to the potency of a male's sexual organs. Literal translation something close to "worthy of entering a female."

Princeps (pr. n.) Highest level of the vampire aristocracy, second only to members of the First Family or the Scribe Virgin's Chosen. Must be born to the title; it may not be conferred.

pyrocant (n.) Refers to a critical weakness in an individual. The weakness can be internal, such as an addiction, or external, such as a lover.

rahlman (n.) Savior.

rythe (n.) Ritual manner of asserting honor granted by one who has offended another. If accepted, the offended chooses a weapon and strikes the offender, who presents him—or herself—without defenses.

the Scribe Virgin (pr. n.) Mystical force who previously was counselor to the King as well as the keeper of vampire archives and the dispenser of privileges. Existed in a non-temporal realm and had extensive powers, but has recently stepped down and given her station to another. Capable of a single act of creation, which she expended to bring the vampires into existence.

sehclusion (n.) Status conferred by the King upon a female of the aristocracy as a result of a petition by the female's family. Places the female under the sole direction of her *ghardian*, typically the eldest male in her household. Her *ghardian* then has the legal right to determine all manner of her life, restricting at will any and all interactions she has with the world.

shellan (n.) Female vampire who has been mated to a male. Females generally do not take more than one mate due to the highly territorial nature of bonded males.

symphath (n.) Subspecies within the vampire race characterized by the ability and desire to manipulate emotions in others (for the purposes of an energy exchange), among other traits. Historically, they have been discriminated against and, during certain eras, hunted by vampires. They are near extinction.

talhman (n.) The evil side of an individual. A dark stain on the soul that requires expression if it is not properly expunged.

the Tomb (pr. n.) Sacred vault of the Black Dagger Brotherhood. Used as a ceremonial site as well as a storage facility for the jars of *lessers*. Ceremonies performed there include inductions, funerals, and disciplinary actions against Brothers. No one may enter except for members of the Brotherhood, the Scribe Virgin, or candidates for induction.

trahyner (n.) Word used between males of mutual respect and affection. Translated loosely as "beloved friend."

transition (n.) Critical moment in a vampire's life when he or she transforms into an adult. Thereafter, he or she must drink the blood of the opposite sex to survive and is unable to withstand sunlight. Occurs generally in the mid-twenties. Some vampires do not survive their transitions, males in particular.

Prior to their transitions, vampires are physically weak, sexually unaware and unresponsive, and unable to dematerialize.

vampire (n.) Member of a species separate from that of *Homo sapiens*. Vampires must drink the blood of the opposite sex to survive. Human blood will keep them alive, though the strength does not last long. Following their transitions, which occur in their mid-twenties, they are unable to go out into sunlight and must feed from the vein regularly. Vampires cannot "convert" humans through a bite or transfer of blood, though they are in rare cases able to breed with the other species. Vampires can dematerialize at will, though they must be able to calm themselves and concentrate to do so and may not carry anything heavy with them. They are able to strip the memories of humans, provided such memories are short-term. Some vampires are able to read minds. Life expectancy is upward of a thousand years, or in some cases, even longer.

wahlker (n.) An individual who has died and returned to the living from the Fade. They are accorded great respect and are revered for their travails.

whard (n.) Equivalent of a godfather or godmother to an individual.

PROLOGUE

Qhuinn, son of Lohstrong, entered his family's home through its grand front door. The instant he stepped over the threshold, the smell of the place curled up into his nose. Lemon polish. Beeswax candles. Fresh flowers from the garden that the doggen brought in daily. Perfume—his mother's. Cologne—his father's and his brother's. Cinnamon gum—his sister's.

If the Glade company ever did an air freshener like this, it would be called something like Meadow of Old Money. Or Sunrise Over a Fat Bank Account.

Or maybe the ever popular We're Just Better Than Everyone Else.

Distant voices drifted over from the dining room, the

vowels round as brilliant-cut diamonds, the consonants drawled out smooth and long as satin ribbons.

"Oh, Lillie, this is lovely, thank you," his mother said to the server. "But that's too much for me. And do not give Solange so much. She's getting heavy."

Ah, yes, his mother's perma-diet inflicted on the next generation: Glymera females were supposed to disappear from sight when they turned sideways, each jutting collarbone, sunken cheek, and bony upper arm some kind of fucked-up badge of honor.

As if resembling a fire poker would make you a better person.

And Scribe Virgin forfend if your daughter looked like she was healthy.

"Ah, yes, thank you, Lilith," his father said evenly. "More for me, please."

Qhuinn closed his eyes and tried to convince his body to step forward. One foot after another. It was not that tough.

His brand-new Ed Hardy kicks middle-fingered that suggestion. Then again, in so many ways, walking into that dining room was going into the belly of the beast.

He let his duffle fall to the floor. The couple of days at his best friend Blay's home had done him good, a break from the complete lack of air in his family's house. Un-

fortunately, the burn on reentry was so bad, it made the cost/benefit of leaving nearly equal.

Okay, this was ridiculous. He couldn't keep standing here like an inanimate object.

Turning to the side wall, he leaned into the full-length antique mirror that was placed right by the door. So thoughtful. So in keeping with the aristocracy's need to look good. This way, visitors could check their hair and clothes as the butler accepted coats and hats.

The young pretrans face that was reflected back at him was all even features, good jawline, and a mouth that, he had to admit, looked like it could do some serious damage to naked skin when he got older. Or maybe that was just wishful thinking. Hair was all Vlad the Impaler, spikes standing up straight from his head. Neck was strung with a bike chain, and not one bought at Urban Outfitters—he'd taken it off his twelve-speed. All things being equal, he looked like a thief who had broken into the mansion and was prepared to trash the place looking for sterling silver, jewelry, and portable electronics.

The irony was that all the Goth bullcrap wasn't the most offensive part of his appearance to his family. In fact, he could have stripped down, hung a light fixture off his ass, and run around the first floor playing José Canseco with the art and antiques and not come close to how much the real problem pissed off his parents.

It was his eyes.

One blue. One green.

Oopsy. His bad.

The glymera didn't like defects. Not in their porcelain or their rose gardens. Not in their wallpaper or their carpets or their countertops. Not in the silk of their underwear or the wool of their blazers or the chiffon of their gowns.

And certainly not EVER in their young.

Sister was okay—well, except for the "little weight problem" that didn't actually exist, and a lisp that was going to be dealt with through oral surgery—oh, and the fact that she had the personality of their mother. And there was no fixing that shit. Brother, on the other hand, was the real fucking star, a physically perfect son prepared to carry forth the family bloodline by reproducing in a very genteel, non-moaning, no-sweat situation with a female chosen for him by the family.

Hell, Luchas's sperm recipient had already been lined up. He was going to have to mate her as soon as he went through his transition—

"How are you feeling, my son?" his father asked in a gentle voice.

"Tired, sir," a deep voice answered. "But this is going to help."

A chill frog-marched up Qhuinn's spine. That didn't

sound like his brother. Way too much bass. Far too mas-
culine. Too . . .

Holy shit, the guy had gone through his transition.

Now, Qhuinn's Ed Hardys got with the program,
taking him forward until he could see through into the
dining room. Father was in his seat at the head of the
table. Check. Mother was in her chair at the foot of
the table opposite the kitchen's flap door. Check. Sister
was facing out of the room, all but licking the gold rim
off her plate from hunger. Check.

The male whose back was to Qhuinn was not part of
the SOP.

His brother was twice the size he'd been when Qhuinn
had been approached by a doggen and told to get his
things and go to Blay's.

Well, that explained the vacay. He'd assumed his
father had finally relented and given into the request
Qhuinn had filed weeks before. But nope, his sire had just
wanted the defect out of the house because the change had
come to his brother.

*Had Luchas laid the chick? Who had they used for
blood—*

Their father, never the demonstrative type, reached
out a hand and gave Qhuinn's brother an awkward pat
on the forearm. "We're so proud of you. You look . . .
perfect."

"You do," Qhuinn's mother piped in. "Just perfect. Doesn't your brother look perfect, Solange?"

"Yes, he does. Perfect."

"And I have something for you," Lohstrong said, in a voice that got husky.

The male reached into the inside pocket of his sport coat and took out a small, black velvet box.

Qhuinn's mother started to tear up and dabbed carefully under her eyes.

"This is for you, my son."

The box was slid across the white damask tablecloth, and Luchas's now-big hands shook as he took the thing and popped the lid.

Qhuinn could see the flash of gold all the way out in the foyer.

Luchas just stared at the signet ring in silence, clearly overwhelmed, as their mother kept up with the dab-dab, and even their father grew slightly misty. And Solange snuck a roll from the bread basket.

"Thank you, sir," Qhuinn's brother said as he put the heavy gold ring on his forefinger.

"It fits, does it not?" Lohstrong asked.

"Yes, sir. Perfectly."

"We wear the same size, then."

Of course they did.

At that moment, their father glanced away, like he

was hoping the movement of his eyeballs would take care of the sheen of tears that had come down over his vision.

He caught Qhuinn lurking outside in the foyer.

There was a brief flash of recognition. Not the hi-how're-ya kind or the oh-good-my-other-son's-home stuff. More like when you were walking through the grass and noticed a pile of dog shit too late to stop your foot from landing in it.

The male looked back at his family, locking Qhuinn out sure as if he'd closed an actual door.

Clearly, the last thing Lohstrong wanted was for such a historic moment to be ruined—and that was probably why he didn't do the hand signals that warded off the evil eye. Usually, everyone in the household performed the ritual when they saw Qhuinn. Not tonight. The head of house didn't want the others to know who was in their midst.

Qhuinn pivoted and went back to his duffle. Slinging the thing over his shoulder, he took the front stairs to his room. Usually, his mother preferred him to use the servants' set, but that would mean he'd have to cut through all the love in there.

His bedroom was as far away from the others' as you could get, all the way over to the right. He'd often wondered why they didn't take the leap completely and put him in with the doggen—but then the staff would probably quit.

Closing himself into his quarters, he dumped the duffle onto the bare floor and sat on his bed. Staring at his only piece of luggage, he figured he had better do laundry soon as there was a wet bathing suit in there.

The maids refused to touch his clothes—like the evil in him lingered in the fibers of his jeans and his T-shirts. The upside was he was never welcomed for formal events anyway, so his wardrobe was just wash-n-wear, baby—

He discovered he was crying when he looked down at his Ed Hardys and realized that there were a couple of drops of water right between all those buckles and leather.

Qhuinn was never getting a ring.

Ah, hell . . . this hurt.

He was scrubbing his face with his palms when his phone rang. Taking the thing out of his biker jacket, he had to blink a couple of times to focus.

He hit send to accept the call, but he didn't answer.

"I just heard," Blay said across the connection. "How are you doing?"

Qhuinn opened his mouth to reply, his brain coughing up all kinds of responses: Peachy fucking jim-dandy. At least I'm not "fat" like my sister. No, I don't know if my brother got laid.

Instead, he said, "They got me out of the house.

They didn't want me to curse the transition. Guess it worked because Luchas sure looks like he came through it okay."

Blay swore softly.

"Oh, and he got his ring just now. My father gave him . . . his ring."

The signet ring with the family crest on it, the symbol that all males of good bloodlines wore to attest to their value to their lineage.

"I watched Luchas put it on his finger," Qhuinn said, feeling as if he were taking a sharp knife and drawing it up the insides of his arms. "Fit perfectly. Looked great. You know, though . . . like, how could it not—"

He began weeping at that point.

Just fucking lost it.

The awful truth was that under all his counterculture fuck-you, he wanted his family to love him. As prissy as his sister was, as scholar-geek as his brother was, as reserved as his parents were, he saw the love between those four. He felt the love among them. It was the tie that bound them, the invisible string from one heart to the others, the commitment of caring about everything from the mundane shit to any true, mortal drama. The only thing more powerful than that connection . . . was what it was like to get shut out from its expression.

Every fucking night of your life.

Blay's voice cut in through the heaving. "I'm here for you. And I'm so damned sorry . . . I'm here for you . . . just don't do anything stupid, okay? Let me come over—"

Leave it to Blay to know that he was thinking about things that involved ropes and showerheads.

In fact, his free hand had already gone down to the makeshift belt he'd fashioned out of a nice, strong weave of nylon—because his parents didn't give him money for clothes and the one proper buckle-and-strap combo he'd owned had broken years ago.

Pulling the length free, he glanced across to the closed door of his bath. All he needed to do was tie the thing to the fixture in his shower—God knew those water pipes had been run in the good old days when things were strong enough to hold some weight. He even had a chair he could stand up on and then kick out from underneath him.

"I gotta go—"

"Qhuinn? Don't you hang up on me—don't you dare hang up on me—"

"Listen, man, I gotta go—"

"I'm coming over right now—" Lot of flapping in the background like Blay was getting his shit together. "Qhuinn! Do not hang up the phone—Qhuinn . . . !"

CHAPTER ONE

Present Day
Market Street and 17th
Downtown Caldwell, New York

Oh, shit! Dad is going to kill us—"

"What are you talking about, 'us'? I'm not driving—"

"You're in the car, Terrie! And not because I kidnapped you—"

The two Allaine sisters were talking over each other, talking over the radio that was still playing loud enough to be heard in the suburbs they'd left, talking over the accident that had just occurred. They were also going nowhere, the front grille of the burgundy 2018 BMW 5 series embedded in the face of a dirty, downtown snowbank that loomed big as a mountain.

"I know I'm in the car, *Ellen*," the twelve-year-old snapped. "But you're the one who crashed us!"

"It wasn't my fault, *Therese*!" Elle punched the radio button, which canned the music and turned up the volume on two things she was so not interested in dealing with: whatever wasn't ever going to work again under the hood and her stupid sister's opinion on what had just happened. "Something ran out in front of the car. It was *not* my fault—"

"It's your fault where you steered us, and you're never going to get your full license—"

"You can stop yelling. Anytime."

No airbags. The airbags hadn't deployed. Elle pulled herself up by the steering wheel and looked over the hood. Whatever had shot across the icy road was gone, the black shadow scurrying off as strays did. In contrast, the snowbank they were headfirst into was about five feet tall and a whole block long of going-nowhere. Beyond it? Nothing but a warehouse the color of a mud puddle that was covered with graffiti and absolutely no exterior lights.

Two seconds sooner or later and this would never have happened. The dog would have crossed the street before or after them, and right now they'd be elsewhere—although probably not where she'd meant to be going. She'd been trying to get onto Trade

Street, and she'd thought, as she'd made a bunch of turns after taking the—hello—Trade Street exit off Northway, that it'd be no problem to find her way. Instead, they were . . .

Cranking around in her seat, she looked past Terrie, who was still talking, her hands all animated, her indignity act on a solid roll. The Northway was down about four blocks, at the Hudson River's edge, and Elle pictured herself back on the four-laner going out of town, headlights leading the way home. Too bad there was no on-ramp that she could see and no signs to one, either—plus the highway was super-raised up on pylons. But, like, what did she think she'd do if it were on the level? Bust through a guardrail?

On the other side of things there was . . . nothing much. Just a bunch of dark buildings that offered no help. No security lights on them, either. Were they all abandoned?

"—going to tell Dad everything. How you stole his keys and took us downtown—"

Elle turned to her passenger with the big frickin' opinions. "It's not like I put a gun to your head. You said you were bored, so you were coming."

"I'm twelve, you know, I'm a minor and it's ten o'clock at night, and if you left home I'd be alone there, and that defeats the whole purpose of baby-sitting, doesn't it. And where are we."

Barely a break between words, much less pauses for sentences. If there had even been more than one.

"We're here," Elle muttered. "I mean, don't freak out."

"Who do we call?" her sister demanded. "We can't call Dad—"

"Shut up, Terrie. I'll take care of it."

"Don't tell me to shut up! You know, this is just like the time you . . ."

As Terrie got back on the bitch train, Elle couldn't decide whether she wanted to be home because it was safe and this stretch of Caldwell's downtown felt any-thing but that, or because she could not stand to be in an enclosed space with Terrie the Big Mouth. The good news? Now that the shock was wearing off, she realized the engine was still running, the heater was still on, and she couldn't smell any smoke or anything burning. And hey, "abandoned" meant no one was around to get involved, right?

Get involved = call her father. Or call the police, who would then call her father.

All she had to do was reverse. Reverse was every-thing. And then she was getting them the hell out of here, and never, ever babysitting her sister again.

"You are such an idiot," Terrie announced.

"Shut up."

Putting things in reverse, Elle hit the gas. There was a jerk, and then a *whrrrrrrrr*. So she pushed down more on the accelerator. Whereupon the *whrrrrrrr* from the back end of the car just got higher pitched and louder.

Terrie cocked an eyebrow. "That's not working."

"Thank you, Mr. Faulk." Mr. Faulk was the seventy-million-year-old English teacher at Caldwell Middle School. They'd both had him, and they'd both hated him. It was the only thing they'd ever agreed on. "And it will work."

Elle stomped on the accelerator. And all she got was more volume out of the spinning rear tires, so she eased off. Then tried again, with less gas.

"FYI, this isn't helping us."

Elle put the car in park and thought seriously about pulling out all of her sister's hair. "I'm never taking you anywhere ever again. Like, ever. You're a fucking pain in my ass."

"Just wait until I tell Dad ALL about this. Including that f-word."

"Good. Then you're in trouble, too, because you were supposed to be in bed an hour ago."

"My bedtime was *your* responsibility. He's never going to let you babysit—"

"Who the fuck else do you think is going to sit with you when we're at Dad's and he's on a date?"

"That's two f-words and he can pay someone better than you—"

"Shut up!" Elle slapped the steering wheel. "*Fuck!*"

Before her sister could update the tally, Elle leaned across the console and stared right into Terrie's brown eyes. For once in her life, the girl thought better about speaking. But it wasn't going to last.

With shaking hands, Elle got her cell phone from the drink-cup holder, but she couldn't think of who could help. None of her friends could drive without an adult in the car—well, technically, neither could Elle—and any parental type who would come with them would call her father, which was exactly what she needed to avoid.

And their mom was out of the question.

Terrie crossed her arms over her pink parka. "You're sixteen and only have your learner's permit. This isn't legal, you know."

"You still can't do long division, what the hell do you know." Elle rubbed at her foggy window with the sleeve of her coat. "Hey. Check it. There's a tow truck over there—"

Terrie grabbed her arm. "Lock the doors!"

"They are locked and what are you talking about?"

"It could be a murderer!"

Elle shoved off her sister. "Oh, shut up. And like you have a better idea?"

As she opened her door, the cold made it seem like it was three a.m. and they were in a bad part of town. Then again, she had a feeling this *was* a bad part of town, and ten p.m. might as well be three a.m. when you were alone with your baby sister.

If something went wrong, maybe she could just throw Terrie at the masher and run away. God knew the kid had that machine gun mouth of hers to use as a weapon.

Shutting her sister in, Elle kept her phone in her hand and double-checked to see if anyone, anything, was around. Nope. Just still December air, distant traffic, and a whole lot of wishing she were back home: Not that she'd ever admit it to Terrie the Big Mouth, she was seriously regretting this whole thing. She'd just wanted to drive down to where the clubs with the lights and the banging music were. When you were stuck babysitting your little sister—while your father was out on a date for the first time since the divorce and your mom was sitting in an apartment in the dark 'cuz it was always dark at her apartment—sometimes catching sight of the twenty-one-and-over glory that was just around your corner was the only thing that made you feel better.

Like what if their dad liked that woman? She was terrible. All perfume and LBD when she'd come to their door to pick him up. Like she was somebody special.

"Elle? You're not going to leave me, are you?"

At least that annoying voice was contained inside the car, but Terrie hadn't stayed put. She'd crawled over the threshold separating the two front seats, and she was staring up out of the driver's side window, the ambient gray light of the city sucking the smart-ass out of her expression.

Or maybe the reality they were in was what was doing that: Car stuck, after dark, with no good options.

Elle looked at the tow truck, which was parked a good fifty yards away and facing in the opposite direction. It was red and white, and had a logo that seemed legit: "Murphy's Towing" was done in script and there was a tagline, "We're Always There for You!" They even had the AAA thingie. And a local phone number.

But she couldn't see who was behind the wheel. There was somebody in the truck, though. Smoke puffed out of the tailpipe, and the brake lights glowed red. Why wasn't he coming to help already, though? It was his job, right? And it wasn't like there were any other cars in snowbanks around here.

"Lock the doors," she heard herself say. Like she was a grown-up.

"Oh, my God, you're going to be dead!" Terrie launched herself at the window, smacking at it with the palm of her hand, her voice all muffled. "Let's call Dad! I'll tell him it was my idea!"

"Shh. You're being weird." Elle swallowed through a dry throat. "Just lock the doors. I'm gonna ask if he can help us."

"We're all alone, Elle." Now Terrie was more like the four-year-old she'd once been, all doe eyes and fright, the child coming out from behind the tween-ager. "We're going to die."

"Lock." She jabbed her forefinger at the door. "Now."

When there was a *chunk* sound, she pointed through the glass with another jab, the universal sister sign for *Stay the hell there.*

It was, like, a hundred miles to the tow truck, and as the snow compressed under Elle's boots, the squeaks it made were like a motion-activated alarm system that seemed to be counting down to an explosion. She couldn't see inside the cab even as she closed in on all the winches and pulleys that hung off the back. But whoever was in there had to be able to help, right? Otherwise, why stencil that slogan on the outside of your stupid tow truck?

Right, because all advertising was legit.

Elle's heart was pounding as she came up to the driver's side of the cab. "Hey, mister? Hey. Hey, you in there?"

Maybe she'd luck out and find that it was a missus. That would be so great.

She glanced back at the BMW. Terrie's pale face was mashed up against the window, her eyes wide, her mouth moving like she was talking to herself. Or maybe getting ready to scream when her older sister's spilled blood turned the snow red as those brake lights—

The sound of the window going down brought Elle's head around.

With a gasp, she jumped back. The man staring out at her had gunmetal-gray piercings running up one ear, and another set on his eyebrow, and one on the side of his nose. His hair was jet black and stained with purple. His clothes were black and he was wearing a leather jacket. One eye was blue, the other green, and there was the tattoo of a purple tear under one of them.

He was not smiling.

He looked like he never smiled. Unless he was tearing someone's head off with his bare hands.

As he stared down at her, he was clearly sizing her up for target practice . . . in a way that made where she had gotten lost seem like a war zone.

Elle put her hands up. "Never mind. I, ah, I made a mistake—"

Stumbling away, she started walking fast back to her sister, trying to make it seem like she was, you know, calm. But when the driver's door opened with a creak, she fucked that lie right off and began to run. Slipping, falling, scrambling, she focused on Terrie, who started to scream and pound at the window with little fists.

Like that was going to do anything.

The decision to go out had been a simple whim back home. Now, it was going to cost her and her sister their lives.

All she wanted was her dad.

CHAPTER TWO

The Black Dagger Brotherhood Mansion

Have you ever had wedding cake?"

Blaylock, son of Rocke, looked up from the December 12th issue of *The New Yorker*. Bitty, a.k.a. Rhage and Mary's daughter, was standing just inside the library's archway, a diminutive figure poised to enter the land of wood paneling and leather-bound books. She was wearing leggings and another one of her dad's black button-downs, the tails of the shirt falling below her knobby knees, the sleeves rolled up her thin arms, the collar flopping on her shoulders. Her dark and shiny hair was pulled back into a ponytail, and she had a steno notebook and a pen in her hand. She looked like a reporter on a lead.

He nodded down at her feet. "Nice slippers."

The girl picked up one of the fluffy pink unicorns. The things had silver lamé horns, rainbow manes and tails, and expressions of unease, the smiles not quite stitched on right. Actually, the poor things looked nauseous, like the small feet in their insides were too much of a meal.

"They're part of the uniform," Bitty said.

"For what?"

"The Party Planning Committee."

"Did Fritz mandate this?" Weird. The Black Dagger Brotherhood's butler supreme was more like the spit-and-polish military-shoe type.

"No, Lassiter."

Blay closed his eyes and let his head fall back against the cushions of the sofa. "Well, I think that is just great."

"You don't look like you think it's great. You look like you ate too much."

Ah, so he was imitating the unicorns.

He releveled himself. "Is the Party Planning Committee working on anything specific right now?"

A *Golden Girls*–themed celebration of Taco Tuesday? Rainbow Dash does the second Saturday in December because . . . it was not the first or the third Saturday? No, wait, George's birthday was coming up. Maybe they'd all have hamburgers and play with chew toys to honor Wrath's beloved guide dog?

At least that last one didn't seem so bad.

Bitty tapped her steno pad. "We're gathering a list of parties. Vampire and otherwise. And then we're going to plan them as training."

"Oh, that's smart. And I've never had wedding cake, no. But I'm sure Fritz and the *doggen* can whip one up for you."

"That's our idea. I mean, I know we don't do wedding cakes. As a species, I mean. But they're really pretty."

"They are. I've seen pictures."

"What did you serve at your mating ceremony with Uncle Qhuinn?"

Blay opened his mouth. Closed it. "Well, we just had a party of sorts. I mean, not a ceremony. It was more like a . . ."

"Like what?" When he didn't immediately reply, Bitty said, "So you're not properly mated?"

"Oh, we are. Definitely."

"Then you saw the Scribe Virgin before she left us?"

"Well, not exactly."

"But I thought when people got mated, that's what

happened. They did their vows, and she blessed the union if it's a good one, and then the carving in the back of the *hellren* comes. After that is the party with cake that's not for a wedding, but that might have many layers separated by raspberry jam, with butter-cream frosting on top."

Blay thought back to the night he and Qhuinn had finally gotten their act together. God, there had been so much denial and confusion and pain, on both sides, for so many years. And then the false starts and worse heartbreak and all kinds of never-going-to-happens. Finally, though, he'd gone to that club and found his male sitting alone at the bar, turning down offers for sex. Which had been kind of like watching Rhage go "I couldn't possibly" to a bag full of Big Macs.

Unprecedented.

He remembered slipping his gold signet ring on Qhuinn's finger and claiming him as family. In that bar. Yeah, because life-changing events didn't neces-sarily happen at beaches in the moonlight or in front of roaring fires with champagne flutes. Instagram pics were great, but they were curated to be great. Real life went down when and where it did, regardless of whether things were photogenic.

"But it's different for us," he said. "Uncle Qhuinn

and I have known each other our whole lives. And when we decided to commit to each other, we had a lot of history behind us. A base of knowledge and familiarity."

"What's that have to do with a ceremony?"

"You don't need the ceremony if you have that much history. And we had a great party. Everyone in the household dressed up—even Uncle Qhuinn had on a tuxedo. My parents came, and he and I danced to 'Don't Stop Believin'' in the foyer."

"Journey."

"You know the song?"

"Uncle Zsadist sings it the best."

"I agree with you on that. And as for the back carving and everything, we've always meant to do that."

But since that night when potential had turned into actual, when happily-never-after had lost its "n," a lot of shit had happened. They had the twins now, and young were some next-level overwhelm, capable of layering a whole new level of exhaustion on top of fighting to protect the vampire species and living a regular life. Still, he wouldn't change a thing, and Rhamp and Lyric were starting to show their personalities, which was exciting: Rhamp was fierce as his sire, meeting you right in the eye even as you cradled him in his blanket—despite the fact that the full ex-

tent of the kid's fighting arsenal was explosive diar-
rhea. Which, okay, fine, could clear a room faster than
a flash-bang. Lyric, on the other hand, was a watcher,
and much more reserved than her brother. But when
she smiled? She was the sun.

"Being mated officially doesn't affect who we are to
each other," Blay said.

Bitty smiled. "Oh, I know that. Your eyes change
color when you look at him."

"Really?"

"Uh-huh. They get deeper blue. Plus you blush a
lot. Why do you blush like that? Is it something he
does?"

Clearing his throat, Blay ruffled through the pages
of the magazine, watching the line drawings flap by in
the midst of their frames of text. He stopped on one
that depicted a fish on a bicycle.

"Well, ah," he said. "Um, I don't really think I
blush—"

"And Uncle Qhuinn smiles when he's with you. He
doesn't smile much anywhere else."

Blay frowned. "Oh, sure he does. He's really happy.
He's got me and the twins, and Layla and Xcor, who
are excellent co-parents with us. Plus he's a member
of the Brotherhood."

"I guess he's just happier with you." Bitty shrugged.

"Okay, I'm going to put 'wedding cake' down on my sample list."

"What else you got on there?"

"Fourth of July cake. Fruit cake. Bundt cake. Pineapple upside-down cake—"

"What's Fourth of July cake?"

"It's a red, white, and blue cake. Then there's funfetti, red velvet, Black Forest, pavlova, Yule log—"

"Wait, so are you researching holidays and celebrations? Or cakes."

"Both."

He thought of Rhage's famous appetite. "Is your dad on this committee?"

"How did you know?"

With a wave, the girl strode off with her list, and Blay intended to return to the article he'd been reading. Too bad his eyes refused to get with the back-and-forth program. He just kept staring at that fish with its bicycle. The rainbow trout was anthropomorphized, dressed in a suit and pedaling with his back fins, the basket in front filled with what looked like groceries.

None of the drawing made any sense. Not the clothes, not the food, not the breathing without water. Then again, it was just a cartoon, free to be some kind of metaphor, the point of the pen-and-ink artistry unclear to Blay at the moment.

Maybe it was merely a whimsical sketch, like a vase of flowers for the eye in the midst of an article about something serious.

He checked his watch. A little after ten p.m.

The night seemed long as a lifetime, and he couldn't wait for Qhuinn to get back from his shift on rotation. The pair of them were allowed to be in the field together, but they were never paired up, and sometimes, like this evening, one of them was off while the other was working. It was fine. There were always the daylight hours.

Blay smiled as he thought of the bed they shared.

And what they did in it.

Okay, fine, no wonder he blushed so much around his mate. But that was nothing Bitty ever needed to worry about.

Forcing his eyes to get going with the busywork of tracking letters, words and sentences, he had to push aside a lingering distraction. The sense that something was off-kilter in the universe, some kind of calamity due to arrive at any minute, was the worst company a guy could have.

Especially when the male you loved more than anybody else in the world was out in the cold in the field.

Blay let his head fall back again. The ceiling was

about thirty feet up, and it had old beams that were varnished the same tone as all the mahogany wood of the shelves, the hearth mantel, the floor. Whenever he retreated to this room, he always thought that this must be what the inside of a jewelry box was like, the glow of gold from all the spines of the ancient tomes like an extension of the crackling fire, the sense of protection and being among that which was rare making him feel kind of special himself.

He looked to the archway. Voices of *doggen* and Brothers and fighters wove together, some louder than others depending on whether they were next door in the billiards room, coming down from the grand staircase, or out in the dining room.

The mansion was never truly quiet.

And on a night like tonight, when he was on edge for no good reason . . .

It was such a reassurance to know that he was not alone.

CHAPTER THREE

As Elle landed facedown in the snow, she flipped onto her back and braced herself for a knife, a gun, a fist—whatever came at her. Mostly, the defensive response was because she wanted to fight for her life, but she was also a coward because she couldn't watch Terrie's face while she got murdered. She already knew her sister was screaming in the driver's seat. She could hear it. And the fact that this was Elle's fault, all of it, from the drive, to the wrong exit, to the bad turn, to the snowbank, was—

"Relax, kid."

The voice above her was grave and very deep, the

kind of thing a radio-show host would use when making a public service announcement. It was also slightly bored, as if sniveling, panicked teenage girls and their bigmouthed sisters hadn't been on the man's list of things to do tonight.

Elle paused with her flailing on the snowpack. "What?"

"You can stop freaking out, okay. I'm not going to hurt you."

The guy was absolutely enormous as he loomed over her, and she had a feeling he wasn't just a tow truck guy. After all, his leather jacket was open, and there was something strapped, handles down, to his huge chest. Knives? And what else from Fortnite could be under there? Add those piercings and the laser-eye routine, and she was pretty sure that he was speaking in a foreign language and she'd translated "I'm going to fuck you up" incorrectly.

When he extended his arm, she shrank back and covered her face with her hands. When nothing happened and nothing hurt, she peeked out from between the picket fence of her fingers. The man was leaning over her . . . with an extended open palm. That had nothing sharp and shiny in it.

"I'm not going to hurt you," he repeated.

Elle glanced back at her dad's car. Terrie had both

of her hands covering her mouth like she was worried that saying anything, even inside the car, might spook the big man into disastrous action.

The guy rolled his mismatched eyes. "Come on, kid. I don't have all night. Shit or get off the pot."

"You shouldn't curse around children," Elle mumbled.

"Children aren't in this part of town at ten o'clock at night. You were an adult when you took that car out, sweetie, and now you've got an adult-level problem. Hearing the word 'shit' better be something you can handle because it's the least of your worries."

Well . . . shit . . . he had a point.

"You talk like my dad."

"That's because I am one, so I have the same rule book yours does."

"Rule book? And you have a kid?"

"Two. So I'm viewing this as a training exercise for when they can drive."

Elle put her hand in the man's and was pulled up to her feet so fast she almost fell on her face again. He kept her upright by planting a palm on her shoulder and steadying her.

"I'll get you out of that snowbank," he said, "and then you gotta head off to wherever you belong. Things aren't safe down here."

As he stomped back to his tow truck, Elle pulled her coat into place around her torso and stared at his stalking stride. God, his black boots were the size of her head, and he might have sounded like her dad, but he sure didn't move like Basile Allaine. This man prowled like you didn't want to mess with him, like he was really strong and knew it, like he might not mind having to set someone straight. Her dad was an international tax attorney.

Elle blinked. For some reason, she thought of how her mom had once been a lawyer. A long time ago. Now, she wasn't anything professional, and that was another reason Elle had wanted to go out tonight. Sometimes, it was too hard to stay inside with all the things going on in her head.

She went back over to the BMW. Before she could hit the door handle, Terrie threw things open and exploded with talk, her words carbonated and shaken up from the scare, releasing in a rush.

"OhmyGodIthoughthewasgoingtokillyou—"

"Just stop, okay. He's going to pull us out."

"Do you have money to pay him?"

"Sure, I do." No, she didn't. "Just relax, will ya."

Instead of getting in, she reshut the door on Terrie because she couldn't handle anything right now. Fortunately, she didn't have to do much else. The tow truck came over and eased front-in to the back of their dad's car, and then the man with the piercings and the knives got out and went to a winch mounted on his bumper. There was a whirring sound, and moments later, a hook the size of a boxer's fist and a wire thick as a boat rope was pulled over to the BMW's rear.

"Um . . ." Elle cleared her throat. "I don't have any money to pay you. I mean, not on me. But I can mail in—"

"Don't worry about it," the man said without looking at her. "I gotchu."

The fact that the guy was fixing a problem for free that she had created on a stupid impulse made her feel small, and not just in terms of physical stature.

"I'm sorry," she said.

The man bent down with a flashlight, and latched the hook to something under the—

Later, Elle would wonder what exactly made her look over her shoulder. It wasn't a sound, and she certainly didn't have eyes in the back of her head. But some tickling sense on the nape of her neck had her turning her head.

The three figures in the shadows were as distinct as ghosts in a fog bank, nothing clear about their outlines or whether they were moving. And yet she was absolutely certain of their presence.

They were watching. And not in a Good Samaritan, how-can-we-help-ya kind of way.

"Um, mister—"

As she pivoted back around, the tow truck guy was already on it. He had straightened from the winch and was staring over her head, at the shadows.

"Hey," he said evenly, "how 'bout you get in your car."

Elle bobbleheaded that idea. "Yup, I'll just—"

"And lock the doors."

"Should we call the police? I mean, can we call the police—"

"Lock the doors. I'll take care of it."

Elle lunged for the driver's side and yanked at the handle. When nothing opened, she glared at her sister, who seemed to be in a cognitive freeze-up as she looked back and forth between the tow man and those three people standing next to the warehouse.

Great. Terrie was broken. Could her sister *never* be a help—

"Open this right now," Elle bit out.

Terrie fumbled with all kinds of switches, her hands slapping at the dashboard, the steering wheel, the console—when there was finally a pop, Elle yanked the door open, and pitched herself inside, slamming things shut and punching the lock mechanism.

"Wh-h-h-hat—who are they?" Terrie said.

Three men came out of the shadows. Three men with ski hats pulled down low over their foreheads and hands that were out of sight as they walked forward through the snow.

"Elle? What are we going to do?"

"It's fine." She punched the locks again even though it wasn't like she could more-lock the doors. "Get down."

"What?"

Without looking away from the approaching trio, Elle shoved her sister toward the passenger side's wheel well. "Shut up, and get down there—"

"I can't fit—"

As Terrie argued, Elle's heart pounded and she put her face into her sister's. "Please. I don't want you to get hurt. It's safer there."

"You said it was fine." Terrie's lower lip trembled. "You told me we were fine. I'm scared."

"It's going to be okay. Just get down."

"What are you going to do?"

At least this was asked as the girl folded herself up under the glove compartment, becoming a pink marshmallow Peep crammed badly into some very non-Easter packaging. Elle went back to staring at those men. The closer they came, the younger they got, until she decided they were only a year or two older than herself. The one in the middle was the shortest, but he seemed to be in charge, walking in front of the taller two. They all had parkas on, gray and black, but not like it was a uniform, more like they had the same style.

She looked to the tow truck man. He was leaning back against the door of his vehicle, his arms hanging casually down at his sides. He seemed totally unconcerned, and was not taking out a cell phone and calling 9-1-1. Had he already done that? No. He couldn't have.

The boys fanned out, like they had done this before, and knew that spreading wide would give them a better attack.

"What you doin', old man," the one in the center said as they stopped in a semicircle.

His voice was muffled on account of the BMW being so well insulated and sealed up.

Did they have guns? Elle wondered. Safety glass didn't go far when it came to stopping bullets.

"I'm never taking you out again when I shouldn't," she whispered. "Ever."

"I'm not going to tell Dad," Terrie said in a small voice.

"Huh?" the punk demanded out by the tow truck. "What the fuck you doin'?"

Elle narrowed her eyes on the tow man. He was staring at the one who was talking, eyes unblinking, body utterly still. She had a thought that the punk needed to be careful. As much as he seemed to think he was in control, something about what was going on here was not in his favor; he just didn't seem to be aware of it yet. Then again, maybe Elle was the one who was reading this wrong.

Yeah, 'cuz really, her judgment had been *so* great tonight already.

Then again, the way the tow truck man was staring at the punk was . . . way too focused.

Like how a cobra might look at a bare foot that had invaded its territory.

She almost cracked the window to yell that the punks needed to run. But it was just a tow truck guy, right? And maybe she was making a dangerous superhero out of him because he was all that stood between her and a whole lot of even-worse happening. She'd thought he was a threat and she'd been wrong. But she was not wrong about the three who had come out into the street.

"You fucking deaf?" the one in front said.

"I'm going to tell him," Elle whispered as her head

got buzzy with fright and she closed her eyes. "I'm going to tell Dad. This was a horrible mistake and I need to be responsible for it."

"I wish he were here."

The fact that it didn't dawn on either of them to call their mother was lost on Terrie, and something that lingered for Elle. But she should be used to it by now, she supposed—

The sound took her back to Labor Day, when her father had been carrying that cooler full of soda and ice and had dropped things: Loud, dull, and with a rattle.

Her lids popped open.

Outside, at the tow truck, one of the taller kids was slumping off the side of the hood, a streak of blood marking the path of his seemingly unconscious flop to the snow. The man in leather didn't pay him any mind. He lunged forward, grabbed the shorter one who'd thought he was in charge by the throat. As the leader of the pack Three Stooges—slapped at what was locked on the front of his neck, all the man with the mismatched eyes had to do was point at the remaining boy—

And the kid took off at a dead run, his ski hat flying off his head.

Elle blinked. And blinked again. But what she was

seeing did not change. The tow truck man just kept squeezing the neck in his grip, the kid clawing at the hold with his gloved hands, boots kicking at the snow . . . until he was lifted up high enough so that just his tiptoes made contact with the icy road. Meanwhile, the man stared with absolutely no expression at that reddened face with its gaping mouth and wild eyes. He might as well have been making himself a sandwich—

Close to where he was standing in the snow, there was a knife, dropped by one of the kids.

The punk who'd had his face banged on the hood flopped onto his side—and saw the weapon at the same time Elle did. Before she could yell, he moved faster than he should have considering he had blood dripping out of his nose and one of his eyes wasn't working right.

Elle yanked the door release, but forgot she'd locked everything. Banging on the window, she shouted, "Watch out!"

The tow truck man glanced toward her—just as the punk got the knife and surged upward, leading with the sharp point of the blade.

"No!" Elle screamed as she threw open her door.

The knife went right into the tow truck man's stomach, buried to the hilt.

"Get back in that car!" he snapped at her.

Then he threw the short one he had by the throat away. Like, literally, tossed the entire body of the kid he'd been strangling off to the side like someone littering with an empty soda can. The former leader of the attack landed in a heap, and he didn't hang around to see what was next. He tore off in a sloppy retreat, snow flying behind him.

Not that the tow man paid any attention to the bye-bye.

He was all about the stabber. Not at all about the knife.

How was this possible?

Even with the blade embedded six inches into his stomach, he bent down to the kid who'd done the deed—who was now back on his ass and staring up with a look of confusion Elle could totally relate to. Clearly, he couldn't believe that he'd stabbed the Terminator, but the tow man didn't give him any time to square up reality with expectation. He grabbed the kid's arm, yanked him to his feet, and forced the limb back until there was a loud *crack!* As the screaming started, and Elle felt a sickening urge to vomit, the man spun his attacker away like a top—with the kid taking the hint and racing off around the building.

Looking down at the handle of the knife, the man seemed more annoyed than anything else. Which was not the typical response when something that could cut steak was at a ninety-degree angle with somebody's belly button.

"Motherfucker," he muttered as he took out a cell phone.

Just before he dialed, he listed to one side. Then he fell down to his knees.

He was still looking annoyed as he slumped to the snow.

CHAPTER FOUR

The Black Dagger Brother Zsadist, blooded son of the Black Dagger Brother Ahgony, bonded of the fair and well-bred Bella, proud sire of Nalla, and brother of Phury, Primale of the Chosen, was cooling his jets on the corner of Market Street and 14th when the first of the punk-ass motherfuckers hauled by him at a dead run, black-and-gray parka flapping, boots stomping, fear scenting the air in his wake with an acrid burn that was a cross between a marshmallow too close to the campfire and Cascade dishwashing pods.

Talk about a snooze. Given that it was after dark

in downtown Caldwell, all kinds of humans were running this kind of footrace, twelve million kinds of bad decision making resulting in exactly this sort of panicked, rethink-sprint.

Like he cared.

Except then number two came tooling along. This guy was wearing a similar parka, which wasn't necessarily a thing, and seemed slightly less terrified—but he smelled like bong water spilled on an old carpet, so it was possible that his body was making a more accurate survival assessment than his THC-dusted brain was. But again, not Z's problem. Humans had an extraordinary capacity for stupidity, and who was he to get in the way of consequential learning—

Inside his ear, there was a low-level *brrrrng*. Then Vishous's voice: "Z? We need you three blocks to the north. Qhuinn's down. Manny ETA four minutes. Abdominal stab."

"Fuck," he muttered as he leaned into his shoulder. "Leaving now."

He would have dematerialized, except you didn't do that unless you knew exactly where you were re-forming and he wasn't far. He started running, the daggers that were holstered handles down on his chest moving with his torso's power as if they were a part of his body that he'd been born with. His guns and his ammo were the same, everything lock-holstered to his shoulders and his hips, nothing slapping against him, the whole arsenal coming with and right in reach.

And what do you know. He was looking to shoot something all of a sudden. Qhuinn was not only a member of the Brotherhood, but he'd also saved Z's life one night. So yeah, there was loyalty all over the place.

When he got to the corner of a storage building that was every bit as bright and shiny as a discarded hubcap, he choked up on his leg churn. Fresh blood on the breeze. Nothing gunpowdery, so no bullets. At least not yet—

Footfalls were coming fast on an approach toward him, and a split second later, a lanky kid with a busted-up, bloody face tooled around the side of the building, right into Z's path. To avoid a head-on collision, Z punched at the fucker's pecs, and like a pool ball on a billiards table, things went ricochet, the body in motion spinning off and slamming into the metal siding with a cymbal crash.

If Qhuinn hadn't been wounded, Z would have grounded the little shit the old-fashioned way.

With a shovel and a grave marker.

Instead, he followed the trail of blood in the snow

to the Black Dagger Brotherhood's tow truck. The vehicle, which was supposed to be reserved for AAA situations of the vampire variety, was front-winch-in to the trunk of a BMW sedan the color of cabernet sauvignon. One of the car's doors was wide open, and a human girl, mid to late teens, was kneeling over a facedown and fetal-positioned Qhuinn. Another human girl, younger, was leaning out of the front seat, one hand clamped over her mouth, eyes the size of basketballs.

The brother was leaking. Badly. And that copper tint to the cold air was the equivalent of a fire alarm, something you couldn't see but made your ears ring.

Z went right for his brother. As he bent down, the girl who was with him backed off.

"Is he d-d-dead? Is he dying?"

"I'm fine," Qhuinn muttered. "I just ate too much for First Meal."

Z wanted to roll the male over and see what was doing, but he didn't have the medical training necessary to do that safely. "Yeah, that Henkel you had for dessert really put you over the edge."

"FYI, I don't think it's that fancy."

"Swiss Army?"

"Prison shank maybe—"

"He w-w-won't let me c-c-c-call the p-p-police."

Z looked at the girl. She had to be seventeen, he was guessing. Jeans. Boots. Parka in pale blue. Nice, middle class, not the kind who should be out in this part of town at this time of night. Instead of fucking around and asking a bunch of questions, he barged into her brain and went directly to her file cabinet of memories.

Ah, yes. Mild rebellion against Daddy run amok— and then things really went wrong.

"Relax," he told her.

"I d-didn't mean for this to happen."

Oops in one hand, shit in the other, see what you get the most of, he thought.

Checking his watch, he figured he had three minutes until Manny arrived so he better get on with it. Rising to his full height, he strode over to the winch and the back of the sedan.

"Don't hurt my sister!"

The older girl had both of her hands outstretched in a way that reminded him of medieval altar pieces, all helpless, Virgin Mary entreaty for him not to do something he had no intention of doing anyway. Uninterested in talking to her, to anyone, he slammed that open door shut and cut the proverbial cord. Unlatching the tow truck's hook from the BMW, he tossed the winch over his shoulder and gripped the underside of the car's bumper. With a grunt, he sank down into his thighs and was careful to lift with his glutes, not his shoulders.

'Cuz really, their snow-locked car was not worth a slipped disk.

Through the rear window, the younger girl in the front seat wheeled about and stared at him, her arms wrapped around the back of the driver's seat like she was hugging it in lieu of a parental figure. As the angle of the tilt increased, the suspension adjusted to the redistribution of weight with an undercarriage creak, and then there was some serious snow-squeak as he relocated the butt while the two tires in front stayed where they were. His human peanut gallery, both the one inside the sedan and the one standing next to him, were jawbone-slacked as he let the back of the BMW drop to the ground again.

Heading to the driver's side, he reopened the door—

"No!" the younger girl screamed as she reared away from him again.

"Oh, please," he muttered, filling the space she'd vacated behind the wheel.

The engine had been left on, so things were warm. Not that he cared. He put the gearshift in reverse and gently eased some pressure onto the accelerator with his right shitkicker. There was a flare of noise from the hood first, and then a subtle shift of position, the tires grabbing at the snowpack with delicate manners. Using what little traction he had, he coaxed those treads to take more of the slippery meal under them, and more, and more—

The BMW rolled away from the snowbank it had been planted in, and he made sure not to run over Qhuinn as he righted its trajectory down the city street. Hitting the park button, he went to get out—

Like a butterfly, a small hand landed on the battered leather sleeve of his wartime jacket. "Mister?" the younger girl said.

He didn't want to look into her eyes. So he stared at the speedometer. "Yeah."

"You're really strong."

Z got out and took his sleeve with him. Facing the older of the pair, he said, "Go home. Don't do this shit again. Your father loves you, that's why he's got rules. You think he wants to ruin your life? He's just trying to make sure you live long enough to trash it on your own terms."

The girl blinked at him. When she didn't move, he opened the door wider and indicated the way in with a hand motion that was more annoyed than gallant elder statesman.

"What's going to happen to him?" the girl asked of Qhuinn.

"You don't have to worry about that."

"But it's my fault. All of this is."

Zsadist frowned. "Why would you care about us?"

As he heard himself speak, he stamped his shit-kicker. He was supposed to have kept that as an internal thought.

"Are you going to call the police?" she asked.

She was so worried. So horrified. So full of self-blame. And even though humans were of less than no concern to him, he had been through those exact trails of brambles so many times. Especially that last one.

"I'm going to take care of him," he told her. "Now you gotta go."

"Promise?" she whispered.

He was about to do another round of what's-it-to-you, but of course she didn't have a clue they were vampires. How could she?

"Do you know how to get back to the highway?" he demanded.

"I go that way?" she said as she pointed deeper into town.

"No." He put his hand on her shoulder and pivoted her around to the river. "That way."

The girl nodded, and for a moment, she seemed

like she wanted to give him a hug. Or maybe get one from him. He took a step back.

As a set of headlights flared and the deep rumble of Manny Manello's mobile surgical unit came down at them, she got into her dad's car. Going around to that back bumper again, Z pushed to help with traction as she turned the BMW in a circle to face the Hudson. At the last moment, just before he let go, he reached into her and her sister's brains. Not only did he scrub their memories, he made sure the one with the provisional driver's license knew exactly how to get back on the highway. Past that, though, she was going to have to get herself to the 'burbs.

"You weren't all that nice to her," Qhuinn muttered as the car rolled off at a snail's pace.

Like its driver was worried that the other snow-banks might spontaneously animate and decide to retaliate for what she had done to their comrade-in-heaps.

Z looked down at his brother as Manny's RV pulled up to them. "Are you going to die right now?"

"Nope. And did you hear what I said?"

"I got them going. That's all that matters."

"You have a daughter. Some night, she may need help from a human. How'd you like him to treat her?"

Zsadist refocused on the taillights as the BMW's

brakes were hit and then a turn signal—to the left, which was the correct way to go—started to blink.

"Whatever," Z said under his breath. "Haven't we got enough to worry about right now?"

"You think Nalla is never going out into the world on her own?"

"No," Z announced as Manny disembarked with his Little Black Doctor Duffle of poke-and-tickle toys. "That will never, ever happen."

As Qhuinn started to chuckle, and Manny began to rapid-fire questions of the how-are-we variety, Z decided that the night was going to get a job-satisfaction rating of zero.

Maybe less than zero.

Then again, it could have been worse. Given his history, you'd think he'd remember exactly how creative destiny could get with the bad news.

CHAPTER FIVE

B lay ran down the underground tunnel toward the Brotherhood's training center, the clapping sound of his leather-soled loafers like a round of applause for his haul-ass. Inside his skin, he was screaming. On the outside, his rigid composure was his armor, the thing he was going into a battle with, and his rational mind was his ammunition, his primary line of defense.

Too bad fate wasn't the kind of thing you could actually fight against.

When he came up to the locked door to the facility, he punched in a code and ripped through a supply closet kitted out with all kinds of OfficeMax. Out the other side, he scrambled by the desk, and from habit, smacked the *Fuck No!* button next to the computer. As the tinny voice expressed what he was feeling, he punched through a glass door and jogged down the concrete corridor. Doc Jane's medical area, which had been constructed and outfitted as an engagement present by V, was state of the art. Thank God. With its fully stocked examination rooms, ORs, and patient rooms, it was the best place an injured vampire could be.

Like, for example, if one had been stabbed in the gut.

Going by the scents, Blay knew exactly where his mate was, and when he came up to the exam room, he wanted to throw his body through the closed door. He forced himself to slow that roll. The last thing he needed was for his panic to cause a golf-sprinkler bleed—

The door in front of him opened and Manny Manello, Doc Jane's clinical partner and Payne's human *hellren*, jumped back. "Oh, good, you're here."

"Last rites?" Blay choked out.

Manny stepped aside as he took off his white coat. "No, awake and asking for you."

Blay's knees went weak as he peered around the surgeon and got a load of his one true love.

"Oh . . . God," he said. "What happened to you?"

Qhuinn was propped up on a gurney, his mismatched eyes bright and alert, his color good, his mouth pursed with mild annoyance . . . like maybe he'd picked the wrong tollbooth on the turnpike or a bad lane at the supermarket check-out. His shirt had been taken off—no, wait, cut off, given the two shredded halves on the tile floor—and for a split second, Blay's libido responded with a hey-there-big-boy.

Then again, all that muscle and smooth skin was distracting—

Yeah, except for THAT FUCKING KNIFE protruding at a right angle to the chip-your-tooth-worthy six-pack.

Blay reached out blindly as his balance went wonky.

Manny caught his arm. "You okay there?"

"Fine," he mumbled. "I'm just—"

"Ehlena, hand me the ammonia—"

"Whatsthatfor—" Blay's vision went checkerboard.

All of a sudden, something that was the nostril equivalent of a sucker punch brought him back to attention. As his eyeballs came online, he got a close-up of Manny's big hand and a cracked-open pill.

"Hit me with that again," Blay stammered.

Annnnnnnnnd *whfff*.

He stood straight up. "That's magic."

"Glad to be of service," Manny said as he ditched the sinus slapper.

Over on the patient bed, Qhuinn held out his arms. "I'm waiting for a proper hello."

Blay rushed across and dropped his mouth to his mate's. The feel of soft, warm lips made his legs go unreliable again.

"What happened?" he repeated. "And how do you get that out?"

"I suggested I could just give it a pull," Qhuinn muttered, "but I got shot down."

Manny propped open the door with his hip. "Yeah, I mean, just because you have half a dozen critical structures and veins in that area, what the hell. Give it a yank. In a non-sterile environment with no backup. Suuuuuurrrrrre. What medical school did you go to?"

Qhuinn flipped the guy the bird.

The surgeon returned the favor. "And Blay, to answer your question, I am going to remove it in the OR. Ehlena's prepping everything. Jane's going to assist. We're ten minutes out."

"Why is he not bleeding to death?" Blay stared down at his mate. "Why are you not passing out from blood loss?"

"Do you want me to?" Qhuinn winked. "You could totally have your way with me then, you know."

"You let me have my way with you anyhow."

"This is true. On that note, how's now sound?"

"I think he's going to be fine," Manny said dryly. "But we need to make sure the removal is done carefully and in a place where if something goes wrong, I can fix it. Now if you boys will excuse me, I'm going to scrub up."

As the human left, Qhuinn reached for the front of Blay's shirt and grabbed on in desperation.

"Should I call him back in?" Blay took that hand and cradled it between his own. "Do you need—"

"You're looking good tonight—"

"What?"

The hand in his returned to the shirt—and released the top button. "You just look so good. And you smell nice. And I want to touch you . . ."

As Qhuinn licked his lips, those blue and green eyes started to twinkle in that way they did when things were taking a turn into naked territory.

"Qhuinn."

"Yes?"

Blay pointed to the knife. "You're not getting horny with that sticking into you."

"You don't think so? 'Cuz I'm pretty sure you're wrong about that. And *mmmm*, sticking things into people."

As the male started to roll his hips, Blay glanced down the bed. Sure enough, behind the fly of those leathers, a thick erection had sprung up out of nowhere—

A hissing noise preceded an abrupt halt of the grind, and as Blay refocused on his mate's face, Qhuinn lost that lovin' feeling: Gone was the sexual speculation. In its place was all kinds of well-shit-*that*-hurt.

Blay kept his I-told-you-so's to himself. "Just rest, okay?"

"We have ten minutes."

"Well, eight now."

"It's a shame to waste them." Qhuinn turned his head on the thin white pillow and stared at the center of Blay's pelvis like there was a bull's-eye hanging off his Hermès belt. "Besides, I have something that's working just fine."

"Your brain is not it."

Qhuinn deliberately licked his lips again and then bit down on his pierced lower one with his fangs. Next up on the roster was some kind of pleading sound in the back of his throat, and his final player on the field was his tongue. Which really wasn't fair. That ball piercing made an extended appearance, the steel catching a glimmer in the light of the exam room as it flicked back and forth—

Blay groaned and closed his eyes. "What are you doing to me—"

"What I'd *like* to be doing to you, is more the point." That hand, that talented hand, went for a stroll down Blay's torso. "I'll be quick about it and it'll feel good for you, I'll make sure of that."

Well, duh, the male always did. The guy's jaw was double jointed—

As Blay felt his own arousal get cupped through his fine slacks, he tottered on his feet—and sure, at least this time the wobble was not from terror. But it was not from relief, either. There was an operation looming, and that knife was still STICKING STRAIGHT UP out of Qhuinn's pancreas.

Or whatever anatomy was playing pincushion.

"Gimme just a taste," Qhuinn growled. "Come on, just a taste . . ."

Blay swayed so badly he had to catch himself on the gurney's edge. "This isn't the time—"

"Oh, I think it is." That hand went for the zipper. "Tell me to open wide for you, Blay. Tell me you're going to fill my mouth up. Tell me you're going to stretch my lips and—"

The door swung open and Blay jumped back so far, so fast, he slammed into the wall, rattling the framed Claude Monet poster that added a slice of color to all the clinical stainless steel and tile. The good news? Ehlena, the clinic's nurse, was busy rolling in a piece of equipment so she missed all the rearranging. On both his and Qhuinn's part.

"—just need a quick EKG," she was saying. "Won't take a moment."

Qhuinn's voice dropped to a whisper as he looked up at Blay. "Six minutes. Still enough time. And my heart's doing a-okay, so we can tell her to go."

Blay glared at the fool. "You are out of your mind."

"I could be out of my pants if you let me."

"Ehlena?" Blay said.

"Yes?"

As Qhuinn got all kinds of hopeful, Blay crossed his arms over his chest. "Can you hook that thing up to his skull? I think that's the area on him we need to check first."

Qhuinn's beautiful lips mouthed: *Party pooper.*

Ehlena laughed. "I'm not going to ask."

"You're a smart female," Blay muttered.

As the nurse started affixing pads to various pulse points, he went still as reality sunk in. Fear, ever a tenacious interloper, made him focus on his mate with such intensity that it felt as though he was seeing that which was intimately familiar for the first time: The teardrop tattoo that had been colored in in purple when Qhuinn had been relieved of his *ah-strux nohtrum* position for John Matthew. Those incredible eyes, one like a piece of jade, the other like a Ceylon sapphire. The slashing brows that could fluctuate from aggression to flirtation in a second. The piercings in the ears, all gunmetal, the hoops running up from the lobe. The piercings elsewhere, winking in the bright light. The black hair that was cut in an asymmetric flop at the moment, part of it colored grape Kool-Aid. The thick neck, the heavy pecs, the rippled arms and broad shoulders.

The sacred scar of the Black Dagger Brotherhood right over the heart.

It was a helluva package. And yet as unforgettable as it was . . . the inside of the male was even more beautiful: The loyalty. The love. The soul that shone with such inner purity.

"I love you," Blay said quietly. "More than the first moment I saw you and less than I will as the sun sets tomorrow."

Ehlena hesitated with the tangle of colorful wires. "Would you guys like a moment?"

"Oh, no, we're good." Clearing his throat, Blay motioned her to come closer. "Sorry. I shouldn't have started babbling—"

Qhuinn grabbed Blay's arm. In a rare moment

of feeling, the male said, "Yes, you should have. You should always tell me what you need me to hear."

Tears, unexpected and embarrassing, sprung to Blay's eyes, making it seem like he was looking through antique glass. In a flash of paranoia, he blinked them away. What if these were their last moments together and he wasted them on blurry vision?

"I love you, too," Qhuinn said softly. "And I'm going to be just fine. I promise."

After everything Blay's true love had been through—from the way his parents had hated and shamed him when he'd been growing up, to the Honor Guard beating by his own blooded brother and three others, to the acting out and acting in of it all after his transition—it was rare for emotion to come through that facade of resolve and strength. As a result, when Qhuinn's feelings were shown, they had a way of stopping the whole world. Blay never questioned his mate's love, and he didn't require the constant expression of it. He wasn't needy like that. But oh, God, when he did see Qhuinn's heart, it was like the sun coming out on a rainy day.

He had to stop and savor the warmth.

In the back of his mind, he heard Bitty's voice: *So you're not properly mated?*

Blay leaned down and kissed his mate. "In all the ways that matter."

"What?" Qhuinn asked.

"Nothing." Blay looked across Qhuinn's bare chest at Ehlena. "I'll get out of your way."

The female in scrubs smiled. "We're going to take excellent care of him. I swear it."

◆ ◆ ◆

Up at the mansion, Zsadist whispered down the Hall of Statues, heavy shitkickers silent over the Persian runner, big body moving through the still, lemon-scented air without a rustle, breathing even and inaudible as he passed by the Greco-Roman warriors that had been carved out of marble by human hands long dead and gone. All the stealth was not something he cultivated and not anything that was required given the safety and security of his home. But he had moved in the shadows as a shadow ever since his twin had gotten him out of Hell. He never liked to call attention to himself if he didn't need to, whether it was traveling through a house, standing in a room, or sitting in a chair.

When you had had attention forced on you, when your body had been taken against your will, when you had been a toy used and abused at the whims of a malicious other, calendar nights could put the distance of an era between you and your nightmare, and geographic miles could likewise reinforce the difference between the there-and-then and the here-and-now, but you never lost your adaptive behavior. Like the slave bands tattooed around his neck and his wrists, and the *S*-shaped scar that intersected his face, and the way he preferred to be invisible even outside of hostility, his marble had been carved in a certain way. And as with the statues he currently walked by, his evolution was as irreversible and structural as their forever-frozen poses.

A millennium from now, the statues would still be as they were—and so he would ever be as he was. His artist was dead, too. He knew this because he had killed her and slept beside her skull for a century . . . and yet there had been a corner turned for him, an unexpected fresh start that had eased him in ways that even he was coming to trust.

Love had done more than turn his black eyes back to yellow.

Yet he still walked in silence.

Stopping in front of one of the lineup of bedroom suites, he went to knock—

The door opened sharply, and on the other side, the Chosen Layla was dressed in jeans and a SUNY Caldwell sweatshirt, her blond hair pulled back in a ponytail, her glowing beauty the kind of thing that didn't need makeup or fancy clothes for enhancement.

The look of abject terror on her face was wholly at odds with all of her casual, night-at-home-with-the-kids attire.

"Qhuinn's going to be fine," Z said. "They're taking him in the OR now, and Manny is confident there's going to be a good result."

"Thank the Virgin Scri—" Layla stopped herself. "Oh . . . sorry, old habits die hard. I keep forgetting She's gone."

"Just please don't bring up Lassiter's name right now, especially if it's with gratitude. He's liable to show up so he can enjoy the praise, and I've had a long night already."

The female smiled. "I will thank our angel in private then."

When there was a cooing sound from deeper inside the room, Z looked in. Across the antique rug, between a museum-quality inlaid bureau of Italian provenance and a Scottish writing desk from the 1800s, the dual Pottery Barn cribs were a splash of modern, some-assembly-required in the midst of all the Old World luxury. One crib was done in pink, the other in blue.

"Would you like to come in and see them?" Layla

stepped back. "They love visitors, and Rhamp particularly adores you."

Z thought of those two human girls, out in the winter darkness alone in daddy's BMW. As he walked across the room, he wondered if they'd gotten home safe.

You have a daughter. Some night, she may need help from a human. How'd you like him to treat her?

He went over to say hi to Lyric first, but that was not how it worked out. In the midst of all the pink frills of her crib, her sturdy little brother was holding on to his feet and doing some kind of baby pull-up thing with his chunky torso. The moment Z leaned over the rail, the kid stopped his infant-robics and shifted his eyes over, those peepers narrowing into an assessment that penetrated into places a grown-ass male would just as soon not have anybody go.

Much less a bag of carbon-based molecules that only had pooping and consuming down pat.

Except then the young started to smile. Instantly, that intensity was cut off and there was nothing but toothy grin—in spite of how ugly Z was with the scar that ran down his face. Then again, one of the things he liked about these young was that they had never not known males who had deformities. Their stepdad, Xcor, had a harelip they were well used to, so there was no scaring them with what was doing on Z's puss.

Although on that note, one couldn't be too sure Rhamp was going to be scared of anything. He was like his sire in that regard. Qhuinn wasn't ever afraid.

"They like to switch cribs," Layla said as she ruffled her son's dark hair. "Rhamp insists on being in Lyric's space sometimes. She doesn't mind. I feel like he's checking the crib rails to make sure she's safe. It's the funniest thing."

"He's right to look after her."

"Well, she looks after him, too."

"That's as it should be."

Z reached out and ran his forefinger down Rhamp's chubby cheek. As the kid grabbed hold and squeezed, the compression was surprisingly strong. Then it was a case of tug . . . tug . . . tug . . . and all the time, the kid was cheery as he stared up. Even though Zsadist was a fully grown male capable of great violence.

"How do they know?"

As Z heard his voice hit the airwaves, he wanted to curse. He'd meant to keep that to himself.

Second time tonight. Maybe he needed to go see Doc Jane for some oral cavity Imodium.

"Know what?" Layla asked softly. "About who to trust, you mean?"

"People are dangerous. Especially to those who are weaker. And you don't get weaker than a young."

"Not everyone is dangerous. Look at you standing over the cribs of my young."

He moved over to Lyric, and as soon as she saw him, she smiled, her eyes twinkling like stars in her baby face.

"You would kill to protect them," Layla murmured.

"Damn right I would. They are my family, even though we are not of close blood." As Z thought of those two human girls again, he was of a mind to try to strip his own damn memories. "Do you worry about them? Out in the world?"

"Not at the moment. Right now they are here, within my reach, every second of every hour. Later, though, I will. I imagine it will be similar to how I worry about Xcor out in the field. So many things can go wrong. A second can change a lifetime forever."

Z rubbed the back of his neck. "I have to go."

And yet he did not move.

"What consumes you, friend," Layla prompted gently.

"I don't like the vagaries of chance."

"What's making you think of fate tonight?"

"Nothing." Just snowbanks. And children. And stabbings. "Nothing in particular."

"Are you going to go see your Bella and Nalla? They were in the playroom last time I checked."

He glanced at the Chosen. "Take care of yourself, and your precious ones."

"I will. Take care of my beloved out in the field? I don't know what I would do if . . ."

"I always have Xcor's back." He pictured the huge fighter with the disfigured upper lip and the jawline of an I beam. "We all watch after each other. Worry not, Chosen."

And yet would it be enough, he wondered as he left.

Probably on most nights, sure. But on every night? Every single night? Mathematical probability said no on that one.

And young needed their fathers.

Guess Rhamp and Lyric were lucky in that regard. They had three of them.

CHAPTER SIX

Outside of the training center's OR, Blay sat on the corridor's concrete floor and leaned back against the concrete wall. The subterranean cold of everything didn't register and he didn't pay much attention to how hard everything was against his body. Hard was what was happening on the other side of that closed door. Hard was opening up someone's insides, seeing a leak that was life-threatening, and being all I-know-how-to-fix-that.

There was a time when he'd thought he would go into medicine. He was getting over that now.

Especially as he imagined what was going on with

Qhuinn's abdomen at the moment. The only thing that made him feel even halfway okay about the knife removal was the fact that the male had had sex on the brain right up until Ehlena had slapped him silly with those EKG wires. Surely that meant something, right?

Blay looked down the hall toward the reinforced steel door that opened into the underground parking garage. Then he glanced down the other way, toward the gym, the Olympic-sized pool, and the target range. He could smell the distant chlorine, and someone was working out in the weight room, the rhythmic metal clanking going on for what seemed like forever. Probably Ruhn. Saxton's male was a big lifter, even compared to the Brothers.

The guy would have been a great asset out in the field, but he was a certified pacifist now, and considering his history, no one could blame him—

The OR door swung wide, and Manny braced it open with his foot, a vision in blue scrubs and his surgical mask. The fact that he kept his hands behind his back suggested there was blood on those nitrile gloves, and as Blay's stomach went storm-surge on him, he was determined not to throw up on himself.

"Qhuinn did great, and the knife missed all the expensive real estate." The surgeon shook his head.

"It's a miracle. As always, someone was watching out for him."

Blay put his hand over his heart, and as his head swam with relief, he was glad he was sitting down. "Thank you so much. Oh, my God, thank you."

"Our pleasure. We're just closing now. You can see him in a little bit."

As the surgeon ducked back into the sterile area, Blay rubbed his face and shuddered inside his own skin. Images of crystal glasses caught just as they fell off the edge of tables, and of fingers narrowly saved from the bite of car doors, and of land mines missed by millimeters, flashed through his mind. And now, as Qhuinn's body was set to rights again, Blay's own part of the healing process could begin. With the mortal danger over, he had to coax his brain back into risk-awareness hibernation: After every narrow-margin save and each near miss, he always had to stuff his panic back in its lockbox.

Otherwise, he'd be perpetually quaking in his boots.

The thing was, they were all at risk, every night they went out into the field—especially with the Omega gone, and the trainees and others seeing a new shadowy threat downtown. At least with the Lessening Society, they'd known what they were fighting—

Shuffling sounds brought his head up.

A hobbling figure in a terry cloth bathrobe was coming down the corridor, its weight braced on a cane, its gait as steady and regular as a case of the hiccups. The head was down; the dark hair, which had begun to thin and go gray, was wet; the scent of chlorine was pervasive.

"Luchas," Blay said. "How are you?"

Qhuinn's brother didn't speak until he was right in front of Blay, and there was effort involved in lifting his head from its permanent loll.

"I am well, and yourself?"

The voice was reedy, but the accent was straight-up *glymera*, something between high-brow British monarchy and French diplomat.

"I'm okay, and so is your brother."

Luchas's gray eyes flared, and he looked to the closed door. "Is Qhuinn unwell?"

As a matter of fact, he's just recovering from a case of poke-itis.

"He's going to be fine."

"He was injured whilst fighting, then?"

"It was minor." Blay blinked away the image of that knife handle sticking straight up. "And you know, he's a tough one."

"Yes, he is." Luchas lowered his head. "He has always been."

It seemed apt that Luchas went to illness first rather than contusion or concussion. The aristocracy was not hardwired for physical combat or the realities of war, and the male's perspective had not changed in spite of what had been done to him by the Omega's son, Lash. And maybe Luchas's abduction and torture were part of it. Even though he had been treated at the training center since he had been rescued from that oil drum, the Brothers and the fighters didn't talk about the war anywhere around him.

He'd been through enough.

"How is your new prosthesis working out?" Blay asked.

That weight shifted in favor of the cane and a molded silicone foot presented itself from under the hem of the robe.

"It is what it is."

"I'll bet it just takes time to adjust." As Blay made the comment, he was aware that he knew nothing about what being an amputee was like. "Have you talked to Phury?"

"He has been most helpful." There was defeat in that voice as the molded foot was placed back on the concrete floor. "One is exhausted by so much, how-ever."

"You've come so far." Blay tried not to notice the thinning hair and the lines that were etched deep into a face that should have been as youthful as his own. He also did not look at the mangled hand upon the head of the cane. "Truly, you have."

"And yet I am no closer to where I wish I was. If you will excuse me?"

As if the male was uncomfortable with where the conversation had gone.

"Of course." Even though Blay was sitting down, he bowed low in the manner of the aristocracy, bending himself over his outstretched legs. "I'll tell Qhuinn you stopped by and asked for him."

"Please do."

In polite recognition of his departure, Luchas also inclined his torso—but a cracking sound let off as if his spine was not as flexible as it should have been. With a grunt of pain, his deformed hand tightened on the cane's grip, and Blay jumped up and caught him as his balance listed sharply to the left.

"Forgive me," Luchas said as he shoved his body back to level. "I am not my brother. I am not tough."

"There are many who would disagree with that. And I am one of them."

Eyes that were gray as a fog stared across the vast distance of experience and destiny between them. To think that they had both started in the same place: Healthy, first-born sons of the aristocracy. Now?

"I am sorry," Luchas mumbled. "Did you tell me exactly what happened to my brother? I cannot recall. Lately, the pain has been making me fuzzy."

As Blay hesitated, the male shook his head. "So it was in the field, was it not?"

"He is okay now."

"You all protect me from things I very well know exist. The monsters are out from beneath my bed, dearest Blay, and not only has it been as such for quite some time, ne'er shall they return thereunder. I live with them in my head." Luchas touched his temple. "I can assure you that there is no fact pattern you can report that comes close to what dwells here in my mind. Especially as my brother appears to have bested whatever attempt was made upon his life."

Blay cleared this throat. "He was stabbed. In the stomach."

That stare returned to the OR's closed door. "He must have been in such agony."

"He was . . . but he handled himself."

"Of course he did. Survival is a learned trait that comes through the mastery of suffering. My brother suffered in our household for all of his most vulnerable years, so yes, he can get through any kind of pain. Endurance is what he learned to do best." Luchas's head relowered into its downward position. "On the other hand, I am not like my brother because I was not like him. I was nurtured and therefore have no strength. Or purpose, for that matter."

"You are well loved here, Luchas. There are many who care for you."

"Take care of me, you mean." That prosthetic foot made a reappearance. "My needs far outstretch my contributions, I'm afraid."

"That is not true."

"And what exactly have I done for the race of late? Or any of you?" Before Blay could respond, Luchas shook his head. "Forgive me. I do not mean to sound churlish. It is just that Qhuinn is the male our parents should have found virtue in. Outward appearance is, after all, a very thin margin of judgment for character, is it not."

"You are more than—"

"More than this broken mess?" Luchas indicated his body and then held up his hand. It was missing several fingers, courtesy of that asshole Lash. "You know, there are times when I believe this was all meant to be. My exterior frailty is simply a reflection of my internal failings. I have become aligned with my nature."

"That's not true." What else could he say, Blay wondered. "Please know, it will get better."

Luchas's face registered the ghost of a smile. "It is apparent why my brother loves you. I quite believe you mean that."

"I do."

Those gray eyes lost their focus, as if the male were seeing something that only existed in his mind. "Alas, my future is what it is."

"So much has changed, though. I mean, everything is different."

"Not from what I witness. The *glymera* may be lesser in number because of the raids, but they are just as great as ever when it comes to censure. I lurk online amongst them and see what they do. As it was, so it continues to be."

"You don't need to have anything to do with them. You're a part of this community now, and with us, you have a future that is not bound by all those discriminations and rules. I mean, look at Qhuinn. Look at how far he's come, he's not only a Brother now, but he's been promoted to the private guard of the King and—"

"I'm sorry." Luchas stiffened. "What did you say?"

Blay frowned and looked around. Like the tunnel was going to help him out, though? "Ah, Qhuinn was elevated to Wrath's personal guard. I thought . . . didn't you know that?"

"No. I'm afraid I did not. When did this occur?"

"That's not important—"

"When?"

"A little while ago?" Blay phrased it as a question, even though there was no lack of clarity around the date. Clearing his throat, he tried to smooth things over. "I'm sure he meant to share the news with you."

"Indeed." Luchas stared at the door to the OR. "As if being appointed to protect the King and First Family is something that easily slips one's mind. 'Tis only the most venerable, august, and respected position within the race."

"Qhuinn is a very brave fighter."

"Of that I am very aware. And allow me to affirm that if there was e'er an individual to deserve such an honor, it is he. I am happy for him, and I can guess why he failed to bring it up. Quite a reversal of station he and I have had over the course of our lives." There was a pause. "Well. I look forward to his full recovery, as I'm sure do you. And to his continued service unto the race."

"Luchas, please . . ." Blay offered his open palms. Like a lame-ass. "I don't know what to say."

"Worry not, old friend." Those gray eyes clouded over. "My brother chose wisely when he picked you. In truth, Blaylock, you are a male of worth."

This time, Luchas did not try to bow as he turned away. Relying on that cane, he shuffled down the clinical area, the robe hem swinging side to side as weight was transferred back and forth, a load borne with unreliability. When he got to the door to his patient room, he tilted his head to the side in its downward position and looked back at Blay. And then he lifted his bony, mangled hand in a wave before disappearing into his private space.

With a curse, Blay remembered the male from before the raids, from before Luchas had been captured and tortured by the Omega's son, Lash, and the Lessening Society. He had been so fit and healthy and perfect, the pride and joy of his parents, of the *glymera* as a whole.

A firstborn son of impeccable pedigree with all his fingers and toes.

And now here he was.

Even as Blay fought the tide of memory, images bubbled up and refused to be denied. Over all the centuries that vampires had fought against the

Omega and his army of the undead, there had been countless truly tragic events. The raids, however, had been nuclear in nature, *lessers* attacking the hidden mansions of the aristocracy, slaughtering not just families, but whole bloodlines. Qhuinn's had been among them, and he likely would have been killed that night, too, if they hadn't kicked him out for his heterochromia iridum.

His blue and green eyes, long the bane of his existence, at least according to his parents and their ilk, had saved him.

At Qhuinn's request, Blay had gone to the house and identified the bodies, and Luchas's had been among them. Blay had seen the remains with his own two eyes—and that was supposed to be where it all ended, the terminal point of the catastrophic losses for that family, the bodies buried on the property. Except, no. Someone from the Lessening Society had returned.

And Lash had brought Luchas back.

The story had never been completely told, and no one had been inclined to press Luchas for details, but a year later, the male had been found in an oil drum at an abandoned site of the enemy's, reanimated and preserved in a swill of the Omega's vile essence. Qhuinn had been the one who found his brother, and the only identifier had been the gold signet ring Luchas been given by their sire the night after his transition.

The torture he'd been put through had been extensive, fingers cut off, broken bones all over his body, bruises, contusions, cuts. And then there had been the psychological trauma of it all. The Brotherhood had brought him here to the training center, and since then, Luchas had lost his lower leg as part of the continuing attempt to keep him alive and functioning.

Considering where the male had started out in life, it wasn't how any of it was supposed to go. If the world had made any sense, if things had gone the way of history's predictions, Luchas would likely be mated by now, or at least locked into an arrangement with a female of comparable breeding. He would be attending meetings of the Council with his sire, and enjoying grand functions and festivals. He would be rubbing shoulders with vampires like himself, secure in the knowledge that he had more money than he would ever need and an unassailable position in society.

But fiction could pale in comparison to destiny.

In ways both good and bad.

For instance, who'd have ever thought Qhuinn would have been made an official member of the Black Dagger Brotherhood?

Or that the male would ever have decided to settle down. With the best friend who had loved him since they were young.

Luchas was right about one thing. The two brothers had traded places.

It was just such a shame that the former's fall from grace had been so devastating.

♦ ♦ ♦

Paper cut.

Huge, weird, inexplicable paper cut.

As Qhuinn came out of anesthesia, his first thought was that someone had taken a manila folder, a crisp, brand-spanking-new manila folder, and whipped it right across his lower abdominals. It was the only way to explain the sweet sting striping between his hip bones, right below his belly button. Except . . . the discomfort wasn't a surface kind of thing. The sensation was deep inside.

So maybe it was more like part of his intestines had decided to lick a Publishers Clearing House envelope.

Just as he was coming to the conclusion that he had been through so much worse in the owie department, his eyes flipped open.

The medical light fixture above him brought it all back, as did the *beep, beep, beep* that seemed to sug-

gest that he had a heartbeat as regular as a metro-
nome.

Another piece of good news—

Without warning, a face appeared above his own.

Manny Manello.

The dark-haired human had a surgical mask hanging loose in front of his neck, like a feed bag he'd emp-
tied of grain. When he smiled, his fangless teeth were
white and his dark eyes were kind.

"You're all set." Manny flashed a thumbs-up. "No
internal damage, but it's a good thing we already took
out your spleen. It's like your organs did some par-
kour and got away from the blade. Considering what
could have been sliced? You're very lucky."

"Thanks, Doc." Qhuinn cleared his throat, which
was sore from the intubation. "Where are—"

"I'll send your people in."

"Is it okay for the—"

"Yup, the kids are fine to join you." Manny patted
his patient's knee. "And you don't have to stay down
here for much longer. You're cleared to head back to
the big house as soon as you're steady enough to walk."

"Awesome. You're amazing."

"Please don't stop with the compliments. And let's
get your family in here."

The surgeon went over and opened the door, and

Layla was the first to come in. The Chosen had Rhamp in her arms, and her beautiful face was worried—but that concern lifted instantly as Qhuinn clapped his hands.

"There's my boy," he said as he hit the button to raise the head of the hospital bed. "And the best *mahmen* there is."

Blay was right behind her with Lyric, and the instant the little one saw her sire, she put out her arms, straining for contact.

"Oh, sweetie, Daddy's okay." Qhuinn took her first, putting aside the remote and settling her on the bedside as he kissed his mate. "It's all good."

Lyric crawled up his chest and snuggled in quick, all chubby and warm and perfect, finding her favorite place in his neck. Closing his eyes, he breathed in deep and smelled Desitin, fresh Huggies, and Aveeno baby wash—and when her little sock-covered foot dug into his belly, he mostly kept his wince to himself.

"No, I've got her," he said to Blay. "I'm okay. And gimme another kiss."

After a brief contact and a shared smile with his mate, Qhuinn reached up and touched his son's soft and round face. Immediately, Rhamp grabbed on to the forefinger and yanked back and forth, as if he were making Qhuinn wave to himself.

"We were so worried," Layla murmured.

"I don't ever want to scare you guys." Qhuinn smiled as Rhamp started talking, all the babbling like the kid was giving him a lecture to stay safe in the field. "Really? Tell me more."

"He's on a roll," Blay remarked with a smile.

"When this big guy starts stringing actual words together, we're going to have quite a ride."

And he couldn't wait. He wanted to know what his son had to say. His daughter, too.

"Where's the last quarter of our fantastic foursome?" Qhuinn asked.

"Xcor's still out in the field." Layla sat on the foot of the bed and settled Rhamp on her lap. "He wanted to be here, but I told him you'd rather he stay on shift."

"Damn right I would. We need everyone out there right now, and I can see him when the sun's up."

"That's exactly how I thought you'd feel."

"You know me too well."

There was a momentary quiet, and then Blay and Layla started talking about the upcoming human holidays, and some kind of Party Planning Committee run by—God forbid—Lassiter. As they clearly made an effort to get back to normal, Qhuinn was glad things moved away from the drama. He'd had to work hard to keep his mind from going into the I'm-going-to-die swamp, and he'd just as soon start putting distance in whatever form it came in between him and the stabbing.

On that note, he shifted Lyric around so she lay cradled in the crook of his arm. Then he smoothed her Boston Red Sox onesie and gently poked her tummy. As she giggled, her newly acquired baby teeth showed, two on the top, two on the bottom.

"I'ma do it again," he murmured to her. "Watch me. Here it comes . . . gotcha."

The onesie was, naturally, a gift from Uncle V and Uncle Butch, who had made it a personal crusade to outfit every kid in the mansion with bureaus full of Red Sox merch: Bitty. The twins. Nalla. Even George, Wrath's dog, was decked out with a collar and a cold-weather sweater with the red *B* on it.

You might have been tempted to tell the guys they'd have even better luck brainwashing the next generation into hating the Yankees if they put flashing neon signs in the front foyer with pictures of Big Papi and bowls of candy in front of 'em. But then you'd run the risk they might actually do it.

"Who's my smart girl?" he said as he booped Lyric again. "Who's daddy's smart girl?"

As she smiled even wider, her eyes, her big green eyes, shone up at him.

Staring into them, he went back into the past. To that moment when he had died and gone unto the Fade.

To that moment when he had seen her face in that shadowy door.

Maybe it was the fact that he had collapsed out on the street in the snow only an hour or two ago . . . maybe it was because life felt extra special when you woke up out of surgery . . . maybe it was a brain fart caused by the lingering anesthesia . . . but for whatever reason, he returned to that night the Honor Guard had been sent after him.

His parents had finally kicked him out of the house. No news flash there. The see-ya-later had been long in coming, and given that Luchas had survived his transition, the social stakes had been even higher. Who the hell was going to mate the guy, considering what his brother was? What well-bred female was going to volunteer to throw her DNA into a gene pool that had already coughed up a corker with mismatched irises?

So Qhuinn had been removed from the family tree, given the boot from the family house, and left to walk off into the night with nowhere to go.

Except his best friend's house, of course.

He hadn't made it to Blay's, though. Four males in

hooded black robes had intersected his path, and he could still picture them clear as day, their faces hidden, their role clear: an Honor Guard sent to punish him and avenge his family's name. And the purpose of the concealment of identity had not been because the males were behaving unlawfully and didn't want anyone to know who they were. On the contrary, they had been sanctioned in their brutality, and the purpose of the masking was that they represented all of the *glymera*. They were the generalized shaming and shunning of the entire aristocracy, not a mere quartet of it, but a hundred of the species, not just Qhuinn's own bloodline, but all of them.

As the attack had commenced, he had put up a fight, as was his nature. But the numbers game had not been in his favor, and once he went down to the asphalt, the beating had really taken off with those clubs.

And then a voice, in the midst of the raining blows.

We aren't supposed to kill him!

His brother, Luchas. Naturally, the firstborn son had had to be involved in it as the representation of the bloodline. It was the way of things, and Qhuinn had never held the participation against his brother.

In their family of origin, neither of them had had any freedom of choice. No one in the aristocracy did, and maybe that was why as a group they were all such fucking assholes.

Not that there were many left after the raids.

As a shiver of unease teased the nape of Qhuinn's neck, he stroked his daughter's blond hair . . . and the sense of warning got worse instead of better.

Back when he had been lying on that stretch of pavement, after the beating had stopped, his weak breath rattling up and down the collapsed trail of his esophagus, he had seen the door unto the Fade. It had come to him, as he had heard it would when the time for death arrived—and he had reached out for the knob because legend held that if you opened the door and stepped through, all your suffering ended and you enjoyed an eternity with those you loved.

Frankly, he'd been shocked that his defect hadn't relegated him to *Dhunhd*.

Except he hadn't turned that knob.

On the flat plane of the white portal, he had seen the face of a young. Lyric. Who at the time had not only been unborn, but was no possibility at all as far as he was concerned. Yet his beloved daughter had appeared before him, her pale-green eyes looking out at him and sending a clear and certain message that as much as he thought it was his moment to transition unto eternity, in fact, it was not his time.

There had been many consequences to the vision, not the least of which was, hello, he was still alive. But an unintended corollary was the fact that until Lyric was born, he'd relied on that vision as a safety vest, a talisman in his reckless engagement and risk-taking in the field: Because until she was safely delivered upon the birthing bed, he was guaranteed life. After all, if he kicked it? She couldn't exist.

Now, though, it dawned on him that his purpose in creating her had been fulfilled.

No more grace period for danger and death. Sure, in the vision, he had seen her green eyes change to reflect his own mismatched gaze, but that didn't mean he could guarantee he'd be around to see the shift happen. And as for what happened tonight? He'd been chilling in that tow truck, not expecting any complications from humans, frustrated that he wasn't on the front lines.

One stab wound later, he was in the OR.

"—okay? Qhuinn?"

Qhuinn looked up. The other two adults in the room were silent in that way that people got when they were expecting the guy in the hospital bed in front of them to throw a clot and expire on the spot with a round of seizures. He wasn't even sure which one was asking him if he was all right.

"Just perfect." He gave Lyric's hand a squeeze with his thumb and forefinger. "I'm absolutely perfect. Come on, with these little guys in my life? And you two plus Xcor? How could I not be?"

The relief that came over the faces that he held so dear made him feel guilty. But sharing the fact that his get-out-of-jail-free card had been stamped didn't seem like a kind or necessary thing to do.

Shit. He would have been way more nervous going into surgery, or even out on that snowy street, if he'd done the math on it all.

He kind of wished he could undo the realization.

Then again, being more careful just made sense, didn't it.

CHAPTER SEVEN

The sound of the shower running was a soft lilt through the otherwise silent bedroom suite, and as Z shut the door to his mated chamber, he closed his eyes and breathed in deep. Shampoo. Conditioner. Soap. But more than that bouquet of cleanliness was the underlying scent that pulled it all together.

His *shellan*. Bella. Mated unto the Black Dagger Brother Zsadist, son of Ahgony, beloved *mahmen* to Nalla, firstborn of a union that was based on true, abiding love.

When he opened his lids again, the water had

been turned off, and there was flapping, a towel being drawn across a naked body with vigor, like the *mahmen* in question was in a hurry.

He walked forward, shedding his jacket, his chest holster with his daggers, and his guns that rode his hips. He put the hardware of his job inside the walk-in closet on a high shelf, out of sight and out of reach of the young. But never out of mind, not for him, not for his mate.

"Zsadist?"

Oh, that voice. The one that he heard every day and night and never grew tired of. The one that roused him from sleep and aroused him anywhere he was and soothed him and made him smile and did a million other things, small and large, with whatever syllables it served.

"Hi." He came to the open double doors of the bathroom and looked across all the white marble. "Good shower?"

Bella wrapped herself up in a towel the size of a tarp. The fact it barely fit around his shoulders when he used it made him think of how small she was in comparison to him—and he liked the weight difference, although not because he cared about thin or fat. It meant he could protect her. Kill for her. Feed her and their young with his bare hands if he had to.

Caring for his mate and Nalla was the highest purpose he served, higher even than saving the lives of his brothers and his King.

"Yes, it was a very good shower." She bent down and wrapped her wet hair up in a separate towel. Flipping the end up as she straightened, she picked her moisturizer off the counter. "I got covered with paint in the playroom."

"Oh?"

"Mmm-hmmm. Nalla's idea of finger painting is more is more. Especially when it's all over her *mahmen*. Those were blue jeans when we started."

When she pointed to the tub, Z glanced down at a wad of Levi's that belonged at a murder scene. The denim was caked with red. "Wow."

"Right? And I'll spare you the fleece I was wearing. All I'll say about that is Fritz was so excited to take it from me. I swear that *doggen* loves cleaning up messes like it's his job." Bella frowned. "I guess it is his job. That made no sense."

As she laughed at herself, he leaned against the archway and enjoyed watching his *shellan's* hands smooth the Neutrogena over her shoulders, her arms, her elbows. As things began to thicken in his blood, ideas of the naked variety occurred to him.

"Is she there still with Bitty?" he asked as his mate bent down and started working on her legs.

Please, dear God, let that babysitter be with her, he thought as his eyes tracked Bella's hand going up her calf and over her knee, the two halves of the towel parting to reveal the skin of her thigh.

"Yup, the pair of them are having the best time— Bitty is just so terrific with her. I swear, that girl is a gem." Abruptly, Bella stopped in mid-application and looked over at him. "What's wrong?"

Z couldn't keep himself from smiling slowly. "Well, at the moment, I'm sorely disappointed that I didn't walk in here ten minutes ago as you were just getting into the shower. But I can work around that setback if I take that towel off of you. With my teeth."

Bella straightened, and, tragically, lost none of her narrowed eye. "What happened tonight. You're home early, aren't you. Is everything okay? Who got hurt—"

"Everyone's fine." Z walked forward. "There's nothing wrong."

He slipped his hands around his mate's waist, the softness of the terry cloth nothing compared to her skin. In response, her eyes went over the features of his face, and he let her look to her heart's content. She was like this. She always knew whatever he didn't speak, and yet he hadn't lied. He'd gotten the group text that Qhuinn had come through the operation just fine. So everything was . . . just fine.

She put her arms around his neck and leaned into him. When she just stared up at him, he knew what she was doing. She was giving him a chance to elaborate, but also letting him have his privacy—and he hated that she had to do the latter. His therapy sessions with Mary were a weekly thing, and they had helped him a lot, but translating his feelings into words, or even just defining them and sorting through them in his own head, was still hard for him.

"I'm sorry," he said.

Her smile was so beautiful, the center of his chest ached. "I love you."

God, those three words covered so much territory, didn't they: *Don't be sorry. I'm here and going nowhere. I accept you how and where you are. You are not as broken as you're telling yourself you are, and you'll talk about it when you're ready.*

Just as he was dropping down to kiss her mouth, there was a knock on the door and Z glared at the wood panels all the way across the room. The fact that their bed, their big, soft, blanket-laden bed, loomed in his peripheral vision, a nirvana that was potentially getting sidetracked, made him . . . what were the right words?

Cranky as fuck.

"What," he ground out over his shoulder.

Through the closed doors, Tohr's voice was all business. "Wrath's called a meeting. I tried your cell phone."

"Fucking hell," Z muttered. And then, louder, "Coming."

Bella ran her hands over his shoulders. "We'll pick this up where we left off later."

He shook his head. "I owe you an apology."

"You can't control when meetings happen."

"Not about that." He ducked his eyes. "I just wish . . . I were easier."

"Are you kidding me? Compared to the likes of Vishous? Wrath? Wait, how about—"

"Lassiter."

"—Lassiter."

They laughed together a little, and then he said, "But I'm really sorry."

Those three words were like the ones she'd spoken to him, covering more territory than just their Merriam-Webster definitions: *As soon as I know what's bothering me, I'll come to you first. I'm okay, truly, and I'm so grateful for your patience. I'm trying to get better at relating, but sometimes I still get stuck and I wish I didn't.*

Oh, and one more: *Right now, my job requirements are a serious pain in my ass.*

And a last one: *I can't wait to be naked with you.*

"You don't have a thing to be sorry about." Bella stroked his super short skull trim. "And you know where to find me."

"Tell my Nalla I said hello? And that Daddy loves her."

"Always."

Sweeping his arms all the way around his terry-cloth-clad mate, he tilted her back so that her weight was his to bear. Then he brought his lips to hers . . . and kissed the ever-loving crap out of her.

When he finally stopped, she was flushed, panting, and fully aroused. "Oh, my . . ." she said in a breathy way.

Well. Didn't that make a male feel two feet taller.

"I really wish I didn't have to go," he growled.

"Yeah. Me, too," she said with a laugh.

One more kiss and then he left the room walking backwards because he didn't want to leave her. And yet he sometimes didn't want to face her, either. After all the time they'd spent together, and the beautiful

young they'd created, and all the love there was between them? Sometimes he disappeared even when
he was standing in front of her.

Yet she understood him enough to let him go to
the spaces he fell into, content to wait for his return.

"Later," he vowed.

Bella smiled in a way that made him wonder how
fast things could happen in Wrath's little frickin'
meeting. "Later, my male. Maybe I'll even run away a
little just so you can catch me."

The tips of Z's fangs started to tingle, and his
upper lip curled back. The animal in him loved when
he got to chase her, and boy, she loved being caught.

He was still growling deep in the back of his throat
as he stepped out into the Hall of Statues. Stalking
his way to the open double doors of Wrath's study, he
was surprised to see everyone already crammed into
the four-walls-and-a-ceiling.

He'd assumed it would just be him, filling the King
and Tohr in on what had happened with the Qhuinn
stabbing. But nope. It was standing room only, every
fighter in their normal positions on and around the
delicate antique French furniture, the big bodies and
loud, deep voices sucking up all the air in the room.
The King was likewise behind his sire's giant desk as
usual, sitting on his sire's giant old throne, the golden

retriever in his lap like a throw blanket with all that blond fur. George, Wrath's guide dog, was looking at everyone and offering wags, even as he would never leave his master's side. Whether he was on the lap, by the feet, or sitting pretty at the dagger hand of the King, George's friendliness was pervasive, but his love and loyalty singular.

Z went over to the corner he usually stood in. Phury, his twin, was there, along with Xhex.

"How's by you?" his brother asked quietly. "Do you know what this is about?"

Wrath spoke up around his dog. "Are we all here? What are we doing? I'm not getting any younger."

The great Blind King, now democratically elected, was already frowning behind his wraparounds like he'd been waiting for twelve hours, his widow's peak and long black hair making him look more than a little evil, especially as he clipped his words.

Then again, the male could work himself into a lather over the delay of a second and a half.

Tohr, who was at the King's side, cleared his throat and spoke up over the din. "We're all here."

"Do your thing then, weatherman," Wrath muttered as the chatter eased off its raucous boil.

Tohr nodded. "Thanks for coming, everybody. So it

looks like we've got a serious snowstorm on the fore-cast tomorrow and—"

The double doors, which had been closed, were thrown open, and what was standing in between the jambs was a sight for no eyes. Like, absolutely, posi-tively no eyes whatsoever. None.

Lassiter, the household and race's favorite fallen angel—at least if you asked him, that was, and if you asked anybody else, you'd get the statistic that there was in fact only one known fallen angel on the planet—struck a pose, hands on hips, chest puffed out, feet planted like he was ready to get his legs judged by *ANTM*.

"What the fuck are you?" someone said.

"We're still trying to figure that out," V muttered as he lit up a hand-rolled. "I volunteer to start the list with moron."

Lassiter sauntered in and did a little turn. "Mr. Freeze, motherfuckers. In honor of the coming bliz-zard."

"Now I know why I'm a Marvel fan," somebody blurted.

Even though Z didn't know Marvel from Mrs. Maisel, he couldn't agree more. The angel had some-how managed to jack himself into a pint-sized costume that was the color of blueberry Kool-Aid and had all the pipes and mechanics of an air compressor. A molded plastic weapon of some derivation or another was hanging off his right arm, and he'd completed the ensemble with a pair of bronze-colored, bug-eyed glasses that had been strapped to his pinhead.

Clearly, the getup had cost at least twenty cents to make. Maybe thirty.

Cue the peanut gallery:

"How did you get all your hair under that bathing cap?"

"Do you actually think any of that fits?"

"Can you please put your junk away—"

"Why, *why* does Amazon Prime offer free shipping. It should offer free burning—"

Lassiter flexed his sizable muscles, especially his glutes. At which point there was a series of tearing sounds.

Which was what happened when you put a five-pound bag over a fifty-pound asshat.

"Oh, my God, if he goes Hulk and flashes his courting tackle, I'm going to poke my own eyes out—"

"I don't care what any of you say," the angel cut in. "You're going to get used to me because this nor'easter coming our way? We're going to be snowbound inside for days. And days. And days—it's gonna be all of us here on the mountain together, sharing and caring."

There was a pin-drop pause of silence. And then V spoke up. "Who wants to leave right now?"

Everyone jacked their dagger hands up on a oner.

Lassiter looked around with the kind of surprise that indicated self-awareness was not in his personality inventory. Then again, the costume proved that as well.

"You guys can all bite me," the angel muttered as he turned on his heel and headed out of the study. "For real."

CHAPTER EIGHT

Down in the clinic, Qhuinn turned his head on a pillow that was cushy as a piece of toast. Right next to him, sitting on a chair that had been pulled up tight to the bedside, Blay was looking at his phone, reading something that had just come through. The overhead light had been turned down, and in the low glow, the male's red hair was all copper and shine.

That fresh fade V had given him was super tight on the bottom, making his jaw look extra strong, and the flop over his forehead was the kind of thing a male wanted to run his fingers through.

Then again, there wasn't much that Qhuinn didn't want to touch when it came to his mate.

"What is it?" he asked.

Everyone had pulled out of the OR, Layla with the kids, and Manny and Ehlena after they'd unplugged all the machines from him. The training center was likewise quiet, no more voices off in the distance, no footfalls, no muffled grunts from people working out in the weight room or the big gym. It must be getting close to Last Meal, or maybe Wrath had called a meeting.

"Tomorrow night's schedule," Blay said with a frown.

"Where am I going?"

Blay looked up, all serious. Which naturally was sexy as fuck. "Nowhere. You're redshirted for injury for forty-eight hours. You know the rules."

"I was hoping they forgot. Are you on?"

"No one's on." Blay turned the Samsung around. "Schedule's empty."

"What the hell happened?"

Blay started texting. "I'm going to find out."

Qhuinn waited patiently, and when the tippy-tapping ended, he snagged the unit and put it face-down on the bedside table. "Hi."

Blay glanced at the phone. "Hi?"

"Come here." To give the guy some guidance, he reached out and took a hold of the front of his mate's shirt to pull him in. "Hi."

Their lips met briefly, and when Blay went to ease back, Qhuinn tightened his grip on that shirt.

"Mmmm," he said as he got more of that mouth.

Things were going in absolutely the right direction as he licked his way into his male, his tongue sneaking in, taking and giving, stroking—

"Fuck," he hissed. And not in a good way.

With a groan, he flopped onto his back again and put a hand over the gauze and packing tape that was on his belly. The weight of his palm alone was enough to further aggravate the sharp-shooter, so he let his arm slide to the side. Besides, like touching the sutures was going to help?

"Let's hold off," Blay said reasonably. As he re-arranged himself inside his slacks.

"No." Qhuinn tugged on that shirt again. "Gimme. You promised."

"I did not." Blay started to smile in a half-lidded way. "I did no such thing."

"Fine, the promise was implied. By your erection." *Tug. Tug. Tug.* "I locked the door. And no one's down here."

"Qhuinn, you can't even get on your side—"

The gasp that cut off all that being-logical was so damned gratifying. And exactly what Qhuinn had been going for as he'd transferred his hand from the buttons on that fine, pressed dress shirt to a rather tented region south of the waistband of those fine, pressed slacks.

Right onto the hard length of Blay's arousal, actually.

"I told you before," Qhuinn murmured as he ran his pierced tongue over his upper lip. "I don't have to move much. You can do the active part. I'll just open my mouth."

"Qhuinn . . ."

Okay, that was a yes. That tone, with its pleading lilt, was a total, fucking, red-hot *yes*.

"All you have to do is put it in. Then pull it out. After that, you push it in deeper, to the back of my throat. And out again. You do the work. I'll just suck on you. Lick on you. Make you come in my—"

The groan that Blay let out was so long, so tortured, so hungry that it made Qhuinn's hips jerk of their own volition.

"That's right," he said as he lowered his lids. "Let me see you unzip and take it out."

Blay looked to the door. "We're locked in?"

"Absolutely."

Now, all things considered, Qhuinn had no problem having sex in front of an audience. Then again, when you were good at something, showing off was hardly a character flaw. His lover didn't feel the same way, though, and Blay's need for privacy was something that was always respected.

And hey, the truth was, Qhuinn liked the fact that his male only shared that side of himself with the one who loved him most in the world.

"Let me see it," Qhuinn prompted as Blay stood up from the chair. "I want to see it . . ."

Blay's hands trembled as they went to the belt, to the button, to the zipper at the front of those slacks. Fumble, fumble . . . then the two halves were yanked wide.

The enormous erection that burst out was exactly what Qhuinn was looking for.

"Commando," he moaned with approval. "It's meant to be."

As his mate's dagger hand encircled the thick shaft, Qhuinn did some groaning of his own. Except then Blay took a sharp step back.

Cue the sound of a needle scratching over an LP.

"Are you sure we should be doing this?" Blay asked. "I mean, what if something bursts open and—"

"The only thing bursting is going to be you, lover mine—"

"Qhuinn. I'm serious."

"So am I." When Blay stayed where he was—way out of hands-on range, much less tongue-piercing reach—Qhuinn tried to level his stare and pretend he wouldn't say absolutely anything to get what he wanted. "They weren't even going to make me take a wheelchair back. I'm allowed to walk on my own. And I already feel soooo much better."

"You can't roll onto your side."

"That's my hips, not my head. And besides, your pelvis is going to do the work, not mine."

It was probably unfair to flick his piercing around, but what was that saying? All's fair in love and blow jobs?

Okay, fine. That wasn't the saying.

"Please," he said. "And I promise I'll tell you if anything hurts."

There was a pause. And then Blay stroked his cock.

"Good," Qhuinn said with a smile.

"I haven't said yes."

"Yeah, you have. You're pumping yourself off."

Blay looked down as if he'd had no clue what his palm was doing. "Traitor," he muttered.

"Are you talking to your hand right now?"

"No. Not at all."

"Just give me my medicine, Blay. You're not going to hurt me."

Worried blue eyes stared over. "I couldn't bear that."

"I know. It's one of the many reasons I trust you."

With the decision finally made, there wasn't any more talking, the blunt head of that arousal coming at Qhuinn's mouth, just as he'd begged for. And yes, he opened wide and took it all, sucking the length in, savoring the heat, the taste, the guttural sound that his mate made. Lifting his eyes, he had the pleasure of watching Blay's head fall back and his arm shoot out to steady a rocky balance on the solid wall behind him.

A smacking noise rose up between his face and Blay's hips, quiet, repetitive, achingly erotic. The rhythm was slow, Blay deliberately taking his time. Which was fine—until it became frustrating, at which point it was even better. Snaking a hand out, Qhuinn grabbed onto the back of his lover's thigh and opened his throat, taking the full tip to base, everything stretching, his head moving back on the pillow.

Blay gasped and started to pump properly, noises

rumbling in his chest, his breath starting to come fast and hard. And yet he was holding back.

Qhuinn pulled himself free of his prize, his lips releasing the head with a pop. "Fuck me. I want you to fuck me. Give me everything."

Those blue eyes flared. But then went to Qhuinn's abs. "It feels so good, but—"

"It could be better." Qhuinn put Blay's hand on the back of his own skull. "Fuck me proper. You know you want to."

"You're just out of—"

To cut the conversation, Qhuinn extended his tongue and deliberately tickled the tip of Blay's arousal with his piercing, the silver ball teasing, tasting . . . tempting, assuming he was doing it right.

"Oh, Qhuinn, God . . ."

Yup, he was doing it right. And what do you know, in return, Qhuinn got exactly what he wanted: Slowly at first, and then with increasing urgency, Blay drove his cock in and out of the mouth that was so greedy for him. In and out. In and out. Harder now. Faster now. And the broad palm on the back of Qhuinn's head was the guide that made it all possible.

Well, that and those hips, those lean hips with the wings of muscle on both sides.

Blay's body had been sculpted by a master, every

part of it. Especially the part that was fucking Qhuinn's mouth.

Ah, yes. This is exactly the kind of medicine he needed.

◆　◆　◆

Blay had been feeling so guilty about the whole thing. For godsakes, his male was lying in a hospital bed, just unhooked from monitoring machines maybe twenty minutes ago, the stitches still fresh from closing a damn stab wound . . .

And here he was, face-fucking the guy—

Qhuinn looked up, his blue and green eyes glowing, his mouth stretched wide, his cheeks flushed from arousal. Then he purred.

Well. Okay, so fine, his mate did seem to be enjoying this. Even though Blay was drilling into Qhuinn's mouth, the male was taking it all—and loving it. If the noises of approval weren't a tip-off for how good it was for him, then the erection that had thickened up under that hospital sheet was another clear sign—

The growling sound in the back of Blay's throat was a drumroll to his culmination, growing in urgency and volume—and *fuck*, he was drilling Qhuinn's mouth now, the thrusting going wilder as he visually focused on what was happening.

The sight of those lips stretched so wide, and his

shaft going in and out, and the gloss on his arousal was too much.

Blay pitched off the cliff, a tremendous orgasm ripping out of him.

Thankfully, Qhuinn took things from there. As Blay grunted and his pelvis locked into his lover's face, his whole body went rigid, all of his muscles from his feet to his shoulders going rock hard. And so Qhuinn was the one who moved now, nursing at the head of the erection he'd treated so beautifully, pulling more and more out of the release, milking it to continue.

The legs that kept Blay upright turned into wire, and he listed back so that he had to brace himself against the wall. The angle was bad, twisting his spine, making his ass strain, but like he cared?

He was just watching what was happening as Qhuinn's blue and green eyes looked up at him—

That tongue, that talented, pierced tongue, lapped around the head of Blay's arousal again, then tickled the tip with the metal.

Blay's eyes squeezed shut again. "You're going to make me—"

Come again. Yup. Here it was, the pleasure peaking for a second time, jets shooting out of him and going right into Qhuinn's mouth. More sucking now. Lots more sucking.

Blay squeezed his eyes shut and fell forward, collapsing across Qhuinn's upper body—and still his male kept going.

And it kept going. For so long. Until Blay completely fell apart and had to stretch out on the hospital bed next to his lover or crush Qhuinn. As he settled in, his mate pulled him close, making sure his head was tucked against the big chest that was marked with the sacred scar of the Black Dagger Brotherhood.

"I should be cradling you," Blay mumbled. "I need to take care of you—"

"Shh." That big hand made slow circles on Blay's shoulder, going up and around. "You did take care of me."

Blay lifted his head. "I can assure you, it was the other way around."

"Not in the slightest."

"I owe you one. Or four, I think it was."

"Five, but who was counting? And I look forward to collecting on that debt." Qhuinn's smile was so honest, so open. "Anytime."

"Just maybe when you're, like, not right out of an operation."

"Nah. Any. Time. Like how 'bout now?"

Blay blinked. "We've already covered this. You can't move."

"All fours is probably out of the question, but I can roll over."

"No, you can't." Blay shifted his head because he knew eye contact was necessary to get the point across. "And I am not doing that to you right now."

"Buzzkill."

As they started at each other, they both laughed. And then Blay got serious as he admired his mate's hard face, and that strong chest, and that constant wellspring of sexual desire that was ever present, ever ready. Instantly, nothing else mattered or even registered, and it was funny—you'd think after all this time, things would stop receding. But it happened again: The hospital bed disappeared. The room disappeared. The clinic, the training center, the mountain, the world. Everything was gone but the male who was looking back at him.

"Your face is a view I never tire of," Blay whispered as he stroked the black-and-purple hair that had been mussed in the process of . . . well, the blow job of his life.

Qhuinn nodded. "And yours is my true north. So there."

With a smile, Blay meant to keep the compliments going. But then it dawned on him—

"Oh, crap, my pants are around my ankles."

"I can think of no better place for them to be."

"Good thing that door is locked—" As Qhuinn went to move, Blay put his hand on the male's shoulder. "Wait, where are you going?"

"Nowhere."

Qhuinn's face tightened as he sat up and sucked in a breath. But when Blay went to pull him back down to the pillow, Qhuinn fought the urging even as it cost him more pain.

"What are you doing?" Blay demanded.

Ah. The blanket that was folded at the end of the bed.

Qhuinn pulled the soft weave free, shook it out of its squares, and placed the softness over Blay's lower body with careful hands. Even as his face lost its color from whatever he was feeling at his wound site, he batted away efforts to help, and covered that which was clearly precious to him.

Abruptly, Blay found himself blinking fast.

There were so many ways that people said *I love you.*

And sometimes, they did it without speaking a word.

CHAPTER NINE

Elle had done something bad last night. And someone had been hurt. In some awful way.

Or at least . . . that was what she had dreamed of.

As her head began to pound again, she tried to stop pushing into the weird void that took over her mind every time she attempted to remember the details of the nightmare she'd had. God knew the straining hadn't gotten her anywhere. She had nothing but a lingering sense of fear and worry. And the headache.

Still, whatever she had dreamed of was like a mental scab—she just had to pick at it. Then again, her guilty conscience had always been a thing. It was like the time she'd stolen one of Uncle Tommy's cigarettes and tried it out behind the garage. She'd felt awful afterward, and not just because she'd coughed her lungs up by the recycling bin.

Taking her father's car out last night with her sister in the passenger seat and absolutely no legal driver's license in her pocket had been a really stupid move. Especially when she was supposed to have been in charge.

So of course her subconscious would hurl something over her mental fence while she was sleeping.

Rubbing her eyes, she attempted to focus on where she was, what time it was, and what she was waiting for. At least she was clear on the first one: She was sitting at the breakfast table in her father's kitchen. She was also certain that it was a little before 6:30 a.m. And as for the third thing on that list? She was dressed for school, with her homework in her backpack, her hair brushed, and her parka over her lap.

Like being all organized and ready for the bus this early could somehow make up for breaking her father's trust.

News flash: She wasn't actually waiting for the bus.

Glancing around, the weak light of morning made everything seem black and white, the pale green cabinets and cheery ivy wallpaper dimmed down to shades of gray, the throw rug under her chair nothing but a shadow, the spines of the cookbooks on the shelves altogether without color. The only light that glowed was the one out by the front door at the base of the stairs, but the illumination didn't go far, a mere patch of false sunshine.

Picking up her phone, she signed in, but then just flipped through her screens.

She had been compulsively checking the local news station's website since four in the morning. There was nothing. No reports of any . . . anything.

But like her little joyride mattered? Like there was some kind of factory-installed tracer on the BMW that notified the police whenever someone with a learner's permit took the thing out alone?

She just needed to get over herself. Yes, she had taken her father's car out when she hadn't had permission and without a valid full driver's license. Yes, her sister had been with her. Yes, that had been dangerous. But they'd made it back here fine, the car was still safe in the garage, and she and Terrie had been in bed like the good little children they hadn't been before their father had come home with that THOT.

End of story.

Right?

Elle went back to the local CBS news channel. Impending snowstorm. Missing dog found safe. Budget cuts coming in the new year. No one hit by a car by a teenage girl driving illegally or anybody stabbed—

As the pain ramped up behind her eyebrows, she looked out to the hall light and the front door. She kept feeling like the police were going to show up at any moment and she was going to be arrested for obstructing justice because she hadn't come forward right away about—

"Stooooooooooooop," she groaned.

Police did not come after people for dreams. She was being insane.

Dropping her phone, she put her head in her hands. Her mind was like an amusement ride, going up and around and upside down.

She hated amusement rides.

On that note, she stared across at the refrigerator. Front and center, on the freezer side, was the school calendar for December. The sheet of blue paper with its squares full of stuff was held in place by two Disney magnets that had pictures from the trip last spring break. Herself, Terrie, and Dad. All smiles.

So the photographs were kind of like this house. Everything but Mom.

And what a lie those smiles were. Their dad had

intended for the vacation to lift everybody's spirits. Instead, Elle had been miserable on all the rides, Terrie had complained about the food, and their father had spent a lot of time staring off into space.

Even though she tried not to reimagine the night before as if the divorce hadn't happened, it was hard not to conclude that if her parents were still together, she'd still be asleep right now.

Antsy and achy, she compared the kitchen she was in to the one she'd grown up with—because even though the past made her sad, it was better than diving back into her phone. Here, the furniture was new, and the room was in a different layout. Terrie's backpack was on the counter in the corner by the landline that no one used and probably wasn't even turned on. There was a pair of running shoes—man-sized—next to some snow boots—little-girl-sized—over by the door out to the garage. The cereal boxes were all kid kinds like Cap'n Crunch and Frosted Mini-Wheats, and there were avocados mixed up with the apples in the fruit bowl and whole-grain bagels with everything spices were left out by the toaster.

If her mom had lived here, the clutter would have been cleaned up, the phone line turned on, and the cereals would have been organic substitutes of brand names that had no sugar added.

Elle and her sister and father had moved into this house, a two-story from the 1990s, about eighteen months ago, and the street had a lot of families on it. Just like at their old address, in the warmer months, bikes sunbathed on front lawns that were mowed by the owners, not fancy lawn services, and now that it was cold and Christmas was coming, there were blankets of red and green lights in all the bushes and twinkling white icicle strings hanging off the gutters.

So it was almost the same.

And completely different.

Funny, she'd always assumed everyone's life was perfect on their old street. Now, it felt like everybody *else's* life was perfect.

Especially after her bad choice last night.

At least Terrie was still asleep in her room upstairs. If Elle had to deal with that mouth this morning? Not going to be good for anyone.

She checked her phone for the time and worried about how much longer her father was going to be working out down in the cellar. She needed to get this conversation over before Terrie woke up. He rode that Peloton bike four times a week—just her luck, to have missed one of his three recovery days.

Tip-tap, tip-tap.

The sound of her short nails on the table made her

think about family dinner. Part of the reason their father pedaled his heart out early in the morning in the basement was because he wanted to be home at six every night for family dinner: Unless he had a work function, they ate together at this four-seater table, the one unfilled seat something Elle was beginning to not dwell on so much. The only time he ever missed the meal was once a week when he was at a work-related event.

Or now, she supposed, if he had a date.

At least he'd come home last night. He'd cracked her bedroom door just after eleven and looked in while she'd pretended to be asleep. She hadn't been ready to talk yet, the right words still ordering themselves in her head, soldiers that had refused to get into formation. Clearly, he hadn't guessed what she'd done, the BMW having been returned to the garage just fine, and with Terrie then asleep, that mouth was on standby.

And there had been more good news as that woman in the LBD had gone home. As her father had reshut her door, Elle had watched the departure from her bed, the headlights flashing across the front of the house as whatever car the date had been driving backed out of their driveway and moved off down their street—

The creaking of the cellar stairs was soft as her father ascended on tiptoes. He was always worried about how much they slept, so he was quiet when he moved around in the early morning.

Elle flushed, her palms getting sweaty, her heart skipping in her chest.

As he opened the basement door, he was in the process of wiping his forehead with a white towel and stopped short.

"Well, hello. You're up early."

Basile Allaine was just over six feet tall, with thick dark hair, a face that always had the shadow of a beard no matter how often he shaved, and a now-much-less-dad-bod than before the Peloton bike purchase.

Elle tried to smile. "Just felt like getting a head start."

"I like the discipline." He looped the towel around the back of his neck. "If you want, we can get your sister up and I'll drive you in? That way you won't have to ride the bus."

"The bus is good. I don't want to make you late."

Her dad frowned. "You okay, Bug?"

She'd been called Bug for so long, she had no idea where the nick had come from. And lately, it had been annoying her. She was sixteen now, and who wanted to be called an insect, anyway? Right now, though, she was hoping it meant he'd go easy on her.

Ties to her younger, cuter, much-less-likely-to-joyride-in-a-car self.

"What's going on?" Her dad came over and pulled out a chair. "Talk to me."

Elle spent some time looking at her nails. She'd painted them black last week, and the tips were already chipping.

"Whatever it is, we can work through it," he murmured.

Which was what he always said.

She looked up. Her father didn't have much of an accent anymore, but she'd been told by many who apparently knew that he looked like the Frenchman he was and would always be. And hey, he also somehow managed to smell good and be all put-together in his black nylon workout clothes even after he'd been pedaling in the basement for an hour. Which seemed French, she guessed.

He was forty-six, if she remembered right. Was that old? It sounded old.

"We need to talk about last night," she said.

There was a jerk in his shoulders, and then he sat back. As his eyes dropped to the table, she felt an urge to cry. Somehow, he must have guessed what she'd done. Maybe by the tire tracks in the driveway or—

You were an adult when you took that car out, sweetie, and now you've got an adult-level problem.

As the random male voice shot through her mind, Elle hissed and put her hands to her temples.

"Are you okay? Elle!"

She batted away her father's palms as he reached forward. "I'm fine. Just slept wrong." When the pain faded, she sat back like he was. "About last night. Dad, I know that you—"

"I should have told you a while ago."

In Elle's head, she finished what she'd been about to say: *—don't let me take your car out without permission and supervision.*

Out loud, she said, "Tell me what?"

That he'd, like, installed security cameras somewhere and already knew she'd snuck the BMW out for a drive?

"About Megan." He took the towel off his neck and pressed it to his face. "I just didn't know how to bring it up, and I was worried about how you guys would feel."

"Megan?" She pictured the woman who'd come to the door, all confident and perfumed, all . . . sexy. "Wait, the one from last night?"

"Yes."

"It wasn't your first date with her last night?"

There was a pause before he answered. And he lowered his stare and shook his head before he spoke. "No, it wasn't."

Elle sat forward. "How long has this been . . . wait, you're seeing her? Like, girlfriend seeing her?"

"I didn't know how to handle it all." He stared across the table. "There's no handbook for divorce, no blueprint for how to do all of this. And I just didn't know what was for the best."

"I'm pretty sure lying to your kids is not on *that* list."

He nodded. "That's fair, and I don't blame you for being mad. But I'm trying to be sensitive to . . ."

"To Mom? Is that who you're really worried about?"

"Look, I know that she's having a hard time. I know that you go over there and it's hard. I know you worry about her. I worry about her, too."

Elle frowned. "So Megan is your girlfriend."

Her father took a deep breath. "Yes, she is."

As the words sank in, all she could do was sit there and blink. And then she looked at those running shoes by the snow boots and the avocados in with the apples. Suddenly, their little four-top in their new "family" house had a smug ghost sitting in the empty chair.

"Holy shit, Dad, since when has this been going on." And then she did the math. "Are you even kidding me. All those business meetings? Those overnight conferences when Auntie Bette came over and stayed with us? They were all because you were seeing 'Megan'—"

"I didn't know how to tell you. I'm really sorry."

"So you've been lying since for how long?" She crossed her arms over her chest. "How long?"

When he didn't reply, a cold wash of dread went through Elle. "Is she the reason you got a divorce? Oh, my God, did you cheat on Mom?"

"No, of course not."

They were the right words. But his eyes had dropped to the table again.

"If you're lying to me now," Elle said in a low voice, "and I find out, I am moving in with Mom and taking Terrie with me. I don't care if that apartment is a mess."

"Elle . . ." He cursed softly. In French. "It was very complicated. Things between your mother and I, especially at the end, were . . . it was all just complicated."

Elle shoved her chair back, and as she stood up, her parka fell off her lap and onto the floor. "That's a

Facebook status. It's not an acceptable reason for killing a family."

For all of her life, her father had been the steady and calm one, the one she could look to for guidance. Now, he seemed as lost as a child.

"Tell me," she demanded.

"Your mom and I had been drifting apart for a while."

"Because you were cheating on her!"

"No, that came later." This was said almost absently, as if he'd meant to keep that to himself. And then he seemed to snap back to attention. "People grow apart, Elle. It's a sad, terrible truth. We started with the best of intentions, but then . . . things changed. Especially after her parents died in that car accident. She just disappeared into herself, and I don't blame her for that."

Hazy memories of the two-for-one funeral surfaced and then were promptly dismissed. She couldn't go there right now.

As Elle collapsed back into her chair, her father cursed and rubbed his face with the towel. "Ultimately, it was my fault. I will be honest about that. It was . . . I was working too much, and she was grieving . . . and we . . . people drift apart."

"But you were married." Elle felt younger than her

sister by ten years as she spoke in a fragile way. "You were in love. Once."

"Things happen, Elle." Her father's eyes teared up. "People get older and events shape your life in ways you'd never predict. But the one thing she and I have always agreed on, and will always agree on, is that you and your sister are the best things we've ever done. That will never change. Ever."

She thought of her mother's dark apartment, and wasn't sure how true that was.

"I'm really sorry, Elle—"

Terrie appeared in the archway, hair a mess, bare feet on the tile under the hems of her PJs, a yawn distorting her face. "What's happening?"

Elle got her parka off the floor and stood up once again, this time with her backpack. "I'm going to go wait for the bus."

Her father reached out. "Elle, it's cold out there—"

"Do we still have school?" Terrie rubbed her eyes. "I thought it was going to be canceled 'cuz of snow."

"The storm's not here yet," their father said. "It's due late in the afternoon."

"Actually, it already came," Elle muttered as she walked out of the kitchen.

It was a relief to leave the house and not look back, even though her father was right. The morning was bitterly cold, and the air smelled like snow. God, she hoped they didn't cancel school.

And who'd have thought that she'd wish for such a thing.

The good news? If there was any?

If Terrie spilled the beans on their little road trip, it was a drop in the fucking bucket after what her father had revealed.

CHAPTER TEN

I t's just a snowstorm. I don't get what all the big deal is. We live in Caldwell, which is second only to fucking Buffalo for accumulation."

As night fell that evening, First Meal was in full swing at the Brotherhood mansion, the household sitting around the thirty-foot-long dining table, platters of food laid out on the sideboards, all chairs filled. Families were gathered in the Vanderbilt-worthy room in lots of three and four, young on laps and in seats of their own, mated pairs side by side, brothers and fighters and the King all together. As it should be.

"I mean, how bad can this nor'easter be?"

Qhuinn glanced at Butch O'Neal, a.k.a. the *Dhestroyer*, who was the one playing indignant forecaster to his left.

"Haven't you lived here for years?" Qhuinn said.

Butch pulled a well-duh double take that did not exactly match the formality of his deep gray Tom Ford suit. "Which is my point. I've been through a shit ton of these storms. The city's been through a shit ton of them. We've got the daytime shutters to cover the glass, and like we don't know from wicked bad wind up here? It's going to be fine."

"To be fair, the radar looks like a Christmas card of the Death Star." Qhuinn cut into his prime rib. "By the way, I heard everyone already voted to leave the island instead of getting stuck here with Lassiter for days and days."

"And this is my point." Butch wagged his sterling silver fork. "Why do we all have to stay in tonight just because a couple of flakes fall? Especially if we're going to get trapped for the day with that angel anyway. That's like knowing you're going to come down with the stomach flu and volunteering for a spoiled hamburger the night before."

"On that, you might have a point."

Qhuinn glanced down the table. When he couldn't quite see Lassiter, he leaned forward over his plate full of food so he could get around the lineup of people. About ten seats past Butch, Lassiter was sitting between Bitty and Tohr, his blond-and-black extravaganza of hair falling over a brilliant yellow MrBeast sweatshirt, all of the gold he wore adding a good four tons to his body weight.

The guy was like an entire Zales jewelry store upright and walking around—

Abruptly, Lassiter turned his head, and as their stares met, nothing about his expression was jokey-jokey. His strange-colored eyes were grave and unblinking, his lips a thin line, his whole affect a mask of composure that belonged in Madame Tussaud's zip code.

A chill went down Qhuinn's spine.

"Do you need a doctor?"

As Blay spoke up, Qhuinn broke eye contact with the angel and looked at his mate. "What?"

"You shivered. Are you okay? That wound isn't getting infected, is it?"

"No, it's fine." He sliced off a piece of—what was on his plate? Beef? Chicken? Couldn't be fish. That was the only thing he was sure of, because the King hated the smell of the stuff and forbade it in the house except for Boo the cat's dinner, which was given nowhere near Wrath. "I'm good."

Granted, whatever he was chewing could have been a piece of the table, and he was, in fact, running a case of the cold sweats like an iced tea on a hot night. But none of that needed a physician's review. Besides, he was embarrassed at his case of the cobbly-wobbles.

Who'd have thought Lassiter in his normal bouncy-castle mood was something to miss.

Caught up in a sense of doom, he refused to look at the angel again, and his eyes skipped over the familiar faces around the table as his awareness retreated deep within himself. Under the fake-it-'til-you-make-it theory, he somehow managed to join the clean-plate club, and talk to Xcor and Layla, and trade off the twins, and get to his own two feet when the meal was over.

All in all, a good performance. Maybe not Oscar caliber—because he could tell Blay wasn't buying it—but certainly worthy of a Golden Globe nomination.

Out in the foyer, there was a dispersing of bodies, people heading upstairs, across to the billiards room, back toward the library. Meanwhile, he stalled out—

Until he realized Blay was standing in front of him with expectation on his face. Something, apparently, had been asked.

"Yeah, absolutely," Qhuinn replied.

He figured that was a good, broad-spectrum answer, capable of treating a variety of inquiries: *Would you like a drink and a round of pool? Would you like to watch a movie? Would you like to head to bed?*

Actually, that last one required more of a *Fuck, yeah.*

Blay frowned. "You want to do that?"

"What?"

"I said, it's Layla and Xcor's night to do bath and play, but Lassiter's got diamond art going on in the library with the other kids, and has asked everyone to join in."

"Why would I want to do that?"

"Exactly." Blay cleared his throat. "What's wrong?"

"Nothing." He flashed his pearlies, hoping to hit the a-okay mark. "I mean, I'm not thrilled with being stuck here all night, but I thought I'd go down to the training center and check in with Luchas for a while. I was going to stop by his room when I got my medical release—but time got away from you and me, didn't it."

Just as a very attractive blush bloomed across his mate's face, a strange sound wove into the background noise, low and persistent. Qhuinn looked to the windows that faced out the front of the mansion.

"Holy crap, is that the wind?"

He walked over and opened the door into the vestibule, stepping through to the cathedral-like portal of the house's grand entrance. When he went to lean outside, he had to put his shoulder into the effort, and you want to talk about a slap in the face? The wind was a one-two punch of cold and powerful, the skin of his cheeks stripping back, his eyes burning, his front teeth humming a tingle tune.

Given all of that arctic-ness, he wasn't exactly sure why he went all the way out. But one minute, he was on the cusp; the next, he was standing at an angle into the gusts and looking in the direction of the distant suburbs . . . and even farther away, to the downtown skyscrapers and the bridges.

Darius, who had built the manse, had chosen a defensible position on the tallest of the mountains just north of the city of Caldwell. The descending acreage, which was extensive and as pine-packed as a Christmas tree farm, was protected from enemies and humans alike thanks to V's *mhis*. But that invisible force field had no dimming effect on the wind at all. The gale-worthy blasts didn't so much weave their way through all those conifers as tear their way past the linked boughs to batter the front face of the mansion.

He actually pivoted and double-checked that the great stone house was holding up all right, but he shouldn't have worried. All those tons of gray rock and all that cement were standing strong, as if the mighty, sprawling construction was part of the mountain as opposed to something built upon it.

"Big storm," someone next to him said, loud enough so he could hear the words over the freight train in his ears.

Qhuinn glanced at V. "Yeah."

Overhead, the sky was a milky white, the cloud cover dense and low and threatening. No snow was falling yet, but the white stuff was coming. There was a thick, winter humidity in the air, the harbinger of flakes aplenty.

"You guys want to come to the Pit?" V said as Blay joined them. "Foosball. Booze. No Lassiter."

Qhuinn glanced at his mate. And then both of them answered, "Perfect."

◆ ◆ ◆

As Blay sat on Butch and V's leather sofa, he was seriously enjoying the view in front of him. Qhuinn was at the far side of the Foosball table, the male's powerful body tilted forward, his eyes tracking the action, his hands twirling the rods and switching grips at a breakneck pace.

Or should that be "breakwrist"?

Across the box of spinning plastic block figures,

John Matthew was the opponent, and seeing the two going at it reminded Blay of the way things had been before their transitions. So many hours playing video games together in his bedroom at his parents' old house, the three of them trading off handsets, trading Doritos for Lay's, trading gummy bears for Tootsie Rolls.

"Swiss Miss, no marshmallows."

A white mug appeared in front of him and he looked up at Butch. "You are a gentlemale and a scholar."

"I barely got through high school and I cuss a lot. I'm not sure I'm either of those."

"Well, you're a good host, how 'bout that."

As the *Dhestroyer* grinned, the male parked it at the other end of the couch and nursed his own mug. When the Brotherhood had moved in together over at the big house, Butch and V, then both mate-less, had bachelor-padded it here in the old caretaker's cottage. Now, their *shellans* were living happily with them, but the Pit, as the place was known, remained a frat house extension of the more formal and very definitely kid-friendly atmosphere across the courtyard.

"Looking at stuff to put under the tree for the twins?" Butch asked.

"Hmm?"

"On your phone there?"

Blay glanced down at the cell in his hand—and decided the fact that his mate could still distract him so much that he forgot what he was doing was a good sign.

"Oh, yeah, actually, I love this bouncy castle. I know they're a little young, but . . . come on. We can put it outside the playroom, you know in that hall by the movie theater? The older kids will enjoy it, and we can sit with the twins in it."

"Great idea. But I think you're going to have to keep Rhage away from the damn thing. I mean, he loves a good bouncy castle."

"I didn't know that."

Butch lifted his mug in salute. "Things you learn in snowstorms, my friend."

"Speaking of kidlets, do you and Marissa ever want any?" Blay shut his phone down and put it away. And then realized that Butch had frozen with his mug halfway to his lips. "Oh . . . shoot, I'm sorry if that's too personal—"

"No, no, it's all good." Butch followed through and took a sip from his mug. "And I don't know. Sometimes we think about it, but it's not a priority. Especially as I watch how hard all you guys work at it—"

The howl started low, as just another round of

wind blowing, but as the sound of the gust grew in intensity and persisted so much longer than all the others, he and Butch looked to the Pit's door. On the outside of the cottage, the decorative shutters whistled and rattled, and then there was a groan, the load-bearing exterior walls complaining—or maybe it was the rafters of the roof?—about the force of the storm. Cold drafts, born from the glass panes of the windows and the main door's loose seal, snaked around Blay's ankles, and even the Foosballers halted their cranking conflict and looked up from their spinning—

More groaning, definitely coming from up above.

Dust filtered down from the old beams, and over at V's Four Toys, a.k.a. the computers from which the security and monitoring systems for all the Brotherhood's properties were run, Vishous got to his feet as if he were prepared to throw himself over his equipment to protect it.

There was a pause, a relenting. But then everything redoubled, the rattling noises, the protests from the little house, the drafts and the eerie whistling, everything rising again like the Creator had His fingers on the volume knob of the world.

Abruptly, some kind of group-think thing happened, and everyone headed for the door to the courtyard at the same time. Well, except for V, who started to type really fast on one—no, two—keyboards.

Qhuinn was in front and opened the door—only to get blown back off his feet. In the blink of an eye, Blay jumped forward and caught his mate, hitching a hold under those big, heavy arms and keeping all that weight from hitting the floor. And even though it might have been inappropriate, for a brief moment, he closed his eyes and breathed in deep, relishing the scent of his male—

The ripping sound was so loud, you could hear it over the storm.

"The fountain cover!" someone shouted.

In the center of the courtyard that separated the mansion and the cottage, a marble fountain the size of a Greyhound bus station was a winterized focal point—and the blizzard's winds had set upon the canvas tarp that covered the basin and the sculpture. With invisible teeth, it had grabbed ahold of that stretch of woven and waterproof, and ripped it free of some of the sandbags that secured it in place. A good half of the expanse was flapping, a flag that was making the most of its freedom.

Blay ran across the snowpack, the cold biting through his cashmere sweater and icing his bare hands, the force of the wind pushing against his chest and making his eyes water. And he almost caught the damn tarp. There was a fleeting moment when one corner of the tear came at him, and a split second when his fingers felt a lick of fabric—but then the heavy-duty canvas twisted around and was gone, gone, gone, heading for the front of the mansion on an up-up-and-away that was no more threatening than a Kleenex fluttering.

Except it had one bag still with it.

One single sandbag was along for the ride, still hanging on—until it didn't.

As the thing went AWOL, breaking free of its tie, the math on the trajectory of the ten-pound projectile was not good.

In a Murphy's law hole-in-one, the tarp managed to toss that dead weight directly at an expanse of diamond-pane windows on the second floor—and what do you know, the old leaded glass shattered like it had been hit by a skull-sized rock.

"Motherfucker!" someone barked.

Yeah, let's not allow that to happen again, Blay thought.

The rest of the tarp was still ragged and wiggling loose, tugging and pulling and flapping against those other sandbags. More tearing. More projectiles likely—

As he got in range again, the fabric slapped him right in the face, whipping at his cheek. But he snatched hold of the canvas and leaned back, pulling the bucking expanse away from the fountain's basin, and out of the grip of the frigid gusts. Qhuinn joined him in the effort, helping the ground-game part of things as they dragged the lineup of bags away from the cobblestone skirt of the marble fixture.

Out of the corner of his eye, Blay got a load of V and Butch hightailing it up the stone steps for the mansion's entrance.

"Did you check on the twins!" Blay yelled over the wind at his mate. "Are they okay?"

Qhuinn held up his phone and nodded. "Layla just texted! They were in the playroom on the other side of the house. She says the sitting room was empty when the glass broke!"

"Let's take this over to the garage," Blay hollered. "Before there's any more damage!"

"You're bleeding," Qhuinn hollered back.

"Breathing? Of course I am. Over there! Let's go over there!"

Qhuinn's mouth was moving, and going by his glower, he was clearly cursing, but he followed the lead. Together, they dragged the ungainly weight toward the garage, the sandbags flattening a path in the snow-covered side lawn like a Zamboni on an ice rink. And Blay would have just tucked the production off to the side of the stone steps, next to the bushes, but he knew that Fritz wouldn't have approved—and that the elderly *doggen* was liable to go outside in the storm and insist on taking it out of sight on a tidy-up.

The last thing the household needed was a Fritz-cicle in the front yard.

Growing colder by the moment, Blay trudged through the snow, his loafers breaking through the icy top inch of the snowpack, all *crunch, crunch, crunch.* As the wind made staying upright a struggle, his white clouds of breath went the house-ward way of the tarp and the ball-busting, window-breaking, sonofabitch sandbag.

Not that he was bitter.

As they approached the closed garage doors, he triangulated in on the keypad mounted on the side wall.

"What's the code?" Blay shouted.

"Try the one to the training center!"

With a half-frozen forefinger, Blay punched in the numbers, hit the pound key—*ta-daaaaaa.* With a laconic trundle—like the goddamn garage door had no clue they were fucking cold and needed to get out of the wind—the panels lifted and rode their track, retracting to reveal a sparkling-clean, concrete-floored equipment corral nearly the size of a soccer field. The storm's gusts barreled into the space as soon as they had even a six-inch opening, rattling the tops of the metal trash cans, blowing over a row of weed whackers, whipping past V's R8 and Manny's Porsche, neither of which would be taken out until spring.

As soon as they could duck under, he and Qhuinn dragged the tarp in and folded it up in a messy way. If Fritz wanted to micromanage that part of things, fine—

Qhuinn was suddenly right in front of him, and before Blay could say anything, his mate took a grip of his chin and brought up a black-and-white bandana.

"What are you—"

When Blay tried to lean away, Qhuinn wouldn't let him, pressing the folded cloth to the side of his face. "Hold still, wouldya. You're bleeding."

As a vicious gust shot into the garage, their bodies got thrown to the side, and Qhuinn must have willed the garage door back down because the panels started to descend again—you couldn't raise the things without the code because they had closing-activated copper locks, but you could drop them into place.

And good thing. It felt like it was getting even

colder. Or maybe that was just his extremities' last gasp of sensation before frostbite turned him into a statue.

"I'm fine," Blay said as he thought about that broken window in the front of the house. "We need to go help—"

The garage door thumped into place, the wind's last foray ending in a high-pitched whistle, the relative silence something you had to acclimatize to after the din.

"—go down to the training center right now," Qhuinn finished in a normal voice as he rubbed his hands together for warmth.

Outside, the howling ascended in volume again, and Blay had a sudden urge to count everybody in the frickin' household. If someone were to get stuck out there? If they left the house on foot and got disorientated? If they took a car and lost traction on the road?

They weren't going to last long.

Shaking himself back to attention, he tried to remember what his mate had said. "The training center? For what?"

"I just told you. You're bleeding."

The door into the house opened and Tohr leaned out. "Everybody okay in here?"

"No—"

"Yes—" Blay batted Qhuinn's nurse routine away from his face. "Did anyone get hurt upstairs?"

"No, the second-floor sitting room was empty," Tohr replied. "We're boarding up the hole and closing the daytime shutters right now. Hey, do you want me to get Doc Jane for that wound?"

Blay glared at his mate and spoke deliberately. "No, thank you. We're not going to bother a doctor about a scratch that is going to heal within the hour—"

"We need to check him out right now," Qhuinn said. "Maybe get a gurney?"

"Are you even kidding me?" Blay rubbed the side of his face to prove he was fine—until the scratch started protesting the attention. Keeping a grimace to himself, he announced, "I am very sure I'm not bleeding out, and someone else might need something."

Tohr smiled. "How about you guys check in later at the clinic if it looks like things are not resolving on their own with the injury?"

As the Brother gave them a little wave and disappeared back into the house, Qhuinn walked around in a tight circle.

"I'd just feel better if someone looked at it. You know, to be sure . . ." He let the sentence fade out as he blew into his cupped hands.

The helpless look in those mismatched eyes was such a surprise. Especially because what was going on was on a shaving-nick level.

Blay went over and put a hand on Qhuinn's shoulder. "You know I'm fine. Come on, a minor scratch is nothing compared to you getting stabbed last night—"

"But you're who matters. Not me."

There was the temptation to laugh . . . until Blay realized the male was serious. With a frown, he shook his head. "I don't understand that statement at all. You are a father, a *hellren*, a Brother. You are everything—"

"None of it matters without you."

Blay just stood there and blinked. The bleak tone was not normal at all.

"Qhuinn, you know I'm not going anywhere." He pulled his male in close. "I'm right here and going nowhere."

The shudder that went through his beloved was the kind of thing that easily translated from one body to the other. And was another testament to something Blay couldn't quite understand.

"I wish you could promise me that."

Blay pulled back at the whispered words. "What are you saying? You don't trust me?"

"It's the world I don't trust." Qhuinn brought the bandana back up, and dab-dab-dabbed at the cut. "I worry about gunshots and knives and car crashes and—"

"Let's stop that list. Your point is taken."

Qhuinn glared over at the tarp. "I didn't even know I had to be concerned about fucking fountain covers."

Okay, time for a redirection of all this, Blay decided. "Let's go inside. See if we can help with that window."

"Yeah." Qhuinn put an arm around Blay's waist as they started walking toward the door into the back hall. "Lean on me if you need to. Like if you feel dizzy or weak."

"You're trying to make me laugh."

"And get you against me."

"I'm all yours."

Qhuinn stopped, his affect instantly lightening up. "Now? Here? What a great idea—"

"No, not here." Blay pulled his lover along with a laugh. "But later."

"Wherever we are? Assuming the coast is clear?"

"Fine."

Throwing out his anchor, Qhuinn had calculation

in his eyes. "Wherever we are. If the time is right, it's wherever."

Dear Lord, what am I agreeing to, Blay thought. But that was the thing, wasn't it. He loved the edge of his true love.

"Deal?" Qhuinn prompted.

Blay felt a naughty smile hit his face. "Deal."

They started walking again, and as they hit the shallow steps into the house, Qhuinn narrowed one last, mean look back at the tarp.

"You know," Blay remarked, "if you've really got it in for that thing, I'll bet Fritz will let you light it on fire."

Qhuinn halted in mid-step and popped his brows. And then he yanked open the door with an expression of total focus.

"Fritz!" he called out. "Get me the flamethrower!"

CHAPTER ELEVEN

They're not shutting."

Zsadist paused his hammer-and-nail routine and glanced down from his perch on a stepladder. "What aren't shutting?"

Payne, who was holding a six-foot-long plywood section to the sitting room's busted window for him, also looked at Tohr.

"You mean the daylight shutters?" she asked. "Because they're fine in here."

The other brother walked across the antique carpet, his shitkickers crunching over broken glass. Bending down, he picked up the sandbag that was next to the silk sofa and then glared around like he was searching for other signs of storm-related vandalism and equipment failure.

And P.S. Z thought, if it was true that the shutters were failing? Fuck the snow, they had bigger problems. Of all the human myths around vampires, those rats without tails had gotten one thing right: No sunlight. Ever. So the mansion, like any other house inhabited by the species, had custom-made shutters that got locked into place during the day.

Windows needed to be covered before daybreak.

"I should amend that," Tohr muttered. "Some of the shutters aren't working. I just needed to check we were covered in here."

"How many are bad?" Payne asked.

"We got three sets across the back, so far. But this is a big house, as you know, and that wind is a bastard. We're definitely going to lose some trees tonight, and that means all the windows should be protected."

Z pounded in another nail, and then descended the stepladder and moved the thing around Manny's *shellan* to the other side of the plywood. Even though he didn't know a damn thing about decor, you didn't need an *Architectural Digest* eye to see that the insta-fix was a frickin' eyesore in the elegant room.

But it was better than having three feet of snow on the Aubusson—

As the wind speed surged again, the gusts whined through the gaps around the window's molding, and he wondered if he should have used screws.

Or maybe bricks and mortar.

Restarting with the hammer, he nailed another twelve four-inchers in a tidy little row down the plywood's flank. With the last one in place, he disembarked from the ladder and—well, hello peanut gallery. All kinds of people had come in and were on the talk train: Rhage was going on about some fuse box, V was checking the exterior cameras on his phone, and Tohr was talking about emptying the rooms that weren't protected to prevent further furniture damage.

"How many shutters failed?" Z asked. "Do we have a total."

This had a silencing effect, and Tohr did the duty on replying. "Still tallying. And fixing them is going to be a bitch. Even the ground-floor windows are ten feet high off the ground, so it's not an easy reach, and so far, the failures are on banks of windows we can't open—so it's not like we can lean out to see what's wrong."

"I'll take care of everything," Rhage announced. "I can get a ladder—"

"No, I'll do it." V stepped forward. "*I'll* get a ladder and—"

Tohr interrupted the pair. "That wind is really dangerous, even if some are on the back side of the house—"

"You guys are *so* cute."

As the male voice spoke up, everybody turned to the laconic commentary. Balthazar, one of the Band of Bastards, was leaning against the sitting room's doorjamb, his long body at ease, a Yoplait strawberry yogurt in one hand, a spoonful of the sweet stuff on the way to his mouth in the other. He'd been letting his brown hair grow out, and the waves were down to his thick shoulders now, a feminine-ish fall that did absolutely nothing to maternalize his muscle-heavy body, his half-lidded, slightly sneaky eyes, or his sly attitude.

The fighter was a snake in the grass, something that moved quietly and dangerously, always tracking everyone and everybody in any room. But Z actually liked the fucker. Balz never apologized for or tried to hide what he was, and he had the one virtue that mattered: He was willing to die for the people under the mansion's roof.

So a snake with a moral compass.

"I mean, really," Balz murmured before disappearing the spoon between his smackers. "So cute."

Vishous went hands on hips, proving, once again, that he had the warm-and-fuzzies of an Uzi. "You want to explain that compliment?"

The *motherfucker* was implied.

Balz shrugged. "Don't get me wrong, you bunch of chest-thumping, I'll-handle-it's are great. But if you want someone to scale a building, especially in conditions like this, you should use somebody who's done it before."

"Well, ain't you Spider-Man."

"No, I'm a thief." Balz made a ring around the inside of the little container, turned the spoon to his tongue, and licked things clean. "I've climbed more shit than you all have stabbed—and in weather as bad as this. Besides, if I slip off and break my head, who cares? Oh, and don't give me that I'll-just-dematerialize-out-of-the-fall bullshit. You get twenty or thirty feet up, freezing cold in a storm, trying to fight with exterior shutters on tracks that were mounted in, what, the seventies? Eighties, in a best case? Good luck going into a free fall and getting ghost in a split second. You will hit hard, even with the snowpack, and hurt something that can't grow back. And need I remind you that most of you—oh, wait, *all* of you—have *shellans* to worry about? Let a dummy like me do this, will ya?"

"You know"—Rhage crossed his arms over his chest like the blond Adonis he was—"he's not talking stupid."

Balz pointed across the sitting room with his spoon. "You, sir, are smarter than you look and you've never looked stupid."

"You're willing to go up on the house then?" V asked.

"Yup. I'll figure out what's wrong and we can fix it together—"

"I'll spot you," Z cut in. "We'll use ropes and I'll be your ground. And fuck off with the you-can-handle-it. Death bores me after all these years. I'm way too familiar with it."

Balz shook his head. "You're going to stand out there in a blizzard for nothing."

Z's eyes flashed black. "You think I can't handle the cold."

Instantly, the Bastard ducked his stare. "Actually, I'm very sure you can—"

Without any brownout or blink warning, the mansion was plunged into absolute darkness, the electricity cut.

"Shit on a shingle," someone muttered. "Does

anyone else think this is going to be a really long night?"

◆ ◆ ◆

Qhuinn was just stepping out of the cold garage and into the warm back hall when everything went dark. Immediately, he reached back and took Blay's arm—and worried his fantasy about the tarp and the flame-thrower was about to get derailed.

"You okay?" he demanded.

"Really." Blay chuckled. "If a piano had fallen on my head, you'd have heard it even in the dark."

The door slammed shut behind them, and Qhuinn stayed where they were, waiting for the emergency generator to kick on. When nothing happened, he looked around. But like that was going to help? He felt like someone had thrown a black felt bag over his head—

Light flared, emanating from Blay's phone, a pinpoint of here-ya-go that diffused into a shallow, blue-bright illumination that pulled the tile floor out of the void. The beam moved around, illuminating the closed doors of the mudroom, the snow boots of the *doggen* lined up by an Orvis mat, the outerwear hanging on pegs.

"Twins are safe and sound up in the bedroom," Blay said. "Xcor just had Syphon text us both. He's lit candles, so they're not scared."

Qhuinn's worry deflated instantly. "I love that Bastard."

Down the hall, voices from the kitchen rose in volume and velocity, the *doggen* cooking staff clearly nervous—although knowing the way they thought, they were more worried about Last Meal being late eight hours from now rather than any kind of home invasion.

Then again, anyone tried to get inside who wasn't allowed? Not going to be pretty. And hey, Fritz would have plenty of blood to clean up, which was one of his favorite hobbies. #BOGO

Blay led the way forward with his phone, and as they emerged into the culinary area where preparations for Last Meal were indeed in full swing—or had been until it was lights-out—the *doggen* were clustered together, holding hands in their chef whites.

"Don't worry," Blay told them. "We'll figure this out. Let's get you guys some candles—"

Fritz came in from the pantry with a miner's light on his head and a bundle of wax-and-wicks in his arms. For once, he was not smiling.

"What shall we do about the bread," he said as he began passing out the candles. "Light these, yes, light them, please. We must needs recalibrate our offerings for the end of the night."

As the staff shared a box of matches, pinpoints of lights flared in a circle around the stainless steel island, drawing anxious faces out of the dark.

"You all are safe here," Qhuinn told them. "The shutters are in place in this wing, so nothing is going to get through any windows or the foot-thick stone walls. But we need to check for damage elsewhere."

"Whatever may we do to assist you?" Fritz asked as he tucked his hands up close to his throat. "May we help in some manner?"

"Call your staff down here, all of them. If we know where you are, we don't have to worry about you. God only knows what else has gone wrong."

Fritz bowed low and took out his phone. "Yes, sire. Right away!"

When Qhuinn motioned over his shoulder, Blay nodded, and they walked out into the dining room. Everything from First Meal had been cleared, but there were tall stacks of china and bundles of sterling silver flatware that had already been put out to reset the table.

"Where's the generator?" Blay asked.

"Not a damn clue."

As they entered the foyer, others in the household were gathering at the base of the stairs, various camera phones and candles doing the duty with the light thing. There was a lot of talk, and then a voice broke through.

"I can fix the generator."

All the chaos turned to the male who had spoken. Ruhn, mated of Qhuinn's cousin Saxton, was calm-eyed and handyman-ready in his flannel shirt and his low-hanging jeans.

"Just show me where it is," the guy said. "And I'll figure out why it hasn't kicked in."

"'They,' you mean," somebody said. "We've got three. And right this way."

As Ruhn followed Phury around the base of the grand staircase, Qhuinn decided, not for the first time, that his cousin Sax had picked a real winner. Ruhn was an all-around good guy, quiet and steady.

And hey, the pair were clearly in love—which mostly took the sting out of the fact that Blay and Saxton had had a thing once. For a little while. Because Qhuinn had been a douche and a coward.

"Anyone want to help with the shutters out back?" a voice said in the dark.

"Yes," Qhuinn replied, without knowing the details or caring about them. "I'm in."

Anything to avoid going back to that part of his and Blay's past. Even if the distraction involved minus-four-degree windchill, chapped lips, and frostbite.

Blay stepped in close. "I'm in, too."

Outside the pools of light, Qhuinn reached to the side and found his true love's hand. As he squeezed the palm he so often held within his own, he had a thought.

Why hadn't they been formally mated by now? 'Cuz maybe that was something they needed to get on the goddamn calendar.

Not that he was feeling territorial or anything. Or still a little jealous of his very handsome, yet very happily mated cousin Saxton.

Nah.

There was just something about a power outage in the middle of a blizzard that made a young male's thoughts turn toward romance.

CHAPTER TWELVE

This time they were going to be better prepared for the great outdoors.

As Qhuinn zipped up a Mount Everest—worthy parka from his hips to his chinny-chin-chin, he felt like the Stay Puft Marshmallow Man. Add in a set of Gore-Tex mittens, a hood, and a coat of Chap-Stick on the lips, and he felt like he was going to war out on a tundra.

He also knew what steamed broccoli felt like. Jesus, it was hot under all the thermal gear—and not in a fun way.

Turning his head, the miner's light strapped to his

skull hit Blay's chest. His mate had grabbed a load of wearable duvet as well, and as long as a person didn't focus on the twelve-foot-deep gash on that cheek, the sheer beauty of the male was almost overwhelming. Between that wind-burned face and those bright blue eyes and that red hair, Blaylock, son of Rocke, was positively edible.

And okay, fine. Maybe that scratch on the cheek was just a minor injury, but the thing certainly *seemed* like a mortal wound—

The emergency lights came on, offering a quarter of the normal illumination—and saving all kinds of retina burn.

"Thank you, Ruhn," Blay murmured as he looked to the ceiling fixture.

"Guy's a frickin' genius." Qhuinn switched off his headlamp, but kept the contraption noggin-bound on a just-in-case. "Let's do this."

Hitching an arm through the rung of a five-foot stepladder, he led the way back into the garage. The lights that were motion-activated came on at that re-duced level, but it was more than enough to see by as they tromped along the concrete floor, passing by the riding mowers that were drained and draped for the winter, as well as the thirteen ancient coffins that were lined up like something out of a Bela Lugosi movie.

The damn things freaked him the hell out—not that he'd shared that little slice of pansy with anybody. He always worried Dracula was going to crack open one of those fuckers—which was pretty rich because Qhuinn actually *was* a vampire.

"What about Bela Lugosi?" Blay asked as he unlocked the door to the back forty.

"Just rambling. Hey, did you think Frank Langella was hot?"

Blay glanced back. "In that Dracula movie from way back? I mean . . ."

"You're blushing." Qhuinn laughed. "You so did. You so thought he was hot with those high collars and that widow's peak."

"Whatever. You had a crush on Jordan Catalano—"

Qhuinn pulled Blay's parka forward. "I've got a crush on you. Right now. And forever."

Okay, that giggle was pretty much the high point of Qhuinn's night. No, wait. The true high point was going to be getting the male naked and bent over in front of him—

"Oh, my God," Blay said. "You can't talk like that right now. We've got a job to do."

"Did I say that out loud? For real? Oopsy. You want to spank me for being a naughty boy? Please? Commmmme onnnnnnnnnnnnnnnnnn."

Blay was laughing as he stepped out of the garage, and this was the intention. It was always good to hear that sound and know that Qhuinn was the reason for it—especially on a night like tonight, when a strange, paranoid feeling was not only persisting, but being egged on by things like broken windows and moaning wind and electrical failures.

Outside in the back, they didn't run into any wind at all. The great stone house was a helluva buffer, the front taking the lashing, the rear spared. Overhead in the sky, the snow had finally started to fall, the flakes rushing by up high illuminated by the exterior security fixtures that were back on at half-power, the variegated angles of the roof acting like the aerodynamics of a car, the airflow whipping past the peaks and valleys in a fixed, organized pattern. Not that there weren't some icy anarchists. Some of what was coming down—or across, as the case was—broke free of the masses and drifted toward the ground, clearly exhausted with all the frantic, conforming congestion.

"Over here," Blay said.

Qhuinn humped the ladder across to a row of

three windows that were only halfway shuttered. "Okay, let's have a look at this."

"I'll hold the ladder base."

"Perfect." Qhuinn set the thing up and put a foot on the first step. "And please feel free to ogle my assets. Don't be shy about it, either."

Blay laughed, his breath leaving in puffs of white. "You're ridiculous."

"You should also feel no obligation to keep your hands to yourself. And this is more than a mere suggestion."

Down at the other end of the house, at the library, there was another group gathered with a bigger ladder. Because yes, sometimes size did matter. Balz and Z were focusing on the second-story windows of Wrath's study, and that was a heck of an elevation.

"I wonder how many other shutters failed," Blay murmured.

"More than we want, for sure."

Qhuinn went up to the second-to-the-last step and surveyed the shutter's nonfunctioning landscape. As he came to absolutely no viable conclusion, he tried not to envy Ruhn's obvious Mr. Fix It confidence—and he sure as shit wasn't going back down to the ground until he figured things out.

The steel shutters that were mounted over every

single piece of window glass around the mansion were not just sunlight blockers. They were wind-proof, bulletproof, fireproof, vampire-proof, and anti-tamper. Every sash setup had a set custom made for it, and the protective suits were painted the gray color of the stone wallings and set on tracks so the inter-locking panels could unroll from their top mounts and click into place. Like little garage doors.

Only these weren't coming down.

Qhuinn grabbed the lower lip with his gloves and pulled. And pulled again. "Yeah, it's frozen in place."

"As in ice frozen or not-moving frozen?"

"I don't know. Gimme a screwdriver."

Putting a hand down, he got the slap of the tool's handle against his glove. "When in doubt, force it, right?"

"Usually, you just shoot things."

"And you were worried I wouldn't mellow with age."

The flat head went right into a ridge on the lower lip like the shutter had been designed for just this kind of hard-muscled persuasion. After a test lean, Qhuinn put his shoulder into it. And then his whole upper body. And nothing happened—

All at once, the stuck became unstuck and Qhuinn pitched forward. But not to worry, his face caught his body weight—with a ringing bang followed by an old school washboard scrub as the shutter continued down its track.

"—don't fall!" Blay reached up. "Oh, God!"

Qhuinn shoved himself off the house and mostly kept the wince to himself. "It's okay. I needed to shave anyway."

And hey, the frigid temperature had created a nice numbness. Plus, bonus, his nose was still attached: He knew this because he could poke at it with his puffy glove.

Secure in the knowledge that no aesthetic damage had been done—in spite of the fact that his schnoz now had its own heart rate—he clomped down and moved the ladder over to the next window in the lineup of three. The process was repeated, with the absence of the face-plant because now he was ready for it.

"One more to go—"

Just as he was about to step down again, a sensation like he'd been tapped on the shoulder startled him. With a wrench-around, he glanced over the back gardens and the forest rim beyond them.

"What is it?"

Qhuinn's eyes searched the darkness outside the reach of the dimmed security lights. Familiarity with

the estate filled in the winter details he couldn't visu-
alize fully: the pool, which was drained and covered
for the season; the flower beds and blooming fruit
trees, which were likewise on lockdown and draped
with burlap; the snow-covered sloping lawn on the
far side of the brick walkways. And after all that, the
tree line's boundary of coniferous sentries.

"What's wrong, Qhuinn?"

Shaking himself, he intended to look down at his
mate. But his eyes would not leave the back forty.

"Nothing," he lied. "It's . . . nothing."

◆ ◆ ◆

Over at the other end of the house, by the library, Z
was coiling up a rope that was locked on Balthazar's
waist. The Bastard was not paying attention to any
of the safety shit, and not surprisingly, he was already
starting up the side of the house.

Oh, and not using the ladder that had been leaned
into place.

Because why the fuck would you use the ladder.

No, no, the twenty-footer, which had been properly tilted and footed for safety, had been eschewed
with the dismissal of a race car driver being offered
a tricycle. Instead, Balz was somehow managing to
tiptoe his way up the stone, his fingertips and toes
cruising along the mortar joints.

"How the hell is he doing that?" Rhage muttered as he came around the corner.

"Bubblegum on his shoes," somebody with the brother answered.

"Is he even wearing shoes?"

"He better be or those little piggies of his are going to be frozen bacon in the next minute and a half."

Z let out a little more lead, and then a little more. After which he felt compelled to call out, "You need to set some hooks now and loop yourself in."

"I will," Balz said. "Just a bit farther."

"You got this, Z?" Rhage asked.

"Yeah. I'll scrape him off the snowpack when he falls off."

"Call us for backup if you need us. We've got those ground-level shutters out in front to deal with."

Z nodded, and stayed focused on the Bastard. And of course, there was no setting hooks and loops going on. Balz just kept crabbing his way up the stone wall, finding fingerholds, toeholds, in the seams of mortar. When he got to the problem window, some twenty feet up, he reached over with his left hand, grabbed on to the track of the shutter, and pulled himself across so he was in the center of the no-go issue.

"Now you tie yourself," Z yelled up. "Before you do anything. Or I'll pull you down myself."

Balthazar smiled under his arm. "You can't do that."

Z yanked the rope to answer that one.

"But I'll shatter into a thousand pieces," the Bastard said. "That's what you're worried about, right? Seems silly to prove the danger by creating it—and then who will fix this shutter?"

"There's a bush under you. FYI."

"Oh! Well, then it's not that dangerous to begin with, and messing about with hooks will not only ruin the structural integrity of this house, but it'll slow me down and accomplish nothing. Kind of like this conversation."

"Has anyone told you you make no damned sense?"

Balz turned back to the faulty shutter. "It's come up once or twice. Fortunately, I can get very hard of hearing when I want to."

Z closed his eyes. When he reopened them—prepared to tell the fucker to go ahead, it was his goddamn life to wager on the asshat wheel of craps—Balz was already in a yank with the bottom of the half-shut shutter, gloved hands locked on like loaves of bread, body arching back. If that thing decided to get with the program, the Bastard was going to free-fall into—

"Not going to budge," Balz puffed. "Shit. Let me try the next one."

"What do you think is wrong with them?" Z said.

Distantly, the wind let out a roar, the sound like that of a train on the approach. Good thing the mansion weighed as much as the mountain or it might get blown off.

"I think the motors have burned out," Balz yelled down. "You can smell the electric fire up here."

The Bastard crab-walked over to the next fixed sash. Pull. Tug. Nowhere.

"Wait, I have an idea." The male took the rope off his waist and tied it onto the bottom of the shutter. "You have better leverage than I do."

"Get out of the way." Before the Bastard could do what he inevitably would with the arguing, Z cut in with, "You're wrong. So shut the fuck up."

"How do you know what I was going to say?"

"History."

But the Bastard still put his gloved hands back on the shutter.

"You're going to fall off the damn house if this lets go." Z shook his head. "Just be reasonable. Please?"

Well. What do you know. The magic word.

Balz backed off with all kinds of muttering. And then Z wound the nylon rope around his hands a couple of times and gave it a try all on his lonesome, easing into the full power of his body like a tow truck trying to get a car out of mud. Finally, he sank down into his glutes, his arms and shoulders straining, his lips pulling away from his fangs.

There was a tremendous screech, and then the shutter came down on a oner.

"Oh, shit!"

Z fell back on his ass, the snow catching his body like a baseball mitt, all support, no cushioning. As the rope went lax and flapped onto his legs, Balz swung loose up at the window, one foot fixed, the other free, one hand locked on the track of the next shutter, the other up and out. He recovered quick, velcroing once again.

"You okay?" the Bastard called down.

Z upped to his feet and brushed the snow off his backside. "I told you so."

"Let's do the same thing on the next one."

Zsadist glanced to the other end of the house. Qhuinn and Blay were working on their set of shutters on the lower level, or should have been. The former seemed frozen as he focused on something off toward the tree line.

Z put his fingers between his front teeth and whistled. As the sound traveled, Qhuinn's focus shifted around.

After a moment, the brother whistled back two short bursts.

"Do they need help?" Balz asked from above.

"All clear." Z nodded to the next failed shutter. "Okay, Spidey, rope me up with that one. Let's get this done and see what else is wrong with this old ark."

CHAPTER THIRTEEN

It was all going to be fine.

That's what was going through Blay's mind as he and Qhuinn reentered the garage with the ladder. The busted shutters were down where they should be and locked into place, the motor lines cut so that there was no malfunction risk when the full electricity came back on. After the storm, there were going to be a lot of repairs, and there would be time to rewire things then. What couldn't be risked was a daylight retraction.

Just as they were heading back into the house, a

muffled roar sounded out somewhere in the distance. And a second. A third.

At which point the lights came back on fully, the generators settling in to a dim, pervasive purr.

"Ruhn is the fucking master," Qhuinn said as they tilted the ladder against the wall in the mudroom and stomped the snow off the treads of their shitkickers.

The cheer of the *doggen* in the kitchen was like that of a group being rescued off a deserted island. By a Carnival cruise ship. With a stocked bar and the buffet already set out. And Charo performing on the Lido Deck.

"Such the man," Blay agreed.

As they walked into the kitchen and were applauded unnecessarily by the staff, Blay unzipped his parka, but kept the puff where it was in case this was just a pause and they would be going out again. In the foyer, people were gathering once more, the check-in happening organically, as if the electricity coming back on required a reckoning—

The crash was loud as a bomb.

And succeeded by shattering glass, a blast of cold air, and a resonant pine smell.

Before anyone could react, Rhage and Butch came running out of the library. The pair of them looked like they'd been in a slap fight, their faces red, noses runny, eyes blinking like they couldn't see. Snow covered their hair, their shoulders, their shitkickers.

"Tree," Rhage panted.

Butch grabbed the front of his own parka like he was having a coronary. "Big tree—"

"Coming after us!"

"What the hell are you talking about?" someone demanded.

"And what just hit the house?" somebody else shouted.

"Fucking tree!" Rhage ground out as he braced his hands on his knees and bent over to breathe better. "And it's *in* the house."

At that moment, up at the head of the grand staircase, Wrath and Beth appeared with their son. The Queen was carrying L.W., the young was carrying his golden retriever stuffed animal—the one that was bigger than he was—and Wrath had his hand locked on George's lead.

"Is everyone okay?" Beth called down. "We heard a crash."

"And smell a whole lot of pretty-much-Pine-Sol," the King said as they started their descent. "What's going on in the library?"

Blay shook his head and glanced at Qhuinn, ready to raise a question about what was going to go wrong next—

When the lights went off unexpectedly.

Where there had been illumination, there was a sudden and pervasive return of the pitch black, no security lights on, no fireplaces lit to glow, the candles canned because of all the Thomas Edison.

Later, Blay would remember wheeling around in space and throwing his arms out toward the grand staircase. It was as if he knew what was going to happen, what misstep was going to occur, what off-kilter was going to result in a tragic fall.

Wrath would be fine on the descent. As a blind male, whether or not there was light did not matter to him. For Beth, however, the abrupt loss of her sight would be a shock—and Blay didn't know exactly what occurred, but he, and everyone else, heard her shout of alarm.

After which came the fall.

L.W. began to wail at the same time a sickening series of bumps and thumps came down the stairs, bruises or worse occurring—and there was nothing to be done. The momentum worked with gravity's inexorable pull to a terrible result, and in the darkness, no matter how far Blay reached forward, no matter how much he strained, there was nothing he could do to stop the inevitable.

It was a hole in one. Nothing planned, certainly not the horrible result.

And all the while, the child screamed.

◆ ◆ ◆

"There's another one," Balz called down from the now-shuttered bank of windows. "There."

Zsadist stood up again from the snowpack and brushed his leathers off. You'd think he'd have developed a core competency in catching his weight on the free fall, but nope. His butt had taken the brunt of things. Three times now.

As he looked in the direction Balz was pointing toward, he got a snowflake right in the eyeball. Rubbing the sting away, he said, "Yeah, we need that closed, too. Take the rope up?"

"Will do."

There was no reason to raise the whole setting-hooks thing again. Balz was right about his climbing expertise. The Bastard's scaling and staying put was totally impressive, and it made a male wonder exactly what the guy had gotten into over the years.

Then again, that wasn't a question Z really wanted answered.

Stepping back, he reviewed the expanse of the house, you know, just in case any shutters had decided to magically retract. Which they hadn't. But a male got paranoid when he thought of his *shellan* and his young. What if one of those things decided to pop loose in the middle of the day? What if the electricity came back on or had a surge or . . . something . . . and suddenly the mansion went wide-open glass at noontime?

Jesus, why hadn't he worried about this before.

As a hot flash of terror went through him, at least his toes warmed up a little in his shitkickers. Meanwhile, the Bastard was already over at the other window, the rope hanging off his ass like a tail, his thin-gloved hands working the upper left-hand corner of the shutter where the motor was, his lower body flush with the exterior wall while his upper torso curved away to give him space to work.

"Almost done," he called out. "Then I'm going to—"

All at once, the window he was at lit up like the sun had risen inside the room on the far side, yellow light cascading out into the night, into the storm.

Unfortunately, that wasn't all.

Sparks exploded from the motor Balz was disconnecting, the electrical charge transferring from the metal to the male, the blue arc of the lightning-like flash going right into one of the Bastard's hands.

And through his body.

As a brownout registered the transfer of voltage, Balz was thrown back into thin air, his body stiff as a board, arms and legs fully extended.

Z reacted without conscious thought. He triangulated the fall and got under the male, bracing himself for the impact, arms cupped like he was going to catch a hay bale. At the last moment, as Balz dead weighted down toward the ground, Z pivoted, realizing he needed to be sideways to the load he was going to try to cradle.

Talk about electrical burns.

As he captured the heavy load, a whiff of burned flesh along with a metal tang hit his nose, and then he wasn't thinking about smells at all. Lying the male out in the snow, he checked for breath and found none. Reaching for his own shoulder—

Fuck, no communicator. 'Cuz they were at home, not in the field.

Z whistled loud and long as he ripped off his gloves and felt for a pulse at the jugular. Faint. Or . . . maybe there wasn't one? Yanking open the Bastard's parka, he dropped his head down to make sure there was no breathing still. Then he put one of his palms on top of the other in the center of that big-ass chest, interlocked his fingers, and started straight-arming CPR.

"Stayin' alive, stayin' alive," he said under his breath as he compressed with his doubled-up hands. "Ah, ah, ah . . . ah . . . stayin' alive . . ."

He paused to give the male two breaths. Which, yes, he was aware was not what the American Heart Association recommended anymore, but he was hardly a casual bystander and rescue breaths were fine with him.

As he resumed chest compressions, he called out with various "Hey!" "My brothers!" "Fritz!"

He didn't yell *Help*. He never had, and he wasn't starting now.

Time to breathe for the Bastard again.

Inhale. Forced puff into that lax mouth. Inhale. Forced puff. And then more with chest compressions and the yelling.

Jesus Christ, what did he need to do to get someone's attention around here?

CHAPTER FOURTEEN

In the mansion's foyer, the security lights came back on with the same lack of warning that they went out, and Blay braced himself for a paralyzed *mahmen* and a young with horrible injuries, for Wrath to be crazed with grief, for—

Halfway down the grand staircase, there was a tableau of off-kilter, and the great Blind King was in the center of it. L.W. was hanging from the back of his onesie in Wrath's fist, the young screaming and red-faced—but safe from a fall that would have killed him for sure. And on the other side of the King, Beth had been caught by the arm, her whole body leaning out over the rest of the red-carpeted steps, only one foot planted, the other on a high kick to nowhere.

As for the fall? Down at the bottom of the steps . . . L.W.'s favorite toy, the nearly life-sized golden, with its beanbag paws and loosely stuffed legs, was lying in a tangled heap on the hard mosaic floor.

Wrath had saved his Queen and his son.

And beside him, George, the real-life dog, was frozen and panting in a panic, as if the animal knew that things had almost been a tragedy.

As everyone standing around exhaled in relief, the King pulled his loved ones into him, cradling both his *shellan* and his young close, L.W. settling down as soon as his *mahmen* was back in range and all was okay.

"Shit," Qhuinn breathed. "I mean . . . just shit—"

There was a hiccup in the electricity, things faltering before surging again—and then the sconces on the walls flared back fully to life, the chandelier in the dining room reigniting and all kinds of illumination streaming from sources you only noticed when they weren't working.

"I got you," Wrath was saying in a soft voice. "I got both of you."

Beth trembled as she hung on to the King's enormous upper arm. "How did you catch us?"

"Eyes aren't everything, *leelan*." Wrath tucked her head under his chin and stared out into space, his wraparounds hiding his expression. "And I've got a knack for knowing where things are. It's what keeps me on my feet."

The feel of a hand on Blay's waist brought his head around. As he looked into Qhuinn's eyes, he mumbled, "I can't even."

"I know. Come here."

It seemed unmanly to turn to his mate and drop his face into that strong neck and close his eyes. But like he gave a fuck? All he could see against the backs of his lids was a pile of bodies, all broken bones and blood spilled on the tiles.

Before he could think of what to do, what to say, he felt his hand get taken in that warm, solid grip he knew so well—and the next thing he was aware of was being drawn into the billiards room by Qhuinn. As the pair of them hit the layout of pool tables, he had no clue where they were going, but then—presto!—they were at the bar.

"Sit."

Qhuinn pulled out a stool and arranged Blay like you would a potted plant: He saw a flat place and put something on it.

Blay wasn't inclined to argue. At least not with the

ass support. "I thought we weren't drinking tonight, though."

"We're not drinking. This is medicinal."

Two shot glasses were outed, and then came the I. W. Harper's. Qhuinn's hand wasn't completely steady as he poured a splash in each, and that was not what you wanted to see in your mate—but when you were quaking in your own boots, it was nice to know you weren't alone with your shimmies.

"Drink up."

As all kinds of talk bloomed out in the foyer, they did the shot together, and Qhuinn doled out another. After the two, they stopped and put the glasses in the sink—

That was when Blay heard the whistle. Or at least . . . he thought he did.

It was hard to tell because there were so many voices in the echo chamber around that grand staircase, people burning off their adrenaline with are-you-sure-you're-okay conversations.

Looking to the open pocket door that led into the library, Blay closed his eyes and ordered his ears to sift through the other bird-like sounds the wind was making as it winnowed through the nooks and crannies on the front of the house—as well as the big-ass hole some tree had made in the back.

"What is it?" Qhuinn asked.

Blay got off his stool and proceeded over to the pocket door—oh, *shit*. A pointy evergreen the size of the one the Big Apple put up for the holidays at Rockefeller Center had barged in through a set of French doors, bringing with it snow and cold and all kinds of outdoor.

Not exactly a redecorating job that went with all the priceless books and the wonderful old rug.

"Well," Qhuinn hedged, "at least we won't have to cut down something to drape the garland and lights on."

"So that's what was chasing Rhage and Butch—"

The shout outside was muffled, but distinct enough.

Blay rushed forward, but not to the tree, to the other banks of French doors, which were still shut and locked. As he yanked open one set, more of the cold rushed in, but he didn't pay attention to the deep freeze.

In the security lights, he saw the two figures, one back-flatted in the snow, the other crouched down and pumping at a chest.

Blay pivoted and shouted, "Medic! We need a medic!"

Then he and Qhuinn were out in the storm. Z was the one doing the compressions, Balthazar the person in cardiac arrest.

"Do you need me to take over?" Blay asked as he fell to his knees.

"You breathe for him when I say so. Three . . . two . . . one . . . *breathe*."

Blay pinched Balz's nose, sealed the male's lips, and pushed oxygen into those lungs. When he backed off and took another deep inhale, he smelled the burn. Skin . . . and something metallic.

He's not dead, Blay told himself. *He can't be dead*.

"Breathe!" Z commanded.

Blay went back down again, forcing air out of his own lungs and into the other male's. Beside him, Qhuinn had taken Balz's hand and was rubbing it. Or maybe praying over it.

"Where are they?" Blay said as he wrenched around. "*Medic!*"

Jesus Christ, the fighter was dead—

Without warning—because hey, nothing was coming with any warning tonight—Balz arched back and hauled in a breath so big, it was as if he had been animated by an outside force, some dark magic rushing through him and bringing him back to life.

The male's eyes popped wide, and the dilated pupils focused upward. Then the head swiveled toward Z.

In a voice that sounded all wrong, Balz said in the Old Language, "*She is here. The demon is back.*"

◆ ◆ ◆

An hour later, Z was down in the training center. Instead of crowding the clinic, where everybody else was, he was over by the gym.

Every time he blinked, he saw Balthazar in the snow, white face turning to him, eyes rapt and yet unfocused, that haunted voice like something from the other side.

The demon is back.

Z rubbed his eyes and turned away, walking farther down to the pool. Those four words that had been uttered across that cold air had been unconsciously spoken. Z knew this because when Doc Jane and V had come out, assessed Balz, and cleared him to be moved back inside, the real Bastard had returned.

What had spoken those words had been someone halfway back, a ghost with a corporeal shell, the message eerie because it emanated from a place other than mortal consciousness.

When they'd gotten him into the library, he'd

jerked again and then glanced at the tree that had broken through one of the sets of doors.

"Who put that in here?" he'd mumbled. "It doesn't fit."

There had been such relief at that point, a bubbling happiness for everybody as the stabilization and recovery had presented itself. Balz had still been taken down here, of course. And his fellow Bastards were inside the exam room with him. He was going to be fine, though—no lingering aftereffects anticipated, according to the doctors.

Except they were wrong about that. Although not with respect to Balz.

Z stopped at the glass entrance of the pool area. Those four words were causing a rift in reality for the male they'd been spoken to.

But Z's demon was *not* back. He'd been through this before. His rational side knew this.

And yet . . .

The decision was made before he was aware of coming to any kind of crossroads of choice. His feet were clearly committed to a new course of action, however, turning his body away from the pool's enclosure and taking him to the office, through the office, into the supply closet.

He fought the direction he was headed. He didn't want to go into the mansion's cellar, to that corner far, far in the back, to the cardboard box that he had brought down there—

As Z stepped out into the tunnel, he happened to take a deep breath, and that was when he smelled something that made no damned sense.

Looking to the right, to the darkened void at the far end, he frowned and took another deep inhale.

Fresh air? What the hell?

Given the number of things that had gone haywire tonight, he pivoted and headed in that direction. As he continued along, motion-activated ceiling lights illuminated his way, his footfalls echoing around. God knew there was pelnty of distance to travel. The tunnel connected four things: the Pit, which was one terminal; the mansion and the training center in the middle; and at the far, far opposite end, there was a hidden escape hatch that dumped out on the mountain a quarter of a mile away.

No one should have gone in or out of it.

So why was the scent of the storm, of the night, of evergreens, in this part of the Brotherhood's complex?

As he got close to the steel hatch, the lineup of emergency weapons, survival packs, and outerwear put in an appearance, everything ready to get grabbed in the event of a dramatic departure. And on the other side of the triple-locked portal? There was a shallow cave with a blacked-out Chevy Tahoe and several snowmobiles, the vehicles sheltered from the elements and camo'd from prying eyes and trespassing.

Glancing around, he frowned.

Nothing was out of place.

No damp footsteps were drying on the concrete floor.

No empty pegs were in the collection of equipment. No scent of gasoline, either.

Weird. But maybe V had decided to check everything. Considering how things were going tonight, who could blame him for the paranoia?

CHAPTER FIFTEEN

The classroom was the last one in the training center's lineup, and as Blay pushed through its door and turned on the light, he looked to the place where he'd once sat as a student with John Matthew and Qhuinn. Back in their pretrans days, when they'd been in the Brotherhood's training program here, they had stuck together. Part of it had been protecting John Matthew from Lash. More of it had been the simpler, enduring ties of friendship.

As Qhuinn followed him inside, the male had a curious expression on his face. Like everyone else, they'd waited outside Balz's examination room and had been relieved to get confirming good news—and not just about the patient, although that was the most important thing. Tohr had also announced to everybody that even though the storm was in full rock and roll, all of the shutters up at the mansion were locked down, the tree in the library had been removed, and there was plywood covering the French doors the evergreen had broken open.

So considering the way things had started out?

Qhuinn went over to the blackboard—no dry-erase for the Brothers, none of that fancy new stuff—and picked up a piece of chalk. The heart outline he drew was yellow, the color of a lined legal pad. In the center, he wrote: "Q+B = 4EVA"

As he put the chalk back, he clapped his palms clean. "So I'm twelve, okay? Sue me."

"I think you're romantic."

"Do I hit on you too much?" Qhuinn pivoted around. "I mean, am I—"

Blay answered that question by taking the bottom of his cashmere sweater and lifting it up and over his head. Then came the button-down shirt, the one that he'd chosen because it was blue and coral checked and complemented the blue sweater.

Qhuinn froze where his stood. Then his eyes flared.

"I locked the door," Blay said. "And no, I don't think you hit on me too much—" He put his palms out to stop his mate. Then he pointed forward. "Oh, no you don't. I want you to sit there. Where the teacher would."

With a sloppy shuffle, Qhuinn planted himself behind the empty desk—and did a piss-poor impression of a professor. Instead of looking like he was in charge, he linked his fingers together, put his hands primly in front of himself, and sat, spine rigid, like a good little boy praying he got a cookie for behaving nicely.

Splaying out his arms, Blay slowly turned in front of his mate. He was not an exhibitionist by any sense of the word, but he liked how the sight of his body made his lover feel.

For example, the groaning? Coming from behind that desk?

Best sound in the world.

Approaching Qhuinn, he put his left boot on the desk lip, angling his hips so that across the wood top, the bulge behind his fly was very obvious. He took his time with the de-lacing, and enjoyed the way Qhuinn's eyes roamed around his bare shoulders and chest, his abs and his erection. And then it was the other side, again with the de-looping, the pulling free, the shucking out.

The tile floor was cold underneath his feet as he backed away. Then turned away.

Putting his hands to his fly, he made quick work of the button and the zipper. He hadn't bothered with a belt because of the sweater—and because they'd been delayed in the shower—and he was glad he didn't need to fuss around with buckles right now.

Although, actually, the anticipation was working for them both: Qhuinn's bonding scent was flaring all kinds of dark spices—which made Blay wonder what people passing by out in the tunnel might think.

Then again, everybody had returned to the mansion after Doc Jane had sounded the all-clear on Balz's recovery. And with the storm, who was going out into the parking lot anyway?

Blay's fine wool pants were loose enough so that he could have just let them drop, but where was the fun in that? He went the inch-by-inch route, slowly letting Qhuinn see what he wanted. And it was clear that things were going exactly the way Blay was hoping because a pumping growl percolated through the classroom.

And then there was a gasping inhale.

Followed by panting.

Moving slowly, Blay stepped out of the slacks and glanced over his shoulder. Qhuinn had lost the linked-hands routine. Now he'd planted his palms and was leaning forward, his blue and green eyes fixated and hot, his fangs descended, his lips peeled back. He looked bloodthirsty—in a good way. In the best way.

Blay stretched himself, undulating his body from ass to nape, and then he turned around.

His own arousal stuck straight out from his pelvis, and he decided that it needed a little attention. Sweeping his hand down his pecs, he paused to play with one of his nipples and then continued down over the ridges of his abs.

"Touch it for me," Qhuinn said in a guttural voice. "That's right . . . stroke it—oh, *fuck.*"

"You like this?" Blay moved his palm up and down on his thick shaft. "You want this?"

"Yes . . ." Qhuinn started to get up, the chair squeaking. "I need—"

Blay turned back around and ran his free hand down his ass. "Or do you want this?"

"I want everything. All of it," came the growled response.

With another arch, Blay bent over one of the tables. "Then why don't you come and get it."

◆ ◆ ◆

Fuck the desk.

Qhuinn wasn't going to waste time going around it; he went over the bitch, jumping up and pushing off into the air. He covered the five feet between where he had been and where he needed to be in one stride, and he managed to out his arousal on the way.

Blay was arched and looking over his shoulder, and he knew what was going to hit him: He grabbed on to the corners of the table and braced himself, his shoulder muscles flexing up, the ones that fanned out along his spine rippling under his smooth skin.

Spitting into his hand, Qhuinn did a pass on his erection, and then he went in, going deep. Beneath him, Blay's head rose up and he called out, the desperate sound making every inch of Qhuinn's skin prickle with awareness—except then his hearing was lost as the sensation of constriction and heat overrode everything.

The movement was instinctual and compulsive, the pumping rhythm stronger than he wanted it to be. There was no stopping it, though—

"Harder," Blay groaned. "Hard-er . . ."

Qhuinn gripped the tight waist over Blay's hip bones and sank his fingers into the taut flesh. "How much harder," he grunted.

Blay's arms butterflied as he held himself against the onslaught, the front of Qhuinn's pelvis slapping into the back of that spectacular ass, the climax coming so soon—not that there was a reason to fight it—

The orgasm tackled Qhuinn from behind, shoving his torso over Blay's back, his hips jerking and locking into place. The ejaculations were sharp points of pleasure, so acute they were sweetly painful.

And he didn't stop. Reaching around, he pushed Blay's hand out of the way and took over the stroking as he kept pumping, countering the forward penetration with the pull down on the shaft, the retraction of his cock with the palm moving out to the head. It required coordination.

But he'd had so much practice, hadn't he.

Blay came next, hot jets covering Qhuinn's hand and palm, everything slicking up. In both places. There was no stopping either of them, and Qhuinn loved being on this erotic plane with his male, the two of them riding the waves of pleasure, the intensity of the experience uniting them.

Until Qhuinn pulled out. And rolled his mate over.

Usually, Blay was an elegant, lithe mover. Not right now. He landed face-up in a boneless flop, his blue eyes glassy, his mouth parted in a pant, his color high from the exertion. Grabbing one of his mate's thighs, Qhuinn curled up the knee and angled himself back in.

This time, he went slow.

"Look at me, Blay," he whispered.

When those beautiful peepers managed to focus, Qhuinn brought his glossy hand to his mouth. One by one, he licked his fingers, drawing them in, savoring them, extending his tongue and running it up his palm.

Blay moaned and came hard, ejaculating all over his own abdominals.

Which gave a male something to clean up, didn't it.

But that was going to have to wait while he—

"Oh, God," Qhuinn grunted as he found another release of his own, his head falling back, his eyes squeezing shut, his body doing what it did best.

Which was showing his true love exactly what the male meant to him, and how beautiful Blay was.

CHAPTER SIXTEEN

D addy?"

As Z opened the door to his bedroom suite, the little voice brought a smile to his face, even though the night had been full of things that were far from happy. Yes, Balz had survived. And yes, the house had been patched up. But for so many reasons, Z's soul was tossed and turned, an ocean that was raging.

And yet that one word, spoken in that voice?

Zsadist lowered himself down to his knees, even though he wasn't yet over the threshold of his family's private space. Suddenly, though, he didn't care who might see him in this moment when he was so vulnerable.

Besides, he knew nothing else but what was coming across the antique rug at him.

Darling Nalla, sweet, darling Nalla, who was toddling and babbling and living her very best life, was walking toward him, her arms outstretched, her legs chugging along, her healthy body tilting from side to side. The very best part? She was beaming at him.

As if they had been separated by a century, instead of a mere hour or two.

He still couldn't believe it. He still couldn't believe that he and his *shellan* had created this miracle together—and just as wondrous was the fact that in spite of every ugliness inside of him, in spite of the filth that lurked beneath his skin, even with the slave bands that were tattooed around his neck and on his wrists, and his hideous scar . . .

"Daddy! Love you, Daddy!"

With total abandonment, Nalla threw herself at him, knowing he would catch her, secure in the faith that he would always protect her, ever keep her safe. As his huge arms went around her small, warm body, he was gentle with the pressure.

"Daddy!" In response to his embrace, her arms wrapped around his neck and squeezed tight, her soft cheek against the side of his face. "You're back!"

Every time she saw him, she spoke in exclamations, as if his return to their suite, her bedroom, the house, the dining room, the playroom, was the single most exciting thing that had ever happened in her entire life. He kept expecting her to get over this, bracing himself for the time she got used to him or maybe didn't love him with such distraction . . . but it didn't seem to be happening.

He wasn't aware of having shut his eyes until his lids opened.

Across the room, Bella was leaning back against the bureau, her arms linked over her chest, her face cast in a dreamy way.

Like the sight of him with their daughter was her favorite thing in the world.

And instantly, his seas calmed, the churning waves easing.

Z stood up, transferring Nalla's weight into the crook of his arm. Kicking the door shut, he went over to his *shellan*. As he approached, she lifted her lips, and as soon as he was in range, he dropped his mouth to hers.

With a shudder, he remembered Balthazar flipping off the side of the house and falling down to the ground. Then he saw the male's extremities twitching, the gloves patting at the snow, the soft shoes that had found those crevices in between the stones kicking at the base of legs that otherwise did not move.

The final image was of the snowflakes, few and far between, that drifted down onto the open eyes that stared out of that frozen face.

"What time is it?" Z asked roughly. Not that he really cared.

"Last Meal is coming soon. It's about five?"

"I'm hungry," Nalla announced.

Z smiled at his daughter. "Well, then, let's go down and get you fed."

"Yay!"

More with the hugs, and as Z closed his eyes again, he found himself back outside in the cold, hearing what Balz had said as he'd come back from wherever he had been—

Right back open with those lids. Yup. He was not shutting the damn things for any longer than a blink right now. And maybe for the next five years.

"I'm ready to eat, too," Bella said as they headed for the door.

Stepping out into the Hall of Statues, Z smelled the fresh plywood from down in the sitting room, but there were other scents on the air, too, aromas of well-cooked food reminding him they were all going to get through the storm. In fact, they had gotten through it. Things were raging outside, the wind ferocious and the snow no doubt falling by inches that would turn into feet. But they were safe and warm and dry—all who lived in the house, not just his own little family.

Downstairs in the dining room, people were gathering, and as they came up to their three seats, he passed Nalla off to Bella.

"Where going, Daddy?"

"I'll be right back." He touched his daughter's cheek and then smiled at his mate. "Just going to check that no one needs any help."

"That's a good thing to do," Nalla said gravely. "Then you come back."

"Yes, I'll come right back."

As he walked off toward the pantry, the lie stung, but he told himself he wasn't going to be gone long. This was just . . . a compulsion he hadn't felt for a very long time.

One that he knew he better act on or there would be no rest for him.

The steel door into the basement had recently been upgraded, and it was painted to look like the old wooden ones that filled the jambs in the kitchen and the pantry: But for the pattern of bolts around the various panels, you might be fooled into thinking it was made of ash like all of the others throughout the house.

As he went to enter the code, he was glad that the *doggen* were all too busy getting Last Meal on the table to pay much attention to him—which meant he only fielded four inquiries about whether he needed anything, and one nervous drive-by from Fritz, who was apparently checking that the four no-thank-you's Z had given were in fact what he'd meant. As always, it was like wading through a morass of hospitality, and in the past, this obsequious obstacle course had driven him insane. Now, he understood it was just the way of the *doggen* and he was used to it.

The steel portal was like a barricade, and he put his shoulder into the effort of opening the damn thing, the well-greased hinges offering no protest at being called into service. The descent down the steps was a familiar one, and when he got to the lower level, he knew his way through the rabbit warren of spaces. V's forging room was down here. So were the massive furnaces. And the storage areas.

The latter was what he was looking for.

Each family had their own unit, the lineup of closed doors unlocked because even though everyone in the mansion knew everybody else's business, privacy was respected.

His was the one on the far end, and there were motion-activated lights along the ceiling that woke up as he went along the concrete hallway. The smell was damp air and the minerals in the groundwater that was right under the poured floor. The second he took notice of the musty scent, he felt bad, as if he'd betrayed Fritz in some way.

If that *doggen* knew there was any humidity down here? He would hit this hall with a fleet of dehumidifiers and enough hot water and suds to scrub down a naval carrier.

When he got to the door to his and Bella's unit, he took a deep breath and didn't waste time opening it up. No amount of hanging around was going to change what was in it.

Another light came on inside as he crossed the threshold.

Not much to see. Seasonal clothes for Bella, packed in plastic containers that had been vacuum sealed. Seasonal clothes for Nalla that were likewise put away, but probably wouldn't be worn again because she was growing so fast. No seasonal anything for Z. He wore the same muscle shirt, leathers, and leather jacket no matter the weather.

The only time he mixed shit up was with his socks. Sometimes they were black. Sometimes they were white.

Call him a party animal.

There were a couple of boxes of study books that were Bella's. Quilts that had been brought over from her farmhouse. A sofa and chair from there that were draped with drop cloths.

He thought of that property that Bella still owned, the one that was next to what had been Mary's condo. It was so strange. But for the random proximity of those two pieces of real estate, so much would never have happened: Mary had met John Matthew through her work at the local suicide prevention hotline. Bella had known what John was, even though Mary, as a human, had not. Then the three of them had been brought in to the training center, where Mary had met Rhage, and Z and Bella had met, and John Matthew, an orphan in the human world, had found a set of loving parents in Wellsie and Tohr.

Now, years later, John Matthew was a brother and had found a mate in Xhex. Rhage and Mary were mated and had adopted Bitty. And Z and Bella were parents. Wellsie was gone, though, and that was a loss that would never go away. But Tohr had another love in Autumn, although not as a replacement for his beautiful first *shellan*. There were others who had entered the Brotherhood's world as well, like the Band of Bastards, and the Chosen.

The Scribe Virgin, gone.

The Lassiter era, commenced.

Yet for all the changes, the past was still in the shadows.

Z went to the back of the storage unit, to a Hammermill box that had previously held ten reams of printer/copier paper. The lid was not taped down, the corrugated cardboard forming a sturdy enough seal—and it wasn't like anybody was liable to poke around with it.

Bella knew what was inside.

As Z knelt down to the hard floor, both of his knees cracked, and so did his spine. His fingers trembled ever so slightly as he reached forward. The resistance to opening the box was slight and overwhelming at the same time.

Putting the lid aside, he peered in, the light from the ceiling flowing over his head and shoulders and creating an outline of him in shadow on the wall.

The sleeping pallet was folded up, its felt corpus thick and mottled due to the cheap collection of fibers that had been woven together to form its weight.

Given its size, it took up the whole of the interior, as if the box had been precisely made for the purpose of storing the thing.

Z took the blanket out. Holding what he had slept on for . . . God, years and years . . . he found himself remembering when he had put it away, first in the closet in his bedroom, and then in this box that he'd gotten from the office, and finally down here. He'd been determined to turn his life around. He'd lost the female he had bonded with—

No, even worse, he'd told Bella to leave.

And yet even after she was gone, he'd decided to try to better himself. To learn how to read and write. To stop being so brutally angry.

Destroying his mistress's skull, which he had slept beside since he had killed her, had been part of it. So, too, had been starting to sleep in a bed.

Little had he known that he had been preparing for Bella's return. And it was only after she had returned and, by some miracle, taken him back, that he'd realized what he'd been doing. He'd been afraid he'd fail, however, and that was why he'd had to set her free. After a century of hating himself, he'd had no reason to believe he'd be close to worthy—

Z twisted around with a jerk. "Hello?"

There were a couple of footsteps, and then Mary,

Rhage's *shellan*, stepped in between the open jambs of the storage unit. The female was not vampire, but neither was she human anymore, really. The Scribe Virgin had taken her out of the continuum of time, the result of a bargain Rhage had struck to save Mary's life from her terminal cancer. In return, the brother had to live with his beast for the rest of his nights, and you know what? He seemed very satisfied with his choices—and Z could totally get it. Mary was a bastion of calm and reasonable, the perfect foil to Rhage's out-there.

"Hi." She smiled as she ran a hand through her short brown hair. "I hope you don't mind that I followed you."

Z looked down at what he was holding. "I used to sleep on this."

There was no need to fill her in on anything or provide any context. The two of them had spent hours together, sorting through his past, talking things over, reframing when and where they could. Mary was not just a stellar social worker; she was also very wise and very caring. She had helped him so much.

"You slept on it for a long time," she said as she leaned against the jamb. As usual, she was wearing well-washed jeans and a cozy sweater, the enormous gold Rolex on her wrist not fitting her no-makeup, unfussy-brunette-bob vibe. But she always had Rhage's watch on.

"Any particular reason you decided to revisit that blanket tonight?" she asked.

"I don't know." For a moment, he hoped she would fill in the answer—because dollars to donuts, she was well aware of why he was here. But he should have known better. He had to do the work. "Maybe it's because of what happened to Balthazar."

"Seeing someone you live with that close to death is really upsetting."

"It's also what he said when he came around." Z filled her in on the demon comment. "He was looking right at me when he spoke."

"Did you feel as though it was a message specifically for you?"

"I did."

When he didn't go any further, she prompted, "And do you think that your mistress has returned from the dead to haunt you?"

Z thought that over for a moment. Logically . . . ? "Well, no. But that's exactly where my mind went when I heard the word 'demon.'"

"Makes sense to me."

He looked back down at the folds of the pallet. "But you know . . . it's not just that." He thought about Nalla running toward him in the bedroom. "It isn't all gone. What I think about myself, my insides."

"Can you be more specific?"

"The . . . filthy part." He glanced over at her. "What the voice tells me, you know, about what I really am, what my family fails to see."

"What do they fail to see about you?"

"How dirty I am." His voice became small. "How . . . filthy I am." Before Mary could say anything, he cleared his throat. "But I mean, we've been through all that already. We've spent how much time talking about what was done to me by that female?"

Only silence came back at him. Which was frustrating as fuck.

"Why isn't it gone?" he demanded. "My life is good. I'm in love, I have a daughter. Everything is good."

"Yes, it is."

"So what the fuck?" He frowned. "And I'm sorry, I don't mean to get all pissy with you."

"It's totally understandable. I've been a resource for you, and I've done what I can to help. If you want to direct that animus to me, I can take it."

"But you can't make it go away." He motioned next to his head. "This fucking shit is always going to be with me, huh. No matter how much better I get."

Mary came across to him, kneeling down and

meeting his stare levelly. "When was the last time you felt the need to come down here?"

"It's been . . . well, not since I put this box away."

"And when was the last time that voice in your head kept you up during the day?"

"I dunno. Guess a month, maybe longer."

"And your last nightmare?"

"October."

When she just stared at him patiently, he rubbed his face. "Okay, fine, it's getting better. Compared to the every-waking-minute it used to be. But god-damn . . . I just get exhausted retreading the same territory. The same pain. The same weakness."

Mary nodded. And then said, "You know, I have a theory about injury and healing. It's just anecdotal, from my own personal experience with trauma—which, granted, is nothing measured against your own." She shifted around to sit cross-legged, like she was prepared to stay for however long he needed her to. "In my opinion, souls are no different than limbs. If you break a leg or an arm, it's going to hurt when it happens, sharply and unbearably. Therapy is like what you do to set the bone properly in a cast and monitor its mending. It's the physical rehab, the stretching, the follow-up X-rays. But the limb is never the same. On rainy days, the joint aches. If you run a marathon on it, it will be sore. Maybe the healed part isn't quite right. Souls are the same. There are different marathons we run, whether it's the day-to-day interactions with our spouses or the people we work with. Maybe it's an event like Balthazar getting hurt. Perhaps it's an anniversary of a bad night—or even a good one, like a holiday or a birthday. These are the marathons our souls run, and sometimes, where we have healed aches. Or worse. And that is a nonnegotiable part of being a survivor."

Z stroked the felt with his hand, feeling the coarse nap. "I guess I thought the work was over."

"It's never over. If we want to be conscious in our lives, in ourselves, the work is always necessary."

"Physical therapy forever."

"So that you can function better and feel better and be healthier. You can't undo the injury, but you can always work with what you have."

"I wish I didn't have to." He looked back at her. "Shit. That sounds lame."

"No, that sounds very human." Mary shook her head with a little laugh. "I mean vampire."

Silence eased into the space between them, and in the back of his mind, he thought that Mary's ability to be comfortable in the quiet was one of the many reasons she was the right therapist for him.

Taking a deep breath, he returned the pallet to where it had been and placed the lid back on top. Then he pushed the box into its previous position.

He stayed where he was for a couple of heartbeats. Then he got to his full height and offered his dagger hand to his brother's precious *shellan*.

"Care to hit Last Meal?" he said as he helped her to her feet.

"I want you to keep something in mind." She stared up at him. "You know all the hours we've spent together?"

"Yes?"

"Were they so bad?"

"You mean, did I like them? No. I'm sorry, but that would be a no."

Mary shook her head. "Not what I asked. Were they so bad?"

"No."

"Could you do it all over again? Like from the start 'til this moment right here?" She pointed to the concrete between them. "From when we first met down here to now?"

He thought about the conversations. Some had been like pulling teeth. Some had been kind of easy. Others had wiped him out emotionally. One—or no, two—had actually made him vomit.

A few they had even laughed through.

"Yes," he said. "I could do it all over again."

Mary put her hand on his forearm. "Then you have exactly what you need to continue to heal and survive and thrive. If you can look me right in the eye, and say, yup, I got this. I can continue talking. I can keep learning about myself and my place in the world. I can express my doubts and fears, in a supportive environment, and know that I'm not dirty. I am not filthy. I was abused. I was a victim. And none of it was my fault—nor did it change the purity of my soul or the depth and beauty of my heart. If you can keep working those tendons and ligaments and joints? You will be okay, no matter how many times you feel as you do tonight."

Z took another deep breath. "You know, I try to say those words in my head. When I get like this, when I doubt . . . what I am inside."

"Good." She patted his arm and dropped her hand. "Someday, you'll believe them."

He considered his chaotic, nasty thoughts. "How do you know that for sure?"

She leaned in and kept eye contact with him. "Because, my friend, they're true."

CHAPTER SEVENTEEN

At ten a.m., Elle stepped out of the kitchen and into her father's garage. Hitting the go button on the right side's door, she blinked as the thing opened slowly, brilliant sunshine streaming in and illuminating her father's car, the lawn mower, the row of trash rollers. The post-blizzard glare was so bright she had to shield her eyes with her arm, but things adjusted quick enough.

Not surprisingly, she totally bypassed the BMW.

On the far wall, there was a whole bunch of sports equipment, most of which was her father's: Bats, gloves, balls, the volleyball net that was rolled up around itself, in-line skates, hockey bags. As she went over to the sprawl, the square-toed, hard-soled shoes she'd put on made sharp slapping noises. She'd had to put on three pairs of socks to get them to fit, but like she cared?

The cross-country skis were in an organized lineup at the end of the steel shelves, each pair mated together with bands at the top and the bottom, the poles more loosey-goosey and at a tilt.

She picked the Rossignols because the shoes had the same brand on them and the others said Head.

Getting the stuff out into the yard was a two-tripper, the thin, lightweight skis impossible to control along with the poles, assuming she didn't want to scrape the side of her dad's car—and she'd already been through enough with that sedan, thank you very much.

When everything was in the front yard, she entered the code on the exterior pad and closed things up. Taking a look left and right, she saw . . . a fuck ton of untouched snow. Nothing on the street had been plowed yet, not the road, not the sidewalks, not the driveways, although there were a couple of men just getting out their snowblowers and starting to work on their properties.

Like a dad-bell had gotten rung and it was a race.

Overhead, the sky was an impossible blue, so resonant and clear that she couldn't reconcile it with the storm that had raged through the night. But maybe that was the point. The blizzard had wiped the slate clean, cleared it all.

Would that it had worked its magic in her own life.

Clipping the toes of the shoes into the bindings, she palmed the poles and started off. It was slow going at first, her balance bad, no rhythm to anything. She had only cross-country'd like twice before, but she was on the varsity track team, so at least aerobic capacity wasn't part of her problem.

Soon enough, she found a stride, and it felt good to breathe in the cold, dry air. She proceeded down her street, and when she got to the end, she was hot, so she took off her wool hat and crammed it into the pocket of her parka.

The main road had been plowed, and she stayed to the shoulder, making really good time on the inch of powder that had sloughed back down the banks created after the city trucks had barged the majority of accumulation out of the way. There were few cars out and about, mostly high-clearance SUVs with the drivers looking smug, as if they felt that their automotive choices were being totally validated.

She knew exactly how far she went. Six point four miles.

She'd run the route so many times. In fact, all of that back-and-forthing had been the reason she'd made varsity cross-country.

Terrie, on the other hand, was a couch potato. The joke in the family had been that Elle and Dad were birds of a feather and Mom and Terrie were loungers without measure.

Not that anyone was making those comparisons anymore, even if Terrie was still playing on her iPad most of the time.

Elle knew she was getting close when the stores and the bus stops began appearing. More traffic congested the road, so she moved up onto the sidewalk— or where one would have been without the snow dump—and then soon enough, she cut across the narrow lawn of a CVS. After that, it was a diagonal on the Rossignols through the unplowed parking lot of a strip mall, and on the far side, the apartment blocks started, the buildings grouped by exterior paint jobs.

Gray and white. Dark brown all over. Cream and white. Dark green and tan.

The names were fancier than the facilities. Greystone Village. Elmsworth Court. Willowwalk Homes.

As she *shhhhsht-shhhhsht-shhhhsht*'d along, she figured whoever owned the places had chosen the names deliberately. It wasn't that the units were nasty. But they sure weren't old Brownsboro Place–worthy.

Her mother's enclave was second to the last on the street, and Elle skied into the parking lot to find that everything had been plowed—so that all the sedans and minivans parked under the open-area carports were totally blocked in. Not that anybody was making a move to go anywhere. It was a Saturday, after all, and hello, the snow.

Plus who could have gotten any sleep in the whole city with all that wind? It was like Caldwell was gonna get blown off the map of upstate New York.

Her mom's apartment building was two-story and split in half, the double-decker sporting an open-air stairway to feed the upper quartets. Her mom's flat was on the second floor over on the left, and Elle didn't bother to check and see if the Audi station wagon was parked in its spot. It was never not there. And it couldn't have left this morning, anyhow.

Shucking the skis, she gathered them together, and it was messy work getting up the stairs with the poles, too. Fortunately, her mom's door was the first one she came to. She knocked.

No answer.

Elle's heart pounded as she got out the set of keys she had been given. Well, "set" was the wrong word.

The keys she had to her father's house were a set. There was his front door key, the key to her locker at school, the key to her bike lock. For her mom's apartment, there was only the ring and one single, notched dangler.

Unlocking things, she cracked the door an inch. "Mom?"

When there was no answer, she threw open the door. "Mom!"

That was when she heard the shower running. And then a muffled answer through the bathroom's closed door.

"Thank God," Elle whispered. Louder, she said, "I'll just wait, Mom."

Leaving the skis outside, she hoped they wouldn't get stolen as she closed herself in. And then she wasn't worrying about her equipment for the trip home anymore. The interior of the apartment was so dark, she couldn't see, and she stayed right where she was for that reason—and others. After an eternity, she realized she hadn't kicked the snow off her shoes, but before she could step out and stamp on the welcome mat, the bathroom door opened and light spilled into the central room.

"I'll be right there," her mom said as she went into her bedroom.

The other door closed, but with the light still streaming out of the loo, Elle's eyes were able to get to work. The sofa and two armchairs were from the old family house, and they had fit into the living room there. Here, with so much less space, they were crammed in too tight, no room for a coffee table between them, their cushions too big, their backs and arms too tall. At least all the walls were cream so the dark red didn't exactly clash, but neither did it really fit. The color was way too vivid, the tan carpeting making it look like raspberries on oatmeal.

Everything was neat—which was a relief—nothing out on the tiny three-top table in the galley kitchen, no dishes around the sink, no cereal boxes on top of the fridge or debris on the countertop. As always, Elle told herself that that meant everything was okay. She'd seen *Intervention* and *Hoarders*.

Tidy meant it was okay.

Right?

"Not even close," she mumbled to herself as she rubbed her nose.

The smell was stale and dusty, and that, coupled with all the closed blinds, made her feel like she was in a damp cave.

Figuring she better do something about tracking in snow, she took her cross-country'ing shoes off and set them on the rubber mat just inside the door. Then, in her three pairs of socks, she padded over to the kitchen table and sat down. As she waited, it was hard not to notice how barren the front of the refrigerator was: No school calendar. No pictures of her and Terrie. No coupons, or birthday cards, or notes.

Just like there were no framed glossies of her and Terrie in their school uniforms on the mantel over the electric fireplace. Nothing hung on the walls, even though their mom had left with a couple of landscapes that were actual oil paintings rather than posters. No plants; then again, the venetian blinds were all cranked down tight, just a glow around the gaps between them and the jambs showing.

So no way to grow anything in here.

As she took a deep breath, she smelled the same shampoo her mom had always used, and had to rub her stinging eyes.

"I didn't expect you."

Elle dropped her hands. "Hi."

As her mom stood in the doorway to her bedroom, she seemed on the surface to be exactly the same person who had always been there in the mornings making breakfast, in the afternoons after school, in the evenings at the dinner table. She still had thick chestnut brown hair, and dark eyes, and a dimple on one side as she smiled. But she was like a house that had been deserted, the lights on with no one home.

There was nothing behind that stare.

When had she left them? Was it when she'd learned about Megan?

She must know, right?

Elle opened her mouth. But instead of giving airtime to her questions—or confessing that she had been told something private about her parents' marriage—she said, "I called. You know, to tell you I might be coming over."

"I'm sorry." Her mom turned on the hall light and walked over to the kitchen. "I've been trying to charge it."

"Not your cell phone." Well, she'd called that, too. "The home line."

Not that this was a home.

"Oh." Her mom turned to the wall-mounted unit, which, along with the thick paint and old appliances, was a testament to the age of the apartment. "That should have worked. Maybe I was in the shower."

As her mom took the receiver off the wall and put it to her ear, and then tapped the toggle thingy, Elle looked into the bedroom.

No surprise, it was dark as night in there, but the light from the hall fixture penetrated the shadows. The bed was a mess, layered with all kinds of twisted sheets and fallen blankets like someone had dropped a bomb in the middle of the mattress. There were also wrappers on the floor . . . potato chip bags and Hershey's candy bars, mostly. And Coke cans lying on their sides. Wadded-up Kleenex. Rolls of paper towels.

"I'm not sure went wrong," her mom said. "What went wrong, I mean."

There was a click as the receiver was replaced.

"Would you like me to make you something to eat, Elle?"

"Um . . ." Elle looked away from the clutter. "Yes. Please."

"Okay, then. Let's see what we have."

Memories of the way things had been before surged, and Elle recalled delicious sandwiches whipped up on the fly, and fancy dinners that took hours to prepare, and homemade bread and handmade ice cream and cookies that were from that gingersnap recipe from two generations back.

"Oh. I was supposed to go grocery shopping today."

Elle glanced over. The refrigerator had a bottle of ketchup in its door, a mostly empty thing of ranch dressing on its top shelf, and seven bottles of white wine stacked on their sides like cordwood on the bottom.

Her mom shut the fridge and began opening cupboards.

"It's okay, Mom. I'm actually not hungry. I forgot that I already had breakfast."

"Oh. Okay."

Her mom came over, pulled out the other chair, and sat down. "So how's school going?"

"Good."

"Are you ready for Christmas break?"

Elle fiddled with her parka sleeve. Then decided she was hot and took the Patagonia thing off. "I guess so."

"I'm looking forward to having you girls with me for a week. We'll have so much fun. It'll be a sleepover."

Elle glanced toward the bedroom. "Ah . . ."

Her mother's chair made a squeak on the bare floor as she stood back up and went across the apartment.

"It will be *so* much fun." She closed the door. "I can't wait."

As their eyes met, Elle nodded. "Sure. Me, too."

"Unless you want to stay at your dad's during the nights? Maybe you'd rather sleep in your own beds. You could just come for a couple of visits."

"Okay. If that's easier."

"Really, it's what you girls want. But we can have fun for a couple of afternoons."

"Okay."

Her mom sat down again and smiled. "Perfect. I'm so looking forward to it."

Elle stared at her hands. As she tried to think of something to say, she realized she had come over here with questions to ask, questions about things that were really none of her business. Yet the divorce, though it had been between two people legally, had affected four lives, hadn't it.

"I guess I better go back."

"You're so grown up now, driving everywhere."

"Actually, I came on cross-country skis."

As she pointed over her shoulder to the door—like either one of them had X-ray vision—her mom smiled in a vacant way. "Out for some exercise, then. You know, you should take up running, you were always good at it as a child."

"I'm on the track team, remember?"

"Oh, yes, of course. How silly of me."

Elle cleared her throat. "Do you—there was a snowstorm last night. Did you notice?"

"Was there?"

"The roads are really backed up. With snow."

Her mom smiled some more. "Oh. Well, I'm glad you have those skis, then."

"Yes. I'm glad I have them, too." Elle stood up and put her parka back on. "Okay. Well. Call me if you need anything?"

Holding her arms up, her mom stayed seated. "Hugs, Bug. Hugs for Bug."

Swallowing hard, Elle went over. As she leaned down, she realized that her mother had put her turtleneck on backwards, the outline of the tag that was stitched on the underside right in front.

"Bye, Mom," Elle said roughly.

"Tell Terrie I love her, too."

"Okay. I will."

Straightening, Elle went over to the door and shoved her feet back in the square-toed shoes. Then she fumbled with the knob.

"Drive carefully out there," her mom said from the table, her eyes focused somewhere in the middle ground between them.

"I will, Mom," Elle murmured as she stepped out and let go of the door.

The metal panel slammed shut. And for a moment, she stood there and looked out at the snow-packed parking lot, the cars all covered with powdered sugar, the gouges from a plow's effort ruining the soft undulations of what had fallen during the night and been blown into drifts by the wind.

In her pocket, her phone started to vibrate, and when she went to get it, she found that she had put her gloves back on, zipped up her parka, and returned her hat to her head. When had all that happened, she wondered.

Biting off her glove, she got her phone out.

The name on the call was three letters long. "DAD."

She let it go to voice mail, picked up the poles and skis, and started down the stairs. When she got to the bottom, she dropped the Rossignols and glanced around, blinking at the brilliant light. One by one, she clipped in the tips of her shoes. And then she started off, following the path she had made on the trip in, her breath leaving her mouth and drifting over her shoulder in puffs.

It used to be easy to go home, she thought.

Then again, a lot of things had been easier.

CHAPTER EIGHTEEN

Quinn had a spring in his step as he came through the training center's office. Night had fallen, First Meal was through, and he was off rotation. The storm had passed, the damage to the house had been repaired, and everybody was safe.

He'd also gotten no sleep during the day. For the very best reasons.

He and Blay had spent the daylight hours getting very naked up in their bedroom. It was amazing how many positions there were, and how many different places you could get it on: In the bed, of course. In the tub. The shower. The walk-in closet—which had been a surprise. Who knew that rug burns could be such a trophy?

He was walking funny from them. And wasn't that awesome.

Out in the corridor, he went by the weight room, and when he heard music banging, he leaned inside. "You're a fucking beast, Hollywood."

Across the floor mats and through the thickets of lifting machines, a shirtless Rhage was in the middle of a set of chin-ups on the bar, and with every up-and-down the brother did, that tattoo of a dragon across his back moved and seethed along with his flexing muscles.

"You know it," the brother gritted out.

With a wave, Qhuinn kept going. Down past the exam rooms and the OR, he stopped at the last door that was part of the clinic area. Tugging his sweatshirt into proper place over his Adidas training pants, he made sure his hair was not completely crazy.

Although no amount of brushing was going to hide the fact that part of it was the color of Violet Beauregarde.

Not that it mattered to Luchas. Still, old family habits died hard, even when they weren't necessary anymore.

Knocking with his knuckles, he then pushed his way in. "Luchas, my man, how are—"

Qhuinn paused. No one was in the patient room. But at least the wheelchair was parked in the corner. So the male was using his cane as he'd been told to.

"Good," Qhuinn murmured. Then louder, "Luchas, you in the loo?"

The door over there was closed, but there was no shower running. No sink, either. Content to wait, Qhuinn sat down in his brother's reading chair and chilled, taking out his phone. After checking his email, he looked to the bathroom.

"Luchas? You okay in there?"

Getting to his feet, he put his phone away and walked to the door. Leaning into the panel, he listened. "Luchas?"

When he knocked and there was no answer, his throat closed up. "I'm coming in, Luchas—"

As he pushed his way inside, the motion-activated lights came on. No one was there, either: The bathtub was dry. The towels were folded precisely on the rods. The toothbrush, toothpaste, and shaving accoutrements were all orderly around the sink. A surge of paranoia made him open the shower stall's frosted door. Just in case. But there was no blood from a cracked-open head. No body, either.

Just as he started to worry, he exhaled in relief and felt like a fucking fool.

Heading back out into the corridor, he pushed his hands into his track bottoms and whistled a tune as he backtracked his route. Rhage was still doing chin-ups as he went by the weight room, and he said hi to Manny as the surgeon came in through the office.

The pool was Luchas's favorite place to go. Made sense. Given the extent of his physical issues, the buoyancy must feel nice, and the way he could move in water was no doubt so much easier than anything for him on land. The amputation of part of his leg had been necessary to save his life, but the prosthesis had been a tough adjustment. He was doing better, though.

Thank fuck.

Stepping into the swimming area's ante hall, Qhuinn sneezed at all the chlorine and stretched his arms over his head. Maybe he'd get in, too—

As he emerged from the second set of doors, he looked at all the still water, the empty benches, the absolute silence in the floor-to-ceiling tiled space.

Hurrying over to the bathrooms, he ripped open the door to the males' side. "Luchas?"

There were two stalls, and he shoved both their metal panels open. Nothing.

Back out at the pool, he went over to the edge of the water, heart in his throat. But there was nothing at the bottom, no twisted body that had sunk after drowning.

There was a logical explanation for where his brother was. There had to be—

"Shit, you dummy," he muttered to himself as he went back out into the corridor.

Luchas was welcome anywhere in the mansion's complex, free to come and go as he pleased, and Qhuinn kept hoping that part of that "coming" would include showing up for First or Last Meal in the dining room up at the big house. He'd offered to come get the male, to save him a seat, even to provide menus in advance if it would help entice him. So far, it was a no-go, but Qhuinn was going to keep making the invitation.

Hard sell, though. Luchas was a loner by nature now, very different from who he'd been before. Still, from a physical standpoint at least, he was getting better every night, and he had every medical advantage from not only the species, but the human side, too. Havers was even available for consults.

So it was going to be fine. Eventually.

As Qhuinn headed for the classroom section of things, he had to laugh. Reading, writing, and 'rithme-

tic were not what had been taught here. Try bombs
and detonators, poisons and gases, fighting, shooting,
defensive driving techniques. He and Blay and John
Matthew had been in the first class of trainees, and
then a second group had gone through. There would
be a third, sometime in the near future.

Once they figured out exactly what they were
fighting now.

The trainees' break room was just what its name
described, a place for the students, or the brothers
and clinic patients, to chill out in, watch a little tube,
have a bite to eat. It was also where Luchas ate all his
meals.

Given the time, Qhuinn should have checked there
first, but whatever. Pushing his way in, he was totally
relieved that—

No one. Not at the tables. Not by the soda machines or the buffet or the fridges. Not in the armchairs by the TV.

Qhuinn told himself not to panic.

But he couldn't stop his heart from going on a
sprint inside his rib cage.

◆ ◆ ◆

Outside of the library, elbow-deep in fresh snow, Blay
fired up the chain saw, the high-pitched whine flaring
and receding when he pumped the gas. As the motor

settled into a purr, the scents of gasoline and oil were thick, but when the low-level wind changed direction, all of that was wiped clean.

"You got it?" he said.

Tohr nodded and leaned into the shitkicker he'd planted on the fallen evergreen's trunk. "Hit it, son."

Blay brought the running blade down on the tree that had broken into the house, the sweet balsam aroma a delicious conifer cologne. As sawdust flew off to the side and the engine sound got loud, the cut went quick, the chain's barbs making ready work of the job. And when the blade broke through on the far side, the tree shimmied like it was relieved the surgery was done.

"Good work," Tohr said as he bent all the way over and took hold of the trunk.

As Blay cut the motor, the Brother stood the conifer up and they both nodded. The pointed top was a good twenty feet off the ground and Tohr's body was completely obscured by the fluffy green branches.

"The kids are going to love it." Blay traded the chain saw for a tree stand. "I'll just slap this on if you can lift our little friend."

Tohr hefted up the tree, and Blay squeezed under on his belly. "Hold on, just getting it—okay, drop it!"

As the fresh-cut stump end was lowered into the

stand's basin, Blay cranked the screws tight—and marveled that he had developed such a core competency in what was exclusively a human tradition. Who'd have thought he'd end up knowing that it was always better to put the stand on outside of the house?

"We're ready," he said as he crawled out from underneath.

He would have offered to help, but Tohr was strong enough to just walk the pine-scented albatross into the library. The Brother also knew where it went, setting it down in the corner by shelves that held all the Charles Dickens first editions.

"Yay!" Bitty said from the boxes of ornaments she was unpacking. "It's perfect! Thank you, Uncle Tohr."

The little girl ran over and threw her arms around the Brother. Which, appropriately, caused the enormous fighter to completely melt.

"Oh, you are so welcome, baby girl." Tohr smiled and put his dagger hand on her slight shoulder. "Do you have everything up from the basement?"

Considering the number of Rubbermaid containers dotting the library's rug? Which were all the size of twin beds? It was hard to imagine there were any more Christmas decorations left in Caldwell: From the strings of lights to the lengths of garland, and the thousand glass ornaments in red, green, gold, and deep blue, it was quite the inventory.

"Okay, hold up, Rhamp, gentle. *Gentle.*"

At the sound of Layla's voice, he pivoted around. The twins were on the floor, and both had crawled over to the careful unpacking job that Bitty was doing. Rhamp, naturally, was reaching for a blown-glass ornament that, if he pounded it into the floor, which he was about to do, was going to shatter into a million sharp pieces.

And his blood on any rug was not the goal. Ever.

"I got him," Blay said as he swooped in and hoisted Rhamp out of range.

Fortunately, the kid loved swooping more than anything, and the giggle he let out was a joy to hear. As chubby hands clapped, that smile was breathtaking. So Blay did it again. And again.

"You won't need a workout tonight," Layla said with a laugh.

She'd moved Lyric into her lap, and the young was playing with a pack of tinsel, the waterfall of silver lengths a source of great discovery and delight. *Mahmen* and daughter were wearing matching red, green, and white Orvis sweaters. Rhamp, on the other hand, had on an Iron Man onesie because he hated sweaters. Then again, he was always moving and running and churning. He was rarely still.

Throw a sweater on that and you'd have a mobile hot-water bottle.

Swinging Rhamp up and around again, Blay's eyes took a snapshot of the room. Tohr had pulled his mate, Autumn, in tight to him, and they were staring at each other with the kind of soft smiles that happy couples shared when they thought no one was looking. Phury and Cormia were knee-deep in garland, laughing as he wound a length around her shoulders. Rehv and Ehlena were sharing the sofa, snuggled in together across from the crackling fire.

And naturally, Fritz had done a drive-by with provisions for everyone: There was eggnog on a silver tray on one of the coffee tables, along with a setup of hot chocolate and candy canes and gingerbread men. Good thing there was so much of it all. Soon, others would join in. It was a communal event, this now-annual tradition of trimming the Christmas tree, and it was especially significant for those in the house who had grown up human.

And in the future, it was going to be important for the twins and the other current young, Blay realized. They would come to see this as part of their pretrans experience—

Out past the library's archway, in the foyer, a figure entered his line of sight.

It was Qhuinn, dressed in the casual clothes he'd put on just before they'd left their room for First Meal: Same track pants, same My Chem sweatshirt, same Converse All Stars in black and white. But something had transformed him.

He was too still, for one thing. For another, he wasn't coming in and joining the happy crowd. And then there was his expression.

His eyes were burning with emotion.

Blay looked casually at Phury and Cormia. "Hey, how'd you guys like to hold a young?"

Cormia smiled and put out her arms. "Gimme, gimme, gimme!"

Rhamp was thrilled to go to her, answering her enthusiasm with a giggle of his own. And Blay took a moment to tweak his son's nose before he casually walked out of the room, hands in his pockets, an easy smile for anyone to see on his face.

He dropped the act as soon as he was out of range.

Striding across the mosaic floor, he said, "What's wrong?"

Qhuinn nodded over his shoulder and didn't start talking until they were in the lee of the grand staircase.

"I can't find Luchas."

Blay frowned. "What do you mean you can't find him?"

Qhuinn's eyes couldn't light on any particular thing, his focus shifting over the balustrade, the door down into the tunnel, the floor at their feet.

"I went to his room to have a visit. Not there. He's also not at the pool. Not in the break room. Not anywhere in the training center. So I came up here and asked Fritz if he'd seen him in the house? I mean, Fritz knows everything."

"And what did he say?"

"He hasn't seen him."

"Did you ask the medical staff?"

"Manny hasn't treated him, Doc Jane hasn't been down there, and Ehlena's off."

Blay rubbed his face. "Okay, there has to be a logical explanation. There just has to be. It's not like he's disappeared."

When Qhuinn just stood there, the helplessness was as much of a shock as the idea that Luchas was lost somewhere in the Brotherhood's compound.

Blay put his hand on the side of his mate's neck. "We're going to find him. Do you hear me? We're going to find him together, all right? I know what to do."

Qhuinn nodded. And then he made a strangled noise.

"Come here," Blay murmured as he pulled his mate in. "It's going to be okay. I promise you, it's going to be okay."

Over Qhuinn's shoulder, Blay noticed that Tohr and Phury had come out of the library. They were hanging back, arms crossed, faces grave. Even though they didn't know what was wrong, they were prepared to help.

But that was the nature of the Black Dagger Brotherhood. When Qhuinn joined that ancient tradition, he went from being an orphan to having a full-blown family.

And they would no more desert him in a time of need than they would cut off their own hands.

"I know what to do," Blay repeated firmly.

CHAPTER NINETEEN

Quinn couldn't think. But he was aware of following instructions: Go here, sit there, wait for five minutes while V signed into his computer. Other than these very rudimentary functions, however, he was not really connected to anything.

For example, it was interesting, in a passing, well-what-do-you-know sort of way, to realize that he was in the Pit. Evidently, he'd been set on the leather sofa like a throw pillow, and he was facing the Foosball table. As he considered the way the game was played, his brain coughed up a random memory from just twenty-four hours before: Him spinning the spindles against John Matthew, blithely unaware of what that fountain tarp was going to do, what was going to happen to Balthazar up by that shutter, how Zsadist was going to have to do CPR in the snow.

As with all of that, he certainly had never anticipated what was happening right now.

In his peripheral vision, he was aware of V typing on one of his keyboards and then staring at the bank of monitors. Right behind the brother, leaning in over his shoulder, was Blay.

This was a relief. Qhuinn couldn't track anything, and there was nobody he trusted more than Blay. His mate would figure everything out and would translate whatever it was to him.

V pointed at the screen. And then glanced back at Blay.

Blay straightened, his eyes not leaving whatever image they were talking about. And that was when it became apparent there were other people in the room, too.

Right beside the pair of them was a lineup of males. Rhage, Butch, Tohr, Phury, Rehv.

Qhuinn appreciated them showing up for . . . whatever this was. But their presence was also a huge source of anxiety. Generally speaking, the more brothers and fighters who lingered, the more serious things were.

"He's probably down in the training center," Qhuinn mumbled to himself. To anybody who might be listening.

To fate, if fate was looking for suggestions about how to resolve Luchas's disappearance—

In the end, no one really needed to tell him anything.

It was the way Blay looked over at him. And how V stayed focused on the monitors, but then turned his head as well.

Blay was the one who came across to the sofa, and he knelt down.

"You found him," Qhuinn said quietly. "You found my brother?"

The sound of his mate clearing his throat was one of the saddest things Qhuinn had ever heard. And yet he refused to let the sorrow sink in.

"We think he went out," Blay said.

"Like in a car? Can he drive?"

"No, as in . . . he left."

"Who took him out?"

"Qhuinn . . . we think he left through the tunnel."

As his brain translated the syllables, he came back online. "Wait, what? Why the hell would he do that? And when did he go?"

"According to the time stamp on the security feed, it was last night. During the storm."

A buzzing noise lit off inside Qhuinn's skull, and it knocked out his hearing for a moment. And then everything became sharp, too sharp. Cutting blade, crystal shard sharp.

"I don't understand." He got up. "This is wrong. I don't know what you saw—"

V didn't argue; he just pivoted one of the screens and pointed at it. The feed was pixelated, but after a pause and recalibration, the contours of the training center's tunnel came into view. The angle of the camera lens was wide, encompassing a long stretch of the concrete wall and then the terminus of the subterranean passageway. The lineup of outerwear and weapons was to one side, the door out into the escape cave on the right.

Nothing was happening. The picture was just static—

The stooped figure entered from the left and moved along slowly. Its gait was uneven and a cane was cocked at an angle, a black robe draping whoever it was from head to toe.

But like the identity wasn't obvious?

"Luchas," Qhuinn mumbled.

His brother stopped in front of the heavy steel hatch. Then that head turned toward the parkas and the snow pants.

"What are you doing?" Qhuinn wiped his brow and fiddled with the sleeve of his sweater. Then he looked at V. "Does he know the code?"

That question was answered as Luchas put his ruined hand out and punched a series of buttons on the keypad. There was a pause, and after that he opened the heavy steel panel with a struggle, fumbling with his cane, catching his bad balance on the jamb.

"Put a coat on. What are you doing? Put a fucking coat on!" Qhuinn shouted at the monitor.

All at once, he remembered that wind. That terrible, howling wind. More than the snow or the cold, those gusts were going to make it impossible for Luchas to stay on his feet.

"What the fuck is he doing?" Qhuinn looked at Blay with panic. "I don't get this."

When his mate just stared back at him, those blue eyes held an answer that didn't bear translating.

"No." Qhuinn shook his head. "That's *not* what happened."

◆ ◆ ◆

It was a parade.

Or . . . more like a funeral march.

As Blay followed Qhuinn down the training center's tunnel, they were not alone. Everyone who had been in the Pit had joined them, but the Brotherhood was hanging back by a good forty or fifty feet. They seemed to sense what Blay knew for sure. Later, when whatever was happening had actually happened, Qhuinn would be grateful for his Brothers' support—but at the moment, you couldn't crowd him.

Blay himself was waiting to be asked to leave. And yet . . . not yet.

With every step he took, he thought of what he'd seen on V's computer screen, Luchas walking where they were now, God only knew what on the male's mind. But he must have known what he was doing. He hadn't hesitated to open the portal, hadn't looked back as he'd stepped through, had closed things up in his wake as if he never intended to return.

And in fact, he had not come back.

Twenty-four hours in the freezing cold? Much less that storm?

As they came to the end of the tunnel, Qhuinn stopped in front of the escape hatch. Putting his hands on his hips, he looked down at his feet.

"Let's put these on." Blay took two parkas off the hooks. "Come on."

He expected an argument. He didn't get one—which was a bad sign. Instead, he was allowed to dress Qhuinn like he would one of the young, helping arms into sleeves, pulling the body of the jacket into place. He even zipped it up the front.

He did not make the move to put the passcode into the reader. He just drew his own jacket on and waited.

Qhuinn opening the portal and following in his blooded brother's footsteps was inevitable. But there was no avoiding the outcome as soon as they did so. Frankly, there was no avoiding it now.

Yet there was comfort in the in between. A sliver of illogical hope.

When Qhuinn finally reached forward, the keypad let out a series of tones as the proper sequence of numbers was entered, the little tune culminating in a hollow clank, the dead bolt on the hatch retracting. Or maybe there were more than one. Who knew how V had fortified this exit—but Luchas had clearly known the code.

Then again, he hadn't been a prisoner.

As Qhuinn pulled the heavy steel free of its jambs, there was a breath of subzero, outside air. When the male looked back, Blay put his palms up.

"Whatever you want," he said. "I don't have to join you if you'd rather—"

"I need you. But only you."

"Then we go together."

Qhuinn walked through first, and Blay took a second to put his palms out to the Brotherhood, to make sure they didn't follow. The lineup of males nodded and stayed frozen where they were. Except for V. He took out his cell phone and no doubt called up the exterior camera feed so he could monitor the search.

It was the same feed that had shown, in footage recorded twenty-four hours before, a lone black-robed figure weaving out into the storm and disappearing into the blizzard.

Blay took a deep breath . . . and went out as well.

On the far side of the hatch, there was a shallow parking area that had a high-riding Chevy Tahoe and a couple of snowmobiles. A camouflage drape covered up the forest entrance to the cave, and pulling it aside, he entered the night.

In the security footage, Luchas had drifted in a westerly direction, but he'd only stayed visible for ten or fifteen yards. After that?

Well, two things had to be true.

One, he couldn't have gone far. He'd struggled to walk distances on level flooring with his cane. In the storm? Out in the snow?

And the second piece of reality had to be—

"Which way?" Qhuinn said as he looked around at the pines and the birches, the snow-covered landscape, the undulations of the ground.

"Do you want to call the others? To help search?" Blay asked

"No, he is mine to find."

Qhuinn started off, and it was all random, the lefts, the rights. There was no logic to it, no grid system that was the gold standard for recovery missions. Maybe they should have brought George? But even as the thought occurred to Blay, he knew that would have been a waste of a good nose.

There was going to be nothing left. The sun had been out all day long. He'd seen it on the evening news, all that sunshine in the storm's wake.

That was the second tragic truth to all of this. Vampires went up in smoke when exposed to sunlight.

So there were going to be no remains, really. Well . . . except for the prosthesis and the cane. The flesh would burn away, but the metal and plastic would not.

Helluva thing to bury, the remnants of all that suffering.

As Qhuinn continued along through the snow, Blay stayed on his mate's heels. There was the temptation to branch out so they could cover more area, but when they found Luchas's ashes, he wanted to be there to catch his mate.

Why did you have to do it, Blay wondered to himself. *Oh, Luchas . . . why—*

From out of nowhere, an image came to Blay's mind and persisted, even as he looked from left to right, searching the powdery, white ground for a scorch mark the size of a fragile body: It was the memory of Luchas in the corridor outside of the OR—when Blay had told him that his brother had been elevated to the King's personal guard, the highest honor within the Brotherhood.

As a cold sweat bloomed across Blay's chest and rode his throat up into his face, he had to unzip the parka and let a little cold air in.

The intention had been to provide Luchas with an example of how things got better, to give some hope and optimism to him in favor of positive change, personal growth, new horizons. But the expression on Luchas's face had suggested the announcement had been taken in a very different way.

Like maybe it had been one more burden on top of all the others, one more accolade that illuminated the male's spiraling fall from grace, position, and health.

What if . . . what if Blay's throwaway comment had been the reason for this?

What if this was all his fault?

CHAPTER TWENTY

On some level, Qhuinn realized that this "search" of his was just an aimless wander. As he trudged through the snow, he was rational enough to recognize that he should form a proper team of people, and draw on the expertise of the folks in the household for procedures and best practices. But he was locked into this directionless walking, his footfalls crunching through the drifts, his body going in whatever direction it wanted, his eyes ceaselessly roaming the ground.

The fact that he wasn't actually looking for remains, but rather an enormous burn mark on the ground was the answer to why he didn't ask for help from anyone. It was also why there was no rush. This was not a rescue mission. In fact, not only was there going to be no one to save, but no body, either.

So he wouldn't even have a chance to say goodbye.

As the first realization that Luchas was truly gone hit him, he coughed. And then coughed some more. When his eyes watered, it was clearly because of the cold—

At first, he thought it was a shadow. After all, the moon was out, and given the forest's tree population, there were a lot of them on the white ground. Yet this one up ahead and off to the right was different. It wasn't long and thin, not bough or trunk shaped. It was also jet black, although only in places—

"Luchas!"

Qhuinn took off, his body surging forward, his breath exploding from his lungs, from his mouth. He covered the distance fast, even as he told himself he surely was imagining this. His mind had to be playing tricks on him—

He slowed.

He stopped.

How was this possible?

On the ground, about ten feet in front of him, was a pile of black robing that had been partially claimed by the snow, the accumulation creeping up the contours of what was under the draping.

Qhuinn took a step forward. And another.

And then he fell to his knees by what appeared to be his brother's remains.

The cane that Luchas had used was right where he had collapsed. And at the hem of the robe, the foot of the prosthesis stuck out. But there were no scorch marks, no ashes, no evidence of combustion.

Qhuinn's hand shook as he reached for the hood.

Before he pulled back the fold, he looked up to Blay. "How is this real?"

"I don't know."

Images from the past filtered behind Qhuinn's eyes: Of the dining room at the family house. Of Solange. Of their parents. Of Luchas, the night he had come through his transition and been presented his gold signet ring—

"Oh . . . God," Qhuinn moaned as he moved the hood away.

His brother's eyes were open, the gray gaze fixated on eternity, unblinking, unseeing. And Luchas's face had frozen into marble, the cast of his hollow cheeks and his too-prominent jaw a death mask of that which had been alive not so long ago, his lips parted and white, his teeth clamped together as if he had been in pain when he had breathed his last.

Qhuinn looked up. Overhead, there were branches, but not enough of a canopy to filter out the sun that had blazed in the wake of the blizzard's departure.

Unable to comprehend both the enormity of what was before him, and the inexplicable nature of the unburned remains, he obsessed over the mystery of how a vampire's body could have survived the sunshine. Death was no insulation for incineration.

"Luchas . . ." he breathed. "Oh, brother mine."

And then none of that mattered.

Curling over the remains, he wrapped his arms around the snow-dusted folds of the robe, resting his cheek on the hard bone of the shoulder.

As he closed his eyes, he pictured Luchas as he had so often been, back in his hospital room, sitting in his reading chair, a leather-bound book held in his ruined hands.

"I'm sorry," Qhuinn mumbled. "I'm so sorry . . . Luchas, why wasn't I there when you needed me? Why . . ."

◆ ◆ ◆

Blay took a handkerchief out of the back pocket of his slacks and pressed it into his eyes. As tears continued to sting, he struggled to draw air into his lungs.

There was no greater suffering than seeing your true love in pain.

Sniffling, he wiped his face. Down at his feet, Qhuinn was draped over his brother like a shroud, that huge warrior's body covering the other male's broken one, a shield that was too late in its protective endeavor. The words being spoken were so soft, Blay couldn't hear them properly, but he didn't need to know the precise syllables. The tone was resonantly mournful, and that was the only translation required.

Unable to hang back anymore—even if that was what Qhuinn might have wanted—Blay went forward and knelt down beside his mate. Placing his hand on that back, he made slow circles—

Oh . . . God. The face.

Luchas's face.

The features were exactly as they had recently been, but as if death would have rearranged them?

Qhuinn straightened some and sniffled. As Blay offered the handkerchief, it was accepted and there was a quick mop-up.

"We need to call—" Qhuinn cleared his throat and returned the handkerchief. "I need help. To move him."

"May I call the Brothers?"

"Yeah. Maybe they can bring those snowmobiles." Qhuinn glanced around. "How will they know where we are?"

"We're not that far."

Qhuinn looked down at Luchas. "Oh. Right. Of course he couldn't have . . . made it very long."

Backing off a little, Blay got out his phone and stared at the thing. It was a moment before he could remember how to work it, his brain seizing up from everything. But then the Samsung was at his ear and ringing.

Who had he called, he wondered—

"What do you need?"

Ah, Vishous. Of course. Because the Brother would know how to use the GPS search function on the phones, just in case they were farther away from the escape hatch than Blay had thought—

"Transport," he said roughly. "We need to bring Luchas back home."

"What . . . wait, is he alive?"

Blay looked over at Qhuinn. With incredible tenderness, he had taken his brother's frozen hand into his own, the ice-cold, mangled digits lying against a warm and vital palm.

"No. He's not."

There was a pause. Then V's voice resumed its

normal clipped tones. "I'm coming right now. You're only a hundred yards out."

Almost immediately, there was a flare of headlights in the darkness and the sound of a vehicle approaching. And that wasn't all. Ghostly figures materialized around the periphery, the Brothers and the other fighters standing among the trees, silent sentries in the subzero darkness.

As V got closer, the headlights were canned, and then the Tahoe halted about twenty feet away.

The Brother got out and just stared for a moment, as if he were catching up on the inexplicable math— and the incomprehensible tragedy.

Qhuinn looked up. "My brother has died."

V nodded grimly. "Yes, he has, son. I am very sorry."

"He went out into the storm last night."

There was a sad pause. "I have a vehicle here, Qhuinn. Would you like to carry him into the back?"

"I would."

The words were stilted. Formal.

"Okay."

After which, no one moved. No one spoke. Then again, there was no hurry, and it was all up to Qhuinn. Yet he seemed frozen.

Blay put his hand on his mate's shoulder. "Let's gather him up, shall we?"

"Okay."

Qhuinn leaned back down, stretching his arms toward the upper torso and down to the thighs. But when he went to push his hands under the remains, he clearly met resistance, the ice and snow fighting the removal of that which it had claimed.

"We can help," Blay said as he motioned to Vishous. "We'll just—"

"No." Qhuinn put his palms out. "No."

But instead of struggling further to pick up his brother, the male sat back on his heels and stared at the folds of the black robe.

"This is where he chose to die. He chose this."

The words were not a condemnation. They were a lonely statement of fact. And maybe a first attempt to try on the reality of what had happened.

Qhuinn looked up, his blue and green eyes searching for, and finding, Blay's stare. "I'm just trying to figure out how to honor a choice that has broken my heart."

As the cold wind wandered through the panorama of grief, Blay felt more powerless than he had in his entire life.

"Whatever you want to do," he said softly, "we support you."

CHAPTER TWENTY-ONE

Quinn was lost, but he wasn't ungrounded in the fact that his brother's remains were frozen to the snow. If he wanted to move Luchas, he was going to have to get rough with that body that had been so badly broken. He was going to have to shove and push, yank and pull—and for reasons that he wasn't clear on, he feared the sound of dead limbs disengaging from the ice.

Then again, was the why of that really such a fucking mystery?

Forcing his brain to work, he tried on the implications of the whole move thing. Like, where would

he take Luchas? "Anywhere but here" was fine, except
for the total insufficiency of that plan. Sure, he could
transport his brother out of this forest, and into the
warmth and shelter of the training center, but then
what?

It wasn't like Manny and Doc Jane were going to
work some medical magic and revive things. And
dead bodies did not rest well at room temperature.
As ghoulish as it was, he couldn't ignore what would
happen as the remains warmed up.

He thought back to Selena's passing, to when Trez
had lit that funeral pyre and the flames had consumed
his love. Qhuinn had been in the wings for all that.
He had never thought he would so soon be on the
main stage.

Yet here he was.

As he sat where he was in snow, he was aware of
the cold clawing past the parka Blay had put on him,
and he had the sense his lack of decision-making was
a delay tactic that made no damned sense. It wasn't
like he was waiting to wake up from a nightmare . . .
or for reality to give him another fact pattern.

One that didn't involve his brother deciding to go
out in that storm.

In a quick series of hypotheticals, he imagined
Luchas stepping free of the cave. Walking forward.

Struggling against the wind, the temperature. He pictured his brother breathing in snowflakes and blinking his eyes against the gusts . . . fighting for his balance, leaning on that cane.

Given how quickly V had arrived with the SUV, it was obvious that Luchas hadn't gotten far. But that wasn't much of a news flash. Luchas had struggled with just walking on level floors.

Staring down at the body, Qhuinn became obsessed with details he would never know. Had Luchas fallen a couple of times and gotten himself back up? Or had he just collapsed here? What had he thought of as he had stared out across the snowy ground? Had there been pain? There must have been. Freezing to death was painful . . . right?

Or had he been so consumed with ending his suffering that the process of dying had been an afterthought?

Qhuinn would never know. The only thing he was sure of was that Luchas had chosen this. After so much agony, after Lash's torture, after the months and years since the raids . . . the male had decided to close the door on hope. On love. On the future.

As a wave of emotion swamped Qhuinn, he knew he couldn't stay in neutral. He had to deal with this.

And that was when he saw Vishous out of the corner of his eye.

Well, not all of the male.

Specifically his gloved hand.

When Qhuinn looked up into the diamond-hard stare of the brother, V's expression was remote. "You sure you want to do that, son?"

"He chose this place. He . . . picked this. I'm just trying to think of what he'd want." Qhuinn shook his head. "And although I don't know much, I'm sure that tearing him up to get him off this ground is not what he would have wished for his remains."

"I'll do whatever you want." V lifted his curse. "But there's no going back."

"There's no going back already."

"Fair enough."

Qhuinn blindly reached for Blay, and as always, his mate was right there, clasping that which had been outstretched.

V dropped to his knees. The brother took his time removing his lead-lined glove, tugging the insulation off his fingers one by one. It was as if he were giving Qhuinn all kinds of opportunity to change his mind.

Qhuinn simply watched as the brilliant glow was

unsheathed. The energy in V's palm was so strong, it burned the eye, but he did not look away.

This was all so terrible. All of it.

And something told him the worst was yet to come.

"Tell me when," V whispered.

"Now," Qhuinn heard himself say.

"You need to get back."

"No. I'm not leaving him."

"You're going to move back a foot, son, or I'm not going any closer to him with this thing."

There was a subtle pull on his shoulder, and Qhuinn followed Blay's gentle pressure, easing over so he was on his butt, instead of his knees.

And that was when something truly awful occurred to him.

"He's already in the Fade, right?" Qhuinn looked at V. "He got there okay, didn't he?"

There was that rumor about suicide, that whispered, so-called rule that if you took your own life, you were barred from the Fade. But surely . . .

"Vishous. He's there, right."

V's eyes lowered. "He was a right and just male, horribly treated by fate."

"That's not an answer."

"That's the best I can do."

Qhuinn rubbed his face. "Let's just do this."

If he got caught up in the unfairness of it all right now, he was going to fucking explode.

Vishous, birthed son of the Scribe Virgin, nodded. And then he slowly lowered the terrifying power that somehow resided within his flesh.

Just before contact was made, Qhuinn had a spasm of doubt, of panic. He almost called it all off—but what had changed? Where else would they take Luchas?

"Oh, God . . ." Qhuinn breathed. "Oh, God, oh—"

The flare of light was intense, the release of energy so great that Qhuinn was thrown into Blay, the pair of them landing in the snow on a sprawl. And he had expected the final act of his blooded brother's life to last awhile, but it was over . . . within seconds. Or at least that's what it seemed.

There wasn't even a scent. He'd braced himself to smell burning flesh and hair, but there was nothing of that sort and not because the wind had changed directions.

As the illumination started to fade, Qhuinn lifted his arm from the shield it had become over his face— he hadn't even been aware of raising it.

There was nothing left.

In the spot where Luchas had lain, there was no

robe, no cane, no prosthesis. There was no frozen body, no face or hands or foot. There was not a torso or a lower body.

Gone, gone, gone.

In the place of his brother, there was a precise outline of the position Luchas had died in, the exact contours of the limbs and the head and the robe represented in a bare spot with no snow or pine needles, even.

Just bald dirt.

Qhuinn extended his trembling hand over the place where the immolation had occurred. Curls of smoke rose up, riding currents of heat that dissipated quickly.

Until it was all stone cold.

CHAPTER TWENTY-TWO

Blay had never seen anything like it. V's glowing hand had extended downward, and then a nuclear-bright flash had lanced through the night, so intense and far-reaching that the entire mountain had lit up like noontime. Or at least that was what it had seemed. And in the aftermath? It was an artist's drawing of the body's position on a strip of barren, snowless ground, wisps of smoke rising for a moment.

Followed by only dark stillness.

It was as if the whole world had stopped spinning: No movement among the forest fauna, no deer careful-footing it through the leafless underbrush or owls calling to each other. No snaps of sticks or quiet moans of a breeze through pine branches. Certainly nothing from the Brothers and fighters, who were as statues in and among the trees.

Meanwhile, Qhuinn was fixated on where his brother had been, his big body shuddering. Then the labored breathing came next, heavy, loud. Finally, the male rolled off to the side and propped himself up on bowed arms. The retching went on and on, but nothing came up and out of his throat.

With utter helplessness, Blay stayed beside his mate, his hand on that heaving back, his own eyes watering. As all that pent-up emotion was released, Blay kept looking back and forth between the bare spot and his one true love.

And then, when there was finally an easing of the pain to his bereaved male, he spoke up.

"Come on, let's go back inside. It's cold out here."

As he helped Qhuinn to his feet, he wasn't sure the guy had any clue where he was. Like a zombie, Qhuinn allowed himself to be led away from where his brother had died, his sneakers taking the path they had forged out here into the forest, his arms crossed over his chest, his eyes focused in front of him. There was no telling what was going through his mind.

No, that was a lie.

Blay could guess and all of it was bad.

And that was why he was so compelled to get his mate back inside. There was nothing he could do to help with the maelstrom in Qhuinn's heart and head, but at least he could get him warm and dry.

As they came up to the Tahoe, V materialized in their path from out of thin air and nodded to the SUV. Blay shook his head. Like the Brother had said, they were only a hundred yards out. That was as far as Luchas had made it. Besides, Qhuinn didn't stop walking, his trudging stride unbroken as he zeroed in on the camouflaged entry to the cave.

When it was time, Blay jumped ahead and held the drape back, and Qhuinn ducked in. Only to stop dead, like he had no clue where to go next.

"Follow me." Blay hitched an arm through Qhuinn's and started walking again. "Not much farther."

The hatch was closed tight, and Blay entered the code and opened things so Qhuinn could keep going. Then he checked over his shoulder. The Brotherhood had closed ranks, but they were holding back, just looking around the draping, not yet venturing in. This was good. Space was good.

Into the tunnel. Pause by the gear, where Blay stripped the parka off Qhuinn and hung it up.

As Qhuinn looked around with seemingly blind eyes, his face was ruddy from the dry heaves, from the cold, maybe from V's flash of light. He looked utterly lost, a young in the body of an adult.

"I didn't want him to go."

"Of course you didn't—"

"Oh, God, Blay, what if he knew, what if he knew . . ."

"Knew what?"

Qhuinn rubbed his eyes and then stared at his hands like they belonged to someone else. "What if he'd read my mind. I mean, I can't tell you the number of times I sat at his bedside and thought to myself . . . what kind of life is this for him? How does he keep going? I couldn't fathom how he handled it. They were hacking parts of him off to keep him alive. He couldn't walk. He couldn't work his hands. He was down there in that patient room, all by himself." Those mismatched eyes shifted over. "What if he read my mind? And knew . . ."

"It was not your fault," Blay said through a tight throat. "You are not responsible for this."

"But I am. I was the one who told them to take his leg. I was the one . . . maybe I could have done more, helped more." Qhuinn dropped his face into his palms. "I thought I had more time with him. He was medically stable, so I thought there was time to talk. Time to help. Oh, fuck, this hurts."

Blay didn't know what to say. So he reached out and pulled his mate against him. As Qhuinn's arms came around him and held on, he took that as a good sign. At least the connection between them was still there.

He had a feeling they were going to need it.

◆ ◆ ◆

The next thing Qhuinn knew, he was in the mansion's foyer. He didn't remember the trip back to the grand, formal space, but he sure as shit hadn't dematerialized his way here—and he was certain about this because: 1) too much steel to get through; and 2) no way he could have concentrated well enough to ghost out.

At this point, he wasn't sure he could concentrate well enough to take a piss.

With a numb disassociation, he looked around and recognized the malachite columns, the staircase that rose with such great majesty to the second story, the sconces, the ceiling high above with its warriors and steeds. And beneath his feet? The mosaic depiction of an apple tree in full bloom was just as it was supposed to be.

If Luchas had been moved up here, if he'd been given a proper guestroom with beautiful things and a marble bathroom . . . if he'd been treated like a member of the family, instead of an invalid who was nothing but his infirmity . . . would it have made a difference? Would he have held on a little longer?

"Why didn't I ask him how he was?" Qhuinn turned to his mate. "I should have asked him."

"You did, many times. I was there for a lot of them."

"It feels like I didn't do it enough."

Every time he blinked, he saw his brother's remains. Each time he breathed, the pain in his chest got worse. With every beat of his heart, he was boomeranged back to the past and then dragged forward to the present. Images assaulted him, memories battering around his head of him and his brother growing up in that house with their parents and Solange, all the strictures, the discipline . . . and in Qhuinn's case, the censure. And then there were more recent memories, of him sitting at Luchas's bedside, the pair of them talking about nothing.

Why had he wasted those opportunities? They'd had two, maybe three, serious conversations where they'd gone deep into how Luchas was feeling about his injuries and what had happened to him. But most of their interactions had been kept on the surface. Safely on the surface.

Because Qhuinn had always thought he'd have

more time. Sure, not an endless number of nights and days—it wasn't like they were immortal—but he hadn't pressed anything, had respected boundaries that might or might not have been there, had given space and kept things light . . . because he'd assumed there was a future readily available to cover the important things.

When it was time.

Whatever that meant.

And now he was here.

He was here on this heartbreaking side of the great divide that had opened up between them, a divide Luchas had chosen to create when he had walked out into that storm.

A divide that potentially was eternal, if that bullshit about taking your own life was true when it came to the Fade.

If only Qhuinn had known that the male was so close to a decision that could not be unmade. If he'd had a clue, he could have talked Luchas into staying in the land of living. He could have reminded him that he had people who loved him, and a niece and nephew who needed their uncle, and—

From out of the corner of his eye, he noted that someone was standing just inside the billiards room, a tall figure that was, at first, indistinct.

Oddly, what caused recognition to click was a

memory from First Meal the night before . . . of Lassiter staring down the table at him, that odd expression on the angel's face, his strangely colored eyes so grave.

Like he'd known what was coming.

All at once, Qhuinn's emotions coalesced into a spearhead, the tip of which was everything he would have done differently if he'd known, if he'd gotten a heads-up, if he could have been down in the training center when it had mattered, standing outside Luchas's room, the physical barrier that was in the way of his brother's conclusion that his life was no longer worth living . . .

. . . so he was going to walk out and die in a snowstorm.

The sound that ripped out of Qhuinn's throat was that of an animal, and then his body launched into an attack without any conscious direction from him.

He closed the distance and threw himself at the angel, grabbing on to the front of the male's neck with one hand while swinging widely with his right fist. And as soon as he made that cracking contact with Lassiter's face, he didn't stop. He swung again, now from the left side, hitting whatever was in the way. Then he locked hold of the head and swung hard, casting the angel out into the foyer, onto the mosaic floor.

People were shouting at him. He heard nothing.

People were pulling at him. He shoved them off.

Qhuinn let loose with pounding fists and kicking legs, mounting the angel's prone body and slamming Lassiter over and over again into the hard floor—

Without warning, Qhuinn was lifted off bodily, dragged back and held off, whoever it was strong enough to keep him from his target.

So he used his voice instead of his fists.

"You knew!" he screamed at Lassiter. "You knew what he was going to do—and you didn't tell me! You cost me my brother!"

He fought against the iron bars that were under his armpits. They held steady.

"Or you could have stopped him!" Qhuinn's voice rebounded all around, all the way up to the ceiling. "You're an angel, you're supposed to save souls—was he not good enough for you? Was my brother too broken for you to bother saving? Why! Why did you let my brother die!"

He was utterly unhinged, his tirade filling the house, calling all kinds of people into the doorways of other rooms. But like he fucking cared? And meanwhile, Lassiter just lay where he had sprawled, oddly colored eyes showing no emotion at all.

Qhuinn surged against whoever was holding him. "He deserved your help! He deserved to be saved—"

"Let him go."

The angel's voice, soft and low, cut through his hollering, and he abruptly became aware that there was silver blood all over the floor, all over his own fists . . . all over the male's face from the split lip, the busted nose, that cut over his eyebrow.

The angel had not fought back.

He hadn't even tried to protect himself.

"Let him go!" Lassiter yelled.

The constriction was released, and Qhuinn fell forward. Unable to catch his balance, he landed hard on all fours.

And still, Lassiter just looked at him, that silver blood flowing like melted sterling.

"You're pathetic," Qhuinn spat. "You're not worth the effort to kill you. I hope you can live with what a fucking *failure* you are as the successor to the Scribe Virgin. You're nothing but a goddamn lazy joke."

Scrambling to his feet, he stumbled, pushed off someone's hands—he didn't know whose. He was alone as he went up the stairs.

That much he was clear on.

Good thing, too.

CHAPTER TWENTY-THREE

As Qhuinn stormed up the grand staircase, Blay stood at the base of the carpeted steps and watched his mate retreat. He wanted to go after him, but it was very clear that he was not welcome. He'd been shoved away.

He didn't know what to do.

So he turned to Lassiter, who was still lying on the foyer's floor and bleeding silver. Others had gathered around the angel, including V, who had actual medical training—but the bodies parted as Blay went over and lowered himself down.

"He didn't mean any of that," he said as he helped

the angel sit up. "Truly, he didn't. I have no clue what he was talking about."

"Help me to my feet?" Lassiter asked as he wiped his face with his forearm.

Blay grunted at the weight of the male. It was as if gravity had a special interest in the angel, his body heavier than even his prodigious muscles suggested, his bones clearly made of solid gold or something.

"I don't need medical help." Lassiter shook his head as V stepped forward. "A little sun and I'll be fine."

"At least let's clean you up," Blay interjected. "Come this way."

Blay took the angel's arm and led Lassiter around to the left of the staircase. Tucked under the steps, the formal powder room was like a jewel box, with rare stone inlays and twinkling crystal fixtures, everything so lush and lovely. And talk about karats. The sink was gold, and so were the filigreed faucets and the tiny little lamps with the hand-tooled silk shades— which were like birthday candles for a tsar.

Pushing Lassiter down onto the silk-covered bench, Blay snagged a monogrammed hand towel. As he wetted a corner, he had a thought that it was a good thing Lassiter bled silver. The fine terry cloth was a pale gray.

Red blood would have ruined it.

"I'm really sorry," he said as he leaned into the angel's busted face.

Lassiter hissed at the contact. Then cleared his throat. "There is nothing to apologize for."

"He's still just . . ." Blay blinked and saw Luchas's face in the snow. "I'm just really sorry. About everything."

"As am I."

Back to the sink. Running more warm water. Rinsing the hand towel out.

Returning to that face, Blay focused this time up by the eyebrow. As Lassiter cursed and jerked back, Blay murmured an apology. Which seemed to be his theme song.

About ten minutes later, most of the silver blood was gone, Lassiter's classically handsome face re-revealed . . . for the moment. The swelling was coming, the bruising not black and blue, but a shimmering under the surface of the skin.

Blay backed up and leaned against the sink counter, crossing his arms. Focusing on his feet, he frowned at his Bally loafers. He'd had boots on, back when he and Tohr had been dealing with the Christmas tree. When had he swapped those for such flimsy footwear?

That he'd taken out to find Luchas.

"I've ruined my shoes," he said absently as he lifted one of his feet and inspected the wet leather. "Funny, I didn't even notice the cold."

On that note, he bent down and took off the loafer. The sock was next. What was revealed was bad news. His toes were a white color he never wanted to see again: They were exactly the same as Luchas's frozen face—opaque, like marble.

Shying away from the image, he stared at his foot. The damn thing was going to hurt like hell when things started to warm up, but he welcomed the physical pain. It would be easier than what was in his soul.

"Here, let me help."

Lassiter reached forward and put his palm underneath Blay's sole. Instead of the fearsome energy that had exploded out of Vishous's curse, this was a warm glow that enveloped and revived: Over the next minute or so, Blay watched as color returned to his flesh, the warm, healthy skin tone coming back.

"Give me your other one."

Blay shucked his remaining shoe and sock, and extended the left side. "It doesn't hurt. It's a miracle."

"That's the plan."

As the magic was worked on his other foot, Blay realized that the angel was not wearing one of his trademark crazy outfits. He was in all black, his wild blond-and-black hair likewise braided and out of the way. For a male who usually went around in spandex leggings, à la David Lee Roth, the reserve was yet another jarring shock.

Nothing was ever going to be normal again. Of this, Blay was quite sure.

"Can I ask you something?" he blurted.

"Anything."

It was a while before Blay could frame the question. "What can I do to help him?"

Okay, fine, it was probably not fair to ask that of the angel, given the attack. But was anybody really thinking right tonight?

"You know the answer to that," Lassiter said.

"No, I really don't."

The angel leaned down and picked up the shoes. The wetness on them receded as soon as he touched them, retreating from the tips and traveling to the heels. Unfortunately, there were stains left behind in the fine leather, that which had been unmarred before now marked with permanent discoloration.

"Yes," Lassiter said, "you do know what to do."

After the shoes changed hands, the angel left, a lonely figure it seemed, in spite of his power and influence. Or perhaps . . . because of it.

Blay, on the other hand, stayed where he was, staring at what had been on his feet. Overhead, the heating came on, warm, dry air drifting downward onto his hair.

"I can't stay here all night," he said aloud.

All things considered, the first part of going anywhere else was putting his shoes back on. His socks were still wet, however, having not benefitted from Lassiter's attentions, and so he wadded them up into soggy fists that he held in one hand. Then he shoved his feet home, the loafers fitting more tightly than they had before.

Out in the foyer, he discovered that everyone had scattered from the drama. Turning to the grand staircase, he pictured Qhuinn upstairs. He knew where the male would be. He would be with the twins—

Blay frowned and looked around the base of the stairs.

A split second later, he fell into a hurried rush.

The angel was right. He did know what he had to do.

* * *

Qhuinn found what he was looking for in the playroom. As he pulled open the door, Layla glanced up from the floor where she was sitting with the kids— and froze while their eyes met.

"Oh, Qhuinn."

She made a move like she was going to get up

and hug him, but when he stepped back sharply, she ducked her eyes and hung her head.

"I'm okay," he heard himself say as he waved at Lyric, who'd started beaming at him, and then to Rhamp, who was shaking a rattle in his direction. "I just want to be with them for a while, all right? Just me and them."

Layla nodded and got to her feet like she was stiff. "Of course. I—ah, a text went out. From Tohr, so . . . I'm so sorry—"

"It's fine."

She recoiled—and then tried to hide her reaction. But he couldn't help her with her awkwardness. He couldn't even help himself right now—and the "fine" thing was just a door to close on her sympathy, her worry, the burden of the referred pain she was feeling as she confronted a tragedy that really only affected him.

"Is there anything I can do?" she said.

"Just give me some time with them."

The Chosen pulled the waistband of her jeans higher up on her hips. Then she pushed her blond hair back as her eyes roamed around the cheerful room—and he was grateful she kept her thoughts to herself. He did not want to be mean, but he was raw—and like a wounded animal, he was dangerously unstable.

"Let me know when you need me back?" she said. Then she shook her head. "Actually, I was going to feed them in about forty-five minutes. Unless you'd like to?"

"That'll be good. I mean, forty-five. That's fine."

"Okay."

There was a moment of frozen silence, and then Layla went over to the door. As she hesitated to push her way out, he cleared his throat.

"I'm not going to do anything stupid," he said roughly. "You don't need to worry about that. I've seen entirely too many dead blooded relations of mine tonight."

Her eyes closed. "Oh, Qhuinn. I am so sorry—"

"Scratch that." He rubbed his eyes, not because he was getting emotional, but because he couldn't stop seeing his brother's face. "Make that for a lifetime. I've seen enough dead relatives for a goddamn fucking lifetime."

She took a deep breath. "I want you to know something—"

"Just come back in forty-five minutes—"

"I took them to see him the night before the storm."

Qhuinn blinked. "What? Wait, what did you say?"

"Lyric and Rhamp. I took them down to see

Luchas two nights ago." Her eyes started to water. "I'd do that from time to time. You know, I mean . . . I just—he loved seeing them. They sat on his bed, and he played with them, and he smiled at them. They always seemed to make him happy."

Rhamp ditched the rattle, rolled over onto his tummy, and hit the ground crawling fast, going for broke toward a big, red inflatable ball in the corner. The kid had the grace of an Army tank, the speed of a motivated turtle, and the fixation of a chess master about to be pawn'd out of a tournament.

"Thank you," Qhuinn said softly. "I'm so glad he got to see them one last time."

"I'm going to miss Luchas. He was such a sensitive soul. We would talk about books and—"

Qhuinn put his hand up. "I'm sorry, Layla. I, like, don't mean to be rude. But I can't talk about him right now. I'm not even on this planet, actually. I'm just trying to find the floor beneath my feet." He lifted his soggy sneakers one after another. "Because I can't feel it—and talking about my brother makes this floating feeling worse."

"Okay. Just please know, there are a lot of us here in the house for you to talk to."

The door eased shut in her wake, and he looked into Lyric's beautiful pale green eyes . . . and prayed his brother had made it into the Fade. Surely, even if the rumor was true about killing yourself, Luchas would be granted an exception for all he had suffered.

Right?

Lyric put her arms out, and that was Qhuinn's cue to scoop—and scoop he did, gathering his daughter up and bringing her to his heart. In response, she made a whole bunch of cooing noises and babbling sounds. She was normally a quiet kid, but in situations like this, when it was just the two of them because her brother was distracted by another one of his missions, oh, she opened up big. It was like she patiently waited her turn, and as such, there was always a backlog of unexpressed opinions and commentary for her to get out.

Meanwhile, across the blue-and-yellow padded floor, Rhamp was up on his feet and throwing punches at the ball. Both of the twins were still a little unsteady when walking, but coordinated activity improved Rhamp's balance.

And he'd found a helluva rhythm.

Qhuinn pictured them at five years old. At ten. At fifteen and twenty. At . . . fifty and a hundred . . . all their lives ahead of them, adventures to be had, love to be discovered, challenges to best and good fortune to find.

"Oh, Luchas," he whispered. "Why couldn't you have stayed for them . . ."

Yet even as that occurred to him, he realized that he was being self-centered. After all, the twins were his young, not his brother's—

The door to the playroom opened—and he tried not to glare at whoever it was.

When he saw it was Layla, Qhuinn closed his eyes in frustration. "I thought you said I'd have forty-five minutes."

Layla's voice was gentle. "You've been in here for an hour and a half."

His lids popped. And he frowned.

Sometime in the last, well, ninety minutes, apparently, he'd sat down against the wall. Lyric was face-up in his lap, sprawled across with her feet draped over one side and her back braced against the other. Rhamp, meanwhile, had come over from his red-ball-abusing session and found the crook of Qhuinn's arm.

They were both fast asleep.

Swallowing hard, he watched their chests rise and fall, heard their gentle breaths through parted mouths, felt their warmth against him.

"I would like to help feed them," he said in a hoarse voice. "And then after . . . I think it's Blay's and my turn for bath."

When there was no reply, he looked up from his young. Layla was standing in the doorway, her hand over her mouth, a tear rolling down her cheek. Behind her, Xcor loomed big as a mountain, silent as the sky. The male's hand was resting on his *shellan*'s shoulder, protectively, lovingly. His eyes were dry, but the sadness in them darkened them nearly to black.

"Yes," Layla said. "I think it is your turn."

Qhuinn glanced down. "They look so comfortable."

Xcor's voice was deep and grave. "That is because they know they are safe with their father."

CHAPTER TWENTY-FOUR

B lay traveled fast through the training center's tunnel. He actually jogged for part of the
way—which he knew was overkill. What he
was worried about happening would not happen. It
was just paranoia that the already horrible situation
they were all in was going to get worse.

At least he was pretty sure it wouldn't happen.

Blasting through the office, he didn't run into anybody, and this was good. Hopefully no one had gotten
to thinking.

As he came up to the clinical area, he wondered

how much time anyone would have had to intervene if somebody had known Luchas had walked out into the storm. Like, if only an alarm had gone off when the hatch had been opened—no, Luchas had used the code. Okay . . . fine. So if some kind of notice had pinged V's phone that there had been a departure . . . maybe Manny and Doc Jane could have been told to run out and turn the male back around.

Blay jumbled to a halt in front of the last patient room. The door was the same as all the others, made of the same wood that had been properly stained— no particleboard or laminated plastic for the Brother-hood, even in the clinical areas—the exact color as all the others.

He was never going to be able to look at the door the same again.

No one else would, either.

His hand was oddly steady as he opened things up. It was his entire body that was shaking.

The inside of the room . . . was exactly as it had always been. The hospital bed was across the way. In the corner, there was a homey stuffed chair and an ot-toman, next to which was a side table with a lamp and a book. And that was . . . it.

No personal effects. No photographs. Not even a pad and a pen.

"Where is it, Luchas," he murmured. "You must have left something for him. You didn't do that without explaining yourself."

Blay went over to the bed, which was made up precisely, with hospital corners Fritz would approve of and a set of pillows that were so centered at the headboard, you'd think a protractor and ruler had been used to put them in place.

"Where did you get the black robe?" Blay murmured. "And why did you wear it—"

He stopped.

Now his hand shook.

As he reached out to the rolling table, he didn't pick up the white, business-sized envelope that had been placed in the corner of the tray. He just brushed his finger over the two words written in thin blue ink: "Brother Mine."

Blay swiped his face with his palm. Then he looked around again.

When he refocused on the tray, he saw why Qhuinn would have missed the missive, especially if he'd been in a panic as he'd looked for his brother: The tray was white, the business envelope was white, and just like the pillows, the letter had been lined up precisely in one corner. It was nearly invisible.

"You okay?"

He pivoted to the voice. Manny Manello was leaning into the room, the doctor's face full of grim expectation. Like he'd seen this specific kind of tragedy before and knew what a head job it did on people.

"Can you—" Blay cleared his throat. "You can make sure no one comes in here, right?"

"Sure, but what is—"

"The note." Blay pointed to the envelope. "It's for Qhuinn. I don't want anyone touching it or anything else in here."

Manny nodded. "Nobody gets in here but him."

"Thank you."

"What can I do?"

Blay looked around again. Then he went over to the bathroom. Pushing the door open, a light came on automatically. There was nothing significant on the counter.

No, that wasn't true. There was a toothbrush in a holder that would never be used again, a half-filled tube of Colgate that would never be finished, and a bar of soap that would remain forever dry. Towels, which had been folded with care, were stacked on some shelves over the toilet and there were others hanging on rods—and they would all remain untouched by the suite's previous occupant. The shower, which was just a curtain and a lip, the threshold for entry no more than two inches high, would no longer be turned on by Luchas's hand, its stool never sat upon by him again, the shampoo and soap forever at the level they had been left.

Taking a deep breath, Blay caught the faded scents of cleanliness and habit.

Death was so strange. When it claimed its prey, there was a hard stop to the heart, the lungs, the body itself. But the artifacts of a person had a kind of kinetic motion that kept them going forward, at least for a little while. Clothes, shoes, medicines, bath products, subscriptions to things . . . all of that detritus of life was like loose objects in a car that had hit a brick wall, still banging around the interior.

Until they were dealt with, given away, put to use by someone else, thrown out, canceled.

Life should be more permanent than a tube of toothpaste with three inches left in its belly, he thought.

Blay rubbed the ache in the center of his chest. Then again, that was what the heart was for. The dead were immortal in the souls of those they left behind, and the payment for that permanence was pain.

CHAPTER TWENTY-FIVE

Qhuinn was sitting by the side of the tub when he heard the bedroom door open and close. The footfalls that came across the Persian carpet were soft, and there was a hesitation before Blay leaned inside the marble expanse.

The sight of that red hair and those blue eyes, of the clothes that Qhuinn had watched the male put on earlier in the night, of his mate's expression of wary sadness, made a wave of emotion crest. But he fought the feelings back, stopping the weakness by recalling that when the dressing had occurred, when he had enjoyed the sight of his mate's naked body in the walk-in closet . . . everything had been different.

The world had been totally altered.

Luchas had been dead for nearly twenty-four hours then frozen in the snow in that black robe. Just no one had known it yet.

Abruptly, Qhuinn had a chilling thought. How many other horrible truths were lurking around the corners of time, waiting to jump out into his path and ruin his sense that life was okay? Disease, an errant bullet in the field, someone else's choices that cratered his own—

Lyric let out a string of babble, and Blay's stare went over to her.

"It's our bath night," Qhuinn said roughly. "I didn't want you to miss it."

"I am so glad you texted me."

Blay kicked off his loafers and came in on bare feet. Lowering himself down at the other end of the tub, he cupped some water and poured it over Rhamp's shoulders.

"Have you done shampoo?" he asked.

Even as the question was posed, Qhuinn knew his mate was already well aware of the answer. Blay would have smelled the Aveeno if it had been used . . .

but sometimes, when there was too much to say, words were hard to come by.

So you just tossed some out there because it was the best you could do.

"No, not yet." Qhuinn nodded at the baby wash. "Do you want the bottle?"

"Sure."

Qhuinn passed the thing over. "Where did your socks go?"

"What?" Blay looked at his feet. "Oh. Um . . . they're around somewhere."

"You never wear socks in the summer with those shoes. In the winter, you always do."

"I was unaware of being so consistent."

"It's one of your best traits." Qhuinn patted the water with his palm in front of Lyric, and in response, she mimicked him. "And not one of mine. I'm sorry I pushed you away. Down in the foyer."

"There's no need to apologize."

"Yes, there is. I just . . . I wasn't in my right mind."

However, he had no regrets about lashing out at the angel. Every time he thought about Luchas's choice unfairly locking the male out of the Fade, he felt that fury threaten to return.

"It's okay," Blay said as he flipped the baby blue

top open. "I can't imagine how you're feeling right now."

"Neither can I." Lyric grabbed his thumb and played at the surface of the tub with his hand. "Sorry, that makes no sense, does it. I mean . . . I'm not even sure where I am at the moment. That's why it's good to have bath time. I know bath time."

The Aveeno made a whoopee cushion noise as Blay squeezed the bottle over Rhamp's head, and the young laughed and reached for it.

"Close the top and let him have it," Qhuinn said. "Let's see what he does with the thing."

Sure enough. Right in the mouth.

"Okay, maybe that wasn't the best idea. Should have seen that coming."

"I don't think it can hurt him," Blay hedged.

"Neither do I."

Blay sat up on his knees and got with the washing program, sudsing up that dark cap of hair, rinsing things with the soft pitcher that was pink. Then it was time for the washcloth, Rhamp's sturdy little body getting a vigorous scrubbing.

"She took them to see him," Qhuinn murmured.

"Huh?" Blay doused the kid with more water, pouring it over Rhamp's shoulders. "What was that?"

"Layla took them to Luchas."

Blay paused. "She did . . . ?"

Qhuinn nodded. "Bless her. She's a good female. Xcor is a lucky male."

"He is." Blay lowered the pitcher. "Did she say anything about . . . how he was?"

✦ ✦ ✦

Blay's heart pounded as he searched his mate's face. In the back of his mind, he answered his own question in ways that only made him feel worse. Frankly, he was shocked that he was even here, surprised that Qhuinn had texted him and asked him to come up, grateful beyond measure that he was even in the same room with the male.

He'd expected to be totally shut out. That was how Qhuinn usually operated.

"No, she didn't say how he seemed." Qhuinn took a deep breath. "Other than, as usual, the young made him smile."

Rhamp took the pitcher and played with it, slamming the water's surface with the base. His sister found this incredibly entertaining and clapped for him, and as she grinned and flashed her four white teeth, Blay pictured her sitting at the end of Luchas's hospital bed.

"I know I said it before, but I just . . . I wish I could have helped him." Qhuinn shook his head. "I didn't know he'd reached his limit with things. He seemed so fine—I mean, not *fine*, fine. But the same. And maybe that was the thing. He clearly didn't feel like he was getting any better and he didn't want to go on where he was. I really wish I—"

"He left you a note."

Qhuinn's head snapped around. "What?"

"In his room."

"I didn't see it."

"The envelope is on the rolling tray, but it's hard to notice." Blay put up his palm. "And don't worry, Manny's making sure no one goes in there but you. So when you're ready, go—and if it's now, I'll take care of these guys."

But first, you need to tell him, Blay thought. *You need to tell him what you did when you spoke to Luchas.*

With a burst of strength, Qhuinn got to his feet. But then he seemed to stall out.

Instead of leaving, he ended up putting the cover down on the toilet and sitting in a way that was angled toward the exit. Like part of him was running down to the training center—and the other part was frozen out of fear of what he would find.

"What if it's my fault?" he whispered.

Blay cleared his throat. "Actually, I think it was mine."

Qhuinn rolled his eyes. "That's ridiculous."

"I saw him the night before the storm, too."

As his mate looked over sharply, Blay wished he could change places with Layla and be the one who'd brought the kids down. No, wait. Then Layla would have said what he had—and he wouldn't want her to carry that burden.

"You were in the OR." Blay was aware of his heart starting to beat even harder, and also that the bathroom, which had previously seemed just fine for temperature, had turned into a sauna. "He was coming from the pool. He stopped and asked how you were doing."

"You giving him a medical update would hardly freak him out—"

"He didn't know you'd been elevated to the King's personal guard." As Qhuinn stiffened, Blay put his palms out. "I never would have divulged the information, but I wasn't aware you hadn't told him. I mean, I just . . . I can understand why you'd keep that to yourself given everything that was going on with him, but . . . I'm so sorry. I didn't know."

Qhuinn opened his mouth. Closed it. Then rubbed his thighs. "Yeah, I thought I had mentioned to you to keep it on the down low. I just didn't want to pile on. You know the *glymera*. A brother who's a Brother? That would be hard on anyone, but where

Luchas was at? And then add on the personal guard shit?"

"I'm really sorry. It's killing me."

"No, listen, it's okay." Qhuinn cleared his throat. "Was he ... bothered by it?"

"I'll be honest. He was surprised."

Oh, God, Blay thought. As he did the math, it was possible that he was one of the last people who had interacted with Luchas.

The idea that Qhuinn's brother might have been an afterthought for everyone in the house broke Blay's heart. And on some level, he knew that wasn't true. The male had been a part of the community, and yet ... everybody had their own lives, lives with mates and young, lives within the war with the Lessening Society and now whatever new threat had come to Caldwell. There had always been injuries and nightly stressors, changes of seasons, problems with cars, supplies that needed reordering, guns to clean, daggers to sharpen.

Life. With all its multi-faceted layers.

And Luchas had had his own. Such as it was.

Had he felt left behind? And why hadn't someone asked him if that had been true?

"I just want to take it back," Blay said in a voice that cracked. "I don't want to have been responsible in any way for ..."

Qhuinn shook his head. "You aren't. There are so many reasons without that."

The words were the right ones—and some part of Qhuinn must have believed them. His voice was steady and not condemning in any way.

But that mismatched stare was elsewhere, not meeting Blay's eyes.

"I have to go down there." Qhuinn got to his feet. "I need to see the note."

"I'll take care of the kids."

"Okay. Thank you."

Justlikethat, Qhuinn was gone, the door to the bathroom opening and closing, a chill entering the warm, humid space.

Or maybe the waft of cold was just how Blay was feeling.

Qhuinn wasn't an unfair male, and the love between them wasn't something Blay questioned. But sometimes there were things you couldn't come back from in relationships. It wasn't that you didn't want to work past them, or weren't willing to try.

But the reality that your mate had contributed to the death of your brother, even if it was inadvertently, was a tough one.

Any way you looked at it.

CHAPTER TWENTY-SIX

A s Qhuinn stood just inside his brother's fifteen-by-fifteen-foot patient room, his brain fired up with an electric storm of shoulda/coulda/woulda's. Maybe if they'd decorated this place? Like, wallpapered things and added a nice rug, hung oil paintings and thrown some expensive sheets on the hospital bed, maybe it would have—

"Shut the fuck up," he muttered as he looked over at the rolling table.

And there it was. The letter.

Blay was right. With the envelope that white color, it blended completely into the tray. And of course,

Luchas had taken care to make sure it was perfectly flush with the corner, arranged with care.

From across the way, the precise lettering, done with a narrow-tipped blue pen, in Luchas's perfect penmanship, gave Qhuinn the chills.

Somehow, even with all his injuries, he'd managed to write beautifully.

Brother Mine.

Qhuinn went over with the intention of picking the letter up, taking out whatever was inside, and absorbing the words that had been left for him. But he ultimately didn't touch the thing, and it took him a minute to figure out why. Then it came to him . . . as soon as he read whatever had been written, it was truly done. His brother was truly gone.

The finality of the death, the shocking, binary nature of finding Luchas's frozen body out in the forest, had been transferred to the missive: As long as he didn't read what was in there, his brother was still alive, in a way. They were both still in the in-between, something still left to be discovered, considered, reflected upon.

Well . . . and then there was his terror about whatever the message was.

Luchas had never been mean, but reality could be devastating.

After all, Qhuinn knew exactly what it was like to be less than, through circumstances completely beyond your control. He hadn't chosen his mismatched eyes; his brother hadn't chosen to be abducted by Lash and tortured. So, yes, the last thing Qhuinn would ever do was rub Luchas's nose in the very obvious reality that there had been a reversal of fortune for them both.

Looking around, Qhuinn focused on the armchair. Usually when he'd come into this room, he'd find his brother there, a book open in his lap, a cup of tea on that table by the lamp. Because Luchas had always been dressed in clean things, and his hair freshly washed, and that cane set aside . . . it had been simpler to believe all was well. Or at least, all was improving, even if it was just at a snail's pace.

Qhuinn went over to the little table and picked up what his brother had been reading. Because it was easier than touching that last missive's envelope.

Ah, yes. A little light diversion before bed: The leather-bound volume was in the Old Language, something that was, given the current status of Qhuinn's head, wholly foreign and totally unreadable to him as he flipped through the pages.

When he got to where a satin ribbon marked Luchas's pause, he felt sick with sadness.

This journey of letters and words and sentences

and paragraphs would never be completed, the eyes that had traced the symbols that had been written now closed forever.

With a sad capitulation, Qhuinn lowered himself into the chair his brother had spent so many hours in. He kept hold of the book, closing it up and cradling it in his hands. As he stared across at the empty bed, he pictured Layla with the twins and wondered exactly where the visit had occurred. It would help him picture it if he knew whether they'd been over there on the bed or here on the chair and ottoman.

He would ask her for the details later.

He wanted to hold on to the memory, even if it was one he had to create on his own.

And maybe it was better that way. He wanted a picture-perfect, happy, imagined storyline of Layla coming down with the young and Luchas sitting in this chair with both of them in his lap. A poignant, final goodbye—

Had Luchas had his plan already set? Or had it been later?

As Qhuinn let his head fall back, he tried to stop his mind from spinning. When that failed miserably, he considered getting a bottle of Herradura. Then he upgraded that plan to asking Manny for some knock-out drops in the form of nice, little white pills that would help him exit this miserable train at the REM Sleep Station.

Surrounded by his brother's few things, he thought back to an evening in his own timeline, one that he had never told Luchas about. One that only Blay really knew of.

Because Blay had been the one who saved him from his own suicide attempt.

And it was because of that that Qhuinn couldn't blame his mate for what he'd said to Luchas. That one comment about the private guard was not the reason for it all—and besides, Blay had already proven himself and his loyalty and his compassion over and over again, throughout his life.

There had been a lot of reasons why Luchas had chosen to walk out into that storm. So many reasons, all of which were tragic, none of which were a mystery.

A news flash about the King's private guard? Drop in the bucket.

Qhuinn's eyes returned to the rolling table. From his current angle, he couldn't see the envelope, couldn't read those two words that had been written upon it, couldn't reach for the thing if he'd wanted to.

And, he realized, he didn't want to.

He didn't want to read whatever was in there. He'd rather have unfinished business forever . . .

. . . as opposed to confirmation that maybe, just maybe, it was his fault because he'd been too busy, too negligent, too self-centered to take care of his own blood and make sure that Luchas was getting not just the medical care he needed, but the psychological counseling that was just as important to health and well-being.

Maybe more important.

CHAPTER TWENTY-SEVEN

One week later, Blay opened the door to his bedroom suite's bathroom and leaned out. Across the way, the light in the walk-in closet was glowing, the illumination spilling onto the Persian carpet, making the jewel tones even brighter. He hesitated. Then retreated back and shut the door again.

Looking around, he saw that everything was the same in the loo. The toothbrushes by the pair of sinks were in their separate holders and the pair of paste tubes, one Crest, the other Colgate, were teamed with their appropriate Oral-B partners. The Waterpik on one side was Qhuinn's.

It had been likewise in the shower, the shampoo and conditioner bottles where they had always been. The bar of soap was just a single in a dish, as they both used Ivory.

Because it was ninety-nine percent pure. Whatever the hell that meant.

At a loss, Blay lowered the toilet seat, rewrapped the bath towel around his body, and sat down. For some reason, it seemed vitally important to cover himself even though no one was in with him—and he remembered Qhuinn sitting in the same place during that bath time right after Luchas had been found.

That was as close as he and his mate had been for the last seven nights.

Oh, physically it had been largely the same, the two of them still sleeping side by side during the day and eating next to each other during meals. And then Blay had stayed on rotation, even as Qhuinn was not cleared to go back into the field yet. He was off until he passed a psych eval.

Which, no surprise, no one had brought up and Qhuinn hadn't volunteered for.

Through the door, a muffled voice: "I'm going to go work out."

Blay cleared his throat and spoke louder than normal. "You're skipping First Meal?"

"I already ate. See you soon."

A moment later, there was a click of the door out into the hallway shutting.

Blay dropped his head in defeat. At this point, he'd almost have preferred a slam, a stomp, a loud word. Instead, there was just this eerie politeness, an autopilot composure that had as much to do with the Qhuinn he knew as a muffler on a Shelby Mustang: His mate had retreated somewhere deep inside his own mind, his body all that remained. He had been like a ghost, floating around the house, skipping meals, working out, spending time alone in Luchas's room.

He hadn't said what was in the letter.

Which scared Blay and made him replay his self-blame game. Again and again and again.

Getting to his feet, he walked out of the loo. His intention was to go and get dressed, but he ended up standing at the base of their bed. Both sets of pillows had indents on them and both sides of the sheets and covers had been halved back, the whole thing a tidy mirror image of itself. Usually, their bed was a mess:

things on the floor, sheets tangled, duvet backwards or hanging off the headboard. In contrast, this disciplined disorder looked like a Sleep Number bed commercial, a stage set created to suggest that two people, a loving couple, had spent the night together.

And that was accurate, he supposed. He and his mate had been on that mattress together, although he didn't think either one of them had actually found any REM cycles. Blay certainly hadn't.

Pivoting to the walk-in closet, he went across and stood among their clothes. As with the pillows and sheets outside, there was a strict division, a his/his demarcation, the left all Blay's, the right all Qhuinn's.

It was the same with the bed. Left was his, right was Qhuinn's.

The arrangement in here hadn't been a particularly conscious thing, just a yours-and-mine that had made sense. They were pretty close in size, but the styles? Not a thing in common.

He'd have been surprised if the guy had ever worn a loafer in his life. Okay, fine, maybe when Qhuinn had been younger and in his parents' house.

With duct tape to keep them on, no doubt.

Blay went for his fighting clothes, taking a set of leathers off the hooks that were screwed into the wall. But then he remembered. He was off rotation tonight. Frankly, ever since Luchas's death, he'd been surprised that he'd been allowed to go out at all, and he supposed that the continued a-okay meant he was doing a good job hiding everything he was feeling.

As a corollary, he was also surprised Qhuinn hadn't brought up his suspension from the field yet. The fact that there was no fight to get back on rotation from him was scary. Just like his weight loss, and his listless disinterest in anything but the kids. Seriously, thank God for the twins. It was clear that Rhamp and Lyric were keeping their father going, the nightly jobs of giving them baths and changing their clothes and feeding them seeming to consume all of Qhuinn's attention and focus.

Trying to stop the mind spins, Blay got dressed, pulling on a random button-down, a random set of slacks, the closest sweater. He was putting on socks when he realized he'd decided to leave the house.

So he put on boots, instead of loafers, and then grabbed his North Face jacket and a pair of puffy gloves.

Leaving his room—their room—he headed for the back stairs, and bottomed out in the kitchen. First Meal had been served about twenty minutes before, so *doggen* were refilling platters with extra eggs and bagels for service. Blay waved to all of them casually, and tried to appear what he very much was not: He was screaming inside.

As he exited through the garage, he remembered himself and his mate putting on all that snow gear to go out and take care of the shutters. Then he recalled Qhuinn being up on the ladder and stopping to look over his shoulder to the forest—as if he'd sensed something. But there was no way he could have caught the scent of his brother. The wind had been hitting the front of the house. Anything in the trees, especially from that kind of distance? Wouldn't have carried to them.

Strange.

Blay took the back door out into garden, and as he emerged, he glanced over at the shutters they'd fixed. Then he closed his eyes. It was a while before he was able to dematerialize.

When he re-formed, it was on the front steps of his parents' house, and he realized that he hadn't texted them that he was visiting on purpose. The last time he and Qhuinn had had problems, he'd come here—and his return tonight suggested they were back in the soup, as the saying went.

No reason to shine a bright light on that possibility.

Or . . . reality was more like it.

He did get out his phone now, though. It took him

three tries to get the breezy, conversational tone right. Then he pressed send, pocketed the Samsung, and rang the—

"Son!" Rocke said as he whipped the door open. "You know you can just walk in."

His sire was just the same as always, wearing his favorite cardigan, khaki pants, and worn leather slippers. With his pipe in one hand and reading glasses on his nose, he looked like he could have been ordered out of the Dad Catalog.

Blay smiled. "I didn't want to intrude."

"Don't be silly. I'm just paying bills in the den, and *mahmen* is making bread." Rocke laughed. "We sound like something in a Hallmark movie. From the fifties."

Blay tried to imagine he and Qhuinn after the child-rearing was done, the two of them rattling around a big house in a happy decline that was going to take a lot of time, living for visits from the grandkids.

He would love that. He would really love that.

"So how are you, son," Rocke said as they embraced. "How's Qhuinn?"

"We're as good as you could expect." And he supposed that wasn't a lie. "It's really hard."

"I can imagine." Rocke squeezed his shoulder as he

hipped the door shut. "We're so sorry, your *mahmen* and I."

As pain lanced through his chest, Blay rubbed his sternum. "Thanks, Dad. Oh, wow, smell that."

"Your *mahmen* is making stew as well."

"You know, I think I'm hungry."

"Good thing. She's going to want to feed you. She always does."

The stuff about the hunger was, in fact, a lie, but he had hope that his *mahmen*'s cooking would wake his stomach up. But even if it didn't, he had other familiar comforts to sink into. On the way toward the aroma, his father started in with what Blay had always considered the six o'clock newscast for the family: Updates on his shipbuilding, the cooking course the two of them were taking, a distant cousin's impending graduation from online human college.

"—really great what they can do with remote learning," Rocke was saying as they entered the kitchen. "Look who's here!"

Blay's *mahmen* paused in the midst of kneading. "So I sensed! I would have come out, but I'm knee-deep in—well, you get it. Actually, I think it's more my elbows. Anyway, come give me a kiss, my son."

It was amazing how he regressed to full-on *mahmen*'s boy whenever he was around her—and like the dutiful young he was, and had always been, Blay went right over and kissed the cheek that was presented to him.

"Now, go in there." She pointed across to the refrigerator with a flour-dusted hand. "Second shelf, in a Tupperware container, is the quiche I served for First Meal. There's fresh fruit next to it, and I want you to make yourself some toast. The bread is over there. You're too thin."

Annnnnnd that was how his *mahmen* communicated: *I love you, I'm so sorry about Luchas, I'm worried about you, and I hope you know that you and Qhuinn are welcome here anytime.*

Rocke shook his head with a smile and went over to the coffee machine. "You better do what she says, or she'll make you have seconds before you have firsts."

"Don't forget to put a place mat down," she said as she went back to work with the dough. "And Rocke, that coffee needs to be lighter than we like it. He doesn't want it too strong."

"Yes, ma'am," Rocke replied with a wink.

There was light conversation as Blay followed instructions, outing the broccoli-and-cheese quiche and the mixed fruit, making himself up a plate, and sitting down—with toast and a place mat—at the table.

As he dug in, he nodded in the right places, laughed when he was meant to, shared surface updates. And yet there was no elephant in the room. At no point did he feel like he couldn't talk about what had happened, and he didn't feel like he was hiding how sad he was.

It was the very best commentary on his parents, he supposed: That he could be honest friends with the people who raised him. And there was the temptation to stay over day, mostly because he was so exhausted with the silent tension between him and Qhuinn.

God, he was so tired.

And lonely.

"Would you like seconds?" Lyric asked as she put the dough back into its bowl and covered it with a damp dish towel.

Blay looked down at his clean plate. "Yes, *Mahmen*. Please."

CHAPTER TWENTY-EIGHT

After Qhuinn worked out down in the training center, he took a shower in the facility's locker room and then changed into surgical scrubs because he'd forgotten to bring an extra set of clothes with him. As he stepped back out into the corridor, he had a thought that he should go up to the big house. Blay was off for the evening, and maybe they could try and find each other.

Or, more likely, he would just stay lost.

He didn't know what to do with himself. There was a gray fog between him and everybody else, including his mate and his kids. Even when someone was standing in front of him, they were merely an outline of themselves, and their voice, no matter how familiar, was a whisper off in the distance. It was the strangest phenomenon, and the disassociation reminded him of when he'd gone up to the Fade, the landscape all indistinct, no one else around him.

Then again, he felt like he'd died last week, too.

Turning to the right, he looked down toward the office and tried to imagine himself walking into the mansion. As his temples started to pound, he shook his head and went in the opposite direction. When he got to his brother's door, he pushed his way in and—

"What are you doing here?" he said as he stopped short.

Over in the armchair, sitting there like he owned the place . . . was Zsadist. As usual, the brother was dressed in leathers and a muscle shirt, his powerful arms on display, his hair freshly buzzed, his long legs crossed at the knees.

His eyes were glowing yellow, not black like when he was going to go off at someone. But they were narrow and they were focused on Qhuinn with a hard edge.

"Come in," he ordered. "And shut the door."

"This is my brother's room. Don't tell me what to do in it."

"Your brother's dead. So this is not his room anymore."

"What did you say." Qhuinn felt a hot flush go through him. "What the fuck did you say—"

"Get in here, and shut the fucking door. Unless you want everyone in the goddamn training center to hear what I'm about to say to you."

Qhuinn's body stepped forward before he was aware of entering. And he shoved the door closed—

"Shut up." Zsadist's eyes never wavered and he didn't blink. "Your brother is dead and that is a tragedy. But you're not bringing him back with this withdrawal shit."

"Excuse me—"

"You're not talking. I am. You respond when I'm done. And before you get all hot and bothered, you think I want to be sitting here, going through this with you? Yeah, you can miss me with that."

"So get up and leave." Qhuinn tossed a casual hand. "In fact, please do us both a favor and quit it before you start. I don't need the public service."

"Yeah, you do."

It was at that point that Qhuinn realized there was something in the brother's hand . . . a toy airplane, one with red and white markings and a spinning prop on its nose. And in response to Qhuinn taking notice, Z flicked the propeller with his fingertip and the blades went for a ride, blurring out for a moment before slowing down so that the two fins became distinct again.

The shit was so random it temporarily distracted him.

"I've been where you are right now," Z stated, "and not for a couple of nights or a month. Or even a year. Try a hundred years."

Qhuinn opened his mouth to fuck that off—except then he noted the slave bands that were tattooed on Z's wrists and around his neck . . . and the scar that ran down the brother's face.

Z raised one eyebrow. Like he was challenging Qhuinn to say something about whose burden had been greater. And yeah, being imprisoned, sexually abused, and used as a blood source for a century? You could argue that was a trump card.

"This is not a competition about pain," Z said. "And I'm not downplaying your loss."

"Sounds like you're doing both, actually."

"Who the fuck else has a chance to get through to you other than me? Huh? Anybody but me, you'd either snow or walk out on. My past doesn't allow you to do that, so I'm here and you're going to listen to me."

Glancing over his shoulder, Qhuinn eyed the door—and knew he wasn't leaving. And he hated that the brother was right about that.

When he looked back, Z shrugged. "Why do you think the only therapist I've ever had is one who's been through terminal cancer. Like I said, I've been where you are, so I know what's going to get through to you."

With a curse, Qhuinn rubbed his head. "Look, I'm not going to argue with you that I'm struggling. But it's been seven nights. Seven. You think maybe you could give me a little more leeway, here? Like a month, maybe?"

"The longer you stay where you are," Z declared in a low voice, "the harder it is to come back. I still fight every night to stay connected, stay here—" He pointed to the floor. "Stay present. What brought me back was love, but my situation was different than yours. I had nothing to lose and nobody but my twin in my life. You, on the other hand, have everything to lose—a mate who loves you, young who need you, people who require your contribution to a concerted effort. So you have to start coping, whatever that looks like to you."

Qhuinn rolled his eyes and shrugged. "Sure. I'll get right on that. No problem—"

"I'm not diminishing your loss. It's about coping with it—because, FYI, the shit never goes away."

"I *am* coping."

"Fine, you want to play footsie with the words? You're coping *badly*."

Qhuinn jabbed his thumb toward the bed. "I haven't followed in his footsteps. I haven't killed myself. So give me some credit, why doncha."

"If that's your standard, you've got a ways to go before 'functioning well' is anywhere near your zip code." Z spun the toy's prop again, a little hissing noise rising up from the plane's tip. "Let's go through the checklist, shall we? You're not at meals, you're working out too much, and you have bags under your eyes you could pack for an over-day in, so you're clearly not sleeping."

Qhuinn shook his head. "Fuck you, I've been to Last Meal at least three times."

"Out of fourteen meals served in the dining room. Congratulations." As Qhuinn opened his mouth, that eyebrow rose again. "Do you really want to debate the facts? We can waste some time with that, but it's just going to prolong the ass kicking."

Crossing his arms, Qhuinn stared off at the wall. "Say your piece. And then I'm leaving."

"Figure out how to cope." Z shrugged. "That's the

message. That's it. Figure out what works for you and do it. But you can't keep going, night after night, day after day, stuck in neutral. The work is going to have to be done, and—" As Qhuinn cranked open his mouth again, Z cut him off. "Nope, I finish, then you go. The work is going to have to be done, and you need to do it not just for yourself, but for your kids and that mate of yours, too. It's not just for you. You do it for them as well."

Qhuinn waited, expecting more.

"Figure out how to cope," Z repeated. "That's it."

"Oh, sure. That's it."

"I'm not saying it's easy. Trust me. I went through hell while I was held as a blood slave. And then I went through hell all over again when I started talking about what had been done to me. But at least the second trip through got me to a better place."

To avoid those clear yellow eyes, Qhuinn walked around, pacing back and forth from the bed to the door. Then he took a trip through the bathroom for shits and giggles.

And still the brother sat there in that chair.

"Why," Qhuinn asked as he came out again. "Why are you doing this to me."

He hated the capitulation in his voice. But like he could change it? Like he could change any part of this?

"You mean aside from my impeccable credentials when it comes to being fucked in the head?" Z twirled the prop again and swooshed the plane around in circles. "Don't you remember our little ride together on FUBAR Airlines? If you hadn't flown me out of that abandoned *lesser* induction site in that piece of shit we found in the hangar? I'd have died. So I owe you."

Qhuinn closed his eyes and remembered that death flight. And what else had happened that night when they'd searched those cabins. "That was when I found Luchas."

"I know. Which is the other reason I'm sitting here in his chair."

"You said he was dead. That none of this was his anymore."

"I said the room isn't his. This chair is."

"Splitting hairs."

"Don't deflect."

The two of them stared at each other for the longest time. And stupidly, Qhuinn kept waiting for the brother to back down, look away, maybe apologize for his tone, even if his content was on point. When none of that happened, Qhuinn didn't want to be the one who flagged out first.

So they just stared.

In the end . . . well, big surprise, he was the one

who cracked. He lowered his eyes, but to make it look like it was just because he'd decided to sit on his brother's bed, he went over . . . and sat at the foot of his brother's bed.

"I don't know what else to do," he said with a defeat he hated.

"So just do something, anything."

"Isn't that the name of a movie?"

"You should ask Rhage that question, not me."

There was a long period of silence. "Can I be honest?" Qhuinn asked.

"With me? Always."

"I'm afraid to know why he did it. I'm afraid it was my fault in some way. And you know, I can live with his death if I have to, but I couldn't live with . . ."

As his voice failed him, he tried to gather the reins, but the next thing he knew he was weeping so hard his back was in on the sobbing, his whole torso wracked with pain. And while he cracked wide open, Z stayed where he was in that armchair, a silent witness to the active mourning.

It turned out the brother was right.

Given everything Z had been through, Qhuinn didn't feel embarrassed or self-conscious—and strangely, if the brother hadn't been there, he wouldn't have released the pain.

Also, if Z had come over and touched him in any way, or said a word, or tried to get help, Qhuinn would have zipped himself up tight—and probably never reopened again.

But the brother not only had a point about the credibility he possessed, he had the sense to know that this solo journey didn't need any intrusions.

It did, however, require a trailhead.

And maybe a guide.

Or two.

CHAPTER TWENTY-NINE

Quhinn's emotional storm passed, as all storms, no matter how strong and overwhelming they might be, did.

And in the aftermath of his breakdown, as he stood in his brother's bathroom and rinsed his hot face with cold water, he felt like he'd been on a long, exhausting trip. One that had lasted months.

He was that tired, and that discombobulated.

When he stepped back out and looked across at Z, the brother was exactly where he had been, still with the toy airplane, big body lounging in the armchair.

"Sorry about that," Qhuinn said as he made another pass of his face with his palm.

Z lifted a brow. "Really. You're going to apologize."

Qhuinn shrugged and tried to ignore the fact that his eyeballs felt like they had sand in them. "I don't know . . . how to handle this. Any of it."

"That's okay." Z clapped his thigh with his free hand and got to his feet. "But there's no apologizing. You do that when you've offended someone or pissed them off, neither of which you've done to me. You also do it when you have some kind of control over your actions—and trust me, like I don't know you'd have avoided that if you could have?"

"Guess I'm an open book to you." Qhuinn looked around the room like there were windows he might be able to see out of. "I'm really not sure what to do now, by the way."

"That's part of how it works." Z came over and held out the toy airplane. "Anytime you're lost, I want you to look at this. You piloted us both back home that night. And you're going to do it again. I believe in you."

"You really haven't given me anything to go on, by the way."

"Everyone is different. The path back is not going to be the same for you as it was for me."

"How did you start?"

"I opened my heart to someone who loved me. And then I opened my mouth to somebody who cared—and who was more than just a concerned friend."

"I don't want to talk to Mary. I mean, I love Rhage's *shellan* and all, and I know she's a trained social worker, but I don't want to have to sit across from my therapist at meals, thank you very much."

"You think it's going to be any easier with a stranger? And fuck off with the excuses. I don't see you skirting work anywhere else in your life. Don't start the lazy now, and certainly not about this."

Whatever, Qhuinn thought. He didn't want to fucking talk to anyone. But he was too tired from the crying jag to fight the point.

"What else can I do?" he prompted.

"Do the hardest thing first. Whatever you think is the hardest . . . get it out of the way."

After a moment, Qhuinn took the toy that was being offered to him. "Where did you get this? It has small parts, so I know it didn't come from the playroom."

"I ordered it off Amazon." As Qhuinn looked surprised, the brother shrugged. "I can do things like that, you know. I'm not just a brooding cloud."

"So you planned this."

"Five nights ago. I figured I'd give you a week. Seemed as arbitrary an anniversary as any other, and it was a helluva lot better than a month or a year."

Qhuinn looked at the brother's slave bands. "It was you. You were the one who was holding me back from Lassiter that night I went after him. I saw your . . . you know, tattoos . . . out of the corner of my eye."

"That fallen angel's the only savior we've got, son." Z went over to the door. "Besides, if he's a trend? We lose him and the universe is going to send us Bozo the Clown next."

"But that's the problem. Lassiter isn't in the savior business."

"I think the question is more . . . who was he supposed to save that night."

"FYI, it was the one who went out in the blizzard," Qhuinn said bitterly.

Z just shrugged and pointed to the airplane. "Anytime you doubt yourself, look at that. And you can always come and find me, day or night."

After the brother left, Qhuinn stared at the toes of his shitkickers. He hated to break the news to the fighter, but he hadn't been all that helpful.

Figure out how to cope.

Yeah, like that was a map with clear markings. It

was as specific as someone standing on the shores of the Old Country, and pointing west to say, *Yeah, the New World is over thataways a little bit.*

Qhuinn went across to the chair, took a load off, and spun the propeller on the toy plane. As the thing fell into a blur, he thought of the nature of travel and destinations. Then he thought of all the things a person could buy on Amazon. Luggage. Extra socks and underwear. Hiking boots, hats, and gloves.

You couldn't buy a real airplane, but who knew what the future might hold. Maybe in another decade, a person could have an eco-friendly bi-wing land on their front yard. For seventy-five thousand easy payments of $12,798.99. Free financing if you pay it off in under fifty years—

Qhuinn frowned as he realized the weird riff his brain was going off on was normal for him. It was the kind of shit his mind did whenever he had downtime, his thoughts just making up little stupid hypotheticals about absolutely nothing important.

Maybe it was a sign he was coming back some.

He glanced over to the bed and remembered curling in on himself and wailing. Man, he'd fucking lost it.

So no, absolutely not—he was *not* going hard into the therapy. Or even lightly. Z could keep all that shrink-couch bullcrap with the Kleenex box and the stories of Mommy and Daddy and how everyone had been mean to him because of his fucked-up eyes. He was not going to talk about that shit—and certainly not going to ... what was the term? ... oh, right, "unpack" the night of his brother's death and how he'd felt as he'd gone from place to place, each time expecting to see the male and being let down, the ever more violent spikes of fear bungee-cording him around in his own skin.

Nope. He wasn't cracking again.

But he was willing to buy in to Z's cope stuff. The question was where to begin, and maybe it made him a pussy, but he couldn't start with the hardest thing. That ... he just could not manage. He did know that the brother was right, though. He couldn't just stay in this limbo.

As he considered various possibilities, it was hard to know exactly when the plan hit him, but he took out his phone and—

Blay had texted him. To let him know that he'd gone to see his parents.

Qhuinn let his head fall back against the armchair's cushioned contours. With a fresh wave of sadness, he pictured that lovely house Rocke and Lyric had built after the raids, the one set all the way in the back of that human development, by a pond. It was a new-built designed to look old, and Lyric had made it clear that she wasn't thrilled with that part of things. Rocke, on the other hand, loved having all of the mechanicals under warranty.

In a lot of ways, the couple was old-fashioned, the traditional sex roles not just embraced years before, but lovingly maintained: Rocke earned the money and paid the bills; Lyric cooked and cleaned; and their home, no matter what house it was encapsulated in, was always warm, inviting, and serene.

He thought of the twins. The good news was that they could choose who they wanted to be. After all, traditional roles were fine, if they weren't forced. He didn't want either of his kids locked into any kind of social rules or expectations. He'd had plenty of that growing up—and the failures he'd racked up, though in large part nothing he'd had any control over, had nearly killed him.

Qhuinn glanced back to the bed. Refocusing, he called up a blank text message, and then tried to figure out what he was trying to say.

In the end, he could only plainly state his request of Vishous.

Not all journeys were literally on foot. Whether they were or were not, however, there was always a first step. And after that?

Qhuinn looked across to the rolling tray.

Abruptly, he frowned. Figuring he was seeing things, he got up and went over . . . to inspect the two burgundy bundles that had been left on the bedside table, next to the remote to the TV, the call button for the nurse's station, and a blue Bic pen.

Which undoubtedly had been the writing instrument used by Luchas when he'd composed his last letter—which remained unopened, exactly where it had been left.

Qhuinn reached out and picked up one of the burgundy wads. Unfurling it, he saw that it was a sock, a cashmere-and-silk-blend sock.

He recognized whose it was, but he checked the tag that had been sewn inside anyway.

"Blaylock," he said softly.

◆ ◆ ◆

Blay returned to the mansion right before Last Meal. He'd ended up helping his *mahmen* in the basement for hours, rearranging plastic tubs of seasonal clothes, family mementos, and decorations. It had been pretty clear from the outset that there was a make-work component to the effort, but he'd been so grateful for the distraction and the parameters of the job. The project had a beginning, a middle, and an end, and it required not only physical effort, but just enough mental concentration that he couldn't juggle the tasks at hand along with worrying about Qhuinn.

There had even been a break for another meal in the middle, and a cup of satisfaction cocoa, as his *mahmen* always called it, at the end.

He had wanted to stay the day, especially after Qhuinn had not responded to his text about where he was going. But Wrath had called a meeting, and however brokenhearted Blay was, his duty to his King was a responsibility he was honor- and duty-bound to carry out.

Hitting the grand staircase, he was fifteen minutes early, so there was time to put his coat away and gather his thoughts. He didn't have to worry about running into Qhuinn. The male would be downstairs in Luchas's room. That was where he always went after he worked out, and for the last four nights, he had stayed there until well after Last Meal.

Blay had tried not to take the withdrawal personally. And failed.

At the top of the stairs, he looked through the open doors of Wrath's study. The Brothers were already gathering, and he lifted his hand in greeting. Several nodded in his direction, and he flashed them a pair of fingers, the universal language for: *I'll be back in two minutes.*

Maybe Qhuinn would join them all tonight.

Maybe Santa Claus was real.

Heading down the Hall of Statues, Blay stripped off his parka and then zipped up both of the side pockets so his gloves didn't fall out. As he opened the door to his room, the familiar scent that greeted him was fresh, not faded . . . and the male who was sitting on the edge of the bed was not a ghost.

Blay stopped dead.

"Hi," the figment, who certainly seemed to be Qhuinn, said. In the correct voice.

Blay stepped in and closed the door. "Hi."

"I, ah, I've been waiting for you."

Keeping a recoil of surprise to himself was a difficult camo job. "You should have called. Or texted. I would have come right away."

"I didn't want to interrupt your visit. How are the 'rents?"

For some reason, the fact that Qhuinn was using the casual term he always did felt like some kind of positive portent. Which was nuts.

"They're good. They send their love—and their condolences."

"I appreciate that." Qhuinn looked at his hands. "Listen, I just want to apologize—"

"Please don't move out—"

They both stopped. And said "What?" at the same time.

"Look," Blay rushed in, "I'm trying to give you the space you require. I really just . . . want to be whatever you need at this tough time. But please, don't give up on me. Don't give up on us."

And don't hate me for my role in your brother's death, he tacked on to himself.

When there was only silence coming back at him, Blay cleared his throat and hugged his parka to his chest. "I'll . . . I mean, I can leave, if you want me to, and go back to my parents—"

Qhuinn burst up from the bed and came over. And the next thing Blay knew, they were holding on to each other, the first physical contact in what felt like forever.

"I've missed you," Qhuinn said roughly.

Blay squeezed his eyes closed. "I've been here all along."

"I know. I've been the one who was gone."

They stayed where they were for a while. Maybe it was long as a year. And then Qhuinn stepped back. For a moment, tension coiled up Blay's spine, making him stand even straighter. But come on, you didn't tell someone you've missed them and then say you're leaving.

Right?

Oh, and fuck that meeting in Wrath's study. The Brotherhood could come and drag him out of here kicking and screaming if they wanted to: Under any circumstances other than that hog-tied hypothetical, he wasn't moving from the room.

"Come here," Qhuinn said.

As Blay felt his hand get taken, he was content to be led anywhere—just as long as Qhuinn wanted him to stick around. And yes, that was pathetic. But he was feeling like this whole unexpected meet-and-greet was like having a bump on your arm and going to see the doctor about it—only to discover that the person in the white coat with the medical degree actually wasn't all that worried it was cancer.

His brain had sure been convinced the freckle was stage-seventy terminal.

They sat down together, and then Qhuinn reached over and picked something off the bedside table—

It was the letter.

From Luchas.

Next to which were the socks Blay had worn the night the remains had been found, the ones that had been left wet when Lassiter had warmed his frost-bitten feet and dried his ruined loafers, a pair of after-thoughts that had ultimately been forgotten.

"I found those in my brother's room," Qhuinn said.

Blay put his hands up. "As I told you, I didn't touch anything. Not one thing. I saw the letter and left."

"I know." Qhuinn picked up the envelope, holding it in his palms as if it were in danger of shattering. "I talked to Manny earlier tonight. He said you told him no one but me was to go into that room."

"It's your private family business." Blay ran a hand through his hair and glanced around at all the neat-as-a-pin, vacuum-and-dusted. "I love the *doggen* here, they're so wonderful—but sometimes they're almost too good at their jobs. I thought it was important that everything be exactly the way it was left for you."

"I really appreciate that." Qhuinn looked over, his blue and green eyes luminous. "And I've decided to do the hard thing first, after all."

"What?"

"I, ah, I wanted to open this with you. If that's okay?"

As Blay's throat tightened, he swallowed with difficulty. "Absolutely."

He might as well learn the truth about his complicity at the same time Qhuinn did. But more than that . . . Qhuinn's stare had dropped back down to the envelope, and it was clear he was terrified—and the fact that he was letting his fear show was so significant. The male didn't share that shit with just anybody.

"It's hard to explain why I've left this for as long as I have," Qhuinn murmured as he stroked over the two words on the front. "But this is my last piece of business with Luchas. Whatever he wrote is our final . . . thing."

Blay nodded, but stayed silent.

"Did I ever tell you about *Seinfeld*?" Qhuinn asked. "Or *The Office*?"

"The, ah, the TV shows, you mean?"

"Yeah." Qhuinn took a deep breath. And then laughed a little. "Not *The Sopranos*, though. That I couldn't resist."

Blay put his parka aside and rubbed his eyes. "I'm so sorry, but I'm not following here?"

Qhuinn turned the letter over so that the flap that had been glued shut was face-up. "I have this weird thing about my favorite TV shows that have ended. I did it for *Home Improvement*, too, come to think about it. See, I refuse to watch the last season. It's this weird thing. Like, back when we had DVDs? I always kept the last season in its wrapper." His thumb went back and forth on the flap. "That way they're never finished, you know? I can pretend in my mind that they go on forever, that they're infinite—because the definition of infinity is no ending. And if I don't watch the ending there hasn't been one." There was a pause and Qhuinn looked up. "That's nuts, right?"

"Not at all." Blay wanted to stroke the male's back, but kept his hands clasped in front of him. "It makes all the sense in the world."

"Now you're just humoring me."

"No, I'm really not."

A ghost of a smile hit Qhuinn's lips, but was quickly lost. "I feel the same way about whatever's in here. As long as I don't read it, my brother isn't gone. Because that's how it works with people, you know? The folks I live with, you, the kids, Layla and Xcor, everybody else in the household . . . I mean, I have countless unfinished conversations, and pool games that need to be played to even out scores, and meals that are up and coming, and nights out in the field. It's all in the middle. We're all in the middle because we're all alive. And there's power in the middle. There's power and potential and this weird, illusory stability that feels so permanent, even though it isn't because any one of us can die at any time. Yet because death happens so rarely, we get used to the middle. We take the middle for granted. We only see how beautiful, how magical . . . how tenuous it is . . . when the end comes."

Qhuinn tapped the envelope in his palm. "When the end comes, the fog of habit lifts, and only then do we see how rare and special the landscape of the in-between is."

After a moment of silence, the male laughed awkwardly. "I'm babbling, aren't I."

Blay shook his head. In a rough voice, he said, "No, you're really not."

They both took a deep breath. Maybe it was for the same reason, maybe for different reasons, but that was the nice thing about being with someone you loved. Often, you came to the same corner, even if it was from opposite directions.

"So . . ." Qhuinn tapped the envelope again. "What do you say we open this . . . together."

As that mismatched stare lifted to Blay's, he did what he had been wanting to do. He put his hand on his mate's back and made a slow circle—that he hoped was as reassuring as he intended it to be.

Some seminal moments were anticipated: Births, matings . . . deaths, too. As well as anniversaries and festivals, graduations and fresh starts. Yet some of the most important moments in your life crept up on you, no less revelatory or significant for their lack of advance notice and fanfare.

This was one of the most significant moments in Qhuinn's life: And he'd waited, maybe for hours, just so Blay could come home and share it with him.

Blay meant to hold the words in, as he still wasn't sure where they stood. But the emotion in the center of his chest chose its method of expression—and it was a conventional one. Tried and true.

"I love you so much," Blay said in a voice that cracked.

Qhuinn lifted his hand up, the hand that had been on the letter his brother had written. And as he brushed at the side of Blay's face, it was tenderly.

"Don't cry," Qhuinn whispered.

"Am I?"

Qhuinn nodded. "I'm going to try to get through this. I don't know what I'm doing, though, and I don't know how long it's going to take."

Blay put his hand over Qhuinn's, and then he kissed that palm. "However long you need, I will wait. Whatever you want from me, I will do. Wherever you go, I will be right there with you. If you still want me like that."

Those beautiful blue and green eyes closed. "I love you so much right now, too."

Instantly, all of the tension disappeared, not just in Blay's own body, but in the air between them. What had been stuck was now unjammed, and the release was so great, Blay trembled.

The kiss they shared was soft. Reverent. More of a vow than anything else.

And then they eased apart, and both stared down at the letter.

Dear God, Blay thought. He hoped that what was in there . . . didn't drive them apart all over again.

CHAPTER THIRTY

Quinn's hands started to shake as he eased a finger under the envelope's flap. There was a lot of resistance, and somehow he wasn't surprised that his brother had taken care to make sure it was properly sealed. Luchas was precise like that.

Had been precise like that.

Opening the envelope slowly, Qhuinn pulled out . . . a single sheet of eight-and-a-half-by-eleven copier paper. The page had been folded in thirds, and there was only writing on one side—and at first, his eyes just focused on the handwriting. The pen was the same Bic that had been used for *Brother Mine*, the same one that was on the bedside table, and the cursive script was beautiful, flowing, yet easy to read, each letter executed perfectly.

"He had such wonderful penmanship," Qhuinn murmured as he ran his thumb down one of the margins. "And look at how straight the lines are. I don't think he used a ruler. I think he just . . ."

Did it the right way, as he'd been trained.

Before Qhuinn started reading, he had a thought that his brother was so much better than multipurpose office paper. Luchas should have had personalized stationery, embossed with his name and address at the top. Maybe with a pen-and-ink drawing of the family house as a header.

As Qhuinn trained his eyes on the salutation, he considered reading the letter out loud—but his throat was too tight for that. So instead, he leaned forward and moved the sheet of paper so that it was in between him and Blay.

Dearest Brother Mine,

Firstly, allow me to apologize. You have always been far braver than I, and I believe that what is about to happen proves this truism once again. I am sorry that I am not strong enough to continue upon

*this path from which I cannot escape, but I am tired.
I am bone weary of the pain and the restlessness,
and of late, the unchanging nature of my body's
compromises. All has worn me down, whereas you
would have persevered. I am weak, however—and the
biggest regret of this weakness is that in my actions
you may search for, and feel that you find, some sort
of personal culpability. Allow me to assuage your
conscience. This is naught to do with you.*

*Secondly, I beg of you a favor. I realize that this
is an imposition. For certain, if you are reading
this, I am gone and you are in pain. It is entirely
unfair of me to ask anything of you in your current
state, and yet I beg of you this. Please go unto our
family home, and into the confines of my former
bedroom. There is a loose floorboard where my
bureau was. Hidden beneath it is a secret I have
kept. There have been times when I nearly broached
this matter that I have kept to myself, but in the
end, I was too cowardly. I think I also had hope that
I would heal enough to be an advocate for mine own
interests. Alas, that did not come to pass. You will
know what to do.*

*Finally, I need you to believe me when I say
that our parents chose the wrong son of whom to
be proud. I am the failure. You, the paragon. You*

should be so proud of all you have accomplished,
and I wish our sire and mahmen *could see you*
the now. You have proved them all wrong, wholly
wrong. You are a Brother. You are a father. You are
the mate of a wonderful male. You are everything
anyone could have wished for in a son or a brother.

As Fate would have it, my own Honor Guard,
the one that I deserved, came and found me. Those
lessers *and their hateful master were no less than*
I deserved, and they killed me many times. In
retrospect, I believe part of their interest in me
was in the reviving. I, however, intend to finish
this night what they started. I am well done with
resurrections of all sorts and I welcome the abyss. I
am through with the seesaw between life and death.

I love you. I pray that you will believe me when I
say that this choice is mine and mine alone. Perhaps
you are angry at me, maybe you are in sorrow. I
wish for you neither of these. I am just so tired. I
want to sleep.

With my most sincere love and affection,
Luchas

Qhuinn closed his eyes. Then he read it all again.
And a third time. By that last go through, he didn't

even see the words. He simply heard his brother's voice in his head, the sound so missed that his heart skipped beats.

"Are you . . ." He took a deep breath. "Are you finished?"

Next to him, Blay nodded.

"I'm going to put it away now." When his mate nodded again, Qhuinn carefully folded up the page and slipped it back into the envelope. "I wish we could have fixed him. I wish . . . our love had been enough."

And he really wished he could have had a conversation about that night he had come home to their parents' house to learn that he'd been sent away on purpose because Luchas had been going through his transition. That night when he had removed his makeshift belt and strung it up to the shower head. That night . . . when Blay had arrived in a nick of time.

"You saved me," he murmured. "That night. In my shower."

There was no need to offer further details. They both knew exactly what evening he was referring to: Sure enough, as he looked over at Blay, his beloved was staring off into the distance. No doubt the male was remembering when he'd had to bust down the bathroom door and manhandle Qhuinn off the shower head.

"I am so glad you called me," Blay said roughly.

"I didn't. You called me."

"Did I?"

"You seemed to know." Qhuinn put his hand on Blay's knee. "You've always known."

As Blay's eyes blinked quick, Qhuinn reached for his mate, and then they were stretched out on the bed, their heads on one king-sized pillow, their bodies so close they were ankle to ankle, hip to hip, as they lay on their backs. The letter and its envelope stayed on Qhuinn's chest, over his heart.

"I'm sorry my brother was in such pain," he said. "And I wish . . ."

Blay turned on his side, and it was automatic, to reposition things so that the male was lying in the crook of Qhuinn's arm.

"You wish you could have stopped him that night?"

Qhuinn put his free hand over the letter. "I wish I could have told him it gets better. I've been where he was. Hopeless, helpless. And now look at where I am. I never could have predicted how my life turned out—I certainly wouldn't have hoped for even half of the good things that happened to me. Maybe the same was just around the corner for him. Maybe if he'd held on . . ."

"We'll never know," Blay said sadly. "And neither will he."

"I wish I knew that he got into the Fade."

"That has to be a cautionary tale—that whole 'suicide keeps you out of the Fade' thing has to just be a cautionary tale."

Qhuinn frowned at the ceiling. "Does it? It got started for a reason."

"Your brother was a just male of worth. It wouldn't be fair."

When was life guaranteed to be fair, Qhuinn thought.

He turned his head. Blay was staring off into the distance, his lashes low, his mouth slightly parted, his hair smudged on one side from his having drawn his fingers through it. His cheek, the one that had been cut by that tarp in the storm, was fully healed, nothing marring the smooth skin.

As Qhuinn remembered the two of them in the garage, him armed with a bandana and thoughts of a gurney, Blay batting his hand away from the minor injury . . . he felt a striking warmth in his chest.

The swell of love permeated his body, filling him up from the inside out, replacing the cold numbness that had frozen him in place even as he had moved and breathed and pretended to be among the living.

With reverence, he stretched over and pressed a chaste kiss to his mate's forehead. "I'm so glad you're here with me."

◆ ◆ ◆

As Blay lay beside his mate, he was grateful for a lot of things. For one, there was the fact that he and Qhuinn were actually lying together on their mated bed—and not just in a side-by-side, separated-by-a-duvet-divide sense. And then there was his inclusion in the reading of the letter. He had wanted to be invited into his male's grief so that he could help in some small way, even if it was just by being witness to the pain—and now it appeared that he had been.

Considering where the night had started, miracles had been granted.

And yet he was still feeling like shit. He'd read the note to himself twice, and what stood out to him were not all the reassuring things, the hopes for peace in the midst of the chaos of the choice Luchas had made. It was the reckoning.

Intrinsic in the words, in the decision, was a vista, a long view on where Luchas had been and where he was—followed by an extrapolation of the future that had provided no relief at all. If anything, the more-of-the-same had no doubt been yet another burden on top of so many others.

Whether or not it was true, Blay had decided that his conversation, which surely had been one of Luchas's last, had provided that view. Or at least perhaps the ledge the male had been standing on as he had regarded the valley of his life as it unfurled before him.

God, if Blay could just go back and not have said a thing. Maybe it wouldn't have changed anything, but at least he would be free of this sickening feeling in the pit of his stomach.

"—glad you're here with me."

Blay forced himself back into focus. And as he did, he felt Qhuinn's lips press to his forehead with incredible gentleness. When the male eased back, their eyes met and held.

You may not be holding me responsible, Blay thought to himself. *But I cannot forgive myself.*

"I didn't want any of this for your brother," he said sadly. "I only knew him from afar, as you know. I mean, my family was not on the same level of yours socially—"

"My parents' level, you mean. I wasn't on their level, either."

Blay shook his head. "You're better than all of them."

"You're biased."

"Not even close." Blay ran his fingertips over the envelope on Qhuinn's chest. "And when it came to Luchas, I believe he was a product of his environment, but he wasn't bad through and through. Some in the *glymera* were. He was not."

"He was the one who stopped the Honor Guard from killing me that night I was jumped. He was with them, and he made them quit the beating. Otherwise, I would have died in the middle of that road."

Blay frowned. "Your family sent him as part of . . . but of course they would have. He was the firstborn son."

"So having him be a part of it was the best way for them to save even more face after they banished me from the house and removed me from the family bloodline. It proved how serious they were." Qhuinn frowned. "And you know, I've been wondering about something. That black robe Luchas had been wearing? I've never known him to have one or wear one before. But somehow he got his hands on it—and I think he wore it because of his guilt over his role in the Honor Guard."

"Did he ever talk to you about that night?"

"He said he was sorry, of course. But I didn't know it was still a thing for him . . . I mean, he clearly saw Lash and the *lessers* as his own version of what he did to me. That had to be the reason he was in that robe. But I wish he hadn't tortured himself so."

Blay nodded. And then said, "Are you going back to your old house? Like he asked?"

"I don't know." Qhuinn frowned and shook his head. "I mean, of course I am. It's just going to be fucked up to be there. I wonder what it looks like now."

"Do you want me to go with you?"

"It's too close to dawn now. And aren't you on to-morrow night?"

"I am, but I'm sure I can get someone to cover."

Qhuinn's brows lowered. "I want to return to work. I asked Tohr. He said I needed to be cleared."

"Medically? Oh, right. Mary."

"Yeah."

Blay wasn't going to touch that one with a ten-foot pole—and as much as he wanted to support his mate, he didn't disagree with the necessity of a mental health check-in. But there was no reason to bring all that up.

"What can I do to help you?" he said instead.

"You already are. Just by being here." As Qhuinn

yawned, the male's jaw cracked, and then there was a long exhale. "I'm suddenly exhausted."

"Why don't you go to sleep?"

"Are you tired?"

These were simple questions, simple replies, every-day/every-night stuff. And like the proximity, physical and otherwise, the normal was something to be grateful for, especially as Qhuinn mumbled something about food: He wasn't ready to go down to Last Meal yet, but maybe after a little nap, they could order something from the kitchen? Or at least that's what Blay thought his mate was saying.

"Yes, absolutely," he murmured in response. "And let me get off your shoulder, it's going to go numb."

Lifting his head, he repositioned the heavy arm he'd been leaning on. As he arranged the limb down at Qhuinn's side and the male didn't move, Blay was reminded of the times he'd found Rhamp in a tangle in his crib, face mashed up against the slats, butt in the air, one arm kinked under his body.

As he brought over the pillow he usually used and crammed it under his ear, he stared at Qhuinn.

And worried about what Luchas had tucked away.

If there was one thing Blay had learned about life in Caldwell, there was always another shoe to drop. And a lot of times, it landed on your head.

CHAPTER THIRTY-ONE

Hands.

Hands were moving over Blay's body.

Wait . . . maybe it was only one. And he knew whose it was.

His and Qhuinn's bedroom was dark, the lights having been willed off at some point, and Blay was lying on his stomach. Next to him, Qhuinn was on his side . . . and the male's sensuous palm was traveling across Blay's lower back and sneaking around his opposite hip. With a groan, Blay rolled to his side, his ass finding the front of Qhuinn's pelvis—and the erection that was there.

Maybe this was a dream.

Maybe this . . . which he'd missed for so long . . . was just something his mind had constructed out of sad desperation—

"Is this okay," Qhuinn said in his ear.

"Oh, God . . ." Blay arched back and rubbed against that arousal. "*Please.*"

"I thought I was dreaming."

"So did I."

They were both fully clothed and lying on top of the covers—where they had been when Qhuinn had meant to take a catnap, and Blay had intended on staying awake and worrying about things he couldn't change. No more sleeping now, though.

And for the very best reason.

As Qhuinn arched over, all bonded male, his lips brushed the side of Blay's neck, and then came the fangs, slowly going up his jugular. Twisting his torso, Blay turned his head—and then they were kissing proper, all tongues, and moaning, and breath coming fast . . . while that hand, oh, that hand, found Blay's erection and started to stroke over the fly of his slacks.

Overcome, Blay reared back once again, grinding his ass on Qhuinn until the male cursed low.

"I'm supposed to take it slow," Qhuinn grunted.

"Says who?"

"Oh . . . *fuck* . . ."

The next thing Blay knew, he was being handled roughly—the way he liked. He was shoved on his back, and then Qhuinn straddled his hips, the male's massive body looming in the darkness. With an erotic surge, Blay willed on a lamp across the room, and he was not disappointed with what he saw. His mate was fully aroused, Qhuinn's eyes burning, his face flushed, his huge shoulders blocking out the illumination.

Oh, and then there was the erection tenting up the front of his track bottoms.

"I'm going to fuck you," Qhuinn growled.

Blay's eyes rolled back. "Now. God, now—"

Harsh hands all but demolished his Hermès belt as the thing was whipped out of its loops. And then his fly was treated with no better regard, dragged down roughly with a jerk.

"Do you give a shit about these pants?" Qhuinn asked harshly.

Actually, they were Blay's favorite pair. He'd put them on to cheer himself up. "Not at all—"

Qhuinn's hands clamped on the two sides and he yanked the front apart, the fabric tearing—

Before Blay could start begging, Qhuinn's mouth was right where he wanted it to be, the male sucking his cock, head going up and down, massive arms bowed out on either side. Blay splayed his legs wide and dug his hands into that thick black-and-purple hair. Pumping his hips, he closed his eyes and gave himself up to the pleasure.

Like the reconciliation and the letter-reading, he hadn't expected this. And one thing continued to be true. Sex with his mate was the great eraser. Even with how scrambled his brain was, this made everything recede. All he knew was Qhuinn.

Well, Qhuinn's mouth, specifically.

Popping his lids, Blay lifted his head. His shirt was all wedged up his abs, his pants were nothing but the leg parts, and his mate was—

Blay let out an animalistic sound as Qhuinn's mouth retracted and the tip of Blay's erection popped out from between those lips. Then it was a case of that tongue extending and that piercing flashing silver in the low light. The flicking was unbelievable, every slip and tickle going through to Blay's sac.

He didn't last long.

And that was clearly his lover's plan. Qhuinn opened wide and sucked it all down, taking the shaft and the head, the orgasms, everything. After the release was over? Blay's hips kept pumping into that mouth, over and over again.

Until it was suddenly a very different position.

Without warning, Qhuinn flipped him over onto his stomach, dragged his hips up, and—

The contact was wet and slick, and Blay totally fucking lost it. And then the penetration—deep and thick, plunging in and retreating. Driving in again. Pulling out.

Faster, harder, as Blay kicked the pillows out of the way and bore down into the sex, giving it all up to his mate. To keep himself in place as the onslaught intensified, he gripped the edge of the headboard and worked with the rhythm, hanging on and then pushing back, and hanging on and pushing back.

The smell of dark spices thickened the air, and sweat slicked his body, and the bed was banging, and—

Oops, bedside lamp was on the floor. Fortunately, there wasn't a crash as it landed on the pillows he'd evicted. It also wasn't the one Blay had turned on.

Qhuinn started to growl, and the smacking sounds behind Blay's body got louder, everything going next level. And then his mate started to come, Qhuinn's hips locking in, his cock kicking deep, everything slipping into perfect, blissful alignment.

As Blay closed his eyes and felt his mate's fangs

sink into his shoulder . . . he prayed that this lasted. All of it.

Forever.

And yet even as he reveled in the releases, he still feared the future.

CHAPTER THIRTY-TWO

ind a way to cope.

As Qhuinn stepped out of the Brotherhood's mansion the following evening, that was his mantra. He'd been saying the words over and over again to himself, ever since he'd woken up, naked and sated, in his mate's arms. By mutual agreement, Blay had stayed on rotation, and after they'd eaten First Meal in their room, Blay had left along with the other brothers to go out into the field.

Qhuinn had chilled on his lonesome for a while, just sitting on the bed and holding his brother's letter. Gathering his courage.

And now he was here, standing on the front steps of the big house, the cold air in his nose and his lungs, his body braced even though there was barely a breeze and no challenge to his balance. He wasn't sure he liked where his head was at, his thoughts all disjointed and wired, but he had a feeling that if he waited until he felt more stable about everything . . . ?

It was going to be fucking spring before he made this trip.

Closing his eyes, he thought maybe he wasn't going to be able to dematerialize. Maybe he was going to have to drive—

His corporeal form scattered into its component molecules, and he willed himself to travel off the mountain, over the farmland, past the suburbs . . . to the wealthy part of Caldwell. As he moved through the night air, he wouldn't have been surprised if he spaced where his old house had been. But like that was possible? Just because you wanted to forget something didn't mean you could. In fact, usually the converse was true. The more you needed to bury a memory, a place, a person, the more the shit stuck with you.

His destination reached, he re-formed behind the groundskeeping shed—

"Fuck!"

Qhuinn jumped back at the same time he threw

his hands out in front of his chest. The building he'd very nearly killed himself on was single-storied and super-shingled—and most certainly had never been on the property when he'd lived on it.

"Jesus," he muttered as he looked around.

Had he gotten the wrong address? Nah, that wasn't possible.

Wondering what the hell was wrong with him, he walked to the corner of whatever outbuilding he'd nearly embedded himself in—

Motion-activated lights flared, and he hissed at them as he willed them off with such force that the one that had pegged him right in the eyes exploded up at the roof, smoke rising, glass shattering.

"Fuck, fuck, fuck . . ." He stopped the cursing as he blinked the retina-shock away—and got a look at the back of his family's old house and yard. "What . . . the *fuck?*"

The last time he had been here, there had been formal gardens and a perfectly maintained lawn, along with a back terrace with old school black wrought iron furniture. Now? Everything but the terrace was gone. In its place? A swimming pool you could stage Olympic trials in, a pool house that could shelter a family of six, and half a dozen modern sculptures the size of SUVs.

All of which were the colors of Lassiter's collection

of zebra tights: Neon pink, acid yellow, kryptonite green.

Rubbing his eyes, he was sure his parents were rolling in their graves—and heard his mother's voice, dripping with censure: *All that money in the wrong hands.*

Frankly, he was surprised that the mansion remained intact—

For one piercing moment, he saw it all as it once had been, his *mahmen* walking among the flowers, pointing out the varieties of white blooms to his sister, forcing Solange to memorize the proper Latin names. Behind them, Luchas and their sire would likewise be strolling at a leisurely pace, their hands clasped behind the small of their backs. They were discussing finance. They'd always discussed finance.

In the warmer months, the four of them had walked together after every First Meal, the females in front, males in back, and never the twain shall mix: Solange was never going to learn about money—it was far too above her. And Luchas would never learn about horticulture—it was far too beneath him.

Qhuinn had always watched them promenade in the moonlight from the window in his bedroom.

And yearned to be asked to join, even just once.

Before he got all maudlin, he stopped the

memories—and decided it was a relief that everything on the estate was so different. It made things less complicated.

Setting himself into motion, he stalked across the lawn, his footsteps marring the pristine snow cover—and when he went by one of the sculptures, he knocked his knuckles on the pink surface. The hollow ring suggested it was metal, and he imagined some interior decorator exclaiming the virtues of its random contours and hard corners. Fuck all knew what the design was supposed to represent. Or maybe that was the point.

Closing in on the back of the mansion, he found that he'd been wrong. There had been renovations to the house, too, and they were . . . pretty extensive. Was that a new room out the back? And the terrace—he'd been wrong about it, as well. The old flagstone was all gone, replaced by some kind of sandstone? He couldn't really tell because of the snow cover, but it was clear from what had melted close to the first floor's edge that the tile was totally different.

When he was in range of one of the windows, he cupped his hands and leaned in to see inside.

"Ooooookay."

Beetlejuice. When the Deetzes took over the Maitlands' nice old farmhouse . . . and turned it into a freak show of bad modern artiste crap. No antiques. No beautiful Persian rugs. No grandfather clocks, and oil paintings, and collections of Imari porcelain. In the place of all that had been venerable and cultivated over generations? Steel and leather furniture, black stone floors, and more sculptures that looked like three-dimensional Rorschach tests.

Like that red hand over there? It was a chair, right?

He'd never thought of himself as a traditionalist before, but frankly . . . he wouldn't have given a plug nickel for the lot of it. But their taste was not his problem.

On the contrary, the motion-detector pods mounted in the corners at the ceiling were. The damn things were obvious 'cuz they had little green blinking lights—and they probably had cameras, too.

On that note, there were no doubt monitoring feeds running out here as well.

These were all his fucking problems.

Because he had to get inside.

One advantage of having to wait until twelve for the humans under this roof to hit the sack was that he'd figured out his coping mechanism. Fuck the therapy and the sniveling. He was going to deal with his brother's death through service: Luchas had broken his heart with pain and revived him with a directive. And in honoring the request that had been put to him, Qhuinn had a job, a purpose, a direction into which he was able to channel his sadness and his sense that he could have changed where things had gone if he'd only been more attentive.

So yeah, he was getting into this fucking house and he was going to grab whatever his brother had left behind under that floorboard.

Utterly resolved, he closed his eyes and dematerialized right into the center of the . . . was it the living room? It had been a study before. Now, the place had couches, and again, was that supposed to be a chair? He guessed you could sit on that palm—

Ah, yes. The alarm.

Instantly, a high-pitched, screaming siren lit off, and given all the absolutely-no-rug, and the walls that were bare as a museum backdrop, the sound echoed around like firecrackers had been set off at his feet.

Three . . . two . . . one . . .

A light flared in the front hall, and then a set of heavy footsteps came down the staircase—along with a male voice that was muttering things about having to work in the morning, and stupid alarms, and whatnot.

Qhuinn calmly pivoted toward the noise and put his hands in the pockets of his track bottoms. His leather jacket was zipped up, but he hadn't bothered to strap any weapons on—which okay, fine, probably proved the point that he wasn't ready to go out into the field yet. But he had other issues to deal with at the moment, fuck him very much.

As he waited patiently, the man of the house went in the opposite direction, the footsteps growing dimmer as he headed for the kitchen end of things. Which made Qhuinn wonder. Shouldn't there be a keypad upstairs? A remote?

Somewhere, a phone started ringing. And then there were a series of beeps.

Finally, off in the distance, that male voice started clipping out syllables that were loud enough to hear clearly.

"—no, I don't need the police. I need a technician to come out and fix the keypad in my bedroom and that goddamn motion detector downstairs. It's gone off again—"

The voice and footsteps got louder. And louder.

And then there he was, coming back to the stairs, the master of the house, in a pair of flannel PJs bottoms and a nylon Nike shirt. He was well into his fifties, but he'd had an eyelift and dyed his hair dark, so he could pass for forty at forty feet. No gut. Fairly good shoulders. Was probably eating keto and smoking weed instead of drinking vodka tonics to save on the calories—while he pickled himself with Botox and collagen injections to preserve as much youth as he could.

Probably on his second wife with his second round of kids.

The human stopped with the walk-and-talk.

When the guy's mouth fell open, Qhuinn raised his hand in a little wave. Seemed rude not to offer some kind of greeting.

As the man grabbed hold of the phone with both hands and took a deep breath like he was about to blab on his midnight visitor, Qhuinn wagged his finger. "Yeah, that's a no-no."

He reached into the human's brain and shut down everything. Then he isolated the two-second-old memory of Mr. I Don't Wanna Be Old finding an intruder in his living room—along with the current signals being sent by those peepers that Qhuinn was standing about ten feet away from him.

Next came the marching orders.

Which were kind of fun.

The man cleared his throat. And then started speaking into the phone calmly, his eyes locked on Qhuinn. "Oh, sorry. No, everything's fine. Like I said, it's just that malfunction again. But please, I'd like to have a technician out whenever is convenient. I'm happy to work around your schedule."

As there was a pause, like the alarm company rep had been unprepared for the change in attitude, Qhuinn was glad he'd tacked on some polite shit as a public service. He had a feeling the guy was one of those self-made sonsabitches who was a fucking prick to people.

"Thanks," the man said to the Jake from State Farm equivalent. "That'll be great. And I really appreciate your help. Of course, I'd love to take your customer satisfaction survey. Just send it to my email. Thanks again. Bye."

The human ended the call. Lowered the portable phone from his ear. And stood there like a robot waiting for instructions on whether he was cleaning the floor or about to do a load of laundry.

"Can I ask you something?" Qhuinn rolled his eyes at himself. "Stupid question. I could ask you for your bank accounts right now."

"Do you need them? They're on my computer upstairs."

"Nah, I'm good. You paid me seven million for this place about a year ago."

"I paid you? So this was your house."

"My parents', actually. How you likin' the place?"

"It's good. I like it fine. It needed updating."

"Well, you've certainly left your mark on it." Qhuinn indicated the phone, which was an old school cordless. "My question is, why you still got a landline, my guy? You don't have the alarm wired into your cell? For like, the security feeds?"

The man's shoulders drooped and he rolled his eyes. "My daughter threw my iPhone in the toilet tonight."

"Bummer. How old is she?"

"Three."

"Cool. Hey, do you know about the rice trick? You put the phone in a plastic baggie full of the stuff. It works. Or you could just buy another."

"I'm going to get another one—"

"Ron?" a female voice called down. "Is someone there?"

As Qhuinn shook his head, "Ron" yelled back, "No. It's just me on the phone with the alarm company. Go back to bed."

"It's cold," came the petulant response. "You need to come back up here."

Like good ol' Ron was her electric blanket.

"Ron?" she repeated.

"Give me a minute, honey." The tone was level, but

the expression was tight, like he was gritting his molars. "I'll be right there."

"You know," Qhuinn murmured, "I don't envy your life, my guy."

Ron took a deep breath and lowered his volume, too. "The three-year-old wants to sleep with us all the time. Susie had to get her mommy-tuck redone two weeks ago. And I think my partner is stealing from the firm."

"Wow. When was the last time you got high?"

"Three hours ago. It's the only way I can shut everything up."

"So I was right."

"About what?"

"Doesn't matter." Qhuinn shrugged. "Well, as much as I've liked talking to you here, Ronnie boy, I've got work to do. So you need to go upstairs and tell your wife again that everything's fine. It's nothing. And then you're going into your office, and you're going to delete the security feeds from tonight. Let's say, from eleven forty-five to two a.m. After that? You go to sleep. Oh, and when that alarm technician shows up here, don't be a fucking douche, 'kay? You got a lotta things going for you, there's no reason to be rude."

"Okay. I won't be. Promise."

"Attaboy, Ron."

"Thank you."

"You're so welcome."

The man nodded and turned away. As he shuffled off, he walked like a man whose lower back hurt. Or maybe it was all those miles running on those fifty-six-year-old knees.

A moment later, there were footfalls ascending the stairs, and then a door shutting. And then more footfalls overhead, walking into another part of the house.

Good ol' Ron, following directions.

Bracing himself yet again, Qhuinn went out into the front hall, and found more of the same decor, the modern, black-and-white, strange-art theme like a rash on a body. Everywhere.

Pausing, he looked to the wall where the big-ass mirror had always hung, the one where guests could check their appearance when they arrived, or his parents could inspect their own whenever they left. Such mirrors were standard issue for *glymera* houses. Always right by the front entry.

No mirror anymore.

Now? It was a picture of four hubcaps. That probably cost more than a Lambo.

Unbelievable.

Qhuinn mounted the steps one at a time. Funny, when he'd thought about coming here, he'd imagined himself rushing through the rooms and the hallways, all scrambled and freaking out. Not it. Instead, he took his time, looking at the weird shit hanging along the staircase's wall—he was pretty sure it was a school of taxidermied goldfish, except they had Barbie heads on them?

What a transformation.

And it was not hard to find a metaphor in all of it. When he'd been here with his parents, he'd assumed everything in the house, like his destiny, had been un-alterable. Not true, as it turned out.

When he got to the head of the stairs, he looked to the right. Just more barren black-and-white floors, and stuff on the walls that could have been created by first-graders. Then he turned to the left. Luchas's bedroom was all the way down at the far end. As the preferred son, he'd been given the second-best-appointed suite in the house, behind only the master and mistress's.

God, his chest hurt, he thought as he started walk-ing again.

When he got to his brother's door, he glanced down at his feet to gather himself—only to have a chilling thought when he focused on the hall's glossy tiles. Mother . . . *fucker*. That hiding space of his brother's. When they'd redone his room, had they pulled up the floorboards, too—

He shoved the door open. And let his head fall back. "Shit."

The whole room was black and white. Including the floor, which had been—surprise!—tiled in black marble. Whatever his brother had hidden there, under that old, loose board? Was no doubt gone.

"Whatcha doing, mister?"

At the sound of the squeaky voice, Qhuinn cranked his head around—and had to look down again. Standing in the hall, in a *Frozen* nightgown, was a human young of about five or six. So not the one who'd sunk the phone in the loo.

The little girl was staring up at the intruder in her house without any fear. "That's my older brother's room," she said.

Qhuinn cleared his throat. "It was my older brother's, too."

"Really?"

"Uh-huh."

As she tilted her head to the side, her hair, which was the color of Ron's, moved over her tiny shoulder.

After a moment, she said with suspicion, "Are you allowed to be here, mister?"

CHAPTER THIRTY-THREE

L ook, you need to just go."

As the words were spoken to him, Blay stopped in the middle of the plowed downtown street and looked over at Z.

"I'm sorry?"

They were deep in the field, walking a row of urban apartment houses, all of which were dark and pockmarked with broken windows. There had been nothing enemy-like anywhere to be seen, but that was not to be trusted. Somewhere in the winter moonlight, shadows were lurking, stalking. Taking orders from the new evil.

"You need to go to your boy." The Brother's yellow eyes scanned around. "That's where your head's at."

"No, I'm here."

"Physically." Z focused on him. "Mentally, you're checked out, so you better head back home and see about him. He needs you."

Blay made a show of looking up and down the street, doing the two-can-play thing. As he thought about how to respond, he was aware of Z just staring at him. So yeah, fronting was not going to be his best option, was it.

Clearing his throat, he said, "He's not at home."

"Where is he?"

"He went home."

Z shook his head. "You just said he wasn't there—"

"Sorry, to his old home. His parents' old place."

"Shit."

"But listen, I can still function out here—"

"After the raids, you buried his parents there, didn't you. And his sister. And you think he's okay going back to that property?"

Blay cursed and rubbed his nose. After he sneezed from the cold, he said, "Luchas sent him there on a mission. According to Luchas's note, he left something in his room and he wants Qhuinn to handle it."

Putting his hands on his hips, Z closed his eyes. Then he cursed and activated the communicator on his shoulder. "Tohr, we're taking ten. I'll check in when we're ready to resume."

Blay started waving his arms. "No, really, I can just—"

There was a soft hiss. Then Tohr's voice: "Roger that. I'm shifting V and Butch over to your quadrant."

"Thank you." Zsadist released the communicator and stared across levelly. "Where are we going? I know what happened at the house, but I never had the address."

Blay linked his arms over his chest and shook his head. "He wanted to go alone. And I'd like to respect that."

"He will be alone."

"No offense, but if we're on the property, that happens how?"

"He doesn't see us." Z leaned in, the ambient light of the city making the black daggers holstered over his heart gleam. "You honestly aren't worried about him?"

"Of course I am. But we lived apart from each other for the last week, even as we were sleeping in the same room. We just got back on track. I don't want to mess that up."

"If you check on him because you're concerned for

his welfare, do you really think he'll hold that against you?"

"I don't know."

Blay let his head fall back on his spine and looked to the sky. But if he was expecting any help with the decision from the muted show of stars, he didn't get any. Besides, there was only one thing to do, wasn't there.

So, yup, he told Z the address, and one after the other, they dematerialized to the street in question. As they re-formed on a sidewalk that had been snow-blown with ruler-worthy precision, Blay had chills—and not from the below-zero temperature.

"It's okay, son," Z murmured. "Let's just gather the breath, shall we."

It was a long moment before Blay could speak.

"The last time I was here . . . was the night I identified the bodies." As he turned and faced the estate's driveway, the treads of his shitkickers squeaked on the snow pack—and with every blink of his eyes, the past came back with greater and greater clarity. "The *lessers* had slaughtered everyone in the house, staff included. I found his *mahmen* and his sister upstairs in a maid's closet. They were slumped together in each other's arms. They had been shot in the head."

"I'm sorry you had to see that, son."

"His father . . ." Blay cleared his throat. "I found

his father out in the back garden. He'd tried to run to escape, but he'd been wounded. There was a trail of blood leading to where his body was. His throat was sliced so deep that he was basically decapitated, and he had gunshot wounds all over him."

Blay could still remember the male's fine suit. Full of holes that smelled like lead, and stained with fresh red blood.

"And where was Luchas."

"In his room. Over by his bureau." Blay winced. "That's where he told Qhuinn he'd hidden whatever it is. He'd probably been stashing it there when they got to him."

"How'd they kill him."

"Does it matter now?"

"Finish the story, son. It's why you started talking. You need to get this out. It's the other reason you've come here. You want to see your part in the story—and your identifying and burying the bodies is where so much of Luchas's narrative began."

Blay looked over at Z, a pit in his stomach. "Does that mean it's my fault?"

"You didn't do the killing on either night, son."

"It feels like I did."

The Brother shook his head. "Don't take this the wrong way, but you're not that powerful. Some things are inevitable, both for joy and for pain. Be honest. If Luchas was so weak, don't you think he would have done what he did last week a while ago? He was a strong male of worth. In the end, though, the injuries were too much—and I'm not just talking about the physical ones. You weren't responsible for his pain, and the choice was one he made for himself."

Blay took a deep breath. "But what if I got him to thinking?"

"About what?"

"Where he was in his life. Whether he was ever going to get out of the clinic. If he had a future other than swimming in that pool, getting treatments for pain, and having hunks of him cut off to control infection?"

"You don't think all of that shit wasn't on his mind every second of every night and all the hours of each day? You really think that his reality was some kind of revelation he was avoiding—up until you said two words to him and all of a sudden he was like, 'Fuck me, I'm here and it's awful'?"

"I told him Qhuinn had been promoted to private guard in the Brotherhood."

"So?"

"What do you mean, so. It clearly changed something for him."

At that moment, an SUV drove past, its heavy tires carving a fresh track in the snow pack. Of course it was a Range Rover. Instinctually, Blay put his hand on the butt of his holstered gun as he tracked its velocity, direction, and driver.

After it had gone by, the icy, too-bright headlights fading, the glowing red brake lamps disappearing, Z shrugged.

"Forgive me for being harsh here, son, but you need to get real. Just because you fear something doesn't mean it's true. Just because you're terrified you're responsible doesn't make you the driver of any of this. I want you to at least try on for size the idea that you were not responsible for any of it. Not the damage done to him by the Omega and Lash, not the success and good fortune enjoyed by his brother. It's not about you, and yes, I know that can be a very hard lesson. I'm just hoping you learn it sooner rather than later because it's clearly eating you up."

"But I am responsible. We all are. He was part of our community and he was suffering. We all should have done a better job supporting him."

"You may be right about that. And I am honestly and deeply sorry for everything he went through, everything that made his final choice seem like the only way forward for him. But I think you need to forgive yourself for what you perceive your role was in the whole thing. I have been where Luchas was. I've walked that path of crushing pain and hopelessness. I can assure you, when I was there? I wasn't thinking about anyone else. My own suffering was all I knew."

Blay looked up the drive. The mansion was barely visible from the street, but that was the way of the neighborhood, everything set back behind majestic gates, all kinds of land around the sprawling homes.

"Stop bargaining with what happened, son. You're at a negotiation table with no one sitting across from you. All you're doing is arguing against yourself—and a set of circumstances that are not going to change, no matter how much torture you put yourself through."

With a harsh laugh, Blay shook his head. "That's exactly what I'm doing. How do you know me so well."

"Because my brother lived it—you're on the Phury side of things. He blamed himself for years for everything that happened to me. He carried that burden around for a century and it nearly killed him. Does Qhuinn blame you?"

"He says he doesn't."

"And you don't believe him?"

"I'm not sure he knows where he is about anything right now."

"You think he's that stupid?"

"I think he's in that much pain."

Z exhaled a curse, his breath a white cloud in the cold. "I hate this for him and I hate this for you. And when it comes to the pair of you, I can't tell you what to do or what to believe, but personally, I'll vote for true love—and that's what binds you together. Qhuinn might be confused about a lot of things right now, but the one thing I'm damn sure he's certain about?"

When the Brother didn't continue, Blay looked across at him.

Like he'd been waiting for the eye contact, Z continued, "What I'm really damn sure he's certain about? The quality and the kindness of the male he's mated to."

Z extended the forefinger of his dagger hand to Blay's chest. "Your heart was, and is, always true. And the people around you have faith in your goodness. So if you can't believe in yourself? How about you take our opinion as fact, son—and let the burden you don't actually carry go."

Blay's head dropped.

Just as he thought he was going to lose his balance, Zsadist, the Brother who never touched anyone, stepped in and held him close. As Blay grabbed on to the male, he looked over that massive shoulder to what he could see of the mansion. It was only the gabled roof with its lightning rods, the silhouette like a crown on top of the rolling estate's royal head.

He pictured his mate inside that house, going upstairs to find the thing Luchas had stashed right before he was killed.

For what turned out to be only the first time.

Abruptly, Blay frowned and pulled back. "You switched partners tonight, didn't you. So you could be with me. I was supposed to be paired with Payne."

The Brother shrugged. "I had a feeling you and your boy might need a helping hand. Or at the very least, a sidebar with someone who's had some personal experience with these things."

Blay glanced at the roof again. "Thank you," he said in a small voice.

"I'm just paying back that one airplane ride Qhuinn gave me."

"Which one—oh, right. Jesus."

"Yup. You bet your ass there was some praying going on that night."

"You know," Blay said as they started walking toward the gate, "I didn't realize Qhuinn could fly an airplane."

After they dematerialized through the slats of the iron work, Zsadist said dryly, "I think it came as a surprise to him, too."

CHAPTER THIRTY-FOUR

Up on the second floor of his parents' transformed house, Qhuinn stared down at the little girl standing in front of him. Then he looked back into the dim bedroom.

"Yeah, I'm allowed to be here," he said in answer to her question. "'Cuz this is the house I grew up in. Like you're doing now."

"Oh, okay. So you're going to hurt us? You look a little scary. You're really tall."

"No, honey. I'm not going to hurt you or your family."

"That's good."

He'd fix her memories in a second. Right now, he was too freaked at the idea he might be fucked on his mission because of these humans' need to change every single frickin' thing about the house they'd bought.

Leaving her be, he walked into the room, the echo of his boots loud on the hard marble floor. Currently, there was a bed over there, a desk opposite it, and then something weird across in the corner—a sofa, maybe? In his mind, he tried to remember things as they had been when Luchas had lived in the suite. The bureau had been centered between the two windows that overlooked the garden. Yes, that was where it had been.

Going over, he knelt down and passed his hand over the smooth stone tile. He wasn't well versed in construction, but it didn't take a Bob Vila to know that if you wanted to put in marble flooring, you had to have a clean slate to work with. So those floorboards, and whatever had been tucked under them, were long gone.

Oh, Luchas, he thought. *Why didn't you tell me what you needed me to do after I got the damn stuff? Why didn't you put it in the letter so I had something else to go on—*

"What are you looking for, mister?"

Ignoring the kid, he tried to figure out his options. He supposed he could go get a hammer and bust up this section of the tile . . . at which point he'd have Ron, the second wife, and at least two kids as a peanut gallery—

"What're you doing, Mouse?"

Qhuinn closed his eyes. Great. Ronnie was back.

"There's this man in the house, Daddy."

"Oh, hi," Ron said as he came into the doorway. "How you doing?"

Like the pair of them were old friends.

As Qhuinn shot a glare over his shoulder, he was ready to fuck them both off—and yet, as he saw the pair standing together, both dark-haired, the little girl leaning onto her sire's leg, the father with his hand on her shoulder, he knew he couldn't curse at them.

He pictured him and Lyric doing the same thing, like, five years from now.

Well, okay, fine. If somebody broke into the mansion, they'd be vaporized before there was any conversation with anybody. But still.

"Hi, Ron." Qhuinn let himself fall on his ass. "How are we doing?"

He asked this on a reflex because he knew exactly how everyone was: He'd lost his shot at helping Luchas, Ron had a vampire in his house, and little

Cindy-Lou Who, or whatever her name was, was recording this whole thing like her brain was the Rosetta Stone.

"Are you looking for those old letters?" Ron asked.

Qhuinn frowned. "What?"

"The stuff in the floor? When we did this room over, we found this bundle of, like, envelopes."

Before Qhuinn had a conscious thought, he was up on his feet. "You kept it? Them, I mean."

"Yeah, I thought maybe someone would ask about whatever they are. But the guy I bought this place from—well, you, actually—see, I didn't ever meet you, and when I tried to get in touch through the real estate agent, they couldn't find your representative."

Fritz was a very good proxy, wasn't he. Present when he had to be, invisible to humans of all kinds when the legal work was done.

Ron rubbed his side like he had an itch on his liver. "They said this house had been in your family for two hundred years. Is that true?"

"Hey, Ron, I'd love to keep chatting, but I don't suppose you could grab those letters for me?"

The kid looked up at her dad. "This was his older brother's room."

"Just like you and Tommy."

"Yup."

"Come on," Ron said to Qhuinn. "They're in the safe in my office."

The three of them walked down the hall together, Ron making a *shhhh* with his forefinger to his lips as they passed the master suite, the universal sign for *Don't wake up the wife.*

Yuppers, Qhuinn agreed. That shit was mission critical.

Ron's office was in what had been a formal guestroom, and there were all kinds of high-tech minimal on the Lucite desk, the computer nothing but a keyboard and a screen thin as a human hair.

"The safe is over here." Ron went across to the opposite wall—which appeared to be covered with leather panels the color of Rhamp's diaper after the kid ate a boatload of peas. "It's hidden."

Ron flapped his hand around. Frowned. Did some more flapping. "Maybe it's over here."

After a couple of tries to get some sort of hidden reader to recognize his palm print, Ron managed to locate that which had been so successfully camo'd that he couldn't find the goddamn thing: A part of the wall slid back, exposing a black-and-gray safe.

After some beeping on a little button pad on the front, there was a *shhhscht*, and then Ron was all about the open-sesame. For a split second, Qhuinn panicked that there would be a mysterious disappearance. Some kind of whoopsy. A spontaneous combustion in front of his very eyes—

"Here they are."

Ron held out a bulky manila envelope. As Qhuinn took it and cracked the flap, he felt like his whole body was shaking.

"You okay?" Ron asked.

Inside, there were a couple of sealed letters, a sheet of paper, and something wrapped in tissue paper.

"Daddy? There are two people out in the backyard."

Qhuinn looked up. The mini-Ron in the Disney nightgown was standing at one of the windows that faced the garden. Her hand was up on the glass, her face worried.

Before her father could get involved, Qhuinn froze the guy where he stood and then went over to check the view.

Out on the lawn, where Qhuinn's *mahmen*'s rose garden had been, two tall figures dressed in black were standing together, facing the house. Even though the moon was partially covered with a bank of passing clouds, it was obvious that one had red hair and the other had almost no hair at all.

Well, at least they weren't trying to hide themselves.

"It's okay." He patted the little girl's shoulder. "They're with me."

She looked up at him. "Are you real? Or am I dreaming?"

"I'm kind of real." Qhuinn turned to Ron and held up the manila envelope. "Thanks for this."

The man nodded. "Something told me I should hang on to it. Was it your brother's?"

"Yeah, it was." Qhuinn held the bundle to his chest. "You're a good guy, Ron."

"Thanks. You, too."

Who the fuck knew what they were saying to each other. "Did you deal with the feeds from the security cameras?"

"Yup, they're all gone."

"Good job. I gotta go now. You take your little girl back to her room."

"Okay. Bye. Come on, Mouse."

As Ron held his arm out, his daughter went readily, and as she was led away, the little girl looked over her shoulder.

That was Qhuinn's chance to strike her memories—and he almost did. But her father would take care of framing things, and there was no reason to risk scrambling her for life when this would all just be relegated to the *huh, weird* bucket in her brain.

You had to be careful with children's minds.

When he heard a couple of doors shut, he glanced around one more time. The manila envelope crinkled in his hands as he switched his hold on it, and then he closed his eyes. He desperately wanted to look through the things his brother had left behind now, but here was not the place.

A moment later, he dematerialized down to the back lawn.

As he re-formed, he faced the pair of interlopers.

Z didn't seem bothered by the getting caught. Blay rubbed his eyebrow with his thumb, like he was trying to think of something to say.

Meeting the two males in the eye, Qhuinn did the only thing that came to mind.

He hugged them both at the same time. Rushing forward, he threw his arms around them and dragged them in close. As his embrace was returned, he closed his eyes briefly, and heard himself speak a truth that surprised himself.

"I'm so glad you're here."

Before things got too gooey with the emotional bullshit, he stepped back and held up the manila envelope. Clearing his throat, he announced, "And I got what Luchas left. Let's go back and see what it is."

"I'm so glad," Blay said as he appeared to brush away tears. "I was worried something might have happened to whatever it is."

"Something did." Qhuinn put up his palm. "Lot of marble floors in that place now—well, it's a long story. Let's ghost."

Blay and Z left first. And just before Qhuinn dematerialized along with them, he glanced back at the house. He knew in his heart that he was never returning here and he was surprised at how numb he was to that reality. Then again, it wasn't his home anymore—if it ever had been in the warm sense of that word. Yet so much of what shaped him had happened here, and even though none of it had been pleasant, his origin story was forever etched in each of the rooms and in all of the acreage.

Yet his parents and Solange were buried in the yard off to the side.

But none of that made him want to do a revisit. He had his memories, and they were more than enough.

With a frown, he looked at the terrace. For all the renovations, he guessed that the bones of the bodies hadn't been found. As long as the remains had not been exposed to sunlight, they would have survived, and Blay would have put in the effort to make sure things had been properly buried.

Maybe he should have asked Ron. Too late now, and besides, that kind of information changed nothing about anything.

Just before he departed, movement in one of the windows on the second floor got his attention. A small figure that barely came up to the first row of glass panes had stepped into view.

Mouse.

Qhuinn lifted his hand. The little girl lifted her hand back.

And then he dematerialized from the yard he had once known so well.

CHAPTER THIRTY-FIVE

Three sealed envelopes that were a little bigger than index cards. A cheap sheet of copier paper that was folded in half. A ball of tissue that had been scotch-taped into something hard as a marble.

Qhuinn gave a double-check shake to the manila envelope, even though he knew there was nothing else inside of it. Then he looked at Blay. The two of them were sitting on their bed, Z having been called for a non-emergent assist at the Audience House.

Picking up the piece of paper, Qhuinn unfolded

it—and the first thing he noticed was the brown stain across the bottom.

"I think that's blood," he said sadly as he rubbed his thumb over it.

Lifting the paper to his nose, he inhaled. Over three years old and dried, yet he still caught the unmistakable scent.

"Yeah, it's blood." As he lowered the note, he said, "I never asked you where you found him. And he never volunteered."

"It was by his bureau," Blay replied quietly. "As I told Z, I think he was stashing all of this just before he was . . ."

When his mate let the sentence drift, Qhuinn closed his eyes and nodded. Opening them again, he focused on what had been written by a trembling hand:

Anna Sophia Laval
746 Greene Court
Caldwell

No zip code, but it wasn't needed. Not for hand delivery.

Each of the envelopes had "A. S." in the center of the front in beautifully executed handwriting, like the initials had been drawn. No trembling when they'd been written.

"Are these love letters?" Qhuinn murmured. "This is a human name."

"Definitely human."

"But my brother had no contact with humans. This makes no sense."

Blay took off his leather jacket, and palmed his cell phone. "How do you spell the last name again? I'm going to check social media."

"L-A-V-A-L." Qhuinn tilted the page so his mate could see. "Maybe it's a fake name, but if he really wanted these to get to her and she was one of our kind? He would have provided her real name."

"Unless he's trying to hide her identity." Blay frowned as he typed things into Facebook. Then Insta. Twitter. "I can't find anything. Let me see about Google." A moment later, he shrugged and flashed the front of his phone. "I'm not coming up with a thing."

"So maybe she is one of us and that's a false name to protect her. I mean, most humans just have to have a presence on the Internet. It's like breathing to them."

"We know who we could ask." Blay held up his phone. "If you want to."

Qhuinn nodded. "I need to find this female. Or woman, if that's the case."

Blay drafted a text and sent it to V. Then put his phone down. "You know, I have to be honest. If she was human—"

"Right? If he had had any relationship outside of the species? He would have kept that shit on the DL like you read about. Holy fuck. Our parents would have thrown a fit."

There was a *bing!* and Blay checked his phone. "V says to come to the Pit. He's happy to help."

"Let's do it." Qhuinn put the letters back into the larger envelope and then frowned. "Actually, can you take a picture of this? I don't want to take this stuff out of our room."

As he held the piece of paper up, Blay snapped an image on his phone, and then Qhuinn put everything in the second drawer of their bedside table. As the two of them headed for the door, he pulled Blay in and kissed his mate.

"I'm glad you came out to the house. I was so happy to see you."

Blay's brows worried up. "I was concerned you'd think we were stalking you."

"Not at all. I wanted to go in there alone, but it was

a relief to see you out on the lawn. You make me feel safe."

The flush that hit Blay's face was pretty much the best thing Qhuinn had seen all night, and he squeezed his mate's hand—then kept ahold of it, especially as they walked down the grand staircase. As much as he loved everyone in the household, he hoped they didn't run into anybody else. There was too much on his mind, too much sapping his energy.

But meeting with V was different.

Figure out how to cope.

As he and Blay went out through the vestibule, the cold was a slap, and he liked it. It seemed easier for him to breathe.

Glancing over at Blay, he frowned. "Do you want my coat?"

He was in the process of taking his jacket off when Blay put his hand on his arm. "No. I'm good."

Qhuinn put an arm around the male and pulled him close. "I'll keep you warm."

"You always do."

Together, they descended the stone steps and went around the fountain—and he noted that a replacement tarp had been secured across the sculpture and its basin. On that note, he glanced back at the mansion over his shoulder. The glass that had been broken on the second floor had already been replaced.

Healing. In the bricks-and-mortar sense.

As they came up to the Pit, they didn't have to knock. Vishous opened things and seemed prepared to go to work: He not only had his muscle-shirt-and-leathers uniform on, he was sporting a lit hand-rolled in one hand and a rocks glass of what had to be Goose in the other.

So yeah, Qhuinn thought, the brother was ready for anything.

"How we doing? What do you need?"

They stepped into the Pit's warm interior, and Qhuinn was aware of a nervousness clutching the front of his throat. Stripping off his jacket, he worried about things he couldn't control: Names, addresses, people who had moved, people who lied about their identities.

You know, the social equivalent of new owners doing the floors over.

He took yet another deep breath. "We need to search for a woman or female my brother might have had contact with before the raids."

V went totally still. But only for a split second.

Then he nodded once and went over to his Four Toys. Sitting down in front of his computers, he put his drink aside and his hand-rolled between his teeth. "Name."

Blay held out his phone and Qhuinn took the thing and put it in front of the brother. He should have said the name. But it felt . . . sacred, somehow.

"There's an address there, too," he mumbled. Like the brother couldn't frickin' read?

V set to typing, his fingers, both the ones in the lead-lined glove and the ones that were not, flying over a keyboard. "Have a seat. This'll take a minute."

Qhuinn and Blay parked it on the sofa, the two of them side by side, their knees together, their backs straight. Like they were a couple of schoolkids trying to make a good impression on the teacher.

Like maybe if they behaved themselves, V would find what they needed—

"Got her."

Qhuinn burst up and tripped over the coffee table on the way back to the desk. And even before he got in range, V leaned to the side in his office chair so there was plenty of room to get close to the monitors.

The central screen was showing the front and back of a current New York State driver's license. The image was of . . . a dark-haired woman staring into the camera with dark eyes. Her height was listed as five six, she had corrective lenses, and she was an organ donor. The name was definitely Anna Sophia Laval.

"The address is different," Blay murmured.

V tapped his hand-rolled over his ashtray. "This is her current address. I found the one on the note as her previous residence."

"So this really is her," Qhuinn said as he moved even closer to the image. Not that it got him any more information about her or any further acuity on her features. "But we don't know if she's one of us—or do we?"

"I've initiated a deep search into the species data-base from the Audience House. In about an hour, I'll know more."

Qhuinn continued to stare at that face. The pho-tograph was not all that distinct, but even if it were in hard focus, it wasn't going to tell him what he wanted to know.

For those questions, he was going to need to speak to the woman.

Or vampire.

Herself.

CHAPTER THIRTY-SIX

The Brotherhood House was typically at its most quiet between one and four p.m. in the afternoons. Those three hours were not only the dead zone between Last Meal cleanup and First Meal prep, they were when the *doggen* themselves retired to their quarters for a brief rest from all their other duties like housework, supply acquisition, and planning. So, yup, as Qhuinn sat propped up against the headboard in his and his mate's bedroom, he just listened to all the silence. Beside him, sleeping on his stomach under a heavy load of covers, Blay was twitching like a Labrador chasing bunnies in his dreams.

"Shh," Qhuinn said as he stroked his male's bare shoulder. "Be easy."

Instantly, his mate stilled. Then there was a turn of the head, Blay's face now in his direction. A big inhale followed, and, finally, a slow exhale.

Qhuinn smiled to himself. "You just rest. I've got you."

As Blay fell back into REM land, Qhuinn repositioned himself against the stack of pillows he'd punched up an hour ago, crossing his arms and staring across the dim room.

So odd.

V could find nothing on Anna Sophia Laval in any of the species databases or social media groups.

Therefore, it was either a code name that she and Luchas had used when together . . . or she was a human. But how was the latter possible? His brother hadn't been raised like that. Not that Qhuinn cared one way or the other—but the family's golden son? Falling in with one of those rats without tails?

He rubbed his face as the whens, wheres, and hows jogged around the inside of his skull like they'd had cocktails made of Adderall and Pepsi.

Insomnia sucked. And he had a feeling he'd better get used to it.

On that note, he leaned to the side, reached into

the bedside table, and got his contraband iPad. Before turning the thing on, he compulsively opened the second drawer and made sure that the letters were where he'd left them. Maybe he should discreetly cut the flaps and take images of the contents? You know, on a just-in-case—except that seemed like an inappropriate violation of privacy.

Yup. Still there.

But really, like they weren't going to be?

Shaking his head at himself, he fired up the iPad and wasn't sure what he was going to do with it—except then he remembered his previous request of Vishous. Not the one about Anna Sophia Laval earlier in the night, but the other one from the evening before. Going into his email, he scrolled down the listing of spam and Amazon order confirmations. There was only one personal missive in the bunch—it was from V and he opened the thing:

Again, I'm really sorry about your brother, son. Let me know if there's anything else I can do.

When he checked the time stamp—because he was afraid of the attachments—he saw that the brother had sent what he'd requested a mere eight minutes after he'd asked for it.

V was a good guy. No matter what he tried to portray to the contrary.

There were four attachments, marked sequentially, and Qhuinn stared at them. It was a while before he could open the first of the videos, and when he did, a sense of not being able to breathe returned.

As the screen blacked out and then flared a gray and white, he propped the iPad on his knees and felt his eyes burn. The image was of the training center's corridor, right outside Luchas's patient room. When things got blurry—on his end, not the security feed's—he wiped his face. Then he pressed play with a sinking sensation in the center of his chest.

Nothing moved. Duh, because the camera was static.

No, wait, that wasn't true; there was a counter in the lower right-hand corner with the date and time: The seconds flipped by quickly, the minutes moved slow, the hours were frozen solid. But he didn't have to wait long. V had been efficient about editing the security camera's recording, and in the back of Qhuinn's mind, he had a thought that the brother had deliberately given him a little time to collect himself—

Before his brother walked out of his room.

The sight of that slight frame in the long black robe was a shock even though he'd thought he'd been prepared for it. Putting his hand over his mouth, he tucked an arm across his aching chest and just watched.

God, that rough gait. The cane.

"Oh, Luchas," he whispered.

Reaching out, he ran his forefinger over the figure—except doing that stopped the footage. It was okay, though. For a while, he just stared at his brother's contours. It had to be among the last moments of the male's life.

Qhuinn thought of pulling back that hood and exposing . . . what had frozen beneath it.

To clear that memory, he continued with the file. When Luchas left the camera's field, there was a cut to another feed. And another. And another, as his brother went down the corridor of the training center. And then the file ended.

The next attachment was from the subterranean tunnel, and Qhuinn witnessed his brother limp along to the right, heading for the hatch. When Luchas came up to it, he hesitated.

And glanced back over his shoulder.

That was when Qhuinn finally got to see his brother's face from under the hood. He froze the feed. There was no fear. No anxiety. Luchas's expression was simply . . . grave. "Resolved" was maybe the better word for it.

With a pounding heart, Qhuinn tried to memorize exactly what it all looked like, the turn of that ruined body, the angle of the cane, the line of the mouth, the cast of the eyes. But that was stupid, right? He could play this file anytime—and if he lost it or deleted it by mistake, not that he would, he could always ask V for another copy.

"I miss you," he whispered. "I wish you were here . . ."

Yet the file had reminded him of how much pain Luchas had been in. How pervasive the agony and untenable the hours must have been. When he considered his brother's suffering, he supposed . . . that it was a blessing of some kind that he could at least understand why his brother might have reached the end of his journey. But that was a sad tally of fortune, wasn't it.

As a groundswell of regret made Qhuinn's heart skip beats, he didn't know how he was going to make it to the end of the files.

He hit play again. It was nearly impossible to watch Luchas turn away, and there might have been some more rubbing of the eyes. And then after Luchas entered the code to the hatch and stepped through, the feed ended. So Qhuinn teed up the next one. This recording was of the parking area in the cave, and it showed his brother walking past the Tahoe and the snowmobiles. Luchas paused again, but he didn't look back once more. He just pulled the camo drape to the side . . . and then with a swirl of snow from the storm, he stepped out of sight.

At that point, the feed switched to an exterior camera mounted somewhere on the lip of the cave. It showed Luchas struggling through the freezing cold onslaught, the winds lashing at him, his body weaving. And then there was nothing but white, the black robes eaten up by the blizzard.

V left no extra time on that one. He just cut it where it was.

One last file. But wasn't this the end of the story?

In danger of losing it, Qhuinn fired up the final attachment, and it took a moment for his eyes to resume proper functioning—at which point, he frowned. The footage was from a camera inside the subterranean tunnel again. There was about thirty seconds of lead time . . . and then someone entered the frame.

"What the fuck?" he said.

As Blay stirred next to him, he absently reached out and soothed his mate. Then he held the iPad closer. Like that was going to make a difference?

Maybe V had made a mistake.

The figure strode along, and when it got to the hatch, it entered the code and stepped out. Then there was footage tacked on from the area inside the cave and then outside, in the storm. Which was still raging.

Even though the time stamp was about five hours later.

Close to dawn. Very close.

When the image stream ended, Qhuinn rubbed his eyes and prayed he was not going to have to kill someone who lived among them all—

He sat straight up.

As a chill of realization came over him, he nearly threw the iPad aside. Instead, so he didn't disturb his mate, he moved slower than he wanted to, peeling the covers back, slipping one foot and then the other out from the warmth. Making sure that Blay was tucked in, Qhuinn padded over to the walk-in closet and willed the light to stay off. Thanks to the illumination from the bathroom, he threw on whatever clothes he came to.

And then he left as quickly as he could, making sure that he closed the door softly behind himself.

CHAPTER THIRTY-SEVEN

The mansion had never felt so enormous as when Qhuinn jogged down the red-carpeted stairs, his bare feet soundless, his heart pounding like he was on a flat-out run for his life. When he hit the foyer's mosaic floor, the cold registered on his soles, but that was not the reason for the goosebumps that rode up his arms and across his chest.

He looked right, into the library. The Christmas tree had been left on, its red, green, and gold lights blinking, its bulbs and garland sparkling. Red skirting had been tucked around its base, and presents were already appearing on the velvet. Likewise, stockings had started to be hung at the fireplace. There would be a countless lineup of them come December 24th, the human tradition fully embraced.

Glancing left, the dining room was closed down, the chandelier dimmed, the table glossy and polished and empty of everything but a huge bouquet of red roses and holly in the center. Beyond that, the kitchen was also silent.

But not all was quiet.

He followed the theme song for *Magnum, P.I.* into the billiards room.

Lassiter was sprawled on one of the couches that faced the new concave TV screen, his blond-and-black hair spilling over the throw pillow he'd wedged behind his head, his long legs stretched out and crossed at the ankles. He was wearing wool leggings that seemed like the lower-body version of a hair shirt, and a My Little Pony T-shirt that shouldn't have been warm enough—and evidently wasn't, given the blanket he'd pulled across his chest.

As Qhuinn stopped in front of the sofa, the angel paused what was on the big screen with the remote and looked up without surprise.

Like he'd been expecting this.

He also didn't jump to his feet and assume a defensive response.

Meanwhile, Qhuinn just stood there like a dummy. "Hi."

Lassiter shifted into a sit, piling the blanket in his lap. "Hi."

"I, ah . . ." Dragging a hand through his hair, he felt himself start to sweat. "Ah—"

"You don't have to apologize." Those strangely colored eyes were steady as they stared up. "I understood in that moment why you went after me and I understand now."

At a loss, Qhuinn looked around at all the things he'd seen before: The pool tables, the mounts of sticks on the wall, the balls arranged in their triangles on the felt. He saw the Persian rugs under each play area, the leather sofas, the bar with its top-shelf liquor bottles and its sparkling glasses.

"You want something?" Lassiter said as he got up.

"Ah . . ."

"That's a yes."

"Are you drinking? 'Cuz you don't usually drink."

"Not alcohol." The angel went behind the bar. "Sit. I'll make us some fruit juice for the vitamin C. You can't be too careful with scurvy."

Qhuinn sidled up to the long, thin granite counter and parked it on a stool. And then he watched in silence as Lassiter sliced four Hale Groves pink grapefruits in half and started to squeeze them on an old school glass mount, the kind that had a ribbed center to do the grinding and a circular base to catch the juice.

Clearing his throat, Qhuinn figured there was no reason to wait for better words. "So the night my brother died—" At that moment, he realized he would never use that other word. As accurate as it was. "—I know that you were in the tunnel. Just before dawn."

Lassiter didn't say anything; he just kept working the halves on the grind part. The juice that filled the base was pink as a blush and smelled like sunshine.

"That's how Luchas's remains were still there the following night," Qhuinn said quietly. "You stayed with him all day long and blocked the sun from him. Didn't you. You protected him . . . so I could see him one last time. Didn't you."

Lassiter tipped the juicer over a rocks glass and then put the serving in front of Qhuinn.

"I repaid you by attacking you." Qhuinn swallowed. "And insulting you. Oh, shit, Lass, I didn't mean what I said. I didn't mean it—"

"It's okay."

"No." Qhuinn reached across the bar and touched the angel's arm. "It's not. Thank you for what you did for him and for me. And I'm truly sorry."

Lassiter paused in the middle of working on his own serving of juice—and his eyes stayed ducked. "Just so you know, I can't really talk about some things. It's the rule."

Qhuinn slowly straightened on the stool, a shimmy of awareness going down his spine and landing in his ass cheeks, causing them to pucker.

It was easy to forget who Lassiter was. What he was. The enormous power he held.

But at this moment, Qhuinn became fully in touch with the fact that he was sitting across . . . from a deity.

"I do what I can," the angel murmured as he tossed the rind and picked up the last of the halves. "I do what I'm allowed to do. You know, to make things easier. My heart broke for you, and yet all I could do was stand on the sidelines and watch the crash. It's fucking torture . . ." As his voice broke, he cleared his throat. "But I do what I can."

Lassiter poured the juice into his own glass and then clinked the rim of Qhuinn's. "Bottoms up."

As the angel tossed his back, Qhuinn did the

same—and had to click his tongue at the tartness. As the burn rushed down into his gut, his stomach rolled—but not from the grapefruit.

"I can't imagine what it's like for you," Qhuinn said.

"Everyone wants to be in charge—until they are." Lassiter put his glass down with such care, it made no sound on the bar. "Why do you think I watch the kind of TV I do? I've got to shut my mind off somehow. Otherwise, I'd go mad."

"Shit."

"All the strands of all the lives, woven in patterns of suffering and joy, the cloth infinite in every direction, the layers upon layers unending. And I see every fiber in every thread, at every moment. I feel the reverberations, too. I am but a tuning fork of flesh, struck by the hand of the Creator. I am but a servant of destiny, yet I am accountable."

As Lassiter spoke the words, his voice grew deeper and deeper, and then behind him, revealed first as a figment of the eye, and then as a glorious, three-dimensional reality, the set of iridescent wings he usually hid appeared at his shoulders. And that was not all. From overhead, cascading down, not from the ceiling of the room, but from the great above, a shaft of light, brighter than the sun, yet not painful to the eye, bathed the angel in a halo that encompassed his entire body.

In his holy form, as a glimpse into eternity and the mystery of fate, Lassiter looked across the bar. And now his lips remained closed, even as his voice permeated the space around them.

Ask what you want to know.

Qhuinn began to tremble, a precipice he had not intended to confront appearing at his feet.

Ask. And I shall tell you.

Covering his face with both his hands, Qhuinn felt like a child, for the answer could well crush him in a way that couldn't be contemplated when you were an adult, when you were big and strong and capable of protecting yourself. The knowledge he sought and feared was of the ruination kind, the sort against which he had no defenses.

"Is my brother in the Fade?" he choked out. "Is he safely in the Fade, even though he . . . ended himself. And therefore cannot be granted a peaceful afterlife?"

Motherfucker, why had he said any of that out loud? He already knew the answer—

Your brother was killed by the blizzard. Murdered by snow.

As Lassiter's voice entered his mind, Qhuinn

dropped his hands. Through tears, he whispered, "So is he in the Fade?"

Lassiter, in all his mystical splendor, nodded. *He is safely in the Fade forevermore. He was murdered . . . by the snow.*

All at once, the magic was gone as if it had never been, the wings disappearing, the pool of golden illumination dissipated, the halo around the body no longer visible.

Qhuinn blinked. "You are the one who makes that call. Aren't you. You're the one who decides where they go—"

"I don't know what you're talking about." Lassiter's tone was brisk as he held up his empty glass. "More grapefruit? I think I'm going to have another—"

"Thank you," Qhuinn croaked out.

When Qhuinn's glass was taken back, he could only watch in silence as more grapefruit was cut and squeezed, the sweet and tangy scent rising up, another round of summer in the midst of December.

In his mind, Qhuinn heard the angel's voice: *I do what I can. What I'm allowed to do. You know, to make things easier.*

"You are the best savior we could ever have," he whispered reverently.

Lassiter didn't respond. He just filled up the

glasses again and returned Qhuinn's. When Qhuinn went to take it, the angel didn't let go.

"You should definitely ask him. He's going to say yes."

Qhuinn drew back with surprise. "What?"

The angel winked. "You know what I'm referring to. Or you will as soon as you think about it."

CHAPTER THIRTY-EIGHT

At nightfall, Blay got dressed in civilian clothes. He wore his second favorite pair of slacks—his first favorite having been so delightfully destroyed two nights before—and chose a Christmas green cashmere sweater, a red-and-green silk scarf, and the camel hair hand-me-down coat he'd gotten off of Butch the season before.

At the last moment, he took one of his nines and clipped it to his waistband. When he pulled the sweater down, you couldn't see it, and that was the goal.

Stepping out of the walk-in closet, he put his arms wide and did a spin. "This good? Do I look okay?"

Qhuinn, who was sitting over on the bed, smiled. "Come here."

As Blay walked over, he was conscious of those mismatched eyes watching every move he made—and not necessarily in a sexual way, although there was heat, as always, in that gaze. It was more—

"You're beautiful, you know that?" Qhuinn said as he wrapped his arms around Blay's waist and put his chin on Blay's belly button.

"You're going to make me blush."

"Good. I like when you do."

Blay could only shake his head slowly and smile like a fool. The truth was, something had happened during the day to his male. He wasn't sure what it was. Qhuinn was still sad. That was obvious. But there was . . . a peacefulness about him. A calmness in the mourning that had not been there before.

"You must have finally slept," Blay said as he stroked that black-and-purple hair back.

"What do you mean?"

"You look . . . rested."

Qhuinn shrugged. "I'm finding a way to cope, I guess. And I'm glad you're coming with me."

"Anything for you."

"I'm nervous."

"I don't blame you." Blay bent down and brushed his mate's lips with his own. "But just know that whatever happens, we'll get through it together."

They departed the mansion about fifteen minutes later. As they left, they waved at everyone who was enjoying First Meal in the dining room. There was no question of them stopping to eat, though. Blay was too nervous to eat as well.

Leaving the mansion, they dematerialized to the address that was on the driver's license V had found. It turned out to be a block-sized apartment building, the two-story split-sides orientated around open stairwells.

"Over here, on the left," Qhuinn said.

They walked across the skirt of parking lot that had been well plowed, scanning the area the entire time. Cars were parked under open-air ports, and there were others in exposed slots. No trucks. Sedans and SUVs. Mostly Hondas, Fords, and Kias. No minivans.

All the apartments had lights on in them, and there were residents getting out of their cars and going into their flats, the human workday done, the nighttime hunker-down arriving for the other species.

Qhuinn led the way up the staircase in question, and they were halfway up when the tenant on the front right of the building opened her door and stepped out. She had her coat buttoned to her neck, her purse at her shoulder, one glove on, the other in her hand. She was mid-twenties, with her hair all loosely curled and a full face of makeup. Given the time? Probably going on a date.

She took one look at Qhuinn, blanched—and ducked back into her apartment. The sound of the dead bolt getting thrown was loud.

"Shit," Qhuinn muttered. "Gimme a second."

He didn't knock on the door. He just leaned into it, his brows tight, his eyes closed. Then he backed off. A second later, the young woman came out again, gave them a cheery smile, and danced down the stairs. They both watched her cross the parking area and get into a Sorento.

"He better not stand her up. She likes him," Qhuinn murmured.

On that note, he pivoted to the apartment directly across from her place. The number on the door was 114B.

"I think you better do the knock and greet," he said. "Assuming she's human, I don't want to scare her, and I'd rather not go into her brain. I don't want to lose any memories she has."

"Okay."

Blay squeezed his mate's shoulder and then put himself solidly in front of the peephole. Curling up a fist, he knocked his knuckles against the cold metal panel.

No answer.

He glanced over his shoulder. Qhuinn had wrapped his arms around his chest and was staring at the concrete landing under his shitkickers. In the tense silence, a breeze whiffled in, carrying the scent of sautéed onions and ground beef from somewhere.

Blay tried again. "The light's on—"

The door opened.

The woman on the other side was, just as the license had stated, five feet six inches tall, with dark hair and dark eyes. Her skin was very pale, and she looked thinner than her government-issued photograph—or maybe it was more drawn, as if she were getting over an illness or struggling in life. She was dressed in a pair of blue jeans and a cream Irish sweater, and she smelled like shampoo and toothpaste.

Beyond her, a barren apartment was clean . . . except for the bedroom in the distance. A light illuminated a messy bed with crumpled snack bags on the floor.

"May I help you?"

The voice was quiet and a little hoarse. The accent was French. And the scent was decidedly human.

"Hi." Blay smiled warmly, but kept his lips together so his fangs didn't show. "Are you Anna Sophia Laval?"

"I am."

At that moment, she glanced to her right. And saw Qhuinn.

Her eyes popped wide, and she put her hand to her mouth. Just as Blay began to worry they were going to have to go into her mind and calm her, she spoke.

"You're Luke's brother. Aren't you."

✦ ✦ ✦

As soon as that door opened, Qhuinn took in every detail of the woman and the apartment behind her. And then she said words he couldn't immediately translate into meaning.

When they clicked, he was overcome with emotion.

"Yes," he replied roughly. "I am his brother."

She stepped back and indicated the way inside with a hand that trembled. "Please."

Qhuinn let Blay go first, and then he hesitated on the threshold. Before he followed his mate, he ducked a hand into his jacket and made sure he had the letters and the Scotch tape ball.

"Won't you sit down," she said formally as the door clapped shut behind them all.

The sofa was the only place to park it, so he and Blay went over even though the last thing Qhuinn wanted was to get physically trapped. He felt a buzzy need to run—although not to get away. He had nervous energy that was hard to contain.

"May I offer you something to drink?"

Qhuinn narrowed his eyes. There was a regal posture to her in spite of her casual clothes and modest surroundings, and he could see Luchas approving of that. But she was a human; she was very definitely of the other species.

"No, we're good," he said. "Thank you."

She went across to a shallow kitchen area and brought over one of the three chairs that were around a little table.

Sitting down, she put her hands in her lap. "You've come to tell me he's dead, haven't you."

Qhuinn leaned forward on the couch and plugged his elbows into his knees. Wiping his face with his palm, he nodded. "Yes. I'm sorry."

As she closed her eyes and sagged, Qhuinn felt a

communion with her, a deep, abiding connection in which he found a curious relief.

He had to clear his throat. "Listen, it feels inappropriate to have to ask this, but how did you know him? Is it okay for me to ask that?"

She took a deep breath. "I haven't seen him for over three years. Is that when he died?"

Qhuinn's mind chewed over responses. And in the end, he went with: "Yes."

Because his brother had been killed in the raids. That was not a lie. And was he really prepared to tell her the whole true story?

"What happened to him?" she asked. "How did he pass?"

"It was natural causes." Or a snow murder, depending on who you asked.

"You look like him." She smiled wanly and then swept him from head to toe with her eyes. "Well, you're different, too."

"I am. But I loved him and he loved me."

Anna Sophia cleared her own throat. "He was easy to love. He was such a good man. I am . . ."

"Here," Blay said, leaning forward with his handkerchief.

The woman took what was offered and patted at

her face. Then she was quiet for a long while. Just as Qhuinn was about to jump out of his skin, she spoke again.

"We met when I was taking a night class in English literature here at the college." She unfolded and refolded the kerchief. "He was in the same class. It ran from six to nine in the evening for twelve weeks."

That sounded like Luchas, Qhuinn thought.

"Luke sat in the back. So did I. I didn't think I belonged, and oddly, neither did he. Which never made any sense to me. He was so brilliant. He was just . . . special." She stared off into the distance. "It started with a hello. And then a smile. He was . . ."

When she didn't go on, Qhuinn prompted, "He was a wonderful male."

"I need to be honest with you." Her eyes flashed across the space. "I was married at the time."

There was a moment of silence, as if she were waiting to be judged. When Qhuinn just nodded, she sighed and traced Blay's monogram with her fingertip.

"I was not looking for anyone." She shook her head. "My husband and I married young. I was very career focused back then, keeping my own name, determined to go far in the law. Basile was very handsome and looking for a wife. As they say, the days were long, the years short, with two kids, two careers. Eventually, I knew he was having affairs, and I found out about his then current one because one night, I followed him to a 'work event.'" She did the air quotes around the words. "I can remember sitting in my car and watching him escort this woman into the restaurant. Oddly, I knew the marriage was over because I didn't feel anything. There was nothing. Here." She paused as she rubbed over her heart. "We have two beautiful children. Elle and Terrie are the best thing to come out of those nineteen years together. But I knew Basile didn't love me anymore, if he ever had. I knew I didn't love him anymore, if I ever had. And truly, he's not a bad man. He's just . . . who he is—and I know this all sounds detached, but I spent too many years angry. I'm not doing it anymore."

"That sounds healthy," Qhuinn said softly.

"Luke was the one who helped me see it that way. We would have coffee after class. He was a total gentleman. He never . . . he never took things further than that, and neither did I. But that time with him, it changed me. After the class was finished, we continued to meet at restaurants or libraries. We would talk for hours and I lied to my husband about where I was. I told him I was taking another class. I'm not proud of that, but I knew what he was doing on his own time. I guess that made it . . . easier."

Anna Sophia smoothed the handkerchief on her knee. "It went on for a year. Until I told Luke I was getting a divorce. I'd finally decided to talk to my husband and just . . . be real about where we were. Basile put up a fight, but not for long. I think he was relieved? It was hard on us to keep pretending everything was okay in front of our girls." She looked up sharply. "I told Luke I had no expectations about him and me. I didn't need rescuing. He seemed surprised by my announcement, but we set another date for a week later . . . I waited for two hours at the restaurant. He never showed up."

"When was this?"

"It was August. Three and a half years ago."

Qhuinn looked at Blay. *The raids*, he thought as his mate nodded back.

"It wasn't like Luke. I phoned him. Several times. But I never heard back. No texts, no calls. That was it . . . I figured I spooked him. That I was good enough when I was uncomplicated, but two kids? Newly divorced single mom? Too much." Her eyes dropped back to the handkerchief. "The next day, I became convinced that something had happened to him. I had no idea where to find him other than his phone, though. I called St. Francis Hospital, feeling like a stalker, a paranoid stalker. They could tell me nothing. I searched the papers and the news. Nothing. But it turns out . . . I was right, wasn't I. Something had happened."

"I'm so sorry." Qhuinn cursed as he heard his words in the tense air. "That's so fucking lame to say, though."

"What else can anyone do?" Her sad stare lifted again. "And I return the sentiment. I'm sorry for your loss as well."

They held eyes for a long moment, and in the mutual mourning, there was again that strange relief to know that his suffering was not solitary—although that was bullshit, wasn't it. Everybody back at the mansion, and Blay, as the male sat beside him, was grieving. But it was different for him.

Different for this woman, too.

"How exactly did it happen?" she asked. "His death, I mean. You said it was natural causes. Was it a heart attack? A stroke?"

For a moment, Qhuinn felt like he did owe her the full truth. But then the species divide reared its proverbial head. How the hell could he explain Lash, and the Omega, and the Lessening Society? And as for the details of what Luchas had chosen to do? He was going to spare her them.

"His heart gave out," Qhuinn said. "His heart . . . just stopped."

Anna Sophia pressed the handkerchief into her face for a minute. When she lowered her hands, her eyes were even more bloodshot.

"He brought so much to my life." She shook her head. "And then after he was gone . . . I just became so lost and I haven't cared about much since then. I am ashamed of my failures with my girls, but I can't seem to resurrect myself. Maybe I was wrong. Maybe I did need rescuing."

Qhuinn reached into his jacket. "I have some things he asked me to give you."

Anna Sophia stiffened. And then she breathed in on a gasp as he leaned forward with the three letters and the little ball of tissue and Scotch tape.

"These are for you," he said.

CHAPTER THIRTY-NINE

An abiding sense of peace and completion came over Qhuinn as the woman took the letters and the little present. At first, she just held on to them. And then she looked at each one in turn.

"Where did these come from?" she murmured.

"He hid them." When she glanced up, he rephrased. "Saved them. For you. At the time of his death, he was working to get to a place where he could present them to you personally, but he never ... I don't believe he ever got there. And I'm truly sorry for the delay. I didn't actually find all this myself until very recently."

In the quiet that followed, while she took the time to examine each of the envelopes and the tightly wound ball, he imagined the Luchas she had known, strong and tall, handsome and well-spoken, a male in his prime.

"I'm scared about what is in these." She glanced up. "Will you stay while I open them?"

"Of course we will."

"Is there an order to them?"

"I don't know. I'm sorry."

She nodded. And then she carefully opened one of the envelopes. Extracting the letter, she lifted the single fold of creamy high-quality stationery. As she absorbed the words intended for her, her eyes went back and forth slowly.

Her tears dropped onto her jeans.

That was the way of it. One after the other, she read each of the three letters, her eyes moving faster and faster. When she finished the last one, she sat back. The tissue paper ball was in her hand, but she seemed to have forgotten everything around her.

Qhuinn didn't move. Neither did Blay.

He wasn't sure any of the three of them were breathing.

And then the words, so soft, so sad . . . and yet wondrous, too.

"He loved me," she whispered. "He said he loved me, and only me."

Her eyes rose, and they were luminous with complex emotion.

Qhuinn nodded at her. "Yes, he did. And I'm glad."

"He said he would have married me if he could have." She frowned. "But the writing is different on this one. Was this right as he was having the heart attack?"

"May I?"

When she gave him the letter, once again it was a shock to see that handwriting of his brother's—but she was right. The script was messy. And the letter was short.

Qhuinn imagined it had been written as the *lessers* had stormed the house. Had Luchas been hearing the screams of their parents, their sister, their *doggen*, as he scribbled this all? And the message was plainly stated. He loved Anna Sophia Laval and he had decided to tell his parents that he was going to be with her, if she would have him.

If he survived the attack, Qhuinn tacked on to himself.

But that was not to be—and not because their *mahmen* and father would not allow him.

It was the start of the nightmare.

Yet it was good to know that Luchas had broken free of their upbringing, just as Qhuinn had. Maybe duress and the threat of death had done it, but in the end, he had chosen love over heritage—and Qhuinn was choosing to believe that the conviction would have stuck if the family had survived.

"This is beautiful," Qhuinn said as he returned the letter to its owner.

Anna Sophia took the missive back . . . and then her hand dipped under the collar of her sweater. As she pulled out a gold cross, he thought of his little grapefruit session with Lassiter.

"You know what," he murmured, "I personally believe that love is immortal, that love abides even after death. And I know that Luchas is up in Heaven, and he's waiting for you there. At the end of your course, I believe you and he will be reunited."

Because the fallen angel who watched over the Fade was going to have it no other way.

Her eyes shimmered. "Thank you for saying that."

"Will you open his gift to you? You don't have to, but—"

"Oh, yes."

She tucked the letters under her hip, and struggled

with the Scotch tape and the tissue. When she got the tangle free, she gasped.

And held out a ring as if she couldn't believe what she was looking at and needed a good second opinion.

It was a diamond solitaire of good size. Two or three karats. Set in a modern setting that had to be platinum. Simple, beautiful . . . a symbol of enduring love.

Qhuinn didn't recognize the piece. It wasn't one that their *mahmen* had owned.

"That's an engagement ring," he said. Like an idiot.

"Is it for me?" As if she were in the same state of shock he was.

And then he realized something about the ring. You didn't go out and buy something like that while there were slayers in your house, murdering everybody. Hell, given its size and the way it sparkled, even in low light? You didn't just waltz out and pick it up at the local mall.

This was an important ring. One that had been chosen with care, over time, and with consideration, for which a tremendous amount of money had been spent.

So Luchas had made his mind up before the raids, before that night.

As that math added up, Qhuinn felt a tremendous swell of pride toward his brother.

"Do you . . ." Anna Sophia looked worried. "Do you need this back? It's very expensive."

"I'm sorry, what—oh, no. That's yours. My brother clearly bought it for you."

"Are you sure?"

"Never surer about anything in my life." Well, except his love for Blay and his young.

Anna Sophia sat back and stared at the ring. Then she slipped it on the fourth finger of her left hand. "I wish he were here."

"Me, too."

"Is it wrong . . ."

"Is what wrong?"

"I'm glad that he didn't just . . . forget me." She looked around the apartment. "I have felt . . . forgotten. By my husband over the last decade of our marriage. By Luke. Especially by Luke. I loved him, too, you see. But . . . you're not supposed to care what others think of you, right. Others are not supposed to define us."

The last sentence was said with resignation, as if it were something she had been trying to convince herself of—with little success.

A sudden fear had Qhuinn leaning forward. "Anna Sophia, I know you don't know me—"

"But I do. You're Luke's brother."

"Well, then, please listen to me. You have things to live for on this side. There's no reason to rush . . . seeing your Luke again. There's time for that. Much later."

It was a relief when she nodded. "You are very right. I have my two daughters. And God knows, I haven't done enough for them lately."

And Luchas had you, Qhuinn thought. *He just didn't trust your love was strong enough to handle his physical suffering.*

Qhuinn reached forward and took the woman's hand, the one that bore his brother's ring. "Luke will be waiting for you, at the end of what I hope for you is a very long life. You're in your middle, though. Not at your end. So you must stay here with your children and carve out your life—now knowing that you were loved by a male of great worth."

He squeezed her hand and then sat back again. At which point Anna Sophia splayed her fingers out. As she considered the ring, her face was cast in shadows of sadness, but there was a light in her eye that had not been there before.

"Thank you," she said. "This gives me closure that I needed. I don't want him to have passed, and I hate that he died so young. But I am . . . this is more than I could ever have hoped for. So thank you."

Qhuinn smiled a little. "It's helped me, too. Just doing this . . . makes me feel like I've done something for him."

Anna Sophia smiled back at him. Then she grew serious. "I'm never going to see you again, am I."

For a moment, Qhuinn considered lying. "No, you're not."

And yet he wasn't going to take her memories. It felt important that she remember this just as much as he did, as if they were in a pact together that swore to the one thing that mattered most to him in this moment: He had honored his brother's last request.

Which had been a beautiful, bittersweet one.

"I'm leaving town," Qhuinn explained.

"Sometimes a fresh start is best." She looked at the ring. Looked at him. "I'm not going to sell this. Ever. Don't worry about that."

Qhuinn nodded. "Wear it in good health. And think of him every time you see the sparkle."

Anna Sophia curled her hand in. "I think I'll put it in a really safe place for a while. It would be hard to explain to my girls. But maybe later . . ."

"The future is yours to decide."

They all stayed where they were for a little while, and then Qhuinn took Blay's hand and they got to their feet. Anna Sophia stood up, too, and tilted her head to one side.

"Is this your husband?" she asked.

"Ah, we don't call it—he's my partner, yes."

"You two look like you fit together."

Qhuinn blinked as a realization hit him hard. And then he slowly turned his head toward his mate.

"We do," he heard himself say. "We do fit together."

CHAPTER FORTY

As they arrived back at the mansion, Blay was the one who went into the vestibule first, and after he stepped through the heavy outside door, he put his face up to the security camera. Almost immediately, the door was opened by Fritz.

"Sires, you have returned! And there is still time for First Meal, come, come!"

The butler seemed concerned as he inched back. Then again Qhuinn's absence at meals had been well noted by everyone—and the butler had a lot in common with Blay's *mahmen*: People needed to eat good, home-cooked food. Or they were in danger of expiring on the spot.

Blay opened his mouth to placate the *doggen* with an order of room service, but Qhuinn spoke up.

"Let's go in," he said. "And see everybody."

"Your place settings are awaiting you!" Fritz clapped his hands like he was giving a rousing round of applause. "Come, come this way."

Like they hadn't eaten at that big table before. Like the huge room, with all the food, was a mystery when it came to its purpose.

Then again, Qhuinn seemed like he was in a daze as they walked over to the archway, and Blay was of a mind to suggest they bail—except then there was a lull in conversation as their presence registered: People paused in the consumption of their eggs and bacon, forks going still in the mid-rise from plates of food, coffee cups hitting saucers too loudly, jaws halting from chewing.

There was a quick recovery, however, the assembled throwing themselves back into the eating thing, trying to pretend that they weren't worried and relieved all at the same time. Qhuinn, on the other hand, seemed to be in a complete stupor.

Their two seats, next to Xcor and Layla and the

twins, had indeed been left vacant, and Blay made sure Qhuinn sat closest to the young. It seemed like a good sign that he greeted both Lyric and Rhamp with smiles and murmured words, but he didn't take either of them into his lap.

Then again, the pile of calories on a porcelain plate that was presented to him was nearly as big as the mountain they were all on.

Blay's plate was no shorter when it came to macros.

Qhuinn picked up his fork. But he didn't eat. He just pushed things around, and Blay felt compelled to leaned back and mouth an *It's okay* to their co-parents because Xcor and Layla looked really concerned.

And he supposed, considering it all, things *were* okay. Qhuinn had closed the circle with his brother's final request, and it had been . . . sad, but lovely.

A secret love. A human. A break with tradition.

It made Blay respect Luchas even more.

Still, it was no wonder Qhuinn was rattled. And hey, he had made the effort to come here for the first time since—

Qhuinn jumped up with such force, his chair went flying backwards. As the thing bounced off the carpet and rattled across the bare floor, everyone went shocked-silent—as Blay wrenched around on his own seat.

Reaching up, he stammered, "What, what what-what—"

Was his mate having an aneurysm? At least Manny and Doc Jane were across the—

Qhuinn's chest was pumping up and down as he dropped to the carpet.

"Medic!" Blay called out as he reached toward Doc Jane. "He's going over!"

"I don't think that's what's happening here," somebody said gently.

Which was when Blay realized Qhuinn was still very definitely conscious. And not collapsing . . .

. . . but down on one knee.

Staring up with blue and green eyes that glowed with love.

Abruptly, the room tilted and spun—and that sensation of spinning got more intense as Qhuinn took Blay's dagger hand into his own.

In a voice that was full of emotion, Qhuinn said, "Thank you for all your support since . . . my brother's passing. And thank you for all the nights and days before that. And thank you for all the nights and days that are ahead of us."

"What are you doing?" Blay breathed.

"I love our middle, Blay. It isn't without challenges, but with you? I believe I can get through them—I believe with you, anything is possible." Qhuinn pressed his lips to Blay's palm and placed it against the side of his face. "I don't want to wait any longer. I want us to be properly mated. Luchas didn't just give me one last way to honor him—he provided me with the example of one sure way to honor you. Let's follow in his footsteps. His end came too soon, but our middle is here now. Mate me, my love? Mate me now, here. Let's not waste even a moment. Please, make me yours. Please, be mine. Officially, before all of our family."

Blay started to blink back tears. And then he was on his knees, too.

As he stammered to give his answer, he reflected that time was never a given, love was never to be taken for granted, and some gifts could not be wrapped and put under a tree.

"Yes. Yes, yes, *yes* . . ." he said over and over again as they kissed.

There was some kind of commotion around them, and when he finally returned to his body, he saw that everyone around the table had gotten to their feet and were cheering and clapping—and every single *doggen* in the house had flooded into the dining room and were jumping up and down.

With a laugh, Blay wondered whether their excitement was also because they were going to have to get ready for a big party.

And there was one other thing he noticed.

Out of the corner of his eyes, he saw Lassiter standing back against the wall, a satisfied expression on his face.

"He was right," Qhuinn murmured as he looked over at the angel as well.

"About what?"

"You said yes."

At that moment, Lassiter bowed to them. And then blew them both a kiss.

Blay refocused on his mate and felt a wave of love come over him. "As if there could ever have been any other answer?"

CHAPTER FORTY-ONE

Talk about a whirlwind.

And yet even though everything came together in a matter of nights, it still felt like the preparations for the mating ceremony took too damned long.

Not that Qhuinn would ever have said so to Fritz. Especially considering that the butler and his staff had worked around the clock. The thing was, though, when Qhuinn had dropped to one knee and asked his true love to properly mate him, he'd intended to have the ceremony then and there.

Like, bring on the daggers, get the salt, let's do this thing.

Cooler heads had prevailed, however—and like he could deny Bitty's party-planning committee a chance to put on its first event?

At least it was all finally going down. Tonight. Right now.

As Qhuinn came to the top of the grand staircase and looked down at the foyer below, everything had been transformed: Black candles flickered from a hundred different stanchions, and a ceremonial table had been set up, also draped with black, and the entire household, along with Blay's parents, were assembled on the mosaic floor, everyone in formal garb.

It was go time. For real.

Wrath was standing behind the table, George on one side, Tohr on the other. And behind them, the Brotherhood was lined up, all of them bare-chested and wearing the same loose black pants that Qhuinn had on.

"You ready?"

At the sound of Qhuinn's favorite voice in all the world, he turned. His mate was stepping out of their bedroom and he took a moment to enjoy the sight of that bare chest and that handsome face and that red hair. On a whim, Qhuinn had gotten ready in the second-floor sitting room, just for this moment—and he was so glad that he had.

"You look amazing," he said as Blay came up to him.

"I'm just in the same thing you are."

"Come here, kiss me." Qhuinn tugged his male forward until their lips met. "I'm more than ready for this. You?"

"I can't believe this is happening. And yes, I'm soooo ready."

Mating ceremonies for members of the *glymera* were highly prescribed affairs—no surprise there. Add in the fact that one of the couple was a member of the Black Dagger Brotherhood? That elevated everything to a celestial realm in terms of propriety—and there was a list of things that traditionally "had" to happen.

Not the least of which was a mandatory mourning period to honor Luchas's death.

Yet he and Blay had decided to do all of this their way, and Wrath had given them his blessing. And as for the mourning period? Qhuinn felt as though this was all partially for Luchas. He had what his brother did not: This moment now, with his true love.

"Let's do this," Qhuinn said.

They each took the other's hand and then they

walked down to the assembly together. When they got to the bottom, they took the twins from Layla and Xcor, who were both glowing with happiness for them, and then they with their young went up to Wrath and the ceremonial accoutrement of two black daggers, an enormous bowl of salt, and a pitcher of water.

Wrath beamed. "I know I speak for all of us when I say this is a blessed occasion. We're happy to do it your way, and I understand there is one tradition that you all feel very strongly about."

On that note, Lassiter stepped out from the crowd. For once, he wasn't in some costume, just a black silk shirt and black slacks, his blond-and-black hair braided into a rope that hung over his shoulder, his gold removed, everything toned down.

Wrath leaned to Tohr and hissed, "Is he in the Elvis suit again?"

"No. He looks normal."

"Great," the King muttered. "They get 'normal,' but I get the Elvis suit . . ."

Lassiter came forward and stood between Blay and Qhuinn, taking their hands. Then the angel closed his eyes—and that illumination rained down on them all, the warmth and grace levitating both them and the young off the depiction of that apple tree in full bloom.

As everyone in the foyer gasped, they were resettled back upon the earth.

"This is a very good mating, indeed," Lassiter pronounced. "Very good."

The Brotherhood let out a mighty yell of agreement. And then the ancient ceremony commenced, sacred words spoken in the Old Language by the great Blind King—none of which registered for Qhuinn at all. He was just standing in front of Blay, looking into those blue eyes as they held their young—in front of everyone they cared about.

Which he supposed, at the end of the night, was all that really mattered. The tradition was great and everything, but what really mattered was the communal acknowledgment of his commitment to his beloved, and his beloved's commitment to him.

The rest was just vocabulary—and a little fun and games with some daggers and salt.

Well, and also, thanks to Bitty and the fallen angel, what looked like some really good frickin' cake.

It was a blur, a total blur—

"Qhuinn?" Blay whispered. "You there?"

"What? Oh, sorry." With a much louder voice, he said, "I do!"

Laughter rippled through the crowd, and Blay leaned in again. "We already did that."

"We did?" Qhuinn flushed. "Then let's get to it with the blades!"

They passed the young back to Xcor and Layla, and then they went to the two black mats that had been laid out in front of the table.

"*You have chosen two to assist you,*" Wrath said in the Old Language. "*I would ask them to step forward at this time.*"

John Matthew and Zsadist broke ranks and walked around the table. Both were smiling as they each picked up one of the black daggers.

Qhuinn and Blay sank down onto their knees. As they planted their palms on the mats, they were facing each other.

And yup, Qhuinn was very aware of the shit-eating grin on his face. God, he wanted this so badly.

"*Blaylock, son of Rocke, I ask you, what is the name of your* hellren?" Wrath said.

Blay's eyes were so beautiful as he spoke. "He is Qhuinn. My beloved . . . is Qhuinn."

"*And Qhuinn, blooded sire of Rhampage and Lyric, what is the name of your* hellren?"

Qhuinn had to clear a sudden lump in his throat. "He is Blaylock. My one and only love is Blaylock."

John Matthew stepped up to Blay. Z did the same for Qhuinn.

Qhuinn and Blay held each other's stare without wincing as the carving happened, the letters of their names inscribed in the flesh across the tops of their shoulders. And then Tohrment poured the salt, first on Blay and then on Qhuinn.

Not once, for even a moment, did either of them look away.

As their names became permanent in their skin.

And their hearts, already paired forever, swelled with love.

◆ ◆ ◆

"Oh, thank you, Father," Blay said as he embraced his dad. "And *Mahmen*, I'm so glad you're here!"

As Lyric threw her arms around him, she squeezed the air out of his lungs. "As if we would ever have missed this! Finally! Now, where are my grand-babies?"

"Over there, by the Christmas tree in the library."

Lyric hooked her *hellren's* elbow. "Let's go! I have to hold my young. And I think I want one of those."

Rocke blanched. "A young?"

"No, silly. A Christmas tree. They're awfully pretty, and when the kids come, I want them to feel at home."

As Rocke rolled his eyes and kissed his mate, he winked at Blay. "Whatever you want, darling."

"That's the right answer, my love," Lyric said as

they walked off through the crowd. "You are *such* a smart male."

All around the foyer, people were talking with animation, drinking spirits, eating—

"Bitty!" Blay called out. "Hey, Bitty—"

The girl came skipping over in her bright yellow party dress, all flounces and smiles. "You're mated!" she exclaimed as she threw herself at him. "I'm so happy!"

Blay hugged the young and set her back down on her patent leather Mary Janes. "I just wanted you to know, I think you did a great job with the planning of all this."

"And Uncle Blay, we have a wedding cake!" She pointed to where the five-layer, chocolate- and vanilla-frosted creation had been set on a platform. "This is your wedding, and that's the cake, so that's a wedding cake!"

Blay smiled. "You are awesome, do you know that?"

"My dad tells me that all the time." She frowned. "And I better go make sure Lassiter's okay. He was worried about the cake—that you wouldn't like it because of the two-colored frosting. So I'll let him know it's just fine."

"It's perfect. Tell him it's perfect."

"Roger that."

The girl danced off, skipping around Phury and Cormia, dashing by Manny and Payne, dodging past Wrath and Beth, who were sharing a kiss over L.W.'s head.

"Hey, *hellren*."

Blay started to smile even before he turned his head. Qhuinn had come up right next to him—and it was weird. Even though nothing had changed, the formality, the carvings in the back, the whole process of confirming their love in front of their community, made it all feel so different. In a good way.

"Hi, *hellren*."

And then they both smiled like idiots.

Absolute idiots.

"Hey listen, can you come over here," Qhuinn said. "You know, to the bathroom—and no, not for nookie."

"Yeah, right."

"No, I mean it. It's not for . . . you know." As Blay laughed, Qhuinn tilted forward and jogged his brows. "But the nookie's coming later today. *All* day."

"I can't wait."

As they went around the base of the stairs, and ducked into the guest powder room together, Blay wondered what was going on. And then they were sitting together on the bench.

When Qhuinn took a deep breath, Blay got anxious. "Is something wrong?"

"No, no. Not at all. This is the best night of my life. But there's something I wanted to do privately. Just for you and me. I mean, not that other people shouldn't and won't see eventually, but I just . . ."

Blay stroked Qhuinn's arm. "What is it?"

Qhuinn shifted his weight to one hip and winced, as the carvings across his shoulders undoubtedly stretched. And then he held up something that glowed with gold.

"Remember when you gave this to me? At that bar?" he said.

Blay instantly recognized what he was being shown. "My signet ring. Of course."

"Here, you take it now."

"Are you giving it back to me or—" Blay stopped talking as Qhuinn flatted his other hand to reveal, in the center of his palm, something that took the breath away. "Oh, God . . ."

It was another gold signet ring, and Blay knew whose it was even before he picked the heavy weight up and noted the crest.

Luchas's ring. The one that had been given to him the night after his transition. The one that had been on his finger when he'd been found in that oil drum—which was the only reason they'd been able to identify him.

The one he'd turned over to Qhuinn.

Because Qhuinn had never been given one by their parents.

"This ring is my most precious possession," Qhuinn said roughly. "For reasons that you are well aware of. And so tonight, on the night of our mating ceremony, in honor of my brother, and as a way to include him, I would like to place it on your finger."

Blay's eyes watered. And then, in the Old Language, he said, "*It is my greatest honor to wear it in his name and yours.*"

Qhuinn took a deep breath and stared at the gold crest.

And then he cleared his throat. "I miss him."

"How could you not."

With an effort, Qhuinn seemed to refocus. And then he smiled a little. "Shall we?"

"Yes," Blay murmured.

They both placed the rings on the other's fingertips. And then, as they tilted in and kissed, they slid the gold home.

They kissed for a bit longer and eased back.

Qhuinn smiled and brushed the side of Blay's face. "You are my warm heart in winter, you know that?"

"And you are mine," Blay said as they both looked down at the same time.

The sight of their entwined fingers, with the rings, seemed like a fitting metaphor for their lives, a melding of histories and experiences, a foundation on which to further build their future together, a vow to raise their young, and love and live and learn, for all the nights destiny provided them.

Together.

Forever.

Amen.

EPILOGUE

It was a week before Christmas when Elle returned again to her mother's apartment. She didn't really want to go, but like she had a choice? She got worried if she didn't personally check in every couple of weeks.

"Don't run into a snowbank again," Terrie said slyly.

As Elle pulled their father's BMW into an empty parking spot, she deliberately pounded the brake so that Terrie jerked forward against her seat belt.

"Ow!"

"Sorry."

"You are not!"

Elle cut the engine and opened her door. With her period of monitored driving finally up, she was now allowed to go out on her own, and their father—who'd been feeling extra permissive since . . . well, since their little talk that morning when she'd gotten up early to confess something she'd ultimately kept to herself—was letting her take out the BMW pretty much whenever it was free to be used.

Getting out, she rolled her eyes as Terrie bitched her way around the far side of the car—but all the sister-stressing dried up as they both stared at the apartment building.

"I don't know why you dragged me here," Terrie whined. "I don't—"

"She's our mother. And it's almost Christmas. And that's why you have to come, too, sometimes."

As they started off for the stairwell, the pit in Elle's stomach got more hollow.

"I'm hungry," Terrie said. "Can we go to McDonald's after this?"

"Sure."

"Really? You'll, like, really take me? Even though it's almost dinnertime."

"Dad's out tonight, remember."

"Oh. Another work event?"

"Yeah," Elle muttered. "Work again. Always with that work of his."

Up on the second landing, at their mother's door, Elle went to knock—

The panel opened, and Elle jumped back in surprise—although not because someone other than their mother was standing there. It was because of the smell. Which was . . .

"Are you making dinner?" Elle blurted.

Their mom nodded. "I thought you girls might be hungry. It's almost six, and I know you like lasagna."

"Is this our lasagna?" Elle demanded. "I mean— wait. What is that?"

She barged in and stared across the shallow living room at the Christmas tree that had been put up in the corner. The thing was four feet high, and had a coordinated decorating scheme of blue and white lights and bulbs.

No garland. But their mother had never liked garland.

"It's not a live one," their mom said. "Without your father to help—well, this was what I could handle. But I think it's pretty, *non?*"

Terrie raced over and skidded on her knees on the carpet. "There are presents! This one is for me!"

Elle narrowed her eyes on their mother as the door to the apartment shut by itself. "What's going on?"

Before their mom could answer, the timer in the kitchen went off. "Excuse me."

Elle looked around again, and wondered if the Upside Down hadn't showed up in Caldwell . . . especially as, through the open door to the bedroom, she saw a freshly vacuumed carpet, and a bed that was made, and a sprig of holly in a little vase on the bedside table.

"Girls, wash your hands, please."

Elle snapped to it without any argument—Terrie, too—because that tone of voice was one she'd spent her childhood respecting. And as she traded off the bar of soap at the kitchen sink with her sister, she tried to remember the last time she'd heard that kind of command.

And look, the table was set for three.

The next thing Elle knew, they were seated together and holding hands, the prayer done in French. And then their mother was serving them from the glass pan in the center of the little table.

"I love this lasagna!" Terrie exclaimed as she accepted her plate.

"Two or one piece?" their mom asked Elle.

Elle looked down at the melted cheese and the perfect layers. "Two. Please."

Their mother even put a piece on her own plate.

As Elle took a test taste, she closed her eyes because they had started to water. It was exactly right, the sauce, the cheese, the noodles. And this . . . was exactly right, too, the three of them together, just like old times.

"So I'm going back to school," their mom announced.

"You are?" Elle said as she flipped her lids back up.

"If I work hard, I should finish my psychology degree two summers from now. And then I want to get a master's in social work."

"I think that would be amazing, Mom," Terrie said. "I want to be a therapist, too."

"I'd love to talk to you about everything I learn," their mom said.

"I want to help people."

With your mouth? Elle thought. *You'd have better luck being a drill sergeant in the Marines.*

"So tell me how school is going for you both." Their mom flushed. "I'm afraid I haven't been asking about it enough. I'm afraid I haven't . . . been present enough. But that's all going to change from here on out."

There was a pause. And then Terrie dropped her fork loudly on her plate and launched herself at their mother. Anna Sophia embraced the girl, and then settled her in her lap. As she stroked Terrie's back and murmured things that were too soft to hear, Elle looked out the window.

The blinds were pulled up, the view one of the parking lot and the shallow ring of trees behind the building.

Confusion warred with a treacherous hope as Elle breathed deep and smelled anew the dinner that had been made specially for her and her sister.

And that was when she saw the tow truck.

It was red and white, the name "Murphy's" written on the driver-side door. As she stared at it, a memory trembled underneath the surface of her consciousness, something that—

From out of nowhere, a headache lit off, and Elle frowned and rubbed her temples.

She had the strangest sense that she had seen the truck before, that it had done something for her, that the night she had taken her father's car without permission, a tow guy had—

"Are you okay?" her mother asked over Terrie's head.

Elle came back to the present. As she focused on what was on her plate, the pounding ache in her skull immediately let up.

"Yes, I'm fine. I just . . . I'm good. Just really hungry."

She glanced out at the parking lot again. The tow truck was gone.

What did it matter, she thought. She had other things to worry about.

"Are you okay?" she asked her mom. "I mean, are you . . . really okay here?"

The smile that hit her mom's face was sad and slow. But the answer that came back was strong and steady. "I am *very* okay. I have you two. And that's all I need going forward."

Elle felt her eyes water. "I've missed you."

Their mom leaned forward and put her hand on Elle's. "I'm missed you, too. And I'm not leaving you ever again, okay? I'm sorry about where I went, but I'm back now."

In a child's voice, Elle whispered, "What . . . what made you return."

Their mom squeezed Elle's palm. "Only the most powerful thing in all the world."

"What's that?"

"Love." Their mom smiled deeply. "What else could it be?"

Elle blinked quickly. Then she took a deep breath, filled up her fork, and took a bite. As the familiar taste bloomed in her mouth, and her mother continued to stare into her eyes with the kind of levelness that had previously been a hallmark . . . Elle found herself nodding.

"Love and lasagna," she agreed. "Are everything."

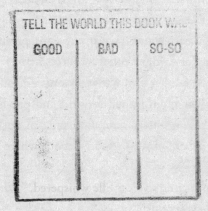

If you, or anybody you know, is suffering from suicidal thoughts, or if you have been affected by suicide and need help, please call the National Suicide Prevention Lifeline at 1-800-273-TALK(8255).

Learn about the warning signs, prevention, and other resources here:
www.sprc.org

ACKNOWLEDGMENTS

With so many thanks to the readers of the Black Dagger Brotherhood books! This has been, and continues to be, a long, marvelous, exciting journey, and I can't wait to see what happens next in this world we all love. I'd also like to thank Meg Ruley, Rebecca Scherer, and everyone at JRA, and Hannah Bratten, Andrew Nguyen, Jennifer Bergstrom, Jennifer Long, and the entire family at Gallery Books and Simon & Schuster.

To Team Waud, I love you all. Truly. And as always, everything I do is with love to, and adoration for, both my family of origin and of adoption.

Oh, and with all my gratitude to Naamah, my Writer Dog II, who works as hard as I do on my books, and to the Archiball!